Safe Haven

OTHER BOOKS AND AUDIO BOOKS
BY JEAN HOLBROOK MATHEWS:

Precious Cargo

The Assignment

Escape to Zion

The Light Above

Safe Haven
a novel

Jean Holbrook Mathews

Covenant

Covenant Communications, Inc.

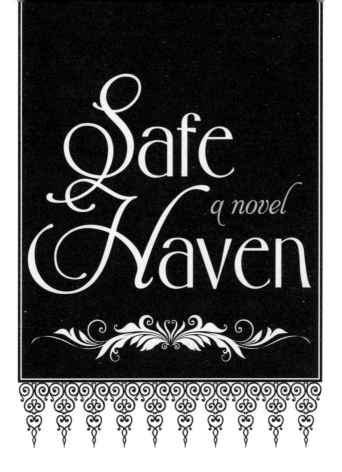

Published by Covenant Communications, Inc.
American Fork, Utah

Printed in the United States of America
First Printing: February 2013

20 19 18 17 16 15 14 13 10 9 8 7 6 5 4 3 2 1

ISBN 978-1-62108-192-0

Dedicated to the women who helped shape my life: Margaret Elizabeth Neal, who taught me to love the English language and a well-written story; Grace S. Wright, who taught me to use my voice and to love real music; Patricia Stewart Keyes, who taught me the importance of getting involved in government and politics; and my mother, Connie J. Holbrook, who taught me the importance of faith by her quiet example.

Foreword

The courage of the Mormon pioneers who chose to cross the North American continent seeking a safe haven from religious persecution during the middle of the nineteenth century has been recognized and respected by historians for more than one hundred fifty years, but too often, the courage and hardships of those pioneers who set out for Zion on the ship *Brooklyn* in anticipation of a vast sea migration, which did not materialize, have often been overlooked.

The pioneers of the *Brooklyn* endured six months of cramped quarters, poor food, bad water, illness, and death. After planting their roots in California, anticipating the arrival of Brigham Young and the rest of the Saints, the faithful were called to relocate to Zion in the Great Salt Lake Valley.

That eastward journey required three months of hardships even greater than those faced by the westward-bound pioneers. They had to cross the seldom traveled, nearly trackless Sierra Nevada Mountains, survive the harsh Nevada desert, and face repeated conflicts with hostile Indians.

This book is a tribute to the courage of those Saints. It is not meant to be a thorough historical account of their experiences aboard the *Brooklyn* or in California. That would require a much longer and more detailed treatment, but this book is a sincere attempt to portray many of their experiences so the reader might develop a greater appreciation of their trials.

In evaluating the experiences of the *Brooklyn* Saints, many would say that the hardships they experienced while aboard the ship and during their eastward journey could have been avoided had they simply united with the westbound Saints in Iowa City or Winter Quarters. Had this been their choice, the future state of California would have lost the substantial contributions of the *Brooklyn* Saints to the development and settlement of that state. California would have also lost one of its most colorful historical characters, Samuel Brannan.

Many of the characters portrayed in this story were actually part of the *Brooklyn* passage or the Mormon Battalion. The primary characters of Susanna, Jane, Jonathan, and their extended family members are, of necessity, fictional but plausible. The events that took place on the ship, in California, and on the trail eastward to the Salt Lake Valley are reproduced as accurately as is practical from existing records and journals but certainly in no way can be considered all-inclusive.

Looking back from our day and time, we must not minimize the personal experiences of the *Brooklyn* Saints. We were not present; we did not participate in those hardships. Perhaps eternity will give us a better, more accurate perspective. It is for us to thank them and offer our respect and gratitude for their faith and courage.

The Author

Part One
Massachusetts

Chapter One

ON THAT PARTICULAR NOVEMBER AFTERNOON, Susanna was simply a shadowy figure making her way through the driven snow and chilling wind that lifted her cloak and sniffed at her ankles. As it pushed her down the street, she held the hood of the cloak tightly closed beneath her chin with a mittened hand to keep the wind from pulling it off. She occasionally had to brush the ice crystals from her face and eyelashes with her other hand, but passersby couldn't help but note the smile she wore.

As cold as the world was, she was aware only of the warmth of the memories that suffused her. She was remembering how she and her family had walked the cobblestones of that street every Sabbath morning from her childhood to attend worship services. Only in the worst of weather did her father get out the horse and buggy. It hadn't mattered whether it was cold or hot or a perfect spring day, her father could always make everyone in the family laugh with his renditions of stories from the Old Testament. That picture in her mind was so clear that for a moment she nearly forgot that he was gone.

Those memories had led her to remember the many times she and Jonathan Burnley had laughed and played in the churchyard from the time they were no more than children while the adults in the congregation socialized after Sunday meetings ended. The games of hide-and-seek had changed as the two of them had grown taller. Games of catch-me-if-you-can eventually turned into quiet walks in the meadow during the spring and summer outdoor church socials. After each walk, Jonathan loved to present her the bouquet of wild flowers he had gathered. Like her father, he could always make her laugh, though they always dropped their linked hands and put on serious faces when Pastor Hutchison was nearby. That bit of proper behavior always brought gales of guilty laughter when they were out of his sight.

The winter months had limited their games and walks. When the weather was cold and families hurried to their wagons and carriages after meeting, they had settled for surreptitiously slipping notes to one another as they passed in the aisle of the church. Susanna had saved every note, even those written years earlier in Jonathan's childish scrawl. She had always believed that he would fill an important place in her life and she in his.

When she saw the comforting familiarity of her home through the falling snow, she allowed the memories to slip away. By the time she reached the front stoop, she became aware of how thoroughly chilled she had become.

She loved this house. Like so many in Boston, it was white clapboard with green shutters, built in the traditional New England saltbox design. The well-built, two-story front rose to the peak of the roof and then the roof swept to the rear, ending above the single-story kitchen. The wind swept around the corners of the house, driving the thick snowflakes into drifts and mounds, and whined like an animal wanting to be let inside as it forced its way between the house and what had formerly been her father's two-story shoemaker's shop. She looked regretfully at the harness shop it had become. *Oh, Papa, we miss you so.*

She held the door against the wind, grateful to step into the shelter of the front hallway, where the clock in the sitting room was chiming five. Despite her efforts, snow swirled in with her. The house was dark except for the light in the kitchen. She quickened her step down the hallway. Her mother was preparing supper and her five-year-old brother was playing in the warmth of the Franklin stove. As Susanna stepped from the darkened hallway into the warm room, her mother took a small loaf of bread out of the bustle oven with a long wooden paddle. She set it on the table and then looked up at her daughter. The worry in her face melted like the snow Susanna had tracked in on the warm kitchen floor.

"'Zanna, where have you been? You could have walked to and from the Fowlers' three times in the hours you've been gone. You must be chilled to the bone."

The lithe young woman tossed back the hood and stomped her feet to scatter the packed snow on her shoes. She shook her cloak and hung it on the peg near the stove. "I stopped to talk to Papa for a little while."

Emily Thayer was genuinely perplexed. "'Zanna, your father has been in the ground these three months. Why would you go to the burying ground in a storm like this? It was a least at mile out of your way, and the snow is coming fast and hard." Her mother shook her head, not expecting an answer. "I just hope you don't catch your death of cold. Supper is ready." She looked at the dark-haired boy playing with a small wooden horse and several lead soldiers. "Georgie, you will have to leave General Washington and his soldiers for a little while and come to supper."

The lamplight accentuated the fact that mother and daughter were so much alike that a stranger might mistake them for sisters. Even friends and associates in their church congregation often said, "She is her mother's daughter," when they spoke of Susanna. And they applied the aphorism to more than just their similar appearance; they also applied the statement to the character of both women. Mother and daughter shared a cheerful and positive nature, but the events of the last few months had left them both more subdued and quiet than normal.

The wind and snow had loosened Susanna's auburn hair from the ribbon at the base of her neck, and it curled in damp ringlets around her face. At seventeen, she was in the full bloom of young womanhood, with a complexion that held a pale undertone of gold dotted with a few tiny golden freckles. She looked at the world through eyes almost as green as emeralds.

Her mother's face was also framed by damp auburn ringlets, encouraged by the heat of the oven. She had married young and over the following twenty-two years had given birth to five children, with four still surviving. Her eldest, James, just barely twenty-one, was trying to establish his career as a solicitor. Rachel, her oldest daughter, had married a farmer two years earlier and moved some miles from Boston. Susanna and Georgie remained at home. Emily's figure was still youthful, but her eyes were gray-green and had become even grayer since her husband's death.

"The wind wasn't so bad when I started, and I felt that I needed to talk to him."

"'Zanna, how can you talk to Papa when he's in heaven?" her brother asked.

As her mother ladled the soup into three bowls, Susanna answered, "Georgie, I think that Papa can still hear us when we talk to him. And sometimes, I can hear him answer me—in my heart."

The three of them held hands while Emily offered grace as they sat around the small oak table. They hadn't eaten in the dining room since Robert Thayer had died.

Susanna tasted the soup that was little more than a few floating cabbage leaves in a thin broth made from a ham bone. The bread was warm, and that compensated for the lack of butter. The last few weeks had required that the remaining members of the Thayer family watch their pennies. The large shoemaker's shop, where Susanna's father had employed twelve apprentices, had been closed within days of his death, and most of the family savings had been used to give the assistants their final pay. All income had stopped for Thayer's widow and her two youngest children, other than what she could raise with her sewing. Rachel and her husband had been able to help with fruits and vegetables after the harvest, but now even their help was limited, and the law office James had recently established was hardly feeding him, so Emily had quietly begun to sell a few of the nicer pieces of furniture.

"Well, tell us what he said—or what you felt he said."

"I told him that you and I had discussed the situation in which we find ourselves, and despite the fact that the proper time for mourning has not passed, and will not pass for some months yet, I asked him if it would be acceptable for me to formally accept the offer of marriage I received from young Jonathan Burnley on my last birthday."

Georgie looked at his sister with a very serious expression for his age. "Do you love Jonathan, 'Zanna?"

"I love him very much, Georgie." Even though the question had been asked by a child, an unexpected blush rose in her cheeks. It was the first time she had stated that fact aloud. "I think Mr. Burnley would be as fine a husband as a young woman could hope for." She paused briefly and then added, "It is his family that concerns me somewhat."

Georgie's expression made it clear that he was not convinced that she had a valid concern. "You wouldn't be marrying his family," he said as he returned to his meal.

"In a way I would. You see, we would live with his parents until we could obtain a home of our own. His father seems to be such a stern, hard man, and Jonathan is planning to join his father's firm of solicitors when he finishes his studies at Harvard in the spring."

"Do you feel your father supports such a decision?" Her mother was following her daughter's words closely.

"I feel that he does not oppose it. When Jonathan and his parents attended the services for Papa there at the burying ground, Jonathan told me that I did not need to give a formal answer to his proposal until we had been given a proper period of mourning." She put down her spoon and looked into a distant future no one else could see. "From the time we were children, I have always believed that we would marry someday." She spoke quietly. "He said that after he had finished his studies and had begun his apprenticeship with his father, we would set a date for the wedding, perhaps in late summer or early fall of next year." She paused and took a sip of soup.

Emily rose suddenly, and to give herself something to do while she arranged her thoughts, she added another piece of coal to the fire in the stove.

"Mama, what's wrong?" Georgie asked. Even he could see that she was agitated.

Her posture relaxed slightly, and she returned to her chair. "Georgie, I was counting to ten—slowly, so I wouldn't say something harsh and judgmental."

"Mama, it's not like you to be judgmental," Susanna's tone reflected her surprise.

After she took a deep breath, Emily looked past her daughter rather than at her, knowing that what she had to say might potentially disturb Susanna's happiness.

"Perhaps it's time for me to tell you why I have not been enthusiastic in my support for your marriage to the younger Mr. Burnley. Several years ago, before Georgie was born, you may remember that your father's father passed away in the epidemic of '38. He left an estate of some size to be divided in three equal portions among your father, your Uncle Thaddeus, and his own sister, your great-aunt Louisa."

Susanna's eyes brightened with a childhood memory. "I remember Uncle Thaddeus. When James, Rachel, and I were young, we went out to his farm in Medford during the summer. He seemed to be a cold man, but his wife, Aunt Leah, was very kind to all of us—but what does this have to do with them?"

Her mother continued, "Within a few weeks of the reading of the will, Thaddeus had hired a solicitor and had taken the matter to court. His solicitor arranged for the matter to be presented before a judge who was a personal friend and sympathetic to his case. Thaddeus opposed the will on the grounds that he had ten children, nine of them sons, and your father had only three children at that time, only one of which was a son."

Georgie interrupted. "But Mama, Papa had two sons, me and James."

Susanna interjected, "You weren't born yet, Georgie. Please go on, Mama."

"He—Thaddeus, I mean, claimed that his father would have wanted the estate to pass down in equal parts to his grandsons. The judge agreed, and Thaddeus was given nine-tenths of the portion that would have otherwise been divided between himself and your father.

"Your father felt it unseemly to oppose the matter in the courts and possibly divide the family for generations, not to speak of making it a public humiliation, so he did not oppose the order of the judge. The portion that came to him was used to retire most of his debts." Emily stopped and put her hand over her mouth to stop her quivering lips. She labored to regain her composure. "Your father believed that he would be able to support his family with his shoemaking skills—after all, he had one of the biggest shops in Boston at the time—so he accepted the court's decision regarding the inheritance to maintain good family relations." Her voice turned bitter. "But there have been no relations whatsoever between our family and Thaddeus since that time. Your uncle and his sons did not even see fit to attend your father's funeral services. And now, we face . . ." She did not finish the thought but bit her lower lip instead.

"But what does that have to do with young Mr. Burnley, Mama?" Susanna's eyebrows were arched in concern.

"The solicitor who cost us your father's inheritance was Jonathan Burnley, Senior."

Susanna caught her breath. After a few heartbeats, she asked, "Do you believe that his son asked for my hand in marriage to soothe his father's conscience?" She spoke slowly, chilled by the thought that anything other than affection had motivated Jonathan's informal proposal.

"I have considered that possibility." Her mother tried to soften the words when Susanna recoiled in hurt. "Or more likely, my dear, the friendship you and he have shared since you were children is not something Jonathan would allow his father to disrupt."

"But his son was not directly involved in the matter. Are your objections to the father sufficient to oppose the engagement?" Her voice was tight, and she held her breath, fearful of her mother's reaction.

Her mother smiled stiffly. "If it is in your heart to marry the young man, I will not oppose it."

Susanna slowly let go of her breath. “I have thought much about it over the last several weeks, Mama. I know that things have become difficult for us since Papa’s passing and will only become more so unless somehow our circumstances are changed.” She hurried on. “If I marry Jonathan, our future would be secure. He has an unmarred reputation and a good future ahead of him, and I love him very much.” The resolve in her voice strengthened. “I am determined to wait no longer. With your permission, I will send him a note telling him that I am ready to formally accept his offer of marriage.”

“If that is what you want, Daughter.” They finished their meal without further discussion of the matter.

That evening, after three attempts, Susanna finally completed a note addressed to Jonathan Burnley, Junior, Care of the Office of Burnley and Caspar, Solicitors, Number 18 Court Street, Boston, Massachusetts.

November 12, 1844

Dear Mr. Burnley,

It is my distinct pleasure to write to you to tell you of my decision to formally accept your proposal of marriage of last June. Our family will continue to mourn my father for many years to come, but we recognize that he would want us to go forward with our lives. I would be privileged to become your wife. I look forward to hearing from you regarding this matter.

I remain your faithful friend,
Susanna Thayer

***

The next morning Susanna wrapped her cloak around herself against the cold and walked to the office of the postmaster, where she paid two pence for sufficient postage to have the letter delivered. She then walked six more blocks to deliver a pair of boots ordered from her father two weeks before his death.

She spoke as she entered the kitchen upon her return. “Mrs. Tarbert wasn’t going to pay me the three dollars Papa and her husband had agreed upon for the boots. She said that we waited too long to deliver them, so she was only going to give me two dollars. I’m so glad Mr. Tarbert heard her answer the door. He gave me the money without saying anything. I think he's a good man." She didn't mention her opinion of his wife, but it hung in the air.

"Let's be grateful for that. Tomorrow, we will walk to Market Square and try to sell the remaining four pair. I think we had better take the best of your father's tools as well. Perhaps we can find a buyer for them."

That evening Emily took her place on one side of the Franklin stove so she could put the last few stitches into the linen shirt she had been commissioned to make for Mr. Saterwaite. The Thayers had attended worship services in the same congregation with him and his wife for many years.

As was her custom, Susanna stood before the books that had been such a part of her father's life and ran her finger over the bindings as she read the titles. The bookcase was filled with histories, biographies, and classics. She had received her love of learning from him, and while her formal education had stopped with the completion of the final grade at the private girls' school she had attended for eight years, she carried an insatiable, bone-deep curiosity that could only be fed but never quieted. She read from her father's books at every opportunity.

"What have you selected this evening, 'Zanna?" her mother asked.

"I think I would like to read from that young English poet, Robert Browning." She sat and opened the book

"I gave that book of English poets to your father for his birthday just a year or two ago. I don't think he ever had the time to read it."

"I think you're right. The binding is very stiff." Susanna smoothed the open book and began by reading the poem "Pauline." When she paused, her mother looked up from her sewing as if to seek an explanation for the silence.

Susanna smiled. "Forgive me, Mama, but I wanted to reread this line. It speaks much wisdom to my heart. 'Measure your mind's height by the shade it casts! Every joy is gain, and gain is gain, however small.'" She leaned back and smiled. "I think that if my joy is gain, then I have gained much, and when our engagement is made public, my gain will be even greater."

Her mother simply smiled and Susanna moved on to read "Pippa Passes."

The year's at the spring
And day's at the morn;

Morning's at seven;
The hillside's dew pearled;
The lark's on the wing;
The snail's on the thorn;
God's in his heaven—
All's right with the world.

"Mama, how I wish it were spring right now. Then all would be right with my world, as my wedding would be much closer."

"Well, 'Zanna, we can change many things, but not the weather or the seasons. Are you going to continue reading?"

She nodded. "I think I'll continue reading from 1 Corinthians, which we started last evening."

Her mother smiled over her sewing. "Yes, the Apostle Paul is usually full of uplifting advice."

After a few minutes of reading from Paul's epistle, Susanna reached the well-loved words, "For now we see through a glass darkly; but then face to face: now I know in part; but then shall I know even as also I am known. Now abideth faith, hope, charity, these three; but the greatest of these is charity."

Susanna grew silent as she concentrated on a thought she had previously tried to push out of her mind. *Will I be marrying into a family lacking in charity?* She closed the Bible and sat quietly wondering if the son would grow to become like the father in the Burnley household. *Charity is such a necessary quality between a husband and wife. A marriage without it would be difficult to endure.*

Her mother had been watching her. "What are you thinking, Susanna?"

"I was just wondering if a man's profession, such as the law, or perhaps the example of his father might interfere with the relationship between him and his wife."

"I think it would depend very much upon the husband."

***

The next morning dawned cold and bitter, not unusual for Boston in November. Wrapped against the chill air, Susanna carried the bulky leather bag containing many of her father's tools, and her mother carried the shirt she had made for Mr. Saterwaite. Georgie insisted on carrying the fabric bag containing the four pairs of shoes they hoped to sell.

As they walked, Emily shared her thoughts. "Susanna, it may be a day or two before we hear from young Mr. Burnley, and at the earliest, a wedding date might be set for late summer, so I must find sufficient funds to keep us housed and fed until then." She paused. "We have been using the funds from the sale of the shop to support ourselves until now, but they are running low."

"I had expected as much."

They walked up Kilby Street, nodding at a few acquaintances as they passed. They turned on Water Street and located the address they were seeking. "I have the shirt you ordered for your husband," Emily stated when the door was opened by Mrs. Saterwaite. The woman motioned for them to step inside the large, federalist-style, two-story brick house. They stood in the entryway while she carefully examined the shirt in the light from the window in the sitting room. "Yes, yes, it will do." After she located her coin purse, she handed fifty cents to Emily and stepped toward the door to let the three of them out.

Emily looked from her daughter to the woman holding the new shirt in one hand with her other on the latch. "Mrs. Saterwaite, you once saw my grandmother's rocking chair and admired it. Would you be interested in obtaining it?"

The question caught the woman off guard, and she paused for a moment before answering. "Yeees," she said slowly, stretching the word as she searched her memory. "If I remember, it was a good, solid oak rocker. I think I might be interested in it. Do you want to sell it?"

"Yes, and right away, as we are in need of money at the moment."

"With a husband newly gone, I can imagine that you might be. How much will you be wanting for it?"

"I think it's worth at least ten dollars, but I would be willing to give it up for eight."

"I will speak with my husband when he returns, and if he is in agreement, he will bring the wagon by tomorrow and pick it up."

They bid her farewell and walked for an additional quarter of a mile, with Georgie changing the bag of shoes from one hand to the other as he grew tired. They turned onto Chatham Street and finally reached Market Street. Their hands had grown cold inside their knitted mittens, and their breath made great, frosty clouds. For the next three hours, Susanna and her mother each stood by one of the great granite pillars outside the front doors of the Quincy Market and offered the shoes to each man or woman who had come to purchase potatoes, winter squash, apples, or other items that were spread out for potential buyers inside the large building. Georgie wandered inside, where it was not so cold.

Susanna realized that her mother hated the necessity of seeking buyers for the shoes in that manner as much as she did. It made her feel almost like a beggar selling lucifers from a tin cup. But this did not stop her from asking, "Sir, would your wife or daughter need a fine pair of leather shoes for a reasonable price?" Only a few were interested enough to stop and examine them.

At one o'clock, Emily laid her hand on her daughter's shoulder. "Step inside with me and warm yourself." Susanna picked up the bag of tools and moved it inside, where she leaned it against the wall.

"I finally sold one pair, the smallest of the children's shoes. I think I will keep the other pair, as they will fit Georgie in a few months." Her mother's face was showing the strain of standing so long in the cold.

Susanna responded, "I sold one pair of the women's shoes. Another woman did show an interest in the other pair. She said she would think about it while she did her shopping." Susanna turned and looked at the leather bag. "What will we do with Papa's tools?"

Before her mother could answer, she saw a man tacking a meeting notice to the market door where other notices had previously been displayed. Susanna stepped over to him. "Sir, would you have a wife or daughter in need of a pair of soft leather shoes? They are of the finest workmanship."

He turned and smiled at her. "I'm sure that my wife is in need of a pair of shoes, but as she is in Nauvoo, Illinois, and I am here, and as I have not a cent to spare at the present time, she will be forced to make do with what she is presently wearing." He pocketed the small hammer he had used to tack up the notice. He removed his hat and bowed from the shoulders toward both women. "Though I cannot purchase from you, I can offer you both something of much greater value than any item you may be selling. Tomorrow evening at eight o'clock, a religious meeting will be held across the way in Faneuil Hall, on the second floor, where a message of the restored gospel of Jesus Christ will be preached, and your questions of who you are and what God expects of you will be answered. I earnestly hope you will attend, and bring any menfolk in your family with you."

"We have no men to bring with us, sir, but may we attend unescorted?" Emily asked.

"Yes, of course. I am Ezra T. Benson, of Nauvoo, Illinois, but more recently sent to spread the restored gospel here in New England. May I ask to whom I am speaking?" His smile warmed his face.

"I am the Widow Thayer, and this is my daughter Susanna. Will you preach tomorrow evening, Mr. Benson?"

"Yes, I anticipate that honor. Additionally, my good friend in the gospel, Mr. Parley P. Pratt, will also address the crowd. I hope you ladies will attend."

"We will, if circumstances permit." At that point, they were distracted by the approach of the woman who had earlier promised to consider the purchase of the pair of shoes Susanna still held. A discounted price of two dollars and fifty cents was agreed upon.

Emily whispered to her daughter, "Take some of the coins and purchase some apples, squash, parsnips, and lard. I haven't very much left in the kitchen to eat." When Susanna returned with her purchases, the items were carefully put in the bag with the remaining pair of shoes. Georgie quietly approached and looked at the apples with wide, hungry eyes. She had never been able to resist her brother's pleading eyes. She handed one to him.

Mr. Benson again tipped his hat and nodded at the women as they retrieved the bag of tools.

When they reached the street, Susanna asked, "Will we attend the meeting tomorrow night, Mama?"

"I think we shall. I'm sure we are both in need of something to distract our minds from our present situation." Susanna shifted the heavy bag from her right hand to her left. Her brother skipped beside her as he nibbled at the apple.

"We will offer the tools to Mr. Sawyer, the shoemaker on Salem Street and hope he will purchase them," her mother said quietly. "There's another shoemaker at the north end of Endicott Street, but it is such a long walk, and it's just too cold to walk that far today."

Susanna's hands and shoulders ached with the weight of the bag by the time they reached the little shoemaker's shop that was not far from the Old North Church. Mr. Sawyer examined each of the mallets, needles, and leather cutters as if he were examining precious jewels.

"The tools are well used and worn, but I can use some of them. I will give you two dollars and fifty cents for the lot."

Emily swallowed hard to hide her disappointment. She had hoped for more. "I will accept your offer, Mr. Sawyer." She took the money and thanked the man.

***

Mr. Saterwaite arrived with his wagon at ten o'clock the next morning. The wheels creaked over the hardened crust of snow. He knocked with a firm hand as he stomped the snow off his boots on the front stoop.

Susanna hurried to open the door. She knew that her mother probably dreaded his coming. It was a harsh reminder of the need to part with beloved belongings, brought on by their failing financial condition.

He was a big man with a frozen waterfall of a gray beard and a full mustache. He removed his hat, exposing a shiny dome with only a fringe of hair around the edge like the ice forming on a pond. "My wife has sent me for the rocking chair." His bulk filled the doorway.

"I'm so glad she wants it. I was hoping to find a good home for it," Emily said as she led him into the sitting room and invited him to sit with a sweep of her hand. He sat down almost begrudgingly and ran his hands along the arms to feel the smoothness of the wood. He rose and nodded to both of the women before handing eight bank notes to Emily. He picked up the rocking chair and Susanna hurried to open the door. Without saying anything more, he carried it out the front door and put it in the open wagon bed.

After the door was closed, Emily sat down in one of the straight-backed chairs with the needlepoint seat cover she had stitched so carefully, and she bit her lip to steady her quivering chin. Susanna watched her for a moment. "Mama, I'm so sorry that you had to part with your rocking chair. I know you loved it."

"Yes, it was full of memories. I have rocked each of my children in that chair. I was holding little Asa in that chair when he died of diphtheria. It was a member of the family, but life's circumstances are often altered, and it is best to accept what we cannot change."

After a moment, she more fully regained her composure. "I will miss it, but it was only a rocking chair. I did not sell those memories with it. I will always have them." She sat up and straightened her posture. "Surely, we will all be fine until your marriage to young Mr. Burnley."

"And you and Georgie will come to live with me after I am married and have a home of my own."

"That would be wonderful." But Emily's tone was unconvinced.

Chapter Two

As the three of them ate supper, the six o'clock bells of the Old South Meeting House could be heard in the distance, the sound muffled by the falling snow. Little was said until the soup and bread were finished.

Emily broke the silence. "Get your coat, Georgie. We're going to attend the meeting Mr. Benson mentioned. You are going to be our escort this evening."

***

The meeting room was bare except for rows of benches in front of an elevated podium. It smelled of wood oil and tobacco and was crowded with more than a hundred people. Many of the men present were smoking or chewing tobacco. As the meeting progressed, some taunted the speakers, but most listened attentively.

After the meeting concluded, the three of them walked briskly toward home. Georgie coaxed, "Hurry, Mama. Hurry, 'Zanna. My feet are cold."

The dark was punctuated by the glow of pale puddles of illumination cast by the intermittent street lamps. The falling snow passed through the light only to disappear into the darkness beyond each one. As they walked, Emily shook her clothing to air out the pipe and cigar smoke. "A most remarkable evening, don't you think, 'Zanna? What did you think of the sermons that were taught?"

"I thought several times that Papa would have liked to have been there. He would have been in agreement with much of what they preached. It's wonderful to think that there may be a new religion—a restored religion, as Elder Pratt explained—that teaches that men are responsible for their own sins and not those of Adam. I remember when Georgie was born, and Pastor Hutchison was insistent that he be baptized, as the rest of us had been."

"Your father had concluded before Georgie's birth, while reading the New Testament, that baptism was unnecessary for innocent infants—in fact he felt that it was an affront to God—but Pastor Hutchinson would not permit us to remain in his congregation with an unbaptized infant unless we increased our contributions substantially. While your father was alive, that was not a hardship, but now . . ." She did not finish the thought.

"Elder Benson said that there would be another meeting next Tuesday evening. I hope we can attend."

Her mother nodded. "If the weather is not too cold, we will do so. Elder Pratt spoke of the need to gather to Zion, but I wonder how people with little by way of resources could ever make such a journey." Her mother did not seem to expect an answer so Susanna said nothing. Instead, she allowed her thoughts to run to her upcoming wedding.

When they had closed the front door, they hurried to the residual warmth of the kitchen. Emily heated a bit of water so they each could have something warm to drink before retiring to bed.

***

For the next five evenings, the scene repeated itself. While Susanna read from her father's books, her mother sewed. As the girl read from authors that included Sir Walter Scott, Keats, Shakespeare, Aristotle, and her father's beloved and worn Bible, Georgie would sometimes sit near her feet; other times he would wander off to play with his lead soldiers.

As she read from *The Bride of Messina,* by Johann Schiller, she paused. Her mother looked up from her work. "What is it, 'Zanna? An unusual word?"

"No, Mama, an unexpected thought. We read the classics to learn wisdom, and sometimes we find a bit. Schiller wrote:

Don't let your heart depend on things
That ornament life in a fleeting way!
Who possesses, let him learn to lose

The eyes of both women met as they thought about the rocking chair.

Georgie had been listening from where he was playing. "What's so special about that, 'Zanna? Only people who have things can lose them. If somebody doesn't have anything, he can't lose it."

Their mother laughed and said quietly, "Out of the mouths of babes."

"Mama, I'm not a babe." Georgie was insulted and he scowled at his mother and sister.

"Yes, dear. You're right," she said with a suppressed smile.

***

Susanna only spoke of her letter to Jonathan Burnley once during the days that passed while she waited for a response, but each evening, before she retired to bed, she smoothed the notes he had given her over the years and reread them with a tender smile.

Her unnatural quiet demonstrated her concern. When seven days had passed without a response, Susanna murmured, "I wonder if Mr. Burnley's intentions might have changed since we last spoke. He seems to be taking an uncommonly long time to respond to my note." She could no longer ignore the knot in her stomach that made it hard to eat.

"How would you feel about a change of feeling on his part?" her mother cautiously asked.

"It would break my heart," she whispered. "I have loved him since we were children, Mama—and I hope it is not wrong of me to see this marriage as an opportunity of obtaining the security we lost with Papa's death. How wonderful it will be to have those things—and the best part will be having a good husband to love and who will love me."

***

The letter finally arrived in the late morning post on the twentieth of November. Susanna slowly turned it over in her hand, hesitant to open it. She knew that its contents would potentially set the course of her life. She sat down, carefully broke the wax seal, and unfolded the sheet, which comprised the envelope as well as the letter. She read silently. It was brief.

Her mother watched her face as it grew so white that her tiny freckles stood out on her cheeks. "What is it, 'Zanna? Are you ill? What does the letter say?"

A cold hand was squeezing her heart so hard that she found it difficult to breathe. She held out the letter with an unsteady hand. Her mother took it and read it aloud:

> *November 19, 1844*
>
> *My Dear Miss Thayer,*
>
> *I am in receipt of your letter of November twelfth. I regret to inform you that at my father's urging, I have very recently*

become formally betrothed to my second cousin, Miss Ann Southwick of the Northampton Southwicks. I hope this is not a great personal disappointment to you. A young woman as lovely and refined as yourself will surely have no difficulty marrying a fine young man who will fully appreciate your many graces.

Your respectful servant,
Jonathan Burnley, Junior

Her chest was suddenly so tight, she felt as if it had been banded in steel and she couldn't breathe. She wrapped her arms around herself and rocked back and forth slightly as if holding a child in need of comfort. "Oh, Mama," she said breathlessly, "I thought he loved me the way I loved him. How could I have been so deceived? What will I do now? What will *we* do now?" Her voice was a heartbroken whisper. Her tears began to fall and dropped onto her skirt, making dark spots of purple in the lavender fabric.

"God will provide, Susanna. God will provide." Her mother could think of nothing else by way of more comforting words. She rose and stood by her daughter, patting her shoulder. Susanna turned her face away and covered her mouth with her hand.

Georgie approached her and said quietly, "I'm sorry, 'Zanna. Please don't cry." He looked at her with wide, worried eyes.

She put her arm around him and hugged him to her. She whispered in his ear, "Georgie, I don't mean to upset you, but I just can't help crying."

In his childish way, he patted her on the back, trying to give her what comfort he could. After a few seconds, she straightened and tried to smile. "You are a good and kind brother, Georgie, and even if I must stop loving Jonathan, I will always love you."

Susanna slept little that night, trying to muffle her weeping so her mother would not know the depth of her loss, but in the morning, her red-rimmed eyes gave away her feelings.

***

The next evening, the three of them were quiet as they walked through the lightly falling snow toward Faneuil Hall. Emily had noted Susanna's silence since she had received the reply to her note to Jonathan but made no attempt to force her into unwanted conversation. As they entered through the downstairs doorway, a man in a black coat and tall hat offered them a handbill. Thinking it might have something to do with the religious meeting to be held on the second floor, Susanna glanced at it in the poor light and pushed it into the pocket of her cloak. The three of them entered the hall and found a place to sit on the hard benches as near the front of the crowd as possible. Elder Benson gave a sermon on the eternal nature of man that silenced the critics in the audience and brought great smiles to the others. When the meeting ended, many of the men pressed around both Elder Benson and Elder Pratt. Emily, Susanna, and Georgie hurried out of the smoky atmosphere and made their way into the still, starlit night. The snow, which had been unrelenting for a week, had ceased to fall. They stood on the street, looking up in silence.

Georgie spoke first. "Look, Mama, no more snowflakes, but it looks like God has spilled his jewels in the sky."

"It is beautiful, Georgie," Emily whispered in awe.

Susanna turned her head to view the sky in every direction with amazement, for a few seconds forgetting the hollowness of her heart. "Perhaps this is a sign from God that Elder Benson spoke the truth when he said that each one of us determines our eternal future by the choices we make in this life." She looked directly at her mother. "It is such a beautiful night, Mama, would you mind if we went to the burying ground, so I can talk with Papa?"

"Of course not, Daughter."

As they reached the first street lamp, Susanna remembered the handbill and pulled it out of her pocket. "Look, Mama, it's an invitation for women to apply for work in the mills." She read it quickly, but as her mother showed little interest in it, she pushed it back into her pocket. Despite her mother's lack of interest, Susanna's mind began to wonder if there was purpose in the fact that the information had come into her hands that evening.

They reached Copp's Hill Burying Ground and made their way between the rows of headstones, breaking the crusted snow with each step. The golden orb of the moon and the starlight shed a brightness over the snow that made dark shadows recline behind each headstone. A hundred feet into the large cemetery, they reached the Thayer plot and stood for a few minutes without speaking. The newest stone read: "Robert Thayer, Beloved Husband and Father, born 1801, died July 16, 1844." It sat next to one that read: "Asa Thayer, Beloved Son, born 1835, died 1837."

Susanna broke the silence. "Papa, we have reached a difficult time and need your guidance. I no longer have an offer of marriage. We must find a way to support ourselves." She paused until the tightness in her throat eased enough to permit her to continue. "If I seek a position as a ladies' maid, it will be insufficient to support the three of us." She paused for a moment. "Perhaps we might open a boarding house, but you know that single ladies of refinement cannot have single men staying under the same roof with them. Mama's sewing helps, but . . . but we need some direction." She pulled the handbill from her pocket and read in silence for a moment. "Perhaps the answer is here in my hand. Should I go to Lowell or Providence and work in the mills? Right now, it seems to be the only thing to do."

Her mother turned to her in surprise. "'Zanna, what put that idea in your head?"

Susanna did not respond for a long moment. Then she said quietly, "I think Papa would agree with me, Mama. I think that perhaps I should go to Lowell and take a position in one of the mills."

Her mother took a deep breath and let it out slowly. "'Zanna, that is not considered acceptable work for a well-bred young lady. It would be a hard life—and we have other alternatives. As James is still without a wife, Georgie and I could live with him in the four rooms above the office. I could save him the money he is paying a housekeeper and Georgie could run errands for him. It could be an acceptable arrangement. You could live with Rachel and her husband, William. With her third child due soon, she could use your help with the other two." Emily was trying to sound cheerful but was not entirely successful.

"Mama, I can't live with Rachel and William. You know I love my sister, but her husband has lascivious eyes and hands he should keep to himself. Why do you suppose they hire only women who can pass for the grandmother of the children? They have been unable to keep a maid for more than three months unless she was as ugly as a post. When I stayed with them for a week after her second child was born two years ago, the situation quickly became intolerable."

"I'm sorry, 'Zanna. You had never said anything about your reason for coming home sooner than we had planned, but I suspected as much. Was it so bad that you would prefer the mills to living with Rachel and her husband?"

"Yes."

In quiet distress, Emily avoided her daughter's eyes for several seconds. "Then I won't close my mind to it. Perhaps we have no other alternative. I've been praying for an answer that would permit the three of us to remain together, but now we must face the fact that such a thing may be impossible."

"We could go to work in the mills with Susanna. Then we could stay together, Mama." Georgie spoke with a child's hope.

Susanna looked at her small brother with a tender expression. "I'm afraid that you and Mama will have to stay here in Boston. There isn't any place for little boys as small as you at the mill." His face fell.

Emily took Susanna's hand and squeezed it as if to strengthen their resolve as they walked toward home. When they entered the kitchen, she lit two candles and put them on the table. "May I see the handbill you were given this evening? I would like to read it."

Susanna laid it on the table and tried to smooth the creases in the paper. Her mother sat and read aloud, "*Seventy-five girls and women from fifteen to thirty-eight years of age wanted to work in the cotton mills in Lowell and Chicopee, Massachusetts, and Providence, Rhode Island.*" She looked up with a crease appearing in her forehead. "I could apply to work there as well, but—but I would have to send Georgie to live with Aunt Louisa in Newburyport, and I refuse to consider such a thing. We hardly know her and spinsters of her age just aren't meant to raise children." She looked over to her son, who had looked up from his lead soldiers when he heard his name. "We will be just fine, Georgie." She tried to speak with confidence, but her voice caught in her throat.

She returned to reading aloud. "*I am authorized by said mills to make the following proposition to persons suitable for their work, viz: They will be paid one dollar per week and board for the first month. It is presumed thereafter that they will then be able to go to work at job prices. They will be considered as engaged for one year, cases of sickness excepted. All that remain in the employ of the mills for eighteen months will have the amount of their expenses to the mills refunded to them. None but active and healthy girls will be engaged for this work.*

"*I will be at the Woburn Hotel on November twenty-second in the forenoon and at Reading House that afternoon to conduct interviews with applicants. Signed, J. M. Boynton, agent for procuring help for the mills.*"

She set the paper down. "The twenty-second is the day after tomorrow. This is not a decision that we have time to dwell upon."

As the three members of the Thayer family knelt before retiring to bed, Emily ended their prayer with the words, "Lord, when Robert died, a door was closed. It appears that Susanna sees another one opening. Please give her the courage to go through it—and give me the courage to let her go."

"Amen," Susanna whispered fervently.

Chapter Three

That night, Susanna slept fitfully, and the following morning, with an outer calmness that belied the nervous feelings in her stomach, she asked, "May I use Papa's carpetbag to pack my things?" Without waiting for a response, she continued in a tone meant to be cheerful, "I'm sure I will never be able to get everything I need into it."

"You are determined to go, 'Zanna?"

"Yes, Mama. During the night, I had a dream which I believe was a prompting from Papa, or perhaps from God. Remember the summer we visited Uncle Thaddeus's farm in Medford—before we lost touch with his family? I was about six years old, and I was playing with the goats. One particular billy goat tried to butt me over and over."

"I remember watching the two of you. I could see that you were frightened, so I called out to you to take him by the horns. Then he would have to stop." Her mother smiled at the memory.

"I followed your advice and found that I could control him that way. In the next few days, that little goat became my friend and followed me everywhere." She smiled at the memory. "I think life is sometimes like that. You taught me that I must 'take it by the horns' and then I'm in control." She looked around the room wistfully and then took a deep breath. "Now it's time for me to pack."

Her mother tried to match her more positive tone. "What will not fit into the carpetbag, we will roll into a quilt. We have all afternoon to pack what you will take with you. You can go by rail on the Boston and Lowell Line in the morning. It stops in Woburn about midmorning, if memory serves me correctly. We have made the commitment. As hard as it will be for me to let you go, we will move forward—this seems the only solution to our situation at the present."

The carpetbag that had belonged to Robert was stuffed with an extra camisole, knickers, shoes, a night dress, comb, brush, dust cap, needles, thread, scissors, and the many other small items of importance to a young woman. Two quilts were laid out to become a bundle for bed linens, her two other cotton dresses, and a shawl.

She looked briefly at the royal blue silk evening dress she had worn to dinner the previous June at the Burnley home. Jonathan had urged his parents, in particular his mother, to invite the Thayers—including her brother James, her sister Rachel and Rachel's husband William, and even little Georgie—to join them and several other guests at a dinner party to mark Susanna's seventeenth birthday.

She regretfully returned it to the wardrobe. There would be no need for such a dress at the mills. She and her mother carefully folded and rolled the quilts into a bundle and wrapped a rope around it in such a way as to make a handle for carrying.

They rose early the next morning, ate an apple, and had a cup of hot water as there was little else in the house. Emily banked the coals in the stove while Susanna looked around one last time, searching through the rooms as much for memories as for anything she might have missed that she might need.

"Here, my dear. Put these apples in your bundle. You may get very hungry on the train." Her mother wrapped a small loaf of bread, baked the day before, in a clean cloth and put it into the carpetbag as well. When they had closed the door behind them, Susanna laid her hand on it for a brief moment as if to absorb the memories behind it. Straightening, she turned with resolve and the three of them started for the train station. She carried the carpetbag and Georgie carried the bundle. When he grew too tired, his mother took it.

They hurried through the cold and arrived at the station a few minutes before eight. The great, black engine was sitting on the track with four wooden passenger cars behind it. An occasional belch of steam demonstrated that it was waiting only for the fireman and the engineer to prod it into life.

Susanna took the money her mother gave her and waited in line to purchase her ticket to Woburn. She returned and sat between her mother and brother with a yellow ticket in her mittened hand. "The train leaves at ten minutes after nine." She smiled bravely at her brother. "If I appear to falter, Georgie, just remind me of the goat."

He laughed. "I will."

Susanna looked around at the other women and girls traveling to Woburn. "I suppose they're going to apply for work in the mills as well."

"I'm glad that you're not embarking on this adventure entirely alone." Emily's smile was stiff and forced.

They took one another's hand as they sat together on the hard bench.

All the other women and girls were gathered in clusters where they laughed and talked excitedly, with the exception of one young woman who sat alone on a bench across from Susanna. She had only a small roll of possessions wrapped in what looked like a dish towel with string around it.

In her usual friendly manner, Susanna set about to make the girl comfortable. "Are you traveling to Woburn to apply for work at the mills?" The young woman simply nodded. She had a thin, pale face and anxious blue eyes. She sat with her shoulders hunched. Her fingernails were bitten to the quick. Her head was bare and her carrot-red hair hung straightly to her shoulders.

"I'm Susanna Thayer, and this is my mother, Mrs. Emily Thayer. I'm going to apply for work in the mills. Are you traveling alone?" Again, the young woman just nodded. "Will you tell me your name?" Susanna pressed.

"Jane O'Neil." She looked at the hands in her lap as she spoke. Her coat was much too thin for the cold weather and was badly worn.

"Are you traveling alone?" Susanna asked again. The young woman gave another nod.

Emily spoke. "You have no head scarf. You will become ill with the cold." She unwrapped the quilt bundle and located the item she was looking for. "Here, please take this scarf. Susanna has another one so she won't need it." She offered the long knit scarf to the timid young woman, who shook her head.

Emily stood and moved to the bench, sitting near the timid girl. "Of course you will take it. It's a gift, and it's not good manners to refuse a gift," she said in a motherly tone. She put the scarf around the young woman's head and wrapped the ends around her neck. She stepped back to look at her handiwork. "It's a good color for you. The red gives you some color in your face."

"My father said that red is a color only wanton women wear." Her voice was so low it was hard to hear her through the chatter of the other waiting passengers.

"Is he traveling with you?"

"No. He died last month. My mother died when I was a child. I have no other family where I am welcome to live any longer, so I am going to work in the mills to support myself."

Seeing a common experience that might help her draw the quiet young woman out, Susanna offered, "My father died about four months ago, and I miss him very much. I'm sure you miss your father as well. Since I'm going to the mills like you, I hope we'll become good friends." Jane was unresponsive. She continued to look at her hands.

At nine o'clock, the conductor called out, "All aboard, all aboard for Medford, Woburn, and points north to Lowell."

Emily and Susanna stood and looked at each other. Without a word, they gave each other a long embrace. Georgie pulled on Susanna's skirt. "Give me a hug, too, 'Zanna. I will miss you."

Susanna knelt and gave her brother a hug. While she held him, she whispered, "Take care of Mama while I'm gone."

He nodded. "I will."

The uniformed conductor cried out again, "'Booooaaaarrrd. All aboard."

"I must go, Mama. I will write as often as I can. Please write back to me. I will miss you both so much." Her resolve melted as an unexpected sob caught in her throat almost like a hiccup. Actually leaving was so much more difficult that she had dreamed it would be.

"Yes, Daughter. Make us proud of you." Emily gave her another quick but firm hug before stepping back.

As Susanna turned toward the train, she tried to smile, to force back the sudden tears that burned at the back of her throat. Jane rose from the bench hesitantly and picked up her small bundle. Susanna waved at her mother and brother and then put her arm through that of the pale girl, pulling her toward the steps of the second passenger car.

Her mother returned her wave and called out, "Take life by the horns, Susanna, by the horns."

Once they were settled on the seat in the passenger car, Jane asked, "What did your mother mean when she said 'Take life by the horns'?"

"I think she means to face life with faith and courage." Susanna turned and looked out of the window. The belches of steam from the engine grew larger and hid the people standing on the platform. Finally, the train lurched into motion. She waved again at her mother and brother where they appeared and disappeared intermittently through the steam that billowed around them. She could see the tears glistening on her mother's cheeks.

When they were out of sight, Susanna swallowed hard and forced a smile as she reached into one of the quilt bundles she was carrying. She pulled out two of the three apples and offered one to Jane. "I had very little breakfast, so I'm hungry. Will you have an apple with me?" Jane hesitated for only a second and then took the apple quickly as if she were afraid that the offer would be rescinded. She held it for several seconds and examined it as if it were a treasure. Then her hunger drove her to eat it very quickly, and soon only the stem and four little seeds were left.

***

Despite the increasing separation from her mother and little brother, Susanna began to feel a growing excitement as the train clacked and lurched along the rails. *This is indeed taking life by the horns,* she thought. They arrived in Woburn in little more than an hour. When she stepped down onto the platform, Susanna asked the conductor, "Where is the Woburn Hotel from here?"

"Just up the street about two blocks on the left," he answered as he nodded and touched his hat. He was asked the same question and responded in a similar manner to several of the other young women as they stepped down from the train.

Most of the women and girls had gathered in little groups on the platform. Susanna took Jane's arm again to offer some encouragement to the timid young woman, and as the two of them moved up the street, the other women and girls followed like an unsteady stream, some talking in nervous whispers and giggles.

Mr. J. M. Boynton sat at a long table on the far side of the hotel lobby wearing a tailed coat, vest, and a self-important expression. As the two young women entered the front door of the stately hotel, Susanna noticed the tasseled, red velvet draperies and the plush seats. As they paused to look around, he called out, "If you're seeking a position in the mills, just step up here one at a time and give me your names." He waved them toward him. "Don't dawdle."

Jane continued to look in wonder around the room at the oak woodwork and floral carpeting. Susanna pulled her toward the table. "Jane, we mustn't keep the man waiting."

As each woman or girl stepped up to the table, Mr. Boynton handed her a piece of paper which restated the information that had been in the handbill that was still in the pocket of Susanna's dress. He looked each one in the face. "Name, please." He wrote briefly and then looked up again. "Are you in good health?" Upon receiving an affirmative answer, he would ask, "Are you willing to commit to work in the mills for at least one year?" After one or two additional questions were asked, more to measure the individual's education than for any answer they would elicit, he handed a blue card to each and told her to be at the station at four that evening to board the train for Lowell. "You will arrive at seven, and at that time you will be assigned to one of the company boarding houses. Vacancies in the boarding houses will be filled in order of availability."

Only two were turned away; one was a thin girl with a hoarse, deep cough, and the other was a young woman who held a small child by the hand. "The mills do not furnish child care for children of any age," Boynton said brusquely. In all, twenty-three women were accepted for positions.

Susanna looked at the blue card in her hand with mixed feelings. It represented the commitment she had made. *Papa, have I made the right choice?* There was no answer to her question.

As the noon hour neared, several of the women left the hotel to locate a market or a small place where they could purchase something to eat. A few entered the hotel dining room. Susanna noted that Jane made no effort to leave the lobby but continued to stand near the window watching the carriage traffic on the main street. Susanna spoke. "Jane, what will you do for something to eat?"

Jane removed the red scarf and tucked it in a pocket of her worn coat. "Nothing, as I have no money," she responded.

"Then you must come with me. We will need something to eat. This may be a very long day." Susanna took Jane's arm and led her toward the dining room. There, the formally dressed maitre d' looked at Jane's worn coat with skepticism but led them to a small table.

Susanna did not look at the menu. She smiled in her most beguiling manner when the waiter appeared at the table. "Two cups of peppermint tea, if you please—and a small knife suitable for cutting bread."

"Is that all, miss?" he asked stiffly.

"Yes, thank you."

When the tea was brought and the knife was laid before her, she smiled her thanks. He asked again, "Will there be anything else I can do for the ladies?"

Susanna shook her head. When he had disappeared, she reached into the carpetbag and pulled out the small loaf of bread her mother had given her, unwrapped it, and deftly cut it into four pieces. She removed the remaining apple and, using the same knife, cut it in half. When the cup of tea, two thick slices of bread, and half of the apple were laid before Jane, she appeared momentarily unable to speak. She ate the bread and apple with a speed that made Susanna realize that her new friend had had little to eat for some time, other than the apple she was given that morning.

When they had finished their meal, Susanna rose. "Let's walk the main street and find a market. We will need to purchase something to eat this evening on the train."

They looked into the windows of each shop as they passed. Susanna tried to draw Jane into conversation, but the quiet girl responded only in monosyllables. Jane had put the red scarf back on, but she kept her arms folded and her bare hands tucked under her elbows. In the window of one small mercantile, they saw a variety of items, but it was a pair of red mittens that caught Susanna's eye. Despite the need to watch her pennies, she thought, *Surely I can purchase those for Jane.* She motioned the quiet young woman to follow her inside. The smells of baked goods, oiled wood floors, licorice, and cinnamon filled the air.

She spoke to the man in the white apron behind the battered wooden counter as Jane looked around the store. The man stepped to the window display and removed the mittens. After she had dropped a few of the precious coins into his hand, he reached for a piece of paper to wrap them.

"No, we will take them as they are." She took them from his hand. "Jane, put on these mittens. I think you will find travel in that unheated train car pleasanter if your hands are warm."

Jane made no move toward her, so Susanna stepped over to her and took her hand, turned it palm up, and laid the mittens in it. "Put them on, Jane." The girl slowly followed Susanna's urging.

Susanna turned back to the man at the counter. "And we would like two of those cinnamon rolls, four crackers, and two pieces of cheese, and please wrap them, if you will, so we can take them with us on the train."

When the man handed her the little package, she thanked him and dropped two more coins into his hand. The girls regretfully left the shop of so many wonderful smells.

"Well, where shall we go now? We have more than two hours before the train leaves." When Jane did not respond, Susanna added, "Let's view the windows of the shops on the other side of the street as we make our way back to the hotel. We'll wait out the afternoon there in the lobby where it's warm."

They found a small alcove in the rear of the lobby, where there was a small settee upholstered in red velvet with a low table in front of it.

"Susanna, the rolls you bought smell wonderful." Jane had been so quiet that her comment surprised Susanna. "I was surprised when you bought something so extravagant."

She answered emphatically, "I am determined not to think of this change in our circumstances as a time of mourning. It's not a wake, Jane. We must think of it as a new beginning, something worthy of a celebration, so I spent a few pennies more than might have been necessary so we won't go hungry tonight."

"I hope it will be a good beginning. Anything will be better than what I left." Jane's voice had dropped. "You are so kind, Susanna. I've never known anyone as kind as you have been."

"What about your family? Surely they were kind to you."

"I have only one family member left since my father died, but she holds no affection for me, nor I for her."

"What a sad thing to say." Susanna's words were heartfelt.

"I was raised without a mother. My father was . . ." She stopped and her face grew even whiter and then colored from her neck to the roots of her hair like a vessel being filled. She started again as if determined to speak truthfully. "My father was a drunkard. He operated a public house for all the years I can remember, and his sister, my Aunt Bertha, kept it from total failure. She would lock up the liquor bottles every evening at closing time to keep him from them. She kept the money and counted the profits, but during the hours when we were serving guests, she could not keep him from drinking with the crude and boisterous men who came in each day." Another pause. "He cared only for his liquor and his drinking companions. He once told me bitterly that it would have been better if I had died along with my mother."

Susanna caught her breath and reached out to take Jane's hand. "I'm so sorry. It's hard to imagine living in a loveless home. Such a sin shall be upon the head of the parents."

"And in that house, upon the head of the aunt. She would cuff me whenever we were out of sight of others. She had only angry words, no matter how hard I tried to please her. I often agreed with my father. It would have been better if I had gone to an early grave with my mother."

She took a shuddering breath and sat silently staring out the window for a few minutes, seeing the old tavern rather than the street that ran in front of the hotel. "I was the cook and often served tables as well. There were those who thought we were a family, but they were deceived. I could do nothing well enough to please her. After my father died three weeks ago, the tavern came to the two of us in joint ownership, according to our solicitor. I tried my best to help her run it, but yesterday, in a fit of rage, she threw my things into the street and locked me out. It was then that I knew that I must go to Lowell to work in the mills. Any place will be better than where I was."

"But those times are over now, Jane. We will make friends in Lowell, and you will put those harsh memories behind you. Things will be better." Susanna's voice was firm with conviction. She fervently hoped she was right.

Chapter Four

At three thirty, the women and girls who carried a blue card from Mr. Boynton began to make their way back toward the train station. Once inside the second passenger car, Susanna and Jane settled themselves on a bench that permitted them to lean against the end of the car, and as the evening darkness closed over the monotone countryside, they watched the farms, hills, and fields slip past the windows and into the darkening evening.

After Susanna divided the rolls, crackers, and cheese between the two of them, she watched as Jane ate her cinnamon roll slowly in tiny, nibbling bites, as if to make it last as long as possible. When she had finished, she licked her fingertips.

"Thank you, Susanna. That was the most wonderful thing I have ever eaten."

"I must admit that it was very good." Susanna's smile was broad.

"I think there will be cinnamon rolls like that in heaven," Jane said as she leaned back, closed her eyes, and smiled.

"That's the first time I've seen you smile, Jane. Your smile lights up your whole face. I hope you will do it often."

"Perhaps I will learn now that I have a friend like you."

***

The motion of the train, the rhythmic click-click of the wheels on the rails, the darkness outside, and the muted light cast by a single lantern hung in the middle of the car enticed the women into the warm darkness of sleep.

In her dreams Susanna relived her last birthday party. The skirt of her blue silk dress with the bodice of velvet had rustled and spread about her as she and Jonathan had waltzed with the other guests in the large parlor of the Burnleys' Beacon Hill mansion. They had laughed and held hands under the table during the formal dinner, and he had leaned over and whispered in her ear, "Someday, we'll have a house like this, when we are married and I have a law practice of my own." It was not the formal proposal that was to be announced eventually, but it was an admission of what they both had assumed would someday come to pass.

The dream ended abruptly when all were awakened by the conductor as he announced their arrival. "Loowwellll, Lowell, Massachusetts, next stop."

The train slowed and finally jerked to a halt. The hiss of the escaping steam filled their ears as it billowed around the cars like great clouds blown on the breath of a dragon.

The girls and women stood, stretched, and began to gather up their belongings. Susanna's heart was beating rapidly. *Take life by the horns,* she reminded herself. The girls and women stepped down onto the station platform, which was lit by several flickering whale oil lamps mounted on the exterior walls of the soot-stained clapboard building. The air was so cold it stung their throats and noses.

The city was a myriad of lights gleaming in the darkness in every direction. It seemed that every light in the windows of the multitude of five- and six-story mill buildings and the smaller boarding houses was lit. Adding to the reflection of the windows in the rivers and canals that cut the city into parcels were glimmering stars that filled the sky and glinted off the water.

The girls couldn't help but stand in amazement and stare. "It looks like a fairyland," one remarked.

Above the sound of steam escaping the train engine was a steady growling sound that covered the city like a blanket.

"It's too cold to be a fairyland," Jane commented under her breath.

A very large man in a black great coat with a booming voice announced, "Mill girls, the wagons are waiting. Get your bags, and be quick about it."

The figures crowded around the several wagons and dropped their bundles in the back before climbing onto the seats. As the reins hit the horses' rumps, the wagons lurched forward one at a time and turned into the frigid wind. One young woman leaned forward and tapped the shoulder of the driver of the wagon in which Jane and Susanna rode. "What's that noise?" she asked.

The driver spoke over his shoulder. "That's the sound of the mill machinery that's driven by the water in the canals. It'll be a whole lot louder when you're workin' in the mill buildings."

Little more was said as those in the wagons tried to bury their faces in their scarves. The sound of the clop-clop of the horses' hooves overlaid by the growling of the mill machinery echoed in the streets, which were lit by halos of light that hovered around each street lamp as if to keep warm. Shadows danced on the dirty mounds of snow on each side of the rutted road. Few people were on the streets, most having the wisdom to be inside on such a bitter night.

The five wagons moved down Andover and turned onto Nesmith Street. As they moved along East Merrimack Street, the lights in the mill buildings began to darken, as though a wind had blown through a thousand unprotected candles. One of the girls lifted her face from her scarf long enough to ask the teamster, "Why are the lights going out?"

"It's the end of the shift. Must be about seven thirty."

The reflected lights in the rivers and canals were also extinguished, and only the stars, street lamps, and lights in individual homes continued to burn. The dark water of the rivers widened at the confluence of the Merrimack and Concord, and the wagons' wheels rattled over a bridge. Even in the dark, it was evident that the mill buildings were huddled close to the rivers and canals and were arranged in military precision. Standing behind or beside them, like chicks huddled against mother hens, were two- and three-story boarding houses, some frame, some brick, their windows alight.

The first wagon stopped before one of the smaller buildings. Four women dismounted at the urging of the driver and located their bundles. He motioned them toward the front door. As they approached the building, the remaining wagons lumbered past that wagon, and the first wagon became the last.

At the next building, five young women gathered up their baggage, and those in the wagons behind them watched as they entered the door in the middle of the ground floor. At the third large building, the driver halted the teams and said to the women huddled on the hard seats, which included Susanna and Jane, "Get your baggage, and report inside. According to my instructions, the house staff has four vacancies here."

Unassisted, Susanna carefully made her way backward down from the wagon seat, using the wheel spokes as steps. The others followed her example. At the back of the wagon, she located her carpetbag and bundle. Jane was the last to dismount from the wagon, hesitant and nervous.

The driver's patience was wearing thin. "Miss, please hurry a bit," he urged. "I need to get the horses out of the cold and into a barn."

The snow on the walkway from the street to the door was trampled with the prints of many feet. As the wagon pulled away, the women moved toward the door with Susanna leading the way. She looked at the young woman beside her. "I'm Susanna Thayer. What's your name?"

"I'm Josephine Parker. Just call me Josie." The young woman paused and looked up at the large building, halting the others behind her. "I'm a little bit scared, but you don't even look nervous."

"Josie, I'm nervous, too. I'm sure everyone is. This is new to all of us."

Susanna looked over her shoulder at the young woman behind her. "I'm Susanna Thayer. What's your name?"

"I'm Francis McKinney." Francis appeared as nervous as Josie.

As Susanna knocked, the door opened. A portly woman in a long black dress with a large white apron greeted them. Her gray curls poked out from under a dust cap. Behind her was a skinny young man of indeterminate age with a head of ginger-colored hair going off in all directions like a fireworks explosion.

"Come in, come in, everyone. Let's not let the heat out. I'm Mrs. Winters, the official head of Merrimack Company Boarding House Number Three." She closed the door behind Jane, who had been the last to enter. "Some of the girls call me their 'house mother.' This is Elijah. He'll show you to your rooms and help you with the heaviest bags." She reached into the commodious pocket of the apron and handed each girl two printed sheets of paper. "Read this before you go to bed tonight."

She turned and pointed to Josie's big valise. "'Lijah, can you get that thing up the stairs?" He nodded. She turned away and muttered, "Seems some girls think they need to bring all the comforts of home." She disappeared down a hallway as she shook her head.

Elijah picked up the valise and started up the staircase that rose from the far side of the entryway. "Follow me." The valise banged the newel post of the banister, where it was apparent that other bags and boxes had also done similar damage over the years.

The four young women followed Elijah up the stairs. On the second floor they glanced toward the south end of the hallway, where they could see two doors on each side that faced each other. On the north half of the building, the arrangement was the same.

Elijah moved to the door on the right side of the hallway and dropped the valise. It hit the floor with a thud. After a moment, the door swung open.

A girl of about thirteen stood facing them. Her long, dark hair was pulled over her shoulder, and she had nearly finished braiding it. "Missy, close the door. Some of us are in our nightclothes," a voice from behind her called out,

She ignored the demand and grinned at Elijah. "Have you got some new roommates for us?"

He didn't respond to her question. He looked at the four young women clustered behind him. "Two of you will room here, and as I'm not carrying that valise any farther, one of them better be the one that owns it."

While he started toward the next flight of stairs, Josie shrugged. "I guess I'll see you all tomorrow," she said timidly to the others as she stepped inside. Francis followed her and Missy closed the door.

They could see Elijah standing with arms folded across his chest at the top of the next flight of stairs waiting with a pained look on his face. "You better hurry, ladies, as I don't want to be standin' here when the lights-out bell rings, and I know it takes awhile for a bunch of girls to get settled."

They hurried up the remaining stairs and followed him to a door on the left, where he knocked. The door opened a crack, and a young female voice said, "Who is it?"

"It's me, 'Lijah. I got two roommates for you." The door opened a little wider, and a girl of about twelve stood looking at the little group in the hall. She wore a frayed, pink flannel nightdress and, like Missy, was braiding a long braid pulled over her shoulder, but hers was black. "Open the door, Abby, so these girls can come in." Elijah had grown impatient.

Abby stepped back and the door opened wider. Elijah turned and, with long strides, quickly disappeared down the stairs.

Abby pointed at a double bed in the corner. Susanna looked around the room. It was only about sixteen feet square and held three double beds as well as the belongings of the girls using the room. Trunks and valises were either pushed under the beds or sitting on the floor at the foot of each one. A small pedestal table sat between the two casement windows, where two candles threw their light around the room. Pegs holding coats or cloaks were mounted near the door, and the only remaining items in the room were two chests of three drawers each; one sat against the wall between the heads of the two beds at one end of the room, and the other sat next to the head of the third bed, where the door could hit it. That bed was pushed against the wall and the mattress was bare.

"Jane, did you bring any bedding with you?" Susanna asked.

"No, all I have are my clothes and a hair brush."

"Well, I have some bed linens in one of the bundles, and with my two quilts, we should be warm enough."

"Each one of us has a drawer in one of the chests for our personal things." Abby, who had opened the door so suspiciously, now seemed more than willing to talk. "Your drawers are the bottom two of that dresser." She pointed at the chest of drawers near the door. Then she introduced the other three girls in an open, almost childlike manner, "That's Bridget over there." Bridget had rust-colored hair, and freckles were sprinkled over her nose and cheeks. "That's Ellen reading her book—she's always reading." Ellen looked up briefly, adjusted her wire-rimmed glasses, and gave a quick smile before turning a page. "And that's Harriett, who's brushing her hair, and I'm Abby. Who are you?"

"I'm Susanna, and this is Jane."

Abby laughed a cascade of giggles. "Jane, I can tell you're Irish. Seems like half the girls in the mills are Irish." Jane colored from her throat to her hairline. "I don't have red hair like so many, but I'm Irish too. I'm black Irish." Abby's voice was as full of pride as if she had just announced that she was related to the queen of England.

"You need to get your bed made and your things put away. Then we can talk until lights go out." This came from Ellen, who was still reading her book.

Susanna opened the bundle and spread a muslin sheet and the quilts on the bed with Jane's help, grateful that her mother had sent the two of them with her. When they had finished, Jane stood still, her eyes roving around the room. "How do you know when the lights will go out?" she asked. "I don't see a clock."

"After you've been here for a few months, you'll get good at guessing the time. We live by bells; bells to get up, bells to eat, bells to go to bed. Bells, bells, bells," Harriett said irritably as she pulled the brush forcefully through her long, chestnut hair.

"Jane, here's a drawer for your personal things. I think you'd better put on your night dress," Susanna urged as she folded her other dresses and put them into the drawer she had selected, along with her other personal items.

"I wanted to read the papers Mrs. Winters gave us."

"Just get ready for bed, and tell us all about yourselves. We can tell you everything that's on those papers that you need to know after the lights go out," Abby stated with an all-knowing tone.

Susanna slipped out of her dress and laid it across the foot of the bed. She dropped her nightdress over her head. Jane did the same, but her nightdress was thin as gauze and worn through at the elbows. It was apparent that she was embarrassed by its condition. They talked with the other girls until a bell rang.

Abby rose from where she had been sitting, made her way over to the candles, and blew them out. "If you have anything else to put away, you will have to do it in the morning. If Mrs. Winters finds out we're burning candles after ten o'clock, she'll insist that we're using more than we're allotted, and she'll have our pay docked."

The light in the room had suddenly been reduced to the spill of weak moonlight that made its way through the worn lace curtains at the windows. Susanna slid under the quilts and moved over next to the wall. As Jane climbed in beside her, she asked, "Can someone tell us what was on the papers we were given?"

Abby responded. "One of the pages says that mill girls can only live in the company-owned boarding houses unless they still live at home with family, and that we are each answerable for any improper conduct, and that we are not permitted visitors at unreasonable hours. Doors are closed at ten o'clock, and no one will be admitted after that time without a good reason."

At that point, Ellen added, "It says that the keepers of the boarding houses must account for the number, names, and employment of their boarders and must report the names of any boarders to the company management who are guilty of improper conduct or are not attending worship services regularly."

"And we will be charged for any damage we might cause to the building or the grounds. If we use too many candles, they dock our wages; if we scratch the walls, they dock our wages; if we're late to work, they dock our wages." Harriett chanted her complaints.

"Harriett, be quiet. Don't discourage Susanna and Jane before they've even begun." Ellen's voice was curt. "Don't let Harriett's complaints discourage you. She always has a complaint."

"Mr. Boynton said that we would be paid one dollar per week plus our board for the first month. What will we be paid after that?" Susanna tossed the question out into the darkness.

Abby answered. "If you do well and give no reason for the mill management to find fault with you, you'll be paid two dollars and fifty cents a week for the next three months and four dollars a week after that. Of course, you will pay your weekly board and room of one dollar and twenty-five cents out of your pay."

"What was on the second paper?" Jane asked quietly.

"That was probably the time table," another voice answered. It was Bridget, who hadn't spoken previously. "During the winter, the first bell rings at five in the morning. The second bell rings at five thirty, and the third at five fifty. We must be at our positions in the mill by six, so we must be out of the boarding house well before the third bell. Otherwise, we must run or be late. On weekdays, the evening bell is supposed to ring at seven thirty, but if there's a big order to fill, sometimes the foreman doesn't ring the bell until eight. On Saturday evening, the bell may ring anytime between four and five, and then we must tidy our area before we can leave."

"I didn't think you were still awake, Bridget," Abby murmured. "Tell her about the meal bells."

"In the winter, we eat a bowl of oatmeal before we leave for the mill, but in the summer, we start earlier, so we get thirty-five minutes to come back to the boarding house for breakfast at eight. Year 'round, the bell rings for lunch at noon, and we have thirty-five minutes to rush back to the boarding house, eat, and get back to our post before the bell rings at twelve thirty-five."

"We don't even have time for manners," Harriett added in a disgusted tone.

"We have the same amount of time for supper. The bell rings at five and we must be back by five thirty-five. If you have any questions about what a bell means, just follow the crowd."

Susanna had more questions, but she could hear the even breathing of at least two of the girls, so she turned toward the wall and closed her eyes. In her dreams, she waved to her mother and her little brother where they stood on the train platform and watched them as they receded into the distance. Then the dream faded into a scene where Jonathan and another young woman stood before a minister. She was unaware of the tears that wet her pillow as she slept.

Chapter Five

When the first bell rang in the dark of morning, Susanna couldn't remember where she was for a moment. It took several seconds for her heart to slow its racing beat. The girls in the other beds rose quickly, and one of them lit the candles. Harriett complained forcefully when her shoelace broke.

Jane was still sleeping soundly, so Susanna shook her shoulder gently. "Jane, you need to get dressed. We've got to get dressed for work in the mill."

Jane sat up suddenly, with her arms raised as if to ward off a blow. After a second, she looked around at the other girls. All she said was, "Oh."

Harriett brushed and tied back her hair, taking longer than the other girls. "If you don't get downstairs with everyone else, you might not get any oatmeal," she said, as she went out the door.

As they descended the stairs, the five thirty bell rang. They located the dining room at the end of the hall on the first floor by the sound of the chatter that flowed out of the door like a river.

The young girl waiting tables quickly took two bowls of oatmeal from the tray she carried and set them in front of Susanna and Jane. "Don't burn your mouths," she admonished them.

Within the next ten minutes, the dining room began to empty. The girls and women hurried to their rooms, donned their coats or cloaks, scarves and mittens, and dashed toward the mill.

Abby came over to their table. "You need to come with one of us so you'll know where to report." She stood there, waiting for them to finish their oatmeal. "If you'll hurry, I'll show you where to go."

After they were dressed to face the cold, they followed Abby down the street and through the early morning darkness to a large, six-story building about a quarter of a mile from the boarding house. A few lights were beginning to brighten the windows in the mill buildings, but the city did not look like the fairyland it had seemed the night before. It looked almost like a great dark cave under a black, leaden sky.

She led them to a building that stood in a row of five similar buildings. Under the lamps that burned on the outside of the building, they could see letters painted on the brick along the street side and above the windows on the first floor which read: "Merrimack Textile Mill Bldg. Four."

"See that door near the end of the building where it says 'Employment Office?' Just go in there, and the man will tell you where you'll be working. Bye." Abby darted away.

Inside the door, twenty women or girls of varying ages already stood in line, facing a man at a battered desk with a nameplate that read, "Jacob Cosgrove, Employment Mgr." Light was furnished by the foul-smelling whale oil lamp that hung from the ceiling. As he read from a list, he gave orders to four men who stood at the side of the room in worn and faded work clothing.

"Jonah, take the first five to the bobbin room." Swiftly, he assigned the women and girls to different stations: the shipping room, the dye room, the finishing room.

When only Susanna, Jane, and Josie remained, he pointed at them. "Ben, you take the last three to the weaving room." Ben was a younger man, straight and tall with youth, but with the remnants of a perpetual sneer on his face. Rather than giving them a nod of recognition, as the other men had, he looked each of the three over in a manner that made Susanna feel uncomfortable.

As they followed him up the stairs to the second level and down a long hallway, he looked over his shoulder and spoke. "Stay close with me. The machinery will be startin' right away, and then it will be hard to talk." As he spoke, a great roar surrounded them, a noise that seemed to fill the air like a palpable fog.

"What makes the noise," Josie cried out as she covered her ears with her hands.

"That's the sound of the gears and leather belts that drive the looms," he yelled at her. "The water has been diverted to turn the machinery."

The weaving room was large, perhaps a hundred feet in length, with eight large, casement windows on the riverside. It was about sixty feet wide, nearly filling the full width and length of the building's second floor. In that room, the noise made by the machinery was increased by the screeching of the wooden frames of the looms as they rubbed against one another, shifting position to permit the shuttles to pass back and forth between the warp threads that were pulled tautly over the frames. Like Josie, Susanna instinctively put her hands over her ears.

In the light cast by four malodorous oil lamps mounted high on the walls, it was a scene of vibrant color radiating from moving sheets of cotton fabrics. Plaids, stripes, and solids were rapidly taking shape on the looms, a thread at a time.

"You'll get used to the noise," Ben yelled. "It's your job to make sure the threads don't get knotted, that the spindles don't run out of thread before the end of a run, that the shuttles don't jam or break . . ." He seemed to deflate with frustration at trying to be heard above the noise. "Just follow me. I'll show you what to do."

He led them to a loom, the first in a row of ten, each one weaving what looked like an endless swath of red fabric about five feet wide. At the top of his lungs, he pointed out the likely places where problems could arise in the machinery. "If there's a problem, you pull this rod out, and the loom will pause." He bent over and demonstrated. "When you have the problem straightened out, push it back in, and the weaving will begin again. Keep your hands and arms out of the way as the loom may jump when the gears are engaged. If you don't, you can get hurt. You understand?" The women nodded hesitantly, not at all sure they understood. "If you're sharp about it, you'll soon learn to tie a knot in a broken thread without stopping the looms."

Ben looked up and motioned with his hand to a young woman who had appeared at the end of the first row. She approached the little group, and Ben introduced her at the top of his voice. "This is Miss Murphy. If you have any questions, she can help you." He turned and abruptly left the weaving room, glad to escape the noise.

Miss Murphy, a tall, thin girl of about eighteen with a twist of black hair pinned on the top of her head, motioned the three young women out into the hallway, and there, somewhat removed from the noise, introduced herself in a raised voice. "I'm Margaret. There are two more girls who work in this room, Ellen and Bridget." Susanna's heart leapt with the hope that they were two of the roommates she and Jane had met the night before. "They're in the back of the room, fixing a broken shuttle. What are your names?" Each girl loudly introduced herself.

"You can put your coats or capes on the pegs on the wall inside the door over there." Margaret stepped back into the room and pointed at the pegs where three coats were hung. After they had added theirs, she waved Josie over to a place at the first row of looms. Raising her voice again, she instructed, "You will watch these, and make sure to keep them running smoothly. If you have a problem you can't solve, pull the rod that will stop the machine, and come and get me." She put Susanna at the second row, Jane at the third, and left them to learn their tasks firsthand. "I'll check on you in a little while."

By this time, the early morning light had begun to labor its way into the room through windows smudged and soiled with the residue of the multitude of chimneys and fireplaces in the city. At eight, Margaret moved around the big room, putting out the oil lamps on the walls, but the rank odor of the whale oil lingered in the air throughout the day, lasting until they were lit again in the late afternoon.

The bell rang at noon, but it could hardly be heard above the noise in the large room. The looms stopped as the water from the canal was diverted. The girls gathered their coats and capes and prepared to leave for lunch. Susanna stepped up to Ellen. "I'm so glad you're in the weaving room with us. Perhaps you and Bridget can answer some of our questions."

"You need to hurry or we won't have enough time to eat," Ellen responded. The women and girls poured out of the mill buildings like water from a breach in a dam, and all continued at a near run toward their individual boarding houses. "Too many of the girls spend their time talking instead of eating. If you have any questions, we can talk tonight," she said breathlessly as they found a place to sit at one of the tables in the dining room.

After a very quick meal of a thin stew and a piece of bread, Ellen and Bridget pushed their chairs away from the table and, still chewing the last bite of bread, rushed toward the front door as they threw their coats around their shoulders. Susanna, Jane, and Josie hurriedly followed.

***

When the evening bell rang at seven thirty, the looms halted. The sudden silence after the day of noise was heavy, almost oppressive. As Susanna and Jane moved toward the coat pegs, Margaret stopped them. "Clean up your area. Pick up the threads and change any empty spools so the looms are ready to start in the morning. Sweep the floor, if it needs it. You both did very well today."

"I think that was more luck than experience," Susanna responded wearily. "Is there any way we might be able to take a few minutes to sit down occasionally during the day? I don't mean to complain, but my feet are so tired—and my back is tired—and my legs are tired." Each statement was like a bead added to a string. "Are you tired, Jane?"

Jane nodded. "But not so much as you, I'm sure. I was always on my feet at the tavern, so I guess I'm more accustomed to it."

"Almost any other position is easier, so when you get out of the weaving room, you will feel blessed. After you have been here a few months, ask for a place in the carding room. There you can sit down, and it isn't so noisy," Bridget explained. "The managers in each building sometimes move the girls around, so we will learn several positions, but the carding room is the easiest."

"We'll remember that," Josie responded with a tired smile.

"How long have you been in the weaving room?" Susanna asked Ellen as they walked toward the boarding house. Most of the girls or women walking in front or behind them were quiet, too tired to talk.

"I've been there three months. Mr. Cosgrove said he might let me move to another position eventually, maybe the carding room or the folding room, when there's a vacancy. I'm going to remind him in a few weeks."

They walked in silence until Susanna was taken with a new thought. "Christmas is almost upon us. What do the mill girls do for Christmas?"

"We go to church services and have the rest of the day off. Most of us spend it writing letters or reading."

"The first day of the new year will come a week after that. I hope 1845 will be a good year for us all. Will we mark the new year in any special way?"

"The mill owners always sponsor a ball for themselves and the managers. The rest of us get a half day off as the mills will close at noon."

That night, Susanna and Jane were asleep long before the candles were blown out. In their exhausted state, they were totally oblivious to the chatter of the other four girls.

Chapter Six

The next four weeks were a series of unchanging days, each the same as the one before, except Saturday evenings when many of the girls attended the lyceum lectures available to the people of Lowell. Most of the recently hired girls, including Susanna and Jane, went to bed early those evenings, unaccustomed to the physical demands of their new occupations. During mandatory Sunday services in the nearby Methodist chapel, they and many of the other girls occasionally dozed through the sermon. After church services on Christmas Day, Susanna and Jane spent the afternoon sleeping soundly.

On the following day, an hour into the work shift, screams could be heard above the noise of the looms, echoing throughout the weaving room and out into the hallway and stairs. The girls working near the looms froze for a fraction of a second, trying to determine what was happening. Jane moved faster than the other girls. She ran past the looms as the screams continued and soon recognized Susanna's form twisted and pulled backward above a loom which was yanking her head back and forth as she continued to scream and pull at her hair. Margaret reached her at the same time from the other direction. "My hair is caught," she screamed. "Help me. I can't stop the loom."

Margaret reached for the emergency rod that disengaged the moving parts. Even after the loom stopped, Susanna sobbed, "I can't get free. My hair is all twisted around the frame."

Margaret could see what had happened. "I'll get help," she called out as she ran from the room. In about three minutes, she was back at a run with the man called Jonah. They pushed their way past the other girls who had gathered around Susanna.

He pulled a clasp knife from his pocket and opened the blade. "Get out of my way," he commanded. He began to whittle at her hair, cutting through the thick locks.

"What are you doing," she cried out.

"Look, girl, this is what happens if you aren't careful around these machines. You gotta keep your hair covered or pinned up on your head so it don't get caught this way."

When he was finished, she straightened up and put her hands to her head, noting the shortness of what hair was left. "My hair is so short that I won't be able to go about with my head uncovered." Her hair was uneven and ragged, most of it three to four inches long. Tears of pain and humiliation were streaming down her face.

"If you're not hurt, get back to work. Clean your hair out of the loom so it don't get woven into the fabric. If you can't clean it out good, your pay will be docked for the loss of the ruined yardage. We can't sell it if there's hair in it." He turned and left the weaving room shaking his head, his disgust showing in his heavy steps.

"Are you hurt?" Margaret asked above the noise in the room. "Last year one of the girls got killed that way. Her neck got broke."

"Susanna, are you all right?" Jane's voice was still panicky and shrill.

Susanna wiped her tears on her sleeve and nodded.

"Get it cleaned out of the loom, like Jonah said, so it can be started again." Margaret's voice was relieved, but not sympathetic. "You know, he's right. You should have had your hair up on your head, out of the way, or under a dust cap. I don't guess it will happen again. It only takes once." Margaret returned to her row of looms nearer the back of the big room.

With Jane's help, Susanna started to untangle the long, auburn hair strands from where they were intertwined with the fabric and wrapped about the loom frame.

That evening she sat in the sitting room of the boarding house to write to her mother and brother. A dust cap covered her mutilated locks. The sitting room was filled with well-worn furniture and an old, very battered, upright piano. Three other girls were reading by the light of the only lamp in the room.

Dear Mama,

It seems that I have been here in Lowell for such a long time. I know it has only been a few weeks since I left Boston, but

I miss you both dearly. Sometimes I wake in the night, thinking I am in my own bed in our cozy home and that Papa will soon be getting up to start work. Then all the memories come flooding back, and I know it is time to get up to go to the mill. I am enclosing three bank certificates for one dollar each, drawn on the Bank of Massachusetts, which I am sure will be honored in Boston. I hope they will help you and Georgie with household expenses. I had to spend some of the money I have earned to purchase the paper, ink, and pen I am using. The work is tiring, as I must be on my feet all the day. The noise in the weaving room is difficult to bear. I am assigned there to watch a row of ten looms. They are large, awkward-looking pieces of machinery that occupy a great deal of space. One of them is as unmanageable as an overgrown child, a very spoilt child. It must be watched in at least a half dozen directions every minute, and even then, it is always threatening to get itself and me into trouble. The looms seem like living creatures, with great, groaning joints and whizzing threads and shuttles, and I feel that some of them are aware of my inexperience in managing them. The one that threatens to cause so much trouble brought that threat to fulfillment as it caused an accident today. While I was reaching into the machinery to try to prevent a tangle in the warp threads, my hair got caught in the shuttle and wrapped around the frame. I thought it was going to be pulled out and leave me as bald as Mr. Saterwaite. To free me, one of the supervisors had to cut it very short, but I will try to make the best of the situation. After all, it will grow back. Until then, I will wear a dust cap or a bonnet when I am out and about. Please give Georgie a kiss from me, and write to me soon.

All my love,
Your daughter,
Susanna

Post Script: I have put one of my locks in the letter so you can remember me by it.

***

A few days later, Ellen entered the dining room at the dinner hour and looked around surreptitiously. She hurriedly moved around the tables where many of the forty-eight young women who boarded there already sat, waiting for the evening meal. She laid a small printed handbill near each place and then rushed back to sit with her roommates. The girls picked up their copies and began to read.

"What is this, Ellen?" Susanna asked.

"Read it. Just read it." Ellen's voice was a near whisper as if by speaking quietly, she might hide the fact that she was the one who had distributed the handbills.

Susanna read aloud: "*Women of the mills, defend yourselves! Better your working conditions! All mill girls are urged to join the recently formed Lowell Female Labor Reform Association, which will meet Tuesday evening at eight o'clock in the main room of the Lowell Public Hall. Join us as we fight for the ten-hour work day!*"

As Susanna looked up from the paper, Mrs. Winters bustled into the dining room, and moving her rotund form with unusual speed, she pulled a copy of the handbill from the hand of a girl sitting at the nearest table. She looked down the long slope of her nose, and holding the paper at arm's length she swiftly read it. She stuffed it into her apron pocket and began to gather up the handbills, literally pulling many of them out of the hands of the startled young women.

"We will have no agitation against the mill owners in this or any other company boarding house. I will not condone such plotting under my roof." A few of the girls tried to hide their copies under their soup bowls, and several others sat on them before she reached their table. She lifted the bowls and collected those copies. "Shame, shame on all of you who demonstrate such disloyalty to the company that gives you your employment—and the very bread you eat each day."

Mrs. Winters swept out of the room like a man-o'-war under full sail, determined to burn the notices immediately in the kitchen stove.

The conversation in the room increased from a few startled whispers to a near roar, like water pouring from an opening spillway on a great dam of curiosity as those in the dining room exchanged opinions and questions on the matter.

After Mrs. Winters had disappeared, Ellen pushed her plate away, pulled a tightly rolled paper from underneath her coat, unrolled it, and used the salt and pepper shakers to hold it open. "Tonight, I'm going to take this letter and petition to every girl in the boarding house and urge her to sign it. It's going to be sent to the legislature to demand that they give us a ten-hour day," Ellen said with determination.

Harriett scoffed. "So you're going to demand a ten-hour day. That is such old news. You're wasting your time. Mill workers have been trying to get a ten-hour day for years. Mrs. Winters told me when I came to work in the mill that about half the girls turned out and refused to work for a whole week way back in '36, and look what it got them—nothing,"

Ellen was firm in her resolve. "No, no, we must keep trying. We can't give up. Here, read it." The paper curled back up as she removed the salt and pepper shakers and offered it to Harriett, who waved it away.

Susanna took it. She pushed her plate away and spread the petition out again. She read aloud as her roommates pressed in close to her. Despite her skepticism, even Harriett listened closely. "*Petition to the Massachusetts Legislature. We, the undersigned peaceable, industrious, and hardworking men and women of Lowell, in view of our condition—the evils of which have already come upon us by toiling from thirteen to fourteen hours per day, confined in unhealthy circumstances, exposed to the poisonous contagion of air, vegetable, animal, and mineral properties, debarred from proper physical exercise, mental discipline, and adequate meals, thereby hastening us on through pain, disease, and privation, down to a premature grave—pray the legislature to institute a ten-hour working day in all of the factories of the state. Signed, John Q. Thatcher, Sarah G. Bagley, James Carle, and . . .*" She paused. "Oh, look at all the other signatures. There must be more than a hundred already here."

"There's nearly two hundred, and I'm going to try to get everyone in this boarding house, and every other, to put their signatures on it as well." Ellen's face reflected the resolve in her voice. After the meal was finished, she marched off to complete her self-assigned task.

"It won't do any good," Harriet muttered as Ellen left the table. "None of us will live long enough to see any good come from that petition or any other."

As Susanna and Jane climbed the stairs to their room, Jane asked, "Are you going to sign the letter, Susanna?"

"I don't believe I will. My mother needs the money I send her. I would not want to give Mr. Cosgrove or anyone else a reason to let me go. Will you sign, Jane?"

"I need this job to support myself. I have nowhere else to go. I don't think I will sign the letter either."

***

Two days later, the announcement was made that the Honorable Edward Everett was to be the Saturday speaker at the lyceum lecture. The importance of the news nearly overshadowed the talk of the organization of the Female Labor Reform Association.

"Who is this man that everyone is talking about, Susanna?" Jane asked quietly, after they had seated themselves at the dining room table for supper on Friday.

"I believe he is a man of great importance. My father respected him very much. He told me that Mr. Everett had served in Congress some years ago, and when I was a child, he was governor of Massachusetts. I believe he is recently back after serving as ambassador to England. My father thought that he should run for president."

"I wish I had been blessed with a father who knew so many important things. All my father knew was that he enjoyed cherry rum more than any other drink." Jane's voice reflected her disgust.

"But now that's all behind you. Let's go to the lecture on Saturday evening, and learn about the world outside of Lowell, Massachusetts."

Jane smiled halfheartedly and nodded.

***

Despite the usual weariness that Susanna felt at the end of each work day, she grew excited when she entered the large meeting room and saw the well-dressed men and women who were waiting expectantly for the speaker to take the rostrum. The man with the dignified shock of white hair was the nation's greatest orator and would someday precede Abraham Lincoln on the dais at Gettysburg. He moved onto the stage with a presence that was almost hypnotic. The eloquent words rolled from his mouth for an hour and a half; his arms and hands gestured gracefully, accenting his phrases as he urged his listeners to step forth courageously as the founders of the nation had and, in their memory, preserve the history, the "holy places of this great nation" where they were privileged to be citizens.

Most of the audience followed every word, with the exception of Harriett, who drifted off to sleep after the first half hour. Mr. Everett was interrupted by applause five times, each time disturbing the exhausted girl. She then slipped back into slumber.

On the way back to the boarding house, Susanna could not hold back her enthusiasm for what she had heard that evening. "I've never heard anyone speak like that. He made me want to stand up and cheer when he finished. I would have if it wouldn't have been so unladylike." She turned and asked the others who were walking with her, "Did you enjoy the evening?"

Each one nodded and agreed with her, with the exception of Harriett, who yawned and said simply, "I don't remember much of what he said."

Abby laughed. "Of course not. You slept through most of it."

"I did not."

"Yes, you did." All the other girls laughed and agreed with Abby, silencing Harriett's denials.

They hurried to their rooms, and Ellen stated, as Harriett closed the bedroom door behind them, "Well, tomorrow I must give the letter back to Sarah Bagley, the woman in Boarding House Four who gave it to me. It needs to be put in the post right away. I'm going to ask one more time if Susanna, Jane, and Harriett will sign it."

Susanna dropped her nightdress over her head. "Yes, Ellen, I will. I think it's time I showed the kind of courage that Mr. Everett talked about this evening. Without courage, America would not be a nation. We would still belong to King George—or Queen Victoria—or whomever the English ruler is now."

"What about you, Jane, and you, Harriett?"

Harriett shook her head. "It's a waste of time and effort."

"Jane, will you sign?"

Jane looked at the floor for a moment and shook her head. Without saying anything, she climbed into bed.

"Well, you have until tomorrow evening after we get back from the mill, in case you change your mind."

"I won't," Jane whispered as she turned over and faced the wall.

***

In late March, a man came to speak in the public hall. His name meant little to the mill girls or the other residents of Lowell, but in the back of her mind, Susanna remembered it. Though the others refused, she insisted that Jane accompany her to the lecture. The hall was not as crowded as usual, and the two young women were able to find a place to sit near the front of the large room.

"Susanna, I wish you had let me stay at the boarding house this evening. I am more tired than usual. Who is this man, Parley Pratt? None of the other girls have heard of him."

"I heard him speak in November, before I came to Lowell. He and another man by the name of Benson spoke in Faneuil Hall, and using the Bible, Mr. Pratt demonstrated some of the differences in the doctrines of several denominations, establishing that the religions of today have strayed from scripture. I think you will find what he has to say very interesting."

***

After the formal lectures by Elders Pratt and Brown had ended, and many in the audience were preparing to leave the hall, Elder Pratt stepped up to the podium again and announced, "We will remain in this city for a few more days. If you are interested in learning more about The Church of Jesus Christ of Latter-day Saints, we will meet in the smaller room upstairs on Tuesday evening at eight o'clock. We hope to see you there."

The two young women walked quickly back toward the boarding house through the chill of the evening. Jane's step was tired, but Susanna's was light with excitement.

"Jane, do you see now why I wanted you to come this evening? I think it was as informative as any of the other lectures, perhaps more so."

"I'm no judge of the content of either of the speeches we heard this evening, as I had never set foot in a church before coming to Lowell, but I admit I did find what was said to be of interest," Jane admitted. They took a few more steps before either spoke again.

"I'm going to attend the meeting on Tuesday evening no matter how tired I am. I wouldn't miss it." Susanna's voice was full of resolve.

"I don't suppose any of the other girls will go. I think from all the talk I've heard that most of the mill girls will be attending the meeting of the Female Labor Reform Association that night, so I'll go with you." Jane added thoughtfully, "I think it might be wise for those of us who do not want to lose our positions to stay away from the agitation that may be caused by the labor association."

Susanna stopped, took hold of Jane's arm in her enthusiasm, and turned to face her with an animated expression. "Jane, I firmly believe that the religious message that was taught this evening is vital for our eternal well-being. It is the moral responsibility of each of us to educate ourselves, and we must use every tool that comes into our hands to do so. Somehow, that message reaches out to me like something I have heard before but somehow forgotten."

They walked in thoughtful silence the rest of the way, arriving back at the boarding house just twenty minutes before the lights-out bell.

Chapter Seven

The Tuesday evening meeting in the upper room of the public meeting hall was disturbed several times by the occasional applause and shouts from the larger room on the first floor, where the mill girls were listening to Sarah Bagley, the organizer of the Female Labor Reform Association. But throughout the evening, Susanna, Jane, and nearly thirty other citizens of Lowell listened closely to Elder Pratt and Elder Brown as they told the story of the establishment of the young religious organization they represented.

Elder Pratt closed the meeting much as he had in November, when Susanna and her mother had heard him speak in Boston. He urged those present who wanted to become members of the new church to make plans to be baptized and gather with the Saints in Nauvoo, Illinois, as thousands of recent converts were doing.

After the meeting had been concluded, Susanna stood aside while both men spoke with several members of the audience and patiently answered the sometimes hostile or outright belligerent questions. When the last questioner had put on his hat and made his way toward the door, she stepped up to Elder Pratt. "I am only one of the mill girls here in Lowell, but I am interested in your message. Will you be returning to Lowell to speak again? I want to learn more."

"I don't know where we will be in the immediate future, but if you will give me your name and address, I will see that you are regularly sent a copy of *The New York Messenger*, our church publication, and when we have a branch of the Church organized here in Lowell, it will be announced in that publication."

"Thank you, Elder Pratt. I will be glad to receive it."

It was a few weeks before a copy of the little newspaper arrived. While most of the other girls were reading *The Voice of Industry*, a publication of the Female Labor Reform Association, Susanna excitedly read *The New York Messenger*. On the banner, beneath the name of the paper, it stated that it was the official organ of The Church of Jesus Christ of Latter-day Saints for members on the Eastern Seaboard. Elder Samuel Brannan was listed as editor.

***

The milder, wetter weather of March had finally arrived when Susanna received her first letter from her mother. When Mrs. Winters handed it to her, she rushed to the sitting room to read it in the light of the lamp. Jane followed, filled with some curiosity. Sitting down without pausing to take off her bonnet, Susanna broke the wax seal and pressed the letter flat on her lap. It read:

Dearest Susanna,

This letter is arriving so very belatedly because I have not previously had sufficient funds to pay the necessary postage. A few days before Christmas, I listed the house with a sales agent, and Georgie and I moved in with James. The three of us are comfortable in the rooms above his office, and Georgie walks each day to the academy a half mile from here where he has begun his studies. James is grateful for my cooking. His practice is growing slowly but steadily. He told something to me the mention of which may bring you some pain, but I thought you would find it of interest. He met Jonathan at the courthouse by chance last week. He greeted Jonathan and they exchanged a brief interest in the events of one another's lives. James said that he thought Jonathan looked strained and unhappy, a situation perhaps brought on by the fact that his wife Ann is with child but ill and bedridden. On a happier note, Rachel's baby was born the first of December. She is a beautiful girl who looks much as you did as an infant. After two very active boys, Rachel is pleased. The house is not yet sold. Without my knowledge, James has been corresponding with your great-aunt Louisa for some months. He mentioned our dire financial condition, and she kindly responded by sending me fifty dollars in bank notes. I hated to accept the gift, as charity was always abhorrent to your father, but the money has been useful to tide us over until the house is sold. Georgie reminds me to tell you to take life by the horns. Please write to us as soon as you are able.

With all my love,
Your loving mother,
Emily Thayer

Susanna sat without moving for a full minute. *How quickly things can change.*

"Is it from your mother? Is all well at home?" Jane had watched Susanna's face as she read.

"Yes, Mother says things are well, but she has been forced to place the house for sale and move in with my brother, James." She slowly shook her head. "How I will miss that wonderful home and all the memories within its walls. I had hoped to return there someday." She studied the letter again. "It's hard to accept the fact that I no longer have a home—that I must truly make my way in this world—but as my father often said, it is from the greatest difficulties that we gain our greatest strengths. It is interesting that my great-aunt Louisa has sent my mother a charitable gift of fifty dollars. I would not have expected it of her."

Jane sat next to her friend. "Why not?"

"I have only one memory of Aunt Louisa. When I was very small, we visited her in her great house in Newburyport. She insisted that I sit quietly all afternoon on a very large, very hard chair while Mama and Papa had tea with her. From what little my mother has said of her over the years, I understand her to be a woman very set in her ways. She never married and evidently has little tolerance for children. I know that my mother dreaded the day that we might be forced to become dependent upon Aunt Louisa's charitable feelings."

"I'm sure it will all work out well for your mother. When we met at the train station, she seemed to me to be a generous and kind woman who would surely be able to take tea with the devil and leave his friend."

Susanna looked at Jane with a startled look. "Take tea with the devil . . ."

"I meant no offense. That's just an old saying I often heard my father use. I think it's a compliment to a person's even and pleasant temperament."

"Oh, I see." Susanna smiled a little. "Well, I will continue to send as much money as I can. I am so glad to learn that she is not penniless, as I can't send very much."

***

After the weaving room had been swept and straightened on the following Saturday evening, the girls had put on their coats or capes and were in the process of putting on their bonnets when Ben stepped into the room. They paused and looked at him with inquiring expressions.

"I'm here to talk to Miss Thayer," he stated curtly. Susanna became apprehensive, though she could not have said exactly why.

When the rest of them did not move toward the doorway, he added, "The rest of you can go." Jane looked back over her shoulder and glanced from the tall man to Susanna with a worried expression as the girls exited the room. He watched them leave before turning to stare at Susanna. He did not see them pause in the hall outside the doorway to listen to what he had to say to their friend.

Susanna cleared her throat nervously. "Ah . . . ah . . . How can I help you, Ben? It is Ben, isn't it?" Her heart was thumping in her chest. Something about the way he was looking at her reminded her of her brother-in-law, William.

"Yeah, it's Ben. I hear that you're the one that got her hair caught in the loom not long after you got here. Is that right?"

She cleared her throat again. "Yes, that was my unfortunate luck."

"That wasn't just bad luck, miss. That was foolishness on your part." As he spoke, he moved closer to her, until she could feel the warmth of his breath. She stepped back. "You see, Miss Thayer, I'm in charge of recommending which girls are to be kept on at this mill and those who will be let go."

"I see. So you work with Mr. Cosgrove?" Her voice trembled a little with nervousness.

"Yes," he pushed closer to her, "and he always follows my recommendations." Susanna's heart was thudding hard in her chest, so hard she thought he might be able to see it move the fabric of her dress. "Do you know what I'm going to recommend to him about you?" She shook her head. "I'm still making up my mind, but you can help me make that decision."

"I'm sure I don't understand your meaning." She stepped backward again.

He chuckled maliciously. "But I'm sure that you do." He stepped toward her, and she retreated until she could go no farther. He stepped closer, and putting his left hand against the wall near her head, he put his right hand on her neck. He leaned toward her as if to kiss her. Susanna froze in fear and revulsion.

Suddenly, something white went around his neck, and he was yanked sharply back. Susanna saw him fall to the floor with the ties of Jane's bonnet around his throat. "You will not touch my friend," Jane screamed at him as she bent over him and tightened the bonnet ties. He struggled to rise, but Bridget and Ellen rushed into the room and sat on him. Josie sat on one of his thrashing legs but was nearly thrown off. Margaret hesitated only a moment before she threw herself over both legs.

"You will not touch her, do you understand!" Jane's face was mottled with rage.

Ben's face was scarlet from the tightness of the bonnet ties. He had ceased to struggle and nodded frantically.

"Before we let you up, you will promise not to touch Susanna or any of the rest of us. Do you understand?" Jane asked again, her fury had not relented.

He nodded again. She released the pressure on the bonnet ties. He gasped several deep breaths. "Let me up." His voice was dry and raspy. "Let me up, and I won't bother any of you again."

The girls rose and allowed him to stand. The compliant attitude forced on him by Jane and her bonnet ties changed immediately. He looked like a man who was no longer able to protect his own self-image but had more than enough rage to keep a stranglehold on shame. His voice was a hoarse whisper. "So you think you can bully Ben Roberson? Well, we'll see who wins this contest. None of you will have a job by Monday."

He turned to leave the room. Margaret called after him, "Do you think you can get the six of us fired? Do you think that your word will stand against all of us? When we tell the other girls what you tried to do, how many of them will come forward to tell Mr. Cosgrove that you have done this kind of thing before? How will your wife receive the news of your treatment of some of the girls?"

Ben stopped. He stood without moving while he weighed Margaret's challenge. He turned slowly. "What're you sayin'?"

It was Jane who stepped forward and spoke. "If you will promise not to touch any of us or any of the other mill girls in the future and do not endanger our positions here in the mill, we will say nothing of this matter to Mr. Cosgrove—or your wife—but . . . if we ever hear of your mistreatment of even one more girl," her words slowed for emphasis, "we will bring you down." Jane's voice was full of a quiet ferocity that none of the other girls would have imagined she harbored.

He wiped his hands on his worn shirtfront as if they were dirty. Belligerently but much more controlled, he responded, "Ah . . . I, ah, all right, you have my word. Now will we all keep our peace?" He looked with narrowed eyes at each girl. Each one slowly nodded. He turned and, with hunched shoulders, left the weaving room with a heavy, quick tread.

The young women looked at Jane in amazement. Susanna spoke first. "Jane, where did you get such courage? Where did you learn to . . . to handle a man in that fashion?"

"My father's public house often catered to rowdies and drunkards. I had to learn to defend myself, as neither my father nor my aunt would." The praise made Jane somewhat uncomfortable.

"You're a wonder, a genuine wonder," Josie whispered.

The six of them walked home, two by two, arm in arm.

Chapter Eight

Another copy of *The New York Messenger* arrived at midmonth. Susanna read a small article announcing the planned formation of a branch of The Church of Jesus Christ of Latter-day Saints in Lowell, Massachusetts. It read: "*All parties interested in learning more about this religion are invited to attend the first meeting, which will be held at the public meeting hall on East Merrimack Street on the fourth Sunday of April. At ten o'clock in the morning, Elder Parley P. Pratt will oversee the organization of the group. All are welcome.*"

Instead of attending the services at the nearby Methodist church the following Sunday, as they had since arriving in Lowell, Susanna and Jane hurried to the meeting hall in anticipation of the organization of the little religious group. Elder Pratt preached eloquently, as he had in the past. Then, to the surprise and pleasure of Susanna, he offered each person present a copy of the Book of Mormon. Those who could were asked to pay twenty-five cents for it. Jane paid for two. When Susanna objected, she responded, "Susanna, you are my friend, and I know that you send every penny you can to your mother. I have no one to whom I must give any part of my pay, so I will share it with you in this way. I do not read well, so you will be obligated to help me with the more difficult words."

Susanna smiled and nodded.

When she and Jane sat at supper that evening, Mrs. Winters approached them. "Is it true that neither of you girls attended services this day? You know that I am required to report any of the girls who do not attend services to the mill management."

Susanna put down her spoon. "We were in attendance at the meeting of another religious group which has begun to meet in the public meeting hall on East Merrimack Street, Mrs. Winters. It's called

The Church of Jesus Christ of Latter-day Saints. Perhaps next week you will come with us."

"Hrumpf," she cleared her throat. "I think not. I am very satisfied with the services at the church I have attended all my life—and you should be as well." Her manner was emphatic and disapproving.

***

On Monday, the first of May, the most recent edition of *The Messenger* and a letter were waiting for Susanna. She hurried to the sitting room and, on the way, glanced at the brief article on the front page of the little newspaper, which announced that Elder Samuel Brannan had returned to the East from a recent visit to Nauvoo, Illinois, and had been appointed to lead the Church in New England.

She dropped the newspaper on the table next to the chair, sat down, and tore open the letter addressed to her in an unfamiliar hand. Five bank certificates, each worth one dollar, tumbled into her lap.

> *My Dear Niece,*
>
> *In my recent correspondence with your brother James, I have learned of the financial difficulties which have forced you to take up employment in the mills. I have sent you these bank notes to help ease your situation. As I have grown older, I have come to regret that I did not share a closer relationship with your parents before your father's death. Should you ever have the means and opportunity to pay me a visit, I would receive you with pleasure.*
>
> *Affectionately,*
> *Your Great-Aunt Louisa Thayer*
>
> *Post Script: Should you desire to respond to my communication or make a personal visit, you can reach me at Thayer Hill, Old Post Road, Newburyport, Massachusetts.*

"How very surprising—and very kind of her," Susanna whispered.

***

The full heat of summer arrived. Two bright spots marked the passage of each week: the lyceum lectures on Saturday evenings and the meeting of the newly organized branch of the Church that met each Sunday morning. The original group of twenty who had become regular attendees at the Sunday meetings had grown to thirty-five, and all had become friends, addressing each other as "Brother" and "Sister." In them, Susanna found a substitute for the family that was so many miles away. She grew especially close to John Joyce and his wife, Marion, who was growing large with child. After each meeting of the group, the members stood and chatted about the potential of making the journey to Illinois to join the Church members there. Susanna and Jane saw no way that they could consider such a journey and usually took their leave as soon as the meeting was ended.

***

"It's been six months since the three of you were assigned to the weaving room when you arrived here at the mill." Margaret spoke as they finished sweeping the big room. The girls had gathered to put on their bonnets. "I've asked to be moved to the carding room, and if any you want to get out of the noise here, you had better ask for a change of assignment right away. A few of the youngest mill girls live here in town with their families, and in June they leave the mill to go to school for the summer. That creates a few openings in the other rooms."

"Who do we ask if we want to make a change?" Ellen had asked the question on the other girls' minds.

"You will need to ask Ben."

"Oh dear, oh dear," Bridget murmured. "He isn't likely to do anything we ask, is he? I think he's still very angry with us."

"Go ahead and ask for a different position. He knows his reputation is in our hands." Margaret seemed more confident than the other girls. "He will need someone to replace me as the weaving room supervisor. I get paid twenty-five cents a week more for that position than any of you, so perhaps one of you will want to replace me."

The girls hurried to the office of Mr. Cosgrove, where Margaret stated, "We need to see Ben. Some of the girls in the weaving room would like to move to other positions." As she spoke, Ben entered the office. Mr. Cosgrove just nodded in his direction.

After assignments were altered for the other girls, Ben turned to Susanna and Jane. They had been standing by, nervously wondering if Ben would be willing to give their requests any consideration. They had, after all, been at the heart of his humiliation.

"Either one of you want to move?" His voice was clipped and hard. "All I have left is one position in the spinning room, so one of you could go there. The one who's willing to stay in the weaving room could become the supervisor like she was." He nodded toward Margaret.

"Susanna, you could do it. I know you could, and the extra pay would be nice," Jane encouraged her friend. "And I will stay in the weaving room with you."

"But Jane, I know you would like to get away from the noise."

"No, I'll stay in the weaving room with you if you become the supervisor there."

Susanna nodded and slowly turned to Ben. "Then I will stay in the weaving room as supervisor."

"Yeah, and maybe you'll be smart enough to remember to tell the new girls to watch out that their hair don't get caught in the looms." His voice had become a sneer, reflecting his satisfaction that the two young women were going to continue in the least desirable of mill positions.

***

Within the week, her friends had moved to new positions, and with the exception of Jane, Susanna had four new girls to train. As much as she hated the noise of the weaving room, she was grateful for the extra pay each week. *If I can save enough money, perhaps I will eventually be able to visit Mother and Georgie.*

As she sat down to eat the evening meal at the boarding house in late June, she hardly saw the plate of potatoes, turnips, and boiled beef that had been set before her. She put one elbow on the table and laid her head in her hand.

"Susanna, are you ill?" Jane asked in concern.

"No, no, I'm just tired," her voice was a near whisper, "and I realized that yesterday was my eighteenth birthday, and I didn't even remember until now. I wonder if I will be here doing the same thing on my nineteenth birthday."

One corner of Jane's mouth turned up into a lopsided smile as she tried to answer philosophically, "I think there are worse places we could be at this time next year—like the poorhouse."

***

On a Sunday in early October, as the two friends walked home from a worship service, Susanna seemed inordinately quiet.

"Susanna, what are you thinking that is making you so quiet?"

"The talk at each meeting of the Saints always turns to the need to unite with the Church in Nauvoo, Illinois, and the thought is with me more and more often—but, Jane, I see no way to do so."

"Are you thinking of leaving the mill and going to Illinois?" Jane's voice reflected her surprise.

"For some weeks now the idea has been constantly in my mind. I suppose I shall have to take a philosophical view of the situation—if it is meant to be, God will open a door."

"I should think it would need to be a very wide door," Jane's voice was warm with determination, "because, if you choose to go, Susanna, I shall go with you."

"Do you mean it, Jane?" Susanna beamed at her friend. "You give me hope that it could happen. We'll go back to the boarding house and calculate our resources."

"Susanna, there is another matter for us to consider. Neither of us has been baptized into this new church. I think that is something that has been mentioned during several of the meetings."

Susanna watched her feet as they walked. "You are right. It is a matter of some importance. We will speak with Elder Brown when we attend meeting next Sunday. Is that agreeable with you, Jane? Are you ready to make such a commitment?"

Jane nodded. "Yes, I am ready."

That evening, they sat on their bed, and while the other girls were busy elsewhere, they calculated their funds on a scrap of paper. "I have twenty-five dollars and fifty cents in the savings bank." Susanna sighed. "I thought that was a great deal of money, until I realized how much more I need."

"I have forty dollars and twenty five cents in the savings bank. That gives us sixty-five dollars and seventy-five cents."

"For someone who has little formal education, you calculated those amounts very quickly, Jane. You cipher very well," Susanna said with an amazed smile.

"I had to take payment and make change for the patrons of my father's tavern from the time I was very young. Let's calculate how much money we will have by the end of the year, if we save every penny we can." She scratched briefly on the paper. "We have nine weeks until Christmas." She was quiet a moment while she calculated the amounts in her head. "Between us, we can each save close to a total of about forty-five dollars. That would give us about ninety dollars."

It seemed such a large amount that Susanna smiled broadly. "I think we are well on our way to saving enough to plan our trip to Zion." She paused. "But I wonder if I am being selfish. I have not asked my mother if she can get along without the bank notes I have sent each month."

"Perhaps you need to write to her and ask her about her situation. You said she had received fifty dollars from your Great-Aunt Louisa. That is a substantial amount of money."

So the letter was written that evening explaining Susanna's plans and put in the post the next day.

At the next Sabbath meeting, Elder Brown raised the subject of uniting with the Saints in Illinois. "It is possible that many of us will make plans to travel to Nauvoo, but each must measure his or her degree of conviction and commitment. There are many who have been attending our meetings with regularity but who have not committed to baptism." Susanna and Jane exchanged a smile. "Some have been baptized but have not seen their way clear to the payment of tithing. I believe that these two matters must be addressed by any individual considering emigrating to join the Saints." He was silent for a few seconds while his words were considered. "Are there any here who have not yet been baptized who will commit to baptism?"

Susanna hesitated for only a moment before she raised her hand. Four others did the same, including Jane. Susanna took Jane's other hand, squeezed it, and smiled broadly.

The following Saturday evening, while the people of Lowell met inside, Susanna, Jane, and the three others gathered in the dark, cold evening on the broad steps of the public meeting house, and Elder Brown met them there with a rented wagon and team. On the floor of the wagon in front of each of the long seats were several hot bricks to use as warming footrests. The loaded wagon made its way east on Pawtucket Street until it reached a spot where the road curved near the bank of the Merrimack River. A long sandbar spread out into the water, where it was gradually submerged about ten feet from the bank. He stopped the wagon. "Here we are. This is where we have conducted baptisms in the past. My good wife has sent several quilts that you can use to keep warm while we return you to your homes."

He held out his hand to Jane, who stepped out of the wagon in the poor light from the lantern, which hung from the front corner of the wagon box. Susanna followed her. The others were assisted out of the wagon and stood clustered on the riverbank.

One at a time, the men were invited into the water and immersed by Elder Brown. As they rose from the water, Susanna could see that the white shirts they wore had taken on a blue cast. She suddenly realized that the water was colored by the indigo dye that one of the mills regularly pumped into the river farther upstream. *I think I'm glad that I wore my blue dress,* Susanna thought as she was led out into the deeper water.

As the cold water closed over her head, shutting out the dark sky sprinkled with stars and the glow of the moon, she suddenly felt as if, inside her body, a bank of coals had burst into flame and was generating a warmth that enveloped her. As she was lifted upward and broke through the water's surface, the stars and moon looked twice as bright as she had ever seen them. She was led to the riverbank and offered a quilt. *I've made the commitment. Now I will move forward into an uncertain future with faith that this is the right course to take.*

The wagon rumbled over the uneven road, and she and Jane were delivered cold and wet to the door of their boarding house. "We will confirm both of you as members of the Church tomorrow at meeting," Brother Brown called out as the young women reached the door. "And please return the quilts at that time or my wife will be most unhappy with me." The girls paused and waved as the wagon departed.

"Jane, I think we've made an important choice this evening," Susanna said as she held the quilt around her shoulders. Several of the girls stood in amazement and watched as they dripped their way up the stairs. While they were changing into their night dresses, someone knocked firmly on the door. Jane opened it as she brushed her hair.

Mrs. Winters stood there with her fists on her hips. Looking down the long slope of her nose as she did when upset, she stated accusingly, "Someone has made a trail of river water up the stairs. It is so blue that I may never get the stain out of the wood. I was told that it was the two of you. Apparently, that is correct. What have you been up to that you come back to the boarding house soaked to the skin with river water?"

Susanna stepped up beside Jane. "We were baptized into our new religion this evening, Mrs. Winters. Perhaps you remember that we told you that we were attending services with the other members of The Church of Jesus Christ of Latter-day Saints."

"I certainly do remember," she stamped her foot. "And at that time, I told you that you should have continued with one of the established religions in this city. I will report this to the mill management, as I am required to do." She turned on the ball of her foot and stalked away in indignation.

Jane looked at Susanna. "What will they do to us? Will they force us out of our positions?"

"If they do, we may find that we must leave the mill before the end of the year. I'm sorry, Jane. I didn't think there could be any objection to our being baptized." Susanna was quiet with disappointment.

During the Sunday meeting the next morning, when the hands of the elders were laid on Susanna's head to confirm her membership in the Church, she heard her father's voice. "This is a good choice, Susanna. I'm proud of you." A glow of warmth flooded through her once more, a sweet confirmation of the rightness of her decision. After supper that evening, she wrote to her mother.

> *Dearest Mother,*
>
> *Yesterday, I entered the waters of baptism and was formally united with a new church, the one Elder Pratt and Elder Benson taught us about there in Boston. I am thoroughly convinced that I have done the right and proper thing. Jane has also joined herself with this group, and we are both alight with hope and faith in the future. Whatever it may bring, we feel better prepared to meet it. There is talk of uniting with the Saints in Nauvoo, Illinois, but that cannot be considered until we have greater resources. I hope you are able to find a group to meet with there in Boston and that you will also affiliate with this new religion. I feel it will change our lives.*
>
> *Your affectionate daughter,*
> *Susanna Thayer*

After the candles were put out that evening, the other girls in the room continued to pepper both of them with questions as to why they had been baptized into the church of the "Mormonites." The questions came fast on one another, hardly giving the girls time to respond.

"Why did you stop attending Methodist services?" Ellen asked.

"Don't you believe in the Holy Bible? I hear that Mormonites have a gold Bible of their own that they believe in." Harriett's voice was critical.

"Weren't you baptized as infants?" Bridget asked. "Why would you be baptized again?"

Finally, one by one, the voices quieted as each girl fell asleep with the exception of Susanna, who was busy with her thoughts well into the night.

The response to her letter arrived the last day of October. Susanna smoothed the letter on her lap and read it by the light of the lamp in the parlor while the room was empty. The other young women, including Jane, were busy elsewhere.

> *My Dearest Daughter Susanna,*
>
> *Your plans of traveling to Illinois to join with the members of the new church you have joined made my heart sink. It is so very hard to have you so far from home, but that would be so much more likely to end my hopes of a future reunion with you. I admonish you to pray fervently about the matter, and if your answer confirms your desire to unite with that religious group in Illinois, then go with my blessing. James has seen an improvement in his solicitor's practice, and we are financially well enough off that Georgie and I can sustain ourselves should your monetary gifts cease. All is well here with family and friends, and you have my prayers, which will follow you no matter where the future may take you.*
>
> *Your loving mother,*
> *Emily Thayer*
>
> *Post Script: Georgie sends his love and prayers to you as well.*

Susanna lowered her head and wiped a tear. *I understand your feelings, Mama. I would only make such a journey with a confusion of feelings. It would be hard to go so far from home and family, but I think I must do what God prompts me to do in this matter.*

Chapter Nine

THE OCTOBER EDITION OF *THE Messenger* arrived by post on the third of November. Susanna read it aloud to Jane as they sat in the parlor. "Elder Brannan has written in an article here that there will soon be a flood of Mormons headed to California. He's going to charter a large ship and lead the group. He goes on to say that Church leaders in Nauvoo are preaching to the Saints that they will soon be forced to leave the United States and relocate to the Upper California Basin. Furthermore, he says that travel by ship will be much easier than traveling overland." She looked up at her friend with excitement in her face. "Perhaps that is what we should do—go by ship to California. Surely we can find a way to finance our trip and support ourselves there, and we would be with many other members of the Church. It couldn't be so difficult if we traveled together."

"But, Susanna, a voyage to California is so much farther away than Illinois. Are you sure you want to travel so far from your family? What would your mother say of these plans?"

Susanna stared out of the window into the dark with a far-away look. "Mother has given me her blessing to go where I am prompted by God to go. As my brother James would say, 'In for a penny, in for a pound.' The Lord has confirmed that I should throw in my lot with the Saints, be it in Illinois or California."

While Susanna continued her introspection, Jane took the paper and read the article more closely. "It says that the United States government and Brigham Young support the effort and that it will be much less costly than going overland." She looked up with some alarm in her face. "But, Susanna, one of the lyceum speakers said that even though the US government has encouraged the settlement in that area, that conflict with Mexico may break out into open warfare very soon. Isn't California part of the territory of Mexico?"

"Yes, I think it is, but perhaps the conflict will be settled quickly. The government and Church leaders surely wouldn't encourage people to settle there if we were about to become enmeshed in a violent conflict." Susanna took the little newspaper back as she continued. "Did you see where it says, near the end of the article, that it's expected that as many as twenty thousand Saints will eventually travel to the Upper California Basin by ship? When we attend Sunday meeting, I'm going to ask if any of the others there are making plans to travel with Elder Brannan. If it is less costly than the overland journey to Nauvoo, surely there will be others who will consider it."

***

After the benediction had been offered at the close of the Sunday meeting, Susanna raised the question. The reaction among those present was mixed. Some members shook their heads and murmured that they could not pay the cost, no matter what it was. Others whispered to one another that they would not undertake such a journey with small children. Brother and Sister Joyce and another couple were planning on making the journey, and six others were considering it.

***

Monday evening, after the looms were still, Susanna and Jane were called into Mr. Cosgrove's office, where Ben stood behind the mill manager with his arms folded across his chest and a crooked smile on his lips. As they stood nervously before the big desk, Cosgrove looked up from the papers he had been studying. "Mrs. Winters has reported to the mill owners that the two of you were baptized into that new church of the Mormonites. Is that true?"

"Yes, sir. It's true." Susanna tried to make her voice firm. Jane stood silently beside her.

"Why would you do a thing like that?"

"Because we believe that it teaches the true gospel, a restored gospel." Susanna brightened and smiled. "Mr. Cosgrove, you would be welcome to attend the meetings. You would find that everything that is taught at these meetings can be found in the Bible."

He snorted. "That's not likely. I've also been told that you, Miss Thayer, signed that petition to the legislature demanding the ten-hour workday. I might have overlooked one or the other of these acts, but both combined demonstrate a rebellion that we cannot tolerate here at the mills. If you want to retain your positions, you will have to separate yourself from that religion. Then I will overlook the signing of the petition. " He paused and watched for her reaction.

"Why would the mill owners ask such a thing? The rules only require that we attend Sunday services. No one has ever said we couldn't attend the religion of our choice." Susanna quickly added, "And many of the mill girls signed the petition."

"All I know is what I've been told. It's up to you," Cosgrove responded.

Without saying anything else, Susanna took hold of Jane's arm, and they left the office. They walked back to the boarding house in silence.

"Jane, you know I'm not going to stop going to Sunday meetings. I believe in this new religion and I'm not going to give it up. I'm sorry if I have gotten you involved in my problems."

"I involved myself, Susanna. You were not responsible. I'm as much a member of this new religion as you are, and I'm willing to accept the consequences, just as you are." Though her words were brave, her voice was quiet.

The girls were silent, each involved with her own thoughts as they walked, until Jane asked, "Susanna, if Mr. Cosgrove lets us go as he has threatened, where will we go? There are no ships leaving for California at this time that we know of.

"I could find a position serving in a public house or," she added with distaste, "or a grog shop, but what will you do? Will you go back to Boston to live with your mother and brothers?"

"No, I can't throw myself upon the charity of James. The three of them live in the four rooms over his solicitor's shop, and though in her letters my mother has tried to put a good face on it, I'm sure it is difficult for them. They surely cannot take another person in." After a few more steps, she took a deep breath and stated, "A few weeks ago, Aunt Louisa invited me to visit her in Newburyport. I do not know how long we would be welcome there, but if we lose our positions, we will seek shelter with her. I still hope to join the Saints, despite our lack of funds. Are you still looking toward that goal, Jane?"

"Yes. My feelings in the matter have not changed."

The next morning as the girls dressed for work, Abby finally asked what was on every one of their minds. "Are you going to go to church services with us on Sunday, or are you going to go to your new church?"

"We are going to go to the meeting of our choice. You are all welcome to attend with us." Susanna's voice was firm but quiet.

"But we heard the rumor that if you continue to attend the meetings of that church, that you could lose your place in the mill. Are you going to attend anyway?" Ellen asked.

"Yes." Susanna threw her cloak over her shoulders and left the room.

A frowning Mrs. Winters greeted the two young women when they sat down to supper that evening. "I warned you both, yet I have been told that you insist on attending the meetings of that strange religious group even after it was made clear that you were to cease. If you do not change your minds, I will have to report you again."

While Susanna sat quietly, trying not to be intimidated by Mrs. Winters's disapproval, Jane's temper flared. She stood and raised her voice. "We will not have anyone telling us where or how we will worship. Our pilgrim forefathers left Europe so they could worship as they felt was right—and so will we."

"Well, we shall see how long you keep your position in the mills with an attitude like that." The woman stormed away.

***

"I'm not surprised. We knew it was coming," Susanna said as she and Jane left the office of Mr. Cosgrove on Friday evening. "But I do feel some regret that we will not get our letter of honorable discharge." They walked briskly toward the boarding house, a cold wind whipping their skirts.

"We will have one more payday on Monday. Mr. Cosgrove probably thinks he was being generous in allowing us to finish out the week." Jane's voice was a little bitter.

"Or it is more likely that he doesn't have anyone to take our places at the present time. I think we shall test the hospitality of my aunt. We will go to Newburyport to visit her, as we discussed. I will put a letter in the post immediately and hope it arrives before we do."

As they reached the boarding house door, several mill girls almost collided with them as they hurried out on their way to another meeting of the Female Labor Association. Other girls were still in the dining room finishing their supper. The food had grown cold and Susanna and Jane ate in silence. As they rose from the table, Mrs. Winters approached them. "As you will no longer have a position with the mill after this week, Sunday evening will be your last night here in the boarding house."

In quiet agreement, they determined that they would say nothing of the loss of their positions to any of the other girls until Sunday evening. Then they would say good-bye to the friends who shared their room, but by the next day, it was known throughout the mill that they had been dismissed.

After the looms had grown quiet late Saturday afternoon, Susanna looked around the weaving room, making sure it had been cleaned properly. *I will not have anyone say that I did not complete my supervisory tasks properly.*

As the two friends put on their bonnets, Ben leaned against the door frame in the doorway of the weaving room with his arms folded across his chest. "No one, especially not you mill girls, will get the best of Ben Roberson." His tone was viciously exultant.

Susanna stopped. "So you had something to do with our losing our positions?"

He leveraged himself into a standing position. "Cosgrove was thinkin' of overlookin' your joinin' that new religion with the gold Bible, but I'm the one that told him that you," he jabbed the air toward Susanna, "signed that petition to the legislature for the ten-hour workday."

They said no more but sidled past him as he stood in the doorway with his hands on his hips and a smug sneer on his face.

On the way to the boarding house, Jane asked, "Should we go to Mr. Cosgrove and tell him what we know of that man?"

"Ben would simply deny our accusations and insist that we were being vengeful over losing our positions. There is little we can do about him. The other girls will continue to watch him, and he knows that. Let's let that sleeping dog lie."

After attending Sabbath meeting the next day, Susanna announced their plans to the members of the little branch. "We will leave on Monday for Newburyport to visit my aunt, and it is our intention thereafter to make our way to New York and eventually take passage on a ship to California with the Saints."

"Have you received the most recent copy of the *Messenger?*" Elder Brown asked. When Susanna shook her head, he handed her his copy, which he had received by post the day before. "You may want to have something to read as you travel." She thanked him and took it.

That evening while they packed their belongings, their roommates stood silently watching. Finally, Abby spoke. "I don't know why you can't just go back to church with us. The pastor is a good man. Then you wouldn't have to leave the boarding house and you could keep your places in the mill." She was close to tears.

Susanna tied off a bundle of her belongings wrapped in the quilts. "Ben has made that impossible, Abby." She looked at each of the young women. "We will miss all of you. Your friendship has been the best thing about living here in the boarding house, but my father taught me that I must to be true to my conscience if I am to have any self-respect, and if I have no respect for myself, how could I expect any from others?"

"But you can attend another church and still respect yourself. I don't see what is so important about this Mormonite religion. I'm perfectly happy being a Methodist," Ellen argued. "Why can't you be too?"

"And I'm happy being a Presbyterian who attends Methodist services," Bridget added, trying to strengthen the argument.

Harriett had been quiet, but she finally had to say what she was thinking. "It will be so lonely without you."

Quiet tears wet Susanna's cheeks as she gave each girl an embrace. "It will be lonely without all of you, too."

None of the girls spoke again before they climbed into bed. There was little more to be said.

***

In the morning, Susanna and Jane regretfully left the bedroom they had shared for a year. They descended the stairs, offering their good-byes to several of the other girls. At the door, they each took a deep breath and stepped determinedly outside, knowing that they were walking into another life. After collecting their pay for the previous week from the paymaster's office, they walked to the bank and withdrew their savings. They hurried to the train station with their breath making frosty clouds in the air. Susanna approached the ticket agent. "We need to go to Newburyport. How far can we go by train?"

"You can take the train as far as Andover, and then go by coach the rest of the way."

"Will there be a train to Andover today?"

He nodded.

"At what time will it leave?"

The agent ran a finger over the small print on the schedule tacked to the wall. "That's the number three-oh-eight, and it leaves at half past eleven this morning. It will stop in Andover at about one ten on its way to Cambridge and Boston. Adult fare is ninety cents."

The girls laid their coins on the windowsill and the ticket agent pushed a ticket through the bars to each. They sat on a hard wooden bench to wait for the train.

Finally Susanna spoke. "Jane, I want you to know that your friendship means more to me than I can express. Since the death of my father, everything has turned topsy-turvy in my life. There has been no safe haven. Nothing is what I had expected life to bring. Having you as a friend makes facing an unknown future a little less frightening."

Jane took her friend's hand and squeezed it but said nothing.

Chapter Ten

On the train, Susanna unfolded the copy of *The Messenger* given to her by Brother Brown. From an article with the headline "Hurrah for California," she read aloud to Jane about the opening of Brannan's travel office at Number Seven Spruce Street in Brooklyn, New York, "for the purpose of arranging transportation for members of the Church to the West Coast of California." She was quiet for a moment then read further. "The article states that it is expected that those traveling by water would be joined by overland companies of Church members who will be leaving the territory of the United States within the next few months to find a place to settle in the Upper California Basin. Brannan writes that 'a flood of Mormons' are destined to follow the sailing of the first group, as the cost of passage by ship is substantially less than outfitting a wagon.

"Estimated cost of passage for an adult is fifty-seven dollars and fifty dollars for each child over six years of age." She laid the paper in her lap and spoke her thoughts. "Where will we find fifty-seven dollars for each of us?"

"Perhaps we won't be able to make the voyage."

"Jane, I am entirely serious about this journey. It offers an opportunity to unite our future to that of many of the other Saints. It seems that it is a decision which we should consider made."

She turned to the next page where the article continued. She excitedly sat upright. "Here it says that Mr. Brannan has promised financial help for those passengers who cannot afford the cost of the voyage—if there are not an overwhelming number of them." Her voice rose with excitement. "If that's true, this might be the answer for us."

"Are you sure you read it correctly?"

Without answering, she returned to reading the balance of the article aloud. "*Captain Richardson will oversee the voyage which is scheduled to depart from the Old Slip on the East River in New York on the twenty-fourth of January.*" She skimmed the instructions. "He advises anyone intending to be part of the group sailing at that time to be in the city no later than the twentieth of January. All are admonished to address each other as Mister and Miss or Missus, rather than Brother or Sister, and religious opinions are not to be openly expressed." Susanna was quiet for a moment before adding, "That seems odd to me. What do you think, Jane?"

"After how we were treated at the mill when it became known that we had joined the Mormons, I think it might be wise."

They both rode in silence for a few minutes, listening to the rhythmic clack of the wheels against the tracks. Susanna watched the new snow swirl against the windows for a few minutes before she returned to the newspaper. "*In his farewell address to his New York congregations, Elder Orson Pratt announced instructions for the Saints to follow his example and leave the United States. He counseled all to go by sea and stated that he hopes to sail about the middle of January. All who can afford an overland outfit should go to Nauvoo, but those who cannot must raise the means to pay their passage by sea around Cape Horn. Elder Pratt stated that such a voyage would cost but a trifle more than the usual expenses from here to Nauvoo.* Near the end of the article it says, *Elder Samuel Brannan is hereby appointed to preside over and take charge of the company that will go by sea, and all who go with him will be required to give strict heed to his instructions and counsel.*"

She folded the little newspaper and tucked it into the carpetbag as the train began to slow and the conductor moved through the car calling out in a nasal voice, "Andover, next stop. Aaaandover, next stop."

Without saying anything more, they picked up their belongings. As they stepped down onto the platform, Susanna turned and asked the conductor, "Where might we find the coach to Newburyport?"

He assisted a woman behind Jane with her large valise before answering. "Two blocks down and one block to the north is the Hotel Andover. It's across the street from the Anglican Church, the one with the tall spire that you can see over there." He pointed. "The coach stops there once a day."

She thanked him and turned to Jane. "That will, of necessity, be our first stop." They started walking briskly, their skirts flapping and their bonnets trying to fly off their heads, as they faced the cutting wind that blew off the Merrimack River.

At the hotel, Susanna asked the man at the registration desk, "Sir, might you know what time the coach to Newburyport will come today?"

He pointed to the large clock behind the registration desk. "It comes each day at two, Miss, and leaves at two thirty."

Susanna noted that it was twenty minutes of two. "What is the fare?"

"For one adult, one dollar and five cents," he responded. "You may pay me as I am an agent for the coach company."

They both counted out the required coins and dropped them into the man's outstretched hand, for which they received a yellow ticket.

After the coach arrived, the driver spent twenty minutes in the dining room over a cup of tea to warm himself. He then walked through the lobby, repeatedly calling out, "Coach to Newburyport leavin' now."

The two young women followed him outside, where Susanna accepted his assistance and stepped up and into the coach. When Jane was seated next to her, he tipped his hat and said, before he closed the door, "Time to get movin' agin' as it looks like there's a storm brewing, a real Nor'easter."

He climbed into his high front seat and whipped the horses into motion. The coach began to move over the rough road filled with ruts of frozen mud.

It was gloomy and dark inside the coach, with only a little light making its way around the sides of the leather window blinds that were rolled down to keep the wind to a minimum. Susanna untied the rope that she had wrapped around her bundle at the boarding house. She carefully unwrapped one of the two quilts. "We can put this over our laps as we ride. It should help keep us warm."

The jolting journey seemed to be nearing an end when the coach left the South Newburyport Turnpike and turned onto High Street. The girls each rolled up one of the leather window shades so they could see something of the town. The prosperous community had been built on the elevated south bank of the Merrimack River where it emptied into the Atlantic Ocean. As the coach passed through the intersection with Green Street, which sloped down toward the harbor, Susanna pointed toward the water. "Look, there's the harbor. You can see the masts of the ships riding at anchor. They look like a great floating forest."

Jane was not interested in the ships. She had been observing the large, brick and frame mansions that lined both sides of High Street. In amazement, she commented, "These houses—they are each for a single family? They look as if all the wealth in Massachusetts is gathered on this street."

The coach slowed and lurched to a halt, the brake squeaking under the foot of the driver. The door opened to the cold wind in front of the Seaport Hotel. The driver tipped his hat in a perfunctory manner as the young women climbed out.

"Can you tell me where we can hire a wagon?" Susanna asked the coachman.

He pointed. "Two blocks down the hill on Low Street, you'll find Josh Allred's livery stable right there on the wharf. He's got a wagon for hire, and either he or his boy will take folks as far as ten miles out of town for a reasonable price."

***

Mr. Allred's wagon rattled over the frozen road, making conversation difficult. On every side, winter had drained the scene of color. The hills, vegetation, and clouds all formed a picture in monotones of gray. The bent, leafless trees on either side of the road reached for the sky like withered, arthritic hands.

On one stretch of about a mile where the road was somewhat smoother, the scene was accompanied by the steadily increasing sound of waves beating against the unseen shore. The wind carried the smell of the sea.

Mr. Allred tossed a question over his shoulder. "Is old Miz' Thayer kin of yours?"

"She is the sister of my grandfather. I met her only once when I was a child. Do you know anything about her?" After so many years, Susanna was hungry to learn as much as possible about the aunt she hardly knew, and she was nervous about the sincerity of the invitation that had been extended in her aunt's letter. *Will we be welcome or was that invitation simply a formality? What if I have brought Jane this far to meet with rejection?*

"'Bout all anyone knows is that her solicitor will die a rich man. Since she has ceased going out and about, he has all but moved up here from Boston and practically lives in the big house. The servants say he's running her estate and spending her money, and she lets him do what he wants. Maybe she's too sick to stop him."

Susanna raised her voice to be heard against the wind and the increasing sound of waves. "You say he's from Boston?"

"Yeah, his name is Caspar, and I hear that he's a partner in some important firm of solicitors there." For a moment she felt that the name had a faint familiarity to it, but it quickly faded. Mr. Allred slapped the rump of the horse with the reins to urge the animal to increase its speed. He wanted to get back to the stable, out of the cold.

The road turned and began to rise toward the coast. Against a background of gray scudding clouds on the crest of the hill rose a large, three-story mansion of hewn stone, a dark silhouette against the sky. The stable owner pointed with a gloved hand. "There it is. You say you been here before?"

"A very long time ago, when I was a child. I don't remember much about that visit."

The wagon turned into a tree-lined drive which wound up the hill toward the house. The offshore winds had forced the dark, leafless branches of the oak trees that lined the long drive into black silhouettes that reached for the sky as if in a plea to avoid being blown away. The shrubs and a lawn of coarse, bleached winter grass bent in the wind where the property sloped toward a precipitous drop a hundred feet from the east side of the house. There, the spray from the pounding waves was occasionally visible above the cliff.

The house faced the south as if to coax the sun to bless it a few months of the year. Like an overdressed matron in an enormous hat, it wore a four-sided, gambrel-style hip roof of cedar shingles. The nearly vertical slope formed the third story, which was punctured by pedimented dormer windows. The rooftop was flat enough to permit a widow's walk bordered by a low but decorative wrought iron fence. *Lest a widow throw herself off the roof in her grief over the loss of a seagoing husband*, Susanna thought as a shudder ran through her. Though she did not recognize the architecture as a combination of Italian Renaissance and French Second Empire, she could sense that some European architect had been given a free hand. As the wagon wound up the driveway, the size of the house became even more evident as they noted a rear wing extending from the west end of the main portion of the building. It was balanced by a similar wing extending from the rear of the east end. The sight of the imposing structure brought on a shudder of nervousness Susanna could hardly suppress.

In a region where even the homes of the rich were usually designed in the more modest brick Federalist or frame Colonialist architecture, this house had been built to make a perpetual display of the wealth of the owner.

Six multipaned windows were prominently spread across the front of the second story. The ornate double front doors were centrally located under a colossal, two-story entrance porch, which was flanked by three windows on each side identical to those of the second story. Each window was covered by a pair of dark green shutters in anticipation of the storm, giving the house the look of many blind eyes, dark and unseeing. Above the carved double doors was a wide fanlight but no light showed through the wavy glass panes. The house appeared uninhabited except for the curl of smoke, which was quickly dissipated by each wind gust, from a chimney at the end of the west wing.

Bare rose bushes grew unchecked on the lee side of the house up to the second level, huddled against the building for protection from the elements. Apprehension made Susanna's hands grow clammy and the knot in her stomach tightened.

The sky had darkened to a slate gray, and the sound of the waves had increased, each one breaking with a roar upon the rocks at the base of the cliff. Jane leaned over and spoke loudly in her friend's ear. "What if no one's at home? I don't see any lights."

"I'm sure Aunt Louisa will be home. Where else could she be?" Her words were carried away by the wind.

By the time the wagon had halted in the circle of gravel in front of the columned front porch, which had been designed to intimidate arriving guests, the rain was splashing down the necks of the three of them like cold fingers. Susanna hurriedly climbed down from the wagon seat, in too much of a hurry to wait for the driver to assist. She ran up the stairs to the double doors and lifted the heavy iron knocker, bringing it down twice. The sound startled her as it echoed back at them.

They stood huddled against the wind for several minutes. The horse impatiently shook his harness. Susanna raised the knocker again and struck the door two more times.

"I can't wait much longer, ladies." The stable owner was almost yelling into the wind. "You will have to decide whether to stay here and wait for someone to let you in or come back to town with me."

"Please, Mr. Allred, give us a little longer. I'm sure someone will respond to our knock." Susanna nearly panicked at the thought of being left there when there had been no answer to her knock.

After another three long minutes of waiting with their cloaks drawn closely about them, a weak light appeared through the glass above the doors. One of them opened slowly as if the world was not welcome in that house. An oil lamp was held by a woman in a black dress with an apron over it. The dress blended into the darkness of the hall behind her. The light of the lamp reflected harshly off her gaunt face, gray hair, and veined hands. Her lips were as straight and narrow as the selvage of one of the gray cotton fabrics produced by the Merrimack Mill in Lowell.

"Yes?"

Chapter Eleven

The greeting was so brief and abrupt that Susanna had to take a deep breath to gather her thoughts. A nervous constriction in her throat caused a slight stammer. "I, ah, I am Susanna Thayer. I have come to visit my aunt, Louisa Thayer, at her invitation." Mr. Allred hurriedly climbed into the wagon, and he and it disappeared back down the long drive.

The door opened wide enough for the two young women to enter. "I am Williams, Mrs. Thayer's housekeeper."

Susanna looked at Jane and then back at the housekeeper and asked, as they stepped over the threshold, "Is that *Mrs.* Williams?"

"Just Williams, ma'am." Saying no more, she led them across the wide foyer. Both the hardwood floor and the oak wainscoting were darkened by age. Even in the poor light, it was apparent that the wide staircase to the second level was meant to be the focal point in the large room. It rose up, wide and straight, to the second level at the far end of the foyer, where the landing led to identical hallways on the left and the right. A wide carpet runner of dark blue covered each stair tread. As they followed the housekeeper, the girls could see a marble balustrade at the second level that connected with the landing at the top of the staircase.

The two young women were led to a set of double doors to the right, where the housekeeper set the lamp on a marble-topped sideboard while she opened the doors that led into a sitting room. While Susanna and Jane stood in the doorway, she removed the dust covers from a settee and a large wingback chair. "Wait here. I will get Mr. Caspar."

"I had hoped to see my aunt upon my arrival." She tried to will her voice to be firm enough to hide her nervousness.

"She doesn't see anyone." The housekeeper removed the glass chimney and lit a lamp that sat on a heavy table near the settee from the one in her hand. Saying no more, she turned and left the room.

Susanna sat in the big chair covered in worn, dark blue velvet that faced the settee, where Jane sat. They both studied the room. The ticking of a large grandfather clock in the foyer was the only sound that broke the silence. The carpet had at one time been a royal blue with a gold border but was now somewhat faded, or perhaps the color was dulled by a thin film of dust. The high, scrolled ceiling was decorated with a plaster medallion of miniature sea creatures and mermaids in a double ring. In the center hung a chandelier of twelve candleholders in glass chimneys. The crystal droplets glistened even in the limited light but it was apparent that it had not been used in some time. It held no candles.

Even though much of the other furniture was still hidden under dust covers, they could see various items displayed in a glass-fronted china cupboard: a jade elephant, a fragile model of a clipper ship, brass vases, a carved piece of whalebone scrimshaw—all things that suggested world travels. A great mirror hung above what was probably a desk or table covered by a dust cloth at one side of the far end of the large room. The light of the lamp on the table was doubled by the reflection in the mirror. On a wall opposite the mirror, a nearly life-sized portrait of a man in a sea captain's uniform stared down at them.

Susanna quietly rose and walked over to the painting. The tarnished brass plate attached to the bottom of the frame read: "Sylvanus T. Thayer, 1730–1798."

As she studied the face, she tried to imagine it without the heavy, dark beard shot with gray and the captain's cap. *Am I imagining it?* She smiled. *No, it's not my imagination. Those are my father's eyes looking down at me.* For a brief moment, her tension eased. She returned to the wingback chair.

The clock in the hall had chimed the quarter hour twice before a tall, spare man dressed in a formal morning coat stepped into the room. His chin was minimal, but his large Adam's apple overcompensated and bobbed when he spoke. His hair had once been blond but was now thin and colorless. He cleared his throat and glanced from Jane to Susanna. "You must be Miss Thayer." His voice was high and reedy but accustomed to giving orders. "I am Mortimer Caspar, your aunt's legal counsel." Looking down his nose, he asked, "And what is the purpose of your visit?"

Susanna stood. "I'm Susanna Thayer, and I have come for a visit with my Aunt Louisa." She extended her hand. He offered no response.

"I see. Did your driver wait? If he has not left, you can return with him to the town." His manner bordered on rudeness.

Taking note of his lack of courtesy, she retracted her hand and tried to project an increase in confidence, more than she was feeling. She felt it would be wise to demonstrate that she was not going to be treated like a servant, but her stomach was still one big knot.

"My Aunt Louisa invited me by letter to visit her several weeks ago. Our circumstances have finally permitted such a visit."

"A pity you did not contact me in the matter as her health is so precarious that she sees no visitors at this time. It would be better if you returned to the town and took rooms there. If your driver has not waited, I will get Dan to bring the carriage around to take you back to town."

"My friend and I have come a long way today, and we are greatly fatigued and have had nothing to eat since this morning—and more importantly, the storm is upon us. You would not expect me to leave this house until I have had the opportunity to meet with my aunt. Surely simple courtesy requires that one kinswoman spend some time renewing acquaintanceship with such a close relative." She tried to stop the nervous opening and closing of her right hand, which she was trying to hide in the folds of her skirt.

Mortimer Caspar, Esquire, seemed somewhat startled at Susanna's firm response. He had expected a young woman of her age to be more compliant. "I'm afraid that your aunt is much too weak and ill to visit with you." He paused, as if irritated.

She clenched her right hand. "As I have stated, Mr. Caspar, it is not my intention to leave this house until I have had the opportunity to communicate with my aunt."

"But as I have told you, she is too ill for visitors." A contest of wills was developing.

"Surely I can judge that for myself when I see her." As if to put an exclamation point to her words, a great crack of thunder over their heads seemed to tear the fabric of the sky.

After a moment of frustrated silence in which his face colored a mottled red, Caspar responded, "I will approach her in the morning and see if she is up to meeting you. In the meantime, please wait here until Williams prepares your rooms for this evening. Dinner will be at eight o'clock." He turned and exited the room without further comment.

After his steps had faded, Jane whispered, "Susanna, you were wonderful. He seemed determined to get rid of us immediately, regardless of the storm. I don't think I like him."

A nervous smile crept around Susanna's mouth. "I must admit that I surprised myself. A year ago, I could never have defended myself in such a manner."

They sat for nearly an hour before Mrs. Williams appeared like a wraith at the doorway. "Your rooms are ready. Will you follow me?"

The housekeeper led them up the wide staircase opposite the front door. At the top, she made a turn to the right and stopped at a room on the seaward side of the house. She pushed the door open. A fire had been started in the fireplace, and a full coal scuttle sat on the hearth. The smell of stale dampness pervaded the atmosphere. She nodded to Susanna. "A room for your friend is just beyond this one. Supper will be served at eight o'clock in the dining room."

"Thank you, Mrs. Williams."

"Just Williams, ma'am." She turned and left the room before questions could form in the minds of either of the young women.

They looked around at Susanna's room. The room was dominated by the massive, four-poster oak bed; a heavy, carved chest of four drawers; and a wardrobe with carved double doors. Above the chest hung a mirror in an oak frame. A basin and a pitcher of water sat on the top with a small towel lying next to it. An oil lamp had been lit and stood on a small table by the bed. Both windows were covered with dark blue velvet draperies. The faded wallpaper was a series of different types of ships on a background of blue.

Jane's room was furnished with the same oak furniture, the same blue draperies, and the same smell of perpetual dampness. A clock chimed seven times somewhere in the big house. "We have an hour before supper. It may be somewhat impudent of us, but I want to explore the house a little. Are you willing?" Jane nodded and smiled conspiratorially.

They climbed the stairs to the third floor, where the servants lived. Some of the rooms there were papered in faded pastel prints that suggested that the rooms may have belonged to young children many decades earlier. They moved back down to the second-floor gallery, where they had noted the balustrade upon their arrival. From the wall there, faces stared down at them from great framed canvasses, ladies in fancy dress of an earlier generation and men in uniforms of the sea. Most of the rooms held only dust and the smell of the damp, and all shared the same blue wallpaper with many ships on it.

As they returned to Susanna's room, they met a maid carrying a tray of food up the stairs, who introduced herself with a curtsey. "You must be Miss Susanna, I imagine. My name is Fiona, Mum." A soft Irish brogue gave her words a musical lilt. “May I ask your friend’s name?” She curtsied toward Jane.

“Fiona, this is my friend Jane.”

Not sure how to greet the maid, Jane put out her hand. Fiona colored and curtsied again but did not make contact. Jane retracted her hand.

To cover the embarrassment of the two women, Susanna asked, “Fiona, where is my aunt’s room?”

“There,” she nodded with her head toward the double doors in the middle of the seaward hall above the foyer. “Those are her rooms. I’m takin’ her dinner right now. And that room at the end of the hall is the one bein’ used by Mr. Caspar.”

Fiona was not long in the room of her mistress, and when she exited, she asked, “Would ye like to see the kitchen and meet Cook?” The young women nodded. There in the warm kitchen, Fiona introduced them to the ruddy, smiling woman simply called Cook, and Dan, the elderly gardener who was eating his supper. Cook handed the soup tureen to Fiona to be carried into the dining room, so she excused herself with a nod.

The gong sounded, and they followed Fiona to the dining room, where Mrs. Williams looked at them sternly. “When you were not in your rooms, we did not know where you had gone. That forced us to ring the gong. I’m sure it disturbed Mrs. Thayer.”

Susanna stifled an impulse to offer an apologetic curtsey. “We are sorry if we have inconvenienced you in any way,” she said with a nearly steady voice. *What gives the housekeeper such power to intimidate?* Susanna wondered.

“If you will take your seats, I will have Fiona serve the soup.”

After they had seated themselves, they each had to stand again to pull the chairs closer to the table. When they were settled, Mr. Caspar sat, his manner suggesting that he was lowering his social standing to eat with them. Fiona began to ladle the chowder into the bowl at each place, under the watchful eye of the housekeeper.

Susanna cleared her throat. “Fiona has told me that Aunt Louisa has been taking her meals in her room for some weeks.”

Mr. Caspar nodded. “She prefers it that way.”

At least he responded. “It sounds like the storm has settled in for the night. I hope it doesn’t keep us awake. Do you think you’ll be able to sleep through the storm, Jane?”

“I don’t know.” Jane had been so quiet since arriving that Mr. Caspar looked startled when she responded.

Jane had not begun to eat. She seemed unsure of what to do with the three forks and three spoons near her plate. Additionally, two crystal goblets stood at the tip of her knife.

Susanna caught her eye and carefully picked up the soupspoon. Jane followed her example. Still determined to draw the lawyer out, Susanna continued, "Does this kind of storm happen often here on the coast?"

"Storms like this are common in the winter." His words were clipped.

"How long do they usually last?"

"Difficult to say. Perhaps a day, perhaps a week." He returned to his soup.

When his bowl was empty, Mrs. Williams began to gather all the soup bowls, regardless of whether or not the young women had finished. Susanna laid down her spoon and said nothing.

Fiona brought out a platter of fried clams and set it on the table. She hurried to the kitchen and returned with a platter of cod and another of roasted pork. Those were followed by a bowl of pickled beets and another of cooked cabbage. Susanna made no further attempts at conversation. When the remnants of the food had been removed, Fiona placed a slice of apple pie topped with a piece of cheddar cheese in front of each one of them.

Susanna had never eaten a meal any better than this one except at the Burnley mansion on her birthday, but considering the strained conversation, she would have gladly eaten a meal of thin stew and a slice of bread if the company had been as congenial as the meals with the girls in the boarding house. When the meal was ended, she pushed back her chair and stood.

"Thank you, Williams. It was an excellent meal. Jane, I think it's time for us to retire. I'm sure that you are as tired as I am from a long day of travel."

Susanna looked at Mr. Caspar as he rose, and in a token attempt to be polite, he stated, "Should the storm make it impossible for you to sleep, the library is across the hall. I'm sure there is a book or two there you might read."

"Would you light a lamp for us so we might visit the library, Williams?" Susanna was beginning to grow accustomed to the housekeeper's genderless title.

Williams looked startled. "Right now—" she coughed. "Why, yes, of course." She took one of the lamps from the sideboard and led the way out of the dining room.

The library was directly across the foyer and had the same high, scrolled ceiling as the other rooms on the first floor. There was a massive, carved mantle above an empty fireplace. Through French doors, a few feet of a veranda could be seen where the rain was a torrent falling from a black sky. It coursed across the flagstones, disappearing into a large garden, where flashes of lightning exposed clumps of sticks, which were probably rose bushes in the warmer months.

Books largely about navigation and the sea filled shelves that rose from floor to ceiling. Williams stood inside the door holding the lamp, her manner suggesting that she feared that the young women might purloin something of value if they were not watched.

"Please don't allow us to keep you from your other responsibilities, Williams. When we find something suitable, we will be off to bed." The housekeeper placed the lamp on a table and begrudgingly left the room.

After Susanna located a copy of *Robinson Crusoe*, they climbed the great staircase. Jane whispered, "What was I to do with all those forks and spoons, Susanna?"

"I learned from my mother before we were invited to eat with the Burnley family that one simply works from the outside in, toward the dinner plate. When a guest has a question as to proper etiquette, he just needs to follow the example of the host or hostess."

Jane nodded, feeling better equipped for her next meal in the mansion, if there was to be one.

After they were changed into their nightclothes, Jane knocked on Susanna's door. When it was opened, she said, "I've never slept in a bed by myself. All those years in my father's tavern, I shared the bed with my aunt and then with you in the boarding house. If I don't rise in the morning before eight, please knock on my door. I may have gotten lost in that great bed and I might need someone to find me."

That was the closest thing to humor that Jane had ever expressed. It surprised Susanna, and she smiled broadly at her friend as she gave Jane a hug. Jane reciprocated with a hesitant smile. After Jane had gone to her room, Susanna extinguished the lamp, added several pieces of coal to the fire, and slipped into the bed.

The storm intensified throughout the night. She lay awake listening to the wind as it rattled the shutters and whistled in the chimney flue. Thunder rolled across the countryside like cannon shots. The storm settled down to a hard, wind-driven rain by five o'clock in the morning, and both young women finally fell into a heavy sleep, disturbed only by the sound of the breakfast gong at eight.

Susanna sat up, wondering for a moment where she was. As recognition came, she dressed in the glow cast by the coals in the fireplace.

The clock in the lower hall had struck the half hour before the young women descended the stairs.

The housekeeper was clearing the dirty dishes at the end of the table. "Mr. Caspar's finished his breakfast. He expected to see his guests at eight o'clock." Her voice was reproachful.

Strange that he considers us his guests, since this is my Aunt Louisa's house. "I'm sure you will forgive us for oversleeping. The storm kept us awake most of the night."

"Well, I'm sure the eggs and porridge are cold by now."

"I'm sure everything will be fine, Williams. Did Mr. Caspar say when I might see my aunt?"

"No, he said nothing to me about it." She left the room.

After the meal was finished, Williams entered and began to clear away the dishes, as if she had been waiting and watching from some hidden corner. Susanna offered her thanks for the meal and added, "If you should see Mr. Caspar, I would appreciate it if you would tell him that I would like to speak with him." The housekeeper made no answer, so they climbed the wide staircase and paused outside Susanna's room.

"I didn't want to say anything while we were in the dining room for fear that we might be overheard, but it is my intention to see my aunt this morning, with or without the cooperation of Mr. Caspar. Are you willing to brave his anger with me, Jane?"

"Every step of the way." Jane's smile softened her words.

Susanna and Jane made their way to the door Fiona had come through the evening before, and as Susanna raised her hand to knock, the door opened. Fiona stood there with a startled expression. She held a tray of dirty dishes. "My stars, Miss Thayer, I didn't know ye were there. Ye did give me an awful start."

"I'm sorry, Fiona, but we have come to visit my Aunt Louisa."

"Did Mr. Caspar say it was all right?"

"It appears that Mr. Caspar has no intention of saying much of anything to us today."

"Well, I don't know if I should let you in . . ."

"Fiona, who's at the door? Is it the doctor? Do show him in." The woman's voice from the other room reflected age but no weakness.

Susanna and Jane looked at each other in surprise.

Chapter Twelve

THE TWO YOUNG WOMEN STEPPED past a befuddled Fiona through the little sitting room with its chairs covered in pink needlepoint and a pink vase in the middle of the pedestal table that probably held fresh flowers in the summer.

Despite the fact that the windows were covered with heavy blue draperies, just as they were in almost every other room, the room was bright, lit with a fire in the fireplace and a large oil lamp. It smelled of a combination of whale oil and the faint fragrance of roses, the fragrance an older woman might favor. The furniture was white, with bright pink roses painted on the headboard and the chest of drawers. On the bed, still rumpled from the old woman's sleep, a pink satin coverlet lay folded at the foot. The room was very warm.

Louisa Thayer sat in a large, straight-backed wheelchair with a lap rug tucked around her and a shawl over her shoulders. Firelight glinted off her white hair, which was arranged artfully on top of her head and held by a jeweled, pink comb. She looked up with small, bright eyes and raised a jeweled lorgnette to look at the two young women who had come unannounced into her room.

"And who might the two of you be?" she asked in a surprisingly pleasant voice.

"Please forgive the intrusion, Aunt Louisa, but this seemed the only way we might have the opportunity to see you. Mr. Caspar seemed determined to prevent our meeting. I'm your niece, Susanna Thayer. This is my friend, Jane O'Neil. We've come for a visit in response to your invitation some weeks ago."

After she had looked both young women over thoroughly, the lorgnette fell to the end of its black silk ribbon. "And you've come all that way unescorted." That did not seem to please the old woman, but she quickly pushed the matter aside. "Come, come and sit, so we can get better acquainted." She motioned to a settee across from her chair, which also had pink and white needlepoint cushions.

After they settled themselves, she lifted the lorgnette again and, after further study, thoughtfully tapped it twice against her chin. "You're quite different from what I expected, Susanna. Though I see a little of your father about your eyes, otherwise you are very much like your mother. Tell me again what brought you here?"

I wonder if her mind is failing. "As I said when we entered, I and my friend Jane have come in response to your letter of invitation of some weeks ago. Mr. Caspar seemed determined to keep me from seeing you. He insisted that you were too ill for visitors."

"That is peculiar. I admit that since I have taken to this wheelchair—rheumatism, you know; this climate is the culprit—I have been taking my meals in my room as it has just become too difficult to go down to the dining room." The elderly woman leaned back and continued, "It has been a lonely existence. To state the situation frankly, Mr. Caspar has not been much company, so I have had little reason to descend the stairs, but I am certainly up to receiving visitors. I am so pleased to have the opportunity to become acquainted with one of Robert's daughters. After he gave up his claim to his father's inheritance, we all drifted apart."

Before Susanna could respond, the woman turned to Jane. "You also are welcome, my dear. You're a plain enough young woman and your dress is a bit too common, but if you are Susanna's friend, you must have some good qualities. You will stay as my guest." Jane's complexion grew red with embarrassment. At that point, Susanna wondered if there was not some virtue in the quality of insincerity. Surely, a little less frankness on the part of her aunt would be kinder.

"I don't know what to say. Your kindness is overwhelming," Susanna responded for both of them.

The elderly woman waved away the praise. "I have selfish motives. Not only will I enjoy having some young people in the house, but from what you tell me, I think I need to have some help keeping an eye on Mr. Caspar to show him that I am not nearing the grave as he seems to have been telling people. Today, with your assistance, I will join all of you in the dining room for our midday meal."

***

The lunch was delayed for half an hour while Susanna, Jane, and Fiona assisted the dignified old dowager, but once she had reached the bottom of the stairs, she walked with no more assistance than the use of a cane.

As Mr. Caspar assisted Louisa into the chair at the head of the table, the housekeeper fluttered around her. "Miss Louisa, are you sure you should be out of your wheelchair? Are you sure you are not overexerting yourself?"

Louisa waved the housekeeper away. "I'm fine, Williams. Stop fussing over me. It seems that you and Mr. Casper would be happier if I actually were ill. I can't imagine why I let you talk me into using that wheelchair like an invalid."

"Miss Louisa, we are only concerned for your well-being." Mr. Caspar looked at her from where he sat with a scowl that belied his words.

After lunch, walking between Susanna and Jane, Louisa was assisted to the library, where a fire was laid. Mr. Caspar followed and begrudgingly remained for the next two hours as Louisa talked of her grandfather whose portrait hung in the sitting room and who had built the great house. When she grew quiet, Susanna only needed to ask a question and more stories would follow. As the old woman talked, Susanna and Jane watched the rain as it blew in great gusts against the windowpanes of the French doors. The sound of the breakers beyond the cliff furnished a continuing background to Louisa's stories.

"I understand that some people cannot bear the clamor of the sea. They consider the unceasing roll, the thunder and splash of the waves threatening somehow, but the sea is in the blood of the Thayer family. You remember that, Susanna. Don't ever fear the sea. It has been the friend of this family for many generations. It lifted my grandfather from second mate to sea captain and eventually to the head of his own shipping company."

Louisa had begun to show a noticeable weariness in her face. "I think I shall go upstairs and lie down for an hour before dinner."

"I will have Fiona bring your meal to your room." Williams had returned to the library and spoke with all her usual efficiency, an efficiency that reflected her expectation that when she spoke, all in the house would obey.

"No, I will join all of you for dinner, as I should have been doing for the past several weeks." The old woman pushed herself into a standing position, refusing offers of assistance from Mr. Caspar. Instead, she put out her arms to be assisted by the two young women. As they moved toward the double doors of the library, she said casually, "My niece Susanna and her friend, Jane, will be staying with us for the foreseeable future. Please treat them with the same courtesy you would extend to me." Both Mr. Caspar and Williams momentarily looked as if they had been turned to ice.

"And Williams, please brighten this old barn of a house with some additional lamps in the hallway and a fire in both the sitting room and library fireplaces. It's much too dark and depressing, especially with the storm outside."

***

The following morning, Louisa invited Susanna and Jane, whom she sometimes referred to as "that plain girl with the red hair," to eat breakfast with her in her rooms. Williams's manner and expression suggested that the task of bringing the trays up to the bedroom was an imposition on both her and Fiona, but she said nothing.

"I'll go downstairs for luncheon and dinner, but considering the storm outside, I thought a cozy little group here in my room for breakfast would be pleasant. Don't you think so, Susanna?" Louisa said as the breakfast tray was set before her.

"Yes, I think it is a lovely idea."

After Fiona and the housekeeper left, Louisa leaned back in her chair and closed her eyes for a moment. "I'm sure you wondered why I did not call Mr. Caspar to task yesterday for telling you that I was too ill to meet visitors, but I think it wise if I play the fool a little while longer. I suggest that you and Jane do the same for the present." The two young women looked at one another with a question in their eyes but nodded.

Mr. Caspar announced during luncheon the following day, "Since Miss Louisa has regained her health and strength and has told me that she is able to assume the responsibilities of running Thayer Hill, I will be leaving today. I have many things waiting for me at my Boston office. Do correspond with me if you have any desire for my further services."

Susanna studied him closely. *What is really behind those eyes?*

His trunk was swiftly packed, and Old Dan hitched the horses to the carriage and took him into Andover to catch the train to Boston.

After Mr. Caspar had left, the house seemed brighter. The storm faded and the weak winter sun seemed warmer. That afternoon Susanna and Jane walked the extensive grounds watching the mist over the water dissipate in the sun. The wind smelled of the sea and the damp earth. "The place is wild and lonely but with a beauty all of its own," she commented to Jane as they stood on the cliff and watched the sun glint off the waves until it hurt their eyes.

The next morning, Louisa ordered the horses hitched to the carriage. It was obviously the finest carriage in the area, being a graceful landau manufactured a few years earlier in England. After the three women were seated with Jane and Susanna facing Louisa, Dan offered to raise the front half of the supple leather folding top to the center position to protect Louisa from the cold wind.

"No, Dan, I'm sure we women can tolerate a little cold breeze to see the scenes of the area."

Dan climbed to the high, upholstered bench seat in the front and slapped the horses' rumps with the reins. The carriage moved down the hill, rising and falling gently on its elliptical springs. Jane looked at Susanna with eyes wide with pleasure but said nothing. Neither young woman had ever ridden in such a fine carriage. Susanna noted that it even surpassed the carriage of Jonathan Burnley, Senior.

***

In the morning, the three women ate breakfast together in Louisa's rooms, with the draperies pulled back and the winter sun streaming in. "Susanna, give me that little jewel casket—the one with the mother of pearl flowers on the top." She took it from Susanna's hand, opened it, and lifted a string of pearls from the box. "My father brought these back from one of his long sea voyages to the islands of the Pacific. I have wondered who should have them since I seldom have any need to wear them. Now they are yours, my dear."

Susanna's throat tightened as the generosity of her aunt nearly overwhelmed her. She held the pearls in her hands, studying their translucence for a minute or two before she was finally able to speak. "Thank you, Aunt Louisa. I will treasure them always and wear them often."

"That would be wise, my dear, as the luster of pearls improves when worn against the skin."

Susanna's letter to her mother that evening recounted her surprise and pleasure at meeting her great-aunt.

Dearest Mama,

I am so glad to tell you that I am no longer at the mill. Jane and I lost our positions, and having an invitation from Aunt Louisa, we traveled to Newburyport, where she has offered us her hospitality for as long as we choose to stay. It has been wonderful to meet her. She is so different than I had always believed. She has told us many stories of her father and grandfather and has given me a string of pearls, a gift from her father. She has offered us a warm and welcoming haven in an otherwise uncertain world. I hope the time will come when you and Georgie, and perhaps James, can travel here to renew your acquaintance. I believe you would come to love her as I have.

Your loving daughter,
Susanna Thayer

Chapter Thirteen

On Christmas Day, dinner included fancy meat pies, roast venison, roast mutton, doves baked in nests of puff pastry, a great ham, cod, quail stuffed with oyster dressing, golden squash, and sweetened cranberry relish. For dessert, Cook made an English trifle.

Louisa spoke to the housekeeper, who had begun to clear away the empty platters. "Tell Cook that the meal was excellent." She looked at Susanna through her lorgnette with a benign smile. "Susanna, I think it is time to tell you that I have written to Mortimer Caspar and asked him to send someone from the firm to draft a new will for me." Startled, Susanna turned to look at her but wasn't sure what to say. Her aunt continued, "I'm determined to put you in my will. In fact, I plan to make you my primary heir. I've come to deeply regret that your father was left with such a pittance for an inheritance, forcing your mother into dire straits upon his death. I want to make sure that you, my dear, are provided for, so that you will never have to return to the mill."

The spoon in Williams's hand clattered to the table. She hurriedly wiped the dollop of cream from the tablecloth to cover her surprise.

Susanna was speechless for nearly a minute. She was finally able to take a deep breath. "Aunt Louisa, your kindness is overwhelming. I have no way to express my gratitude." Susanna could not get her mind around the full implications of the announcement.

Louisa continued, "I have asked him or someone from his firm to return to Thayer Hill as soon as it can be arranged, so I can discuss the specific changes I want made in the will." As Susanna sat there, Louisa continued speaking, but her words did not penetrate Susanna's thoughts. *Here we are, welcome in the home and dependent upon the charity of a woman I knew almost nothing about for most of my life. A week, a day, a few seconds ago, I thought my future lay thousands of miles away in California, and now, heaven has spread a new future before me—effortlessly on my part. God does indeed work in mysterious ways.*

"Either Mr. Caspar or someone from his office will be here no later than mid-January, well after the New Year's holiday is past, when he has arranged his affairs in such a manner as to work my request into his schedule." Her aunt's words pulled her attention back to the events around her. The news had actually made Susanna light-headed.

"Aunt Louisa, there is no way I can ever repay you," she repeated.

"Pishposh. The repayment is long overdue and is owed to you and your dead father."

That evening, Susanna lay in the big bed and thought of the many changes her aunt's bequest would make in her life. *The first thing I will do as the mistress of Thayer Hill is bring Mama and Georgie to live here with me.*

A new thought stopped her for a moment. *Am I being unchristian and improper to even think ahead to the eventual passing of Aunt Louisa? Am I being covetous? Yes, yes, I am.* But her attempts to control her thoughts as she felt the texture of the blessings the money would bring were unsuccessful. She fell asleep thinking of the reunion with her mother and brother the inheritance would make possible.

***

The new year came quietly, and the bitter wind from the sea blew away the perpetual dark clouds. The sun was a fiery but cold circle in the sky. The heavy draperies were opened and the light streamed into every room on the lower level. Doors were opened so the light could make its way into the great hallway, where it entered like a welcome visitor. Louisa ordered that a fire be built in every one of the main rooms on the lower level on a daily basis to heat the big house to a comfortable temperature.

Louisa had taken particular notice of her niece's appearance at breakfast. "My dear Susanna, you look very suitable today. That blue dress sets off the pearls very nicely. All I could possibly suggest is that you pull your hair back from your face. You have perfect cheekbones. They shouldn't be hidden behind those undisciplined curls that insist on falling about your face."

"Thank you, Aunt Louisa. I shall do so."

"Now that you are looking much more like a refined young woman, we must do something for Jane."

Jane, please don't be hurt again by her directness. She does mean well. Susanna smiled apologetically at her friend.

Jane's color rose, but without noticing the young woman's discomfort, Louisa continued, "You need a dress more suitable to your coloring, Jane, not that ugly rust color—something in light blue or pale green—something to draw attention away from that carrot-colored hair and pale complexion—and we must *do* something with that hair. Have you ever learned to curl it, my dear?" Jane just shook her head and stared at her hands in her lap.

Fiona entered to remove the breakfast dishes. "When you have cleared away the dishes, Fiona, I want you to take Jane in hand and show her how you curl your hair. If you need some rags or metal curlers, let Williams know, and she will find them for you. We're going to make Jane into a new young woman."

Aunt Louisa, Jane is not in need of becoming a new young woman; she is my dear friend, and I love her just the way she is. But recognizing that her aunt meant well, Susanna determined not to oppose her but to become part of the transition for her friend, perhaps easing her embarrassment.

Louisa continued, "I have a pale green dress undoubtedly much too large for you, Jane, but I'll have Fiona alter it to fit you, and while she is doing that, she can alter my wine-colored dress for you, Susanna."

"What a thoughtful thing to offer, Aunt Louisa," Susanna agreed. Jane dutifully rose from her chair and followed the maid out of the room.

After spending an additional hour in conversation with her aunt, Susanna returned to her room, where she stood before the mirror above the heavy chest and arranged her hair into a cascade of auburn curls falling from a barrette high at the back of her head. She was glad that her formerly sheared locks had grown since the incident with the loom

Fiona entered her bedroom to sweep and dust. "Oh, Miss Susanna, I didn't realize you were still here. I'll come back after awhile to do the cleanin', mum."

"No, Fiona, stay. I won't be long." Susanna turned and smiled broadly. "Were you able to show Jane how to curl her hair?"

"Aye, I showed her how to twist it in rags. It is the straightest hair I have ever seen in all my days."

Susanna laughed. "With your help, and mine, we will make a beauty of her."

"Oh, Miss Susanna, I wouldn't go so far as to say that." Suddenly embarrassed by the directness of her words, Fiona dropped the dustpan and broom. As they clattered to the floor, she put her hands over her mouth. "I'm s' sorry, mum. I was totally out of place to say a thing like that. Please forgive me, mum."

Susanna turned from the mirror and gave Fiona a quick, impulsive hug. "Jane wouldn't mind, so I shouldn't."

The embarrassed maid dropped a little curtsey. "Yes, mum."

The sound of wagon wheels on gravel drew Susanna to the window. Mr. Allred had brought someone to visit. From the straightness of the stranger's back and broadness of his shoulders, the visitor was a young man. All Susanna could see was the top of his hat and his shoulders. He sat next to the driver on the front seat of the wagon and a large valise lay in the wagon bed. As Susanna left her bedroom and started for the stairs, the boom of the great door knocker echoed through the house.

The housekeeper hurried across the wide foyer. "Yes," was all she said when she opened the door.

She will probably never learn to greet guests properly, Susanna thought with a smile. She started down the stairs. "Who is it, Williams? Please invite him in."

***

When Jonathan had been called into his uncle's office several days after the beginning of the new year, he had expected some simple assignment of the kind that Mortimer Caspar would trust to an underling. That was usually what was delegated to him—the filing of a deed, perhaps. For that reason, he was startled when he was given the assignment of traveling to Newburyport to meet with the dowager Louisa Thayer to redraft her will.

"Both your father and I are much too involved in the insurance claims of the owners of the three ships that have been frozen in the harbor these past weeks to get away from the office just now. Your father is meeting with the captain of the *Sea Wanderer* as we speak." Caspar's high, thin voice was, as usual, authoritarian and crisp. "When I suggested to your father that you were capable of this assignment, he agreed. I mentioned to him that Louisa's great-niece, Susanna Thayer is living there at the present time and that this might cause some small discomfort for you, but he said to instruct you not to allow the young woman's presence to disrupt the completion of the assigned task. Now you have been forewarned. Please return to the office here as soon as the task is complete."

Jonathan drew his thoughts back to the present as Mr. Allred's wagon rattled up the long drive to the great house, Jonathan carefully counted to ten with each breath, letting it out just as slowly, to steady himself as he dismounted from the wagon seat.

***

When Williams answered the door, the young man stood silhouetted against the daylight behind him. He handed a coin to Mr. Allred, who touched the brim of his hat and set the valise down on the porch before he returned to his wagon. As the sound of the wheels grew quieter on the gravel driveway, the young man stepped inside the entryway and removed his hat. Susanna could see a certain familiarity in the silhouette. As he stepped farther into the light cast by the lamp on the side board, she caught her breath at the sight of the familiar cheekbones, the high forehead, and the strong jaw. She knew those dark blue, piercing eyes, that head of thick, dark hair. How well she remembered the tall slenderness, the broad, white smile. He wore a stiff, white collar with a blue tie knotted carefully and tucked into the vest he wore under a perfectly tailored coat with tails. His dress was as formal as if he were scheduled to attend a funeral. Her heart began to pound so hard that she put her hand over it, lest he hear it across the room.

He stopped for a moment when he saw her. Susanna had paused on the lowest stair. She carefully let go of the breath she had taken when she had recognized him. She had never expected to see him again, but here he was.

She wasn't sure how to react. *I will not allow him to see my discomfort,* she resolved. She spoke as she stepped off the last stair. "Mr. Burnley, what brings you to Thayer Hill?" She hoped her voice did not reflect the sudden emotions that were churning inside her. She also hoped desperately that her smile was pleasant and relaxed. It didn't feel that way.

He took several steps toward her while the housekeeper continued to hover about him. "My uncle, Mortimer Caspar, has asked me to visit with your aunt as she has some legal work for our firm. Susanna . . . I mean, Miss Thayer, you are looking well."

The housekeeper was watching both of them with her eyebrows drawn close together. "Sir, if you will wait in the sitting room, I will tell Miss Louisa that you are here." She gestured in the direction of the room, which had been made bright and comfortable by the fire.

He shrugged off his heavy overcoat and, without looking at the housekeeper, held it toward her. His eyes never left Susanna's face.

"Will you be staying long?" The housekeeper's voice was hard and direct.

"At least one night, I think." He continued to stare at Susanna. The housekeeper took the coat and hat and started toward the staircase. "I will have your room made ready."

He said nothing, so Susanna responded. "Thank you, Williams." She noted that he didn't even glance in the housekeeper's direction. Susanna cleared her throat. "Mr. Burnley, it has been some time since we last . . . ah, communicated. I hope all has been well with you."

They were finally near enough for her to stiffly offer her hand. He took it in his own and bowed from the shoulders over it. As he straightened, he responded in a flat tone, "Yes, yes, it has." When he was sure the housekeeper was gone, his voice warmed. "Shall we go into the sitting room?" He offered her his elbow as if it were the most natural thing he could do.

She hesitated, resisting the urge to take it. Instead, she walked with folded hands beside him into the sitting room. "I hope your marriage has been a happy one." It was all she could think to say.

"Ah, yes, yes, it has." But there was no enthusiasm in his voice.

"Are you and your bride making your home in Boston?"

"Yes, yes, we are." Susanna noticed that he suddenly seemed to find making conversation more difficult than she. She sat in the wingback chair, forcing him to sit on the settee.

He cleared his throat. "My uncle mentioned to me that you were staying here with your aunt, but I must apologize for the fact that your presence there in the hallway still caught me off guard. It was a surprise—a very pleasant surprise." He smiled in such a warm manner that the sincerity of his words was apparent.

"Your uncle is Mortimer Caspar?" Without waiting for his response, she continued, "I had forgotten. So your father's firm is truly a family affair." She tried to smile, but her lips felt stiff.

"Yes, one might say that." His eyes never left her face.

"May I ask what kind of legal work has brought you here?" She struggled to keep the emotional turmoil out of her voice. She felt she was playing some kind of game with him, verbal hide-and-seek—hide your feelings, let him seek them out.

"I have been sent to draft your aunt's new will."

"Oh, of course." She swallowed hard. "Was there something that kept your uncle from returning?"

"Yes, there are three great ships stuck in the ice in Boston Harbor, and he and my father are working with the insurance firms to obtain recompense for the ships' owners."

"How long will you be staying?" Her feelings were a mass of confusion; she couldn't tell if she wanted him to stay or wished he would finish his task and hurry away.

"Probably no more than one night, as I don't expect the changes in the will to be complex." He rose from the settee and stepped over to the fire. "The ride in that wagon was a cold one. Please forgive me while I warm myself."

"I'm sure it was." She said no more, deliberately leaving the direction of the conversation open to his choosing. *One night with him in the house—surely I can cope with such a brief situation.* But she suddenly wanted him to stay longer—much longer. His face, his voice were so familiar. While he warmed his hands, she hurriedly dashed away a tear.

He was oblivious to her internal confusion. His conversation continued. "The weather has been so cold that several ships have been caught in the ice this year. It keeps the members of the firm very busy." He paused and turned to face her. "Susanna—may I have leave to address you in that familiar manner? After all, we were—" he searched for a way to put it, "we were very good friends."

Susanna had felt the color rise in her face as he spoke of their "friendship," so she looked away from him, trying to hide the hurt that might show in her eyes. "I don't think that your wife would consider it appropriate for you to address me in that fashion, Mr. Burnley. Perhaps greater formality would be more appropriate."

"Susanna, please don't be brittle." His voice was a quiet plea. "We *were* good friends."

"Yes, we *were*." *After all, that was the point. Didn't he realize that?* Attempting to lead the conversation in another direction, she asked, "And how is your wife?"

The previous warmth in his voice melted away. "She recently gave birth and has not fully regained her strength. The doctor said her recovery would be gradual so we must be patient."

"For the sake of both of you, I hope her recovery is swift." She sincerely meant it.

"Thank you," he said mechanically as he returned to looking into the fire.

At that point, the housekeeper entered the room. "I've had Old Dan take your case up to your room, sir. It is ready for you now. Please follow me."

Susanna stood as he left the room but said nothing more.

***

When the midday meal was ready, Louisa refused the young solicitor's offer of help down the stairs, and with Jane on one side and Susanna on the other, she made it down to the dining room. She did accept his offer to help her into the chair at the head of the table.

"Susanna, you should sit here on my right, and Mr. Burnley will sit next to you." Looking at him, she asked in her direct manner, "May I ask why you have brought your portmanteau into the dining room with you?"

"I have a small gift for you, Miss Louisa, from my uncle. It's a small apology from him for his absence. With your permission, I will present it to you at the end of the meal."

"Of course, of course. Jane, you sit here on my left—and I want you to know that you are looking like a very proper young lady today in that green dress with your hair curled."

Louisa immediately began to direct her attention toward the young solicitor. "Mr. Burnley, tell us about Boston. What is going on there right now? It has been some time since I visited that city."

"The city fathers are extending several of the streets to accommodate an increasing population, and some of the Back Bay has been filled so the housing of the area can be expanded." A desultory conversation mainly between Louisa and Jonathan continued through the meal. Susanna ate little, dabbing at her lips with a serviette and trying not to show her relief when the meal was over. Her proximity to Jonathan was again filling her with confusing feelings.

As Fiona removed the dishes from the table, Jonathan bent and undid the buckles on the straps of his portmanteau and removed a small package wrapped in brown paper and string. He handed it to Louisa. "It's only a small gift."

She removed the string and paper and paused with a perplexed look on her face as she examined a bottle of brown glass of the kind used in most chemist shops. She lifted her lorgnette to examine it more closely.

"Mr. Billings, the chemist at the shop used by my family—" He turned to Susanna. "Surely you remember it, Susanna? It was the shop you passed on your way to attend Sunday meetings when your family attended

Pastor Hutchison's congregation." Without waiting for her response, he turned back to the matriarch. "Mr. Billings said it is a fine restorative, medicinal syrup that is an important part of every physician's medications. It is called calomel, and he credits it with the high survival rate of the last epidemic of diphtheria in the city. He said it is also excellent for stomach upset. My uncle wanted you to have some for your own use, should a siege of ague enter the household."

"How thoughtful of your uncle." Louisa said it as if she were not entirely convinced. "Now, if Mr. Burnley will assist me out of my chair, then you, Susanna, and you, Jane, will assist me up the stairs. He and I will retire to my sitting room, where we will discuss the changes I want to make in my will. You two young ladies will need to entertain yourselves this afternoon."

Susanna suppressed a thrill at the thought that the changes in the will would bring her great material comforts. She immediately reminded herself that her aunt could change her mind and leave only a small bequest. *But even that would be a blessing.*

After two hours, Mr. Burnley returned to his room, where he worked behind a closed door until dinner was ready. Louisa sent Fiona to find Susanna and ask her to come to the bedroom.

When Susanna entered, Louisa was laying on her bed, propped up with several pillows, her face a map of exhaustion. "My dear, Mr. Burnley has gone to his room to write out the will as I have requested. I will look at it in the morning, and if it is written as I have instructed, I will sign it. At the present, I am feeling very weary. I will not come down to dinner this evening, but I wanted to give you something before it slipped from my mind. Please bring the little jewel casket on the dresser to me, the one that held the pearls." Susanna offered it to her, but Louisa said, "Open it. You will find two brooches there among the other things."

"What do they look like, Aunt Louisa? There are several broaches here."

"The larger one is made of whale bone set in silver. It has a ship carved on it. It is an excellent example of scrimshaw. Perhaps it is not the prettiest, but it holds the greatest sentimental value, as my grandfather brought it home from one of his last voyages and presented it to my grandmother. Do pin it on."

Susanna pinned the broach just below the lace at the neck of her dress, framed by the pearls.

"That sets it off beautifully. There's a second broach, not so large but similar, as it is also scrimshaw. I want you to give it to Jane. I want her to have something with which to remember me."

Susanna lifted the smaller broach from the jewel box. "Thank you Aunt Louisa. We will always appreciate your kindness and generosity."

"Hand me the jewel box, my dear." Louisa couldn't support the weight of the box, so Susanna set it on the bed near her. The old woman sorted through the items in it. Settling on a pair of pearl earrings, she reached toward Susanna. "Put out your hand, dear. These will match the necklace."

Susanna put out her hand and her aunt dropped the two earrings into it. "They are beautiful, Aunt Louisa." They glowed warmly in her palm.

"Put them on, Susanna. You were born to wear lovely things like these. Had things turned out differently, you might have worn things like this all you life."

"What do you mean?"

She exhaled in weariness. "If your father had wanted his portion of the family inheritance, you could have lived very comfortably."

"But Aunt Louisa, he did want it. When Uncle Thaddeus hired Mr. Burnley, Senior, to contest Grandfather's will, he felt disinclined to oppose the matter in the courts. He felt such a public family disagreement was inappropriate and would sully the family name."

The old woman closed her eyes for a minute, as though she had fallen asleep. As Susanna stood and started for the door to let her rest, her aunt spoke. "I had no idea, no notion that such was the case," she whispered. She opened her eyes and added more firmly, "There will be a few more changes to the will. Would you go to Mr. Burnley's room and tell him that I will want to talk with him again before I retire?"

"Of course, Aunt Louisa."

"And when I have finished with him, please send Fiona up to help me prepare for bed. It vexes me that I weary so completely at times."

"Yes, Aunt Louisa, I'll do so immediately." Susanna rose to take her leave.

"Give one a kiss," Louisa said, pointing to her cheek. "We are family now. How sad we weren't family long ago." Susanna stooped and put a gentle kiss on the pale cheek before she withdrew from the room.

Yes, how very sad we weren't family long ago, Susanna thought as she quietly closed the door and moved down the hall to Jonathan's bedroom. When he opened to her knock, she noted that his hair was mussed and that he had removed his coat and cravat. There were ink stains on the fingers of his right hand.

"Aunt Louisa would like to speak with you, Mr. Burnley. She is very tired but wanted to do so before she retired."

"I'll go immediately." He pulled on his coat and, without smoothing his hair, hurried to her bedroom door and knocked.

***

After dinner that evening, as Fiona was gathering the dishes, Jonathan turned to Susanna and said quietly, "Could we talk for a few minutes in the sitting room, Susanna?"

The use of her given name did not pass unnoticed, but she simply nodded and slowly followed him out of the room. As she stood near the fire with her back to the room, he pulled the doors to the room closed.

"Susanna, I sense a wide gulf between us. I can only assume it stems from hard feelings on your part. It is difficult for me to bear. Won't you please forgive me and remember the good times we shared as children?" She did not respond. "I did not realize how much I missed our old friendship until I saw you again." He sat on the settee, leaned forward, and clasped his hands.

She felt that there was no appropriate response, so she continued to stand silently. He continued, musing more to himself than to anyone else, "Do you remember how we would sit in the sun on the stairs of the church while our parents socialized after Sabbath meetings and exchange quotes from the classics? I excelled in my literature courses at Harvard because of those hours. 'What is a friend? A single soul dwelling in two bodies.'"

Unable to withstand the temptation to respond just as she had so many times in the past, she involuntarily answered, "Aristotle." Then she tried to send him a message in the quote she selected. "Hope is a waking dream."

He smiled. "Also Aristotle."

She tried again. "Hope deferred maketh the heart sick."

"Proverbs 13:12." He was pleased to have drawn her into the old game, but she felt that he had completely missed the point she had tried to make. When they were younger, playing the quote game had been fun for her, but now it just hurt. He continued:

Cupid is winged and doth range
Her country so my love doth change,
But change she earth, or change she sky,
Yet I will love her till I die.

She swallowed hard to relax the sudden tightness in her throat enough to speak. "Included by Thomas Ford in *Music of Sundry Kinds.*" *Why would he quote that to me now? He still does not understand how his decision wounded me.* She looked at her hands and noted that they were shaking slightly. She balled them into fists to hide the tremors.

He was enjoying the old game. He selected another quote.

> *O many a shaft at random sent*
> *Finds mark the archer little meant!*
> *And many a word at random spoken*
> *May soothe or wound a hearts that's broken.*

She turned to look at him. He had leaned back in a relaxed manner and sat with his right ankle crossed over his left knee, his arms extended along the back of the settee. She responded shortly, "Sir Walter Scott, from *The Lord of the Isles.* Forgive me, Mr. Burnley, but this game . . ." She stopped and took a deep breath. "It has been too long since I played this game. I feel very tired. I think I will retire early." She hurried to the doors, pushed one open, and swept out of the room before he could object. As she hurried up the stairs, Proverbs 28:26 forced its way into her mind. *He that trusteth in his own heart is a fool.*

Jonathan sat up, disappointed and confused by the manner of her departure.

Chapter Fourteen

The morning sun was slipping through the blue draperies as Susanna fastened the pearls about her neck. Fiona's scream suddenly echoed through the great house. "She's dead!" Anguish filled her voice, and sobs tore her words into little fragments. "She's de-ad." Susanna opened her bedroom door and could see the maid running toward her, sobbing, "I took her a breakfast tray, like I always do, but she didn't answer the door." She grabbed Susanna's arm. "She's just lying in the bed, cold as ice. Come with me, Miss Susanna. Come and see."

By this time, Williams had hurried into the lower hallway, and Jonathan and Jane had stepped out of their rooms. "What is it?" Jonathan called out. "What in heaven's name has made Fiona so hysterical?"

As she hurried toward her aunt's rooms, Susanna called to him over her shoulder, "She's saying that something terrible has happened to Aunt Louisa—that she's dead."

A knot had formed in her stomach. *Dear God, don't take my aunt from me, not now after we have so lately found each other.*

She entered the bedroom with a weeping Fiona behind her. It was evident from the old woman's pale face and cold hands that the servant was right. Susanna took her aunt's hand in her own and knelt by the bed. As the reality of the loss swept over her, she leaned her forehead against the bed coverlet while her shoulders shook and her tears dropped onto the pink satin.

Jonathan rushed into the room. "What has happened? Is Miss Louisa ill?" He stopped just inside the room, no longer needing an explanation. He sat down on the chair near the dresser, dropped his head into his hands and ran his fingers through his hair. After taking a deep breath, he looked up. "Susanna, this is terrible. This is just terrible."

Somewhat confused at his extreme reaction, she stood and made a major effort to regain her composure. She was finally able to respond, "I know we will miss her, Jonathan, but she has lived a long life. We shouldn't be surprised. She wasn't feeling well yesterday. I suppose her heart just gave out." Her voice dropped. "We can't oppose God's will." Her voice trailed off into a whisper.

"Susanna, you don't fully realize the situation. She did not sign the new will. It will not be binding. The old will is likely to stand, and there is no mention of you in the old will. The new will would have given Thayer Hill to you. Now it will go to your Uncle Thaddeus. There are small bequests for Williams, Fiona, Cook, and Old Dan. The only other beneficiary will be the law firm of Burnley and Caspar, as they will take twenty-five percent of the estate for handling the will."

Susanna stood unmoving while she mentally dealt with the information. Finally, she spoke. "Oh, I see. I hadn't thought of that." She was suddenly dizzy. She sat down abruptly.

Jonathan rose and stepped over to the bedside table. He picked up the brown bottle he had given Louisa the previous day. "How strange. The bottle is nearly half empty." He turned and looked inquiringly at Fiona, who was standing in the corner of the room sniffing and wiping her tears with a corner of her apron.

"Mr. Burnley, she asked me for a spoon when I helped her into bed yesterday. She said her stomach was troubling her, and she thought the calomel might help. I only gave her one spoonful, honestly, only one."

Susanna was trying to shut her mind to the effect her aunt's death would have on her personally. She rose and stepped over to the frightened maid. As she put her arms around Fiona shoulders to offer some comfort, she whispered, "No one is blaming you, Fiona. You were only doing as she asked you to do. Why don't you go down to the kitchen and have Cook fix you something hot to drink—for your nerves." Fiona hurried out of the room, still sniffling.

The housekeeper had been standing just outside the doorway, listening to all that had happened. She stepped in, wringing her hands. "Mr. Burnley, I sat with Miss Louisa last night for a long while—until she fell asleep. She asked me to give her more of that medicine." She pointed at the brown bottle Jonathan had set back down on the bed table. "Did I do wrong?"

"No, no, you just did what you were asked to do. You must not blame yourself. We must send Dan for the doctor, the constable, and the minister. Do you know which congregation she was attending?"

"She didn't attend any church on a regular basis in the years I have served her, but she had been christened in the Presbyterian Church in Newburyport."

"Then we shall send for the minister of the Presbyterian congregation. I will write a letter to my uncle and my father and instruct Dan to post it when he goes into town to inform the others. While I do that, Williams, I think you would do well to prepare a meal for the household and for the . . . the others who will be coming." The housekeeper nodded and left the room, gray with distress.

"I'm glad you're here, Jonathan. I would not have known what to do under these circumstances." Susanna's voice was husky with emotion.

"Susanna, someone should sit with her," he glanced at the bed, "out of respect, until someone of authority arrives."

"I'll wait with her for the present."

***

The constable arrived after Williams had completed laying out a cold lunch. He interrogated each of the residents of the house and was apparently satisfied. He settled down to a lunch of sliced ham, cheese, sweet cucumber pickles, and cranberry relish on slices of bread baked the previous day.

Pastor Entwhistle arrived an hour later, and after he was introduced to Susanna as nearest of kin, he invited all the residents of the house to join him in prayer at Louisa's bedside. The little room was crowded as he appealed to heaven to accept the soul of Louisa Thayer. At Susanna's request, Jane took her place at Louisa's bedside for the next hour. Susanna invited the minister to join Jonathan and herself in the dining room, where the constable was still eating.

Susanna sat with her hands in her lap while the minister meticulously cut his ham into tiny pieces. He asked between bites, "Miss Susanna, when would you prefer to schedule the church for the services? Do you plan an extended wake?"

Susanna looked at Jonathan for guidance, and he shook his head very slightly before he spoke. "Miss Louisa lived a very sedate and somewhat isolated life, according to my uncle, who was her personal solicitor. Due to her age, I don't suppose she would have very many acquaintances able to attend a wake. I think it would be appropriate to schedule services and the burial as soon as is practical after the constable gives us permission to do so. What do you think, Susanna?"

Susanna simply nodded in agreement. As the morning hours had passed, she had found her composure wearing thin. *How I will miss her. If it were mine to give, I would give every penny of the estate to have her back. How I will miss her.* The thought echoed over and over in her mind.

Doctor Harding arrived as Williams was laying another platter of sliced ham and cheese within reach of the constable. He was taken immediately to Louisa's bedroom and Jane was excused to get something to eat. Susanna's legs could hardly take her up the stairs. She was hoping that she could soon retire to her own room, where she could allow her emotions some release. While the doctor and Jonathan talked in the bedroom, she sat in the adjoining sitting room.

For about five minutes, Dr. Harding and Jonathan spoke in low tones. When they stepped out of the bedroom, the doctor held the bottle of calomel. He sat across from Susanna and spoke in a soft, kindly voice. "Miss Thayer, there is no question that age and infirmity probably played a part in your aunt's passing, but as I told Mr. Burnley, in all likelihood, this calomel contributed to it. I'm sure we will never know, but calomel has fallen out of use among many Boston physicians because it contains mercury chloride. Like many things, the body may be blessed by small amounts of this type of chemical, but in larger amounts, it can do much damage. From the amount left in the bottle, your aunt consumed more of this solution than was safe."

His words tore away the remnants of her composure. "You're saying that she might not have died?" Two tears made their way down her cheeks. Jonathan stepped quickly into the bedroom, where he picked up a linen handkerchief from the bedside table with the initial *L* embroidered on it. He handed it to Susanna, who dabbed at the tears with the handkerchief, which smelled faintly of roses.

She stood and turned as if to run from the room to hide her grief, but Jonathan stepped in front of her and wrapped her in his arms. She laid her cheek against his shoulder and sobbed, "I had come to love her, Jonathan, and here, I had found a home—a haven—and now she's gone." She wept for nearly a full minute before regaining her self-control.

Suddenly embarrassed, she pulled away and stood more straightly, pushing away a stray curl that had fallen in her face. "I'm so very sorry. You must forgive me." She turned to the doctor and whispered, "I'm being selfish. I must learn to accept God's will in all things." She walked hurriedly from the room before Jonathan could stop her.

"Well, it's good to know that she will be adequately provided for," the doctor said as he picked up the medical bag from the table. When Jonathan said nothing, he stopped and looked at him. "She is provided for in her aunt's will, is she not?"

"Her aunt was in the process of drafting another will which would have included her. That is why I am here at the present time, but it was not complete." Jonathan's voice dropped to a near whisper. "I fear she will be left penniless."

The doctor paused as he was putting a scarf around his neck. He looked again at the bottle of calomel he had set on the table near his bag. "Who furnished her the calomel?" His voice was very curious.

Jonathan cleared his throat and shifted his weight with nervousness. "My uncle gave it to me to give to Miss Louisa—as a gift. He thought it might help with her stomach problems—but you believe it may have contributed to her death?" His face was white.

The doctor reconfirmed his earlier statement. "Yes, at her age and frail condition, it is most likely that it contributed to her death."

Jonathan had begun to look ill.

"Are you unwell, Mr. Burnley? Perhaps you should lie down." The doctor was suddenly concerned for the young man.

"No, no, I'll be all right. I'll just sit here for a moment."

***

A less perceptive man than the doctor, the constable saw nothing about which to be concerned when the doctor and he spoke in the dining room. His response was simply, "She lived a long life. None of us can expect to live forever." He turned and looked at Jonathan, who had made his way down the stairs, looking only slightly less pale than he had a few minutes earlier. "You may proceed with the funeral services."

Jonathan ordered the door to Louisa's room locked. When the constable, minister, and doctor had taken their leave, Susanna returned to her room, where she sat on her bed and wept freely, both for the loss of her aunt and for the return to the difficulties in which she found herself once more.

That night she dreamed that she was alone in a desert, terribly thirsty. She tried to capture water from a stream in her hands to drink, but it slid between her fingers and disappeared while her thirst remained. The dream was so troubling that when she wakened, she slipped out of the bed and knelt beside it, and in a pleading prayer, she whispered over and over, "Dear God, where do I go now? What should I do?"

***

The funeral was held two days later. The mourners who stood around the grave were few. Even if the weather had not been so bitter cold, the group would not have been any larger.

Chapter Fifteen

The wagon from the livery stable brought Jonathan's father three days later. He was a tall, broad-shouldered man of fifty with a head of dark hair growing gray above the ears in a distinguished manner. His eyes were pale blue, as if something had diluted their original color. He would have been handsome if a faint, perpetual scowl did not darken his expression, carving downward lines around his mouth and a deep slash between his eyebrows. When he was greeted at the door by Williams, he said to no one and everyone at the same time, "None of the senior partners from the firm could get here any sooner. I imagine my son has handled things properly."

The housekeeper looked behind her, thinking that he had been speaking to someone of higher rank. She took his coat and hat, and he briskly pulled off his gloves and dropped them into the inverted hat she held out for him. Never having met him previously, she wondered who he was for a moment. Then she realized who he had to be.

"Your son is young Mr. Burnley?" He looked at her as if she were stupid, so she quickly tried to cover her embarrassment. "Yes, sir. I'm sure he has,"

"Please tell him that I'm here. Is there somewhere private where the two of us may speak?"

"Yes, sir. I'm sure the sitting room would be suitable." Still carrying his coat, hat, and gloves, she led the way.

"Bring me some brandy."

"Sir, Miss Louisa wouldn't permit hard liquor in the house. We do have some sherry for cooking and medicinal use."

"Then bring me some sherry—and tell my son that I'm here," he repeated. His words sounded harsher than he had intended, but he was cold and had begun to think this housekeeper was dimwitted.

"Yes, sir." She disappeared to hang up his coat and returned in a few minutes with a glass of sherry.

As she left the room, Jonathan appeared in the doorway. "Father, I'm surprised to see you. I thought Uncle Mortimer would be coming." His father was standing before the fire, holding the emptied long-stemmed glass. He set it on the mantle before turning to his son.

"He's still tied up with one of the ships in the harbor. It's going to be frozen in the ice for heaven knows how long. Stupid captain. He had two other ports he could have tied up in, but no, he had to come to Boston in one of the worst winters we've seen in a decade." He moved across the carpet and sat in the large captain's chair near the French doors. "Well, how soon can we have the reading of the will? I need to get this over and get back to the office."

"There's a problem with the will, Father."

***

Susanna had stepped out of her room when she heard the great door knocker, but upon hearing Jonathan Burnley, Senior, ask for his son, she returned to her room. Her eyes were still red and swollen from her grieving. She really did not want to see anyone except Jane, but within a few minutes, the sound of raised voices had drawn everyone else in the house to the lower foyer.

Jane hurried up the stairs and knocked on Susanna's bedroom door. "Susanna, come quickly. Something is happening and I think you need to know about it."

The two young women hurried down the stairs, and Williams, Fiona, Old Dan, and even Cook did not move from where they were standing and listening near the library doors. Susanna waved them away.

As she reached for the door handle, Jonathan's voice rose. She drew back. "But it is unethical, Father, entirely unethical." He was emphatic. "I cannot believe you would insist on doing such a thing. It was Miss Louisa's intent to leave Thayer Hill to Susanna. She was very explicit in her new will. You can see that for yourself. She only had to sign it, which she would have done had she not passed in the night."

"But she didn't, so there is no problem!" The older, heavier voice was hard. "How dare you challenge me in this matter. I know what it is." His voice turned oily. "That young woman has been playing on your sympathies, winding you around her little finger." His voice grew sharp. "What a fool of a son I have raised."

"My feelings for Susanna have nothing to do with this, Father. It is a matter of ethics, legal ethics. Before her passing, I learned from Miss Louisa that Susanna's father did not simply relinquish his claim to his father's estate, as you and Uncle Mortimer led everyone to believe. He refused to oppose you and his brother, Thaddeus, in the courts to avoid dragging the family name through the mud of a very public family fight. He was robbed by his brother, and you held the legal gun to his head."

"You young upstart, you're being absurd and disrespectful." The elder Burnley's voice was as cold as a frosty knife blade. "If you challenge me in this manner, I'll cut you off from the firm. I can certainly blacken your name. If you continue to oppose me," rage filled his voice, "there won't be a legal firm between North Carolina and Canada that will use your services when I'm finished with you."

The younger man's voice dropped. Susanna could hardly hear it. "If you blacken my name, you blacken your own. Have you forgotten that I am the junior to your senior?"

"I will take you to court and force you to change your name!"

"Now who is being absurd?" Jonathan's voice had remained low and controlled, despite his father's loud anger. "I have always been a dutiful son. When you demanded that I sever my friendship and planned engagement to Susanna and marry my cousin, Ann, whom I have always found tiresome, I dutifully complied, believing that you had my best interests at heart. But now I find that you and Mortimer were party to robbing Susanna's father of his rightful inheritance and that Mortimer has included in the old will a provision that the firm be paid twenty-five percent of the estate for handling Miss Louisa's legal matters. You and I both know that such a fee is exorbitant. It appears that your greatest motivation has never been the happiness of your family but your personal fortune."

Susanna had stood still for so long that Jane put her hand on her shoulder, startling her. She whispered to her friend, "Susanna, come away with me. You don't need to hear this. It will only upset you." Susanna shook her head forcefully. She would not be moved.

The brief silence in the sitting room was broken by the older man's voice. "We will read the will this afternoon." The finality in it offered a challenge to anyone who would try to interfere.

"Father, if you insist on ignoring the new will, I will take you to court. I will find a way to force you to honor Miss Louisa's wishes."

"You? Just try it. The ink on your law license is hardly dry. If you drag us into a courtroom, Mortimer and I will destroy you. Now go and tell everyone in the house that I will read the will at two o'clock in the library, immediately after lunch." The subject was closed.

Jane pulled a resisting Susanna toward the stairs, and a few seconds later, the double doors to the sitting room burst open. Jonathan saw the two young women standing at the base of the staircase. He stopped, dropped his head, and took a deep breath. He exhaled slowly as he tried to regain his self-control.

In a voice tight with nervous tension, he said, "Susanna, Jane, Miss Louisa's will is to be read in the library at two o'clock." He took several steps closer to them, and taking Susanna's hand with a firm grip so she couldn't pull away, he dropped his voice to a near whisper and leaned toward her. "I tried to make him see reason. I really did. I won't give up, Susanna. This is not the end of the matter." He gave a slight, somewhat embarrassed suggestion of a bow to both young women.

As he started up the stairs, Susanna spoke to Jane, "I'll tell Williams that lunch needs to be on the table no later than noon." Despite the strain in her face, Susanna managed to make her voice sound almost normal. They stepped into the kitchen and found the housekeeper sitting at the table with her head in her hands. It was apparent that she had been weeping.

Susanna was moved with pity for the woman, suddenly aware that there were others who were grieving her aunt's death. She sat down and patted William's hand. "I understand that you are mentioned in the will. You will not be left without resources. You and the other household servants will need to be present when the will is read at two in the library." She looked up at Cook. "Will you be able to have a meal ready by noon?"

The rotund woman in the white apron just nodded and wiped a tear with the back of her hand. Williams spoke. "Miss Susanna, it isn't my fear of the future that makes me weep. I loved your aunt. She was the only family I had."

"I loved her too," Susanna said tenderly. "We have all suffered a great loss." The words actually seemed to hurt her heart. She stood. "Will you give them my regrets at the reading of the will? My presence is not required."

"You will not be present, Miss Susanna?" The housekeeper's head lifted swiftly.

"No, Williams, as I am not mentioned in the will, I am not required to be present." She turned and started out of the kitchen. "Jane, we need to pack." Her words were left hanging in the air as she left the room.

Before she began to pack the carpetbag, she sat down to write her mother.

January 18, 1846

Dearest Mama,

So much has happened since my last letter. I had written to you some time ago of our possible plans to travel to Nauvoo, Illinois, to join the Saints there, but after our positions at the mill were terminated, we were blessed to take refuge with Aunt Louisa, but that too has ended. The dear soul passed in the night a few days ago, and Jane and I will be leaving Newburyport as soon as possible. I had not written to you of the possibility of our taking passage to California with members of our new religion, but as Aunt Louisa's death has forced us to reassess our situation, we will place our faith in the Lord and move toward that goal. Jane and I have renewed our determination to make our way to New York and take passage to California. How very quickly life's direction can change. Please give my love to Georgie, Rachel, and James, and if I do not see you again, please remember that I love you all.

Your loving daughter,
Susanna Thayer

She made no mention of the inheritance her aunt had planned to leave her. She felt it would do no one any good to add to their sense of loss.

***

The gong for the midday meal was sounded as she started to pack. Jane entered her bedroom. "Are we going to eat with those men?" She looked as though she would rather go without eating if that were required.

"Yes, Jane. Let's go down and show them that we are above the kind of behavior they have displayed this morning. I was brought up with proper manners and I am determined to be gracious." The meal was served by a white-faced Fiona. Susanna brought up the cold weather and, in the hope of drawing either of the Burnleys into the conversation, speculated about its effect on shipping. Her attempts to keep the atmosphere pleasant and conversation light met with only a little success.

Jonathan responded with forced cheerfulness, but his father sat silent, lighting a cigar at the end of the meal without extending the courtesy of asking the young women if they minded the tobacco smoke.

As Fiona cleared away the dishes, the senior Mr. Burnley spoke curtly. "Bring me a sherry."

Fiona looked at Susanna, who responded with a nod. "Have Williams bring the sherry. She knows where it's kept."

***

During the reading of the will in the library, Susanna packed her belongings in the carpetbag. She held the pearls and the broach in her hand carefully before she gently tucked them among her things. *These may be the only things of any real value that I will ever possess—except a mother's love—but God's will be done.*

As she closed the bag, Jonathan appeared in the open doorway. His face was gray with anger and frustration. "It's not done yet, Susanna. I promise you that I will try to find a way to see that you receive a portion of your aunt's estate." He sat down on the straight-backed chair near the door and looked at the floor with hunched shoulders, his folded hands between his knees. "My father has given permission for the two of you to remain here for as long as a week, if you need to. He will catch the train to Boston early this evening." Jonathan suddenly sat up as if propelled by a spring. "I promise you, Susanna, I will not let this matter drop."

"Thank you for your kindness, Jonathan, but I do not expect . . . I do not expect anything . . ." She rose from the bed. "Forgive me, I need to be alone." While she covered her quivering mouth with one hand, she urged him out of the room with a wave of the other. She closed the door behind him and leaned against it, trying to control her renewed grief.

At about seven, she heard wheels on the drive. Old Dan had brought the carriage around to take the senior Burnley to the train. She stood at the window and watched in the light of the lanterns that hung from the front corners of the carriage. Dan lifted the valise and portfolio into the carriage, and after the solicitor climbed in, it disappeared into the darkness as it moved down the driveway.

With the reading of the will behind them, Susanna no longer felt it necessary to put a proper face on the situation. She had dinner for herself and Jane brought up on trays, and the two ate in her room.

When Fiona entered to collect the trays and dishes, she spoke. "Miss Susanna, Mr. Jonathan said it is very important that he see you in the sitting room."

She hesitated, wondering what he could want to discuss with her at this time. *Hadn't everything been said?* She relented. *But I will offer him the courtesy of meeting with him one more time.* "Tell him I'll be there directly." She stepped into her room to brush back her hair and tie it with a ribbon. She smoothed her skirt and walked slowly down the stairs. When she reached the sitting room, she paused at the open double doors. "You wanted to see me, Mr. Burnley?"

He turned from the fire. "Yes, Susanna. Thank you for coming. Please sit down." He motioned toward the settee. He appeared somewhat uncertain as to how to begin the conversation. As she sat, he stepped over to the doors and pulled them closed. "May I apologize for my behavior the day I arrived? I was unbelievably . . . insensitive at that time." He paused for her response.

Ignoring his apology, she whispered, "If you are seeking to keep this conversation private, I suggest that we keep our voices low. The doors offer little by way of genuine privacy."

He cleared his throat in an embarrassed manner. "I see."

She nodded, looking at her hands in her lap.

He sat next to her on the settee but she was grateful that he made no effort to reach out to her in any way. He looked straight ahead. "From the time that we were childhood friends and played catch-me-if-you-can after church services in the churchyard, I believed we would someday marry." He was speaking as if to a third party.

As did I, she thought, but she said nothing.

"Our friendship continued as we grew, and when we celebrated your seventeenth birthday with a joint family dinner, I firmly believed that we would make a formal engagement announcement within less than a year. I believe that both our families held that expectation, and for that reason, my informal proposal was not a surprise to anyone." He stood and stepped over to the fire as if to warm his hands.

"Then your father passed, and my father said that I should give you a period of mourning and not press you for a formal response at that time. I see now that he intended to use that time to convince me to marry Ann. When your note arrived, telling me that you had accepted, he began to tell me how lovesick my cousin was. He said if I did not marry her, she might . . . might do something desperate, and everyone would blame me. When

I resisted his 'suggestion,' he brought up the fact that my sister, Rhoda, had chosen to marry a young farmer, a Quaker, against his will, and he had cut her off. It was a glimpse of him that I had never seen before." He cleared his throat. "He made me postpone responding to the note for several days until he had me convinced that it was vital that I marry Ann."

He silently watched the flames in the fireplace for a moment. "Now that I have seen that side of him again, I realize it was Ann's father's fortune and social position that he coveted." He exhaled long and heavily before turning to face her. "I have failed you, Susanna. You were my best and dearest friend, and I failed you. And I have failed my wife because there is no affection between us. It is a loveless marriage. She was evidently as unwilling to marry me as I was to marry her, though she did not reveal it until after the honeymoon. We were both misled into the marriage to please our parents." His voice became a whisper. "And now I must watch you slip away again, and I can do nothing about it."

She rose and walked toward the fireplace, where she stood near him. "We must accept what we cannot change, Jonathan, but it helps to know that you did love me. When I learned of your engagement to Ann, I wondered what I had done to forfeit your affection."

He turned and took her hands in his. "You have never forfeited my affection and you never will."

"Thank you," she whispered.

After a moment of silence, she pulled her hands away from his and turned her back to avoid seeing the expression on his face. He looked so much like she was feeling, full of regret and pain.

"What will you do? Where will you go? Will you go back to the mill in Lowell?" Without giving her time to respond, he added earnestly, "Susanna, you cannot know of my anger when I learned that you had been forced to take a position there."

She shook her head. "I cannot go back there. When Jane and I left the mill, we had made plans to go to New York, where we hoped to obtain passage on a ship to California. We expected to visit my aunt only for a short while, but my feelings for her and her generous plans to make me her heir diverted us from that plan. I think this may be God's way of putting us back on the right path. I feel strongly that I must close the door on the past. My future lies with the members of our new faith."

He had heard nothing after the words "passage to California." He put his hand on her shoulder and turned her to face him. "California! My dear Susanna, we will soon be at war with Mexico." His look of concern increased to alarm. "Why do you want to travel to California?"

"Jane and I have associated ourselves with a religious group that hopes to settle in the Upper California Basin. We will surely be no richer or poorer there than we would be here. This seems to be the direction God has pointed us."

He returned to the settee and abruptly sat. He rubbed his forehead as if it hurt. "This is entirely my fault, entirely my fault. If I had not listened to my father's deceitful arguments, we would be happily married by now." His voice was filled with quiet anguish. "I would give every last penny that ever might come to me to turn back time."

"But none of us can do that, Jonathan." She stepped near him and put her hand on his shoulder. "Please do not look back. Cherish the child that God has sent to you. We must each move toward the future with faith that God has a plan for us that has not yet been fully revealed."

He stood and put his hands on her upper arms as if he could convince her by the intensity of his feelings and the firmness of his grasp. "Please, you must realize the danger of a long ocean voyage."

"I see no other open door to walk through. By its very nature, faith must be tested."

He let go of her arms and ran his hand through his hair in frustration. "I can at least offer you some financial assistance. Let me give you some money for the journey."

She stepped away from him. "No, Jonathan. I will not take your money. Jane and I have saved enough to get us to New York, and the man organizing this voyage has offered free passage to at least some of those who cannot pay their way."

"You would rather take charity from a stranger than money from me, Susanna?"

"That is the way it must be, Jonathan."

"What will you do if there is no ship leaving Newburyport for New York right away?"

"We will take a room until there is. I will not stay here any longer than absolutely necessary. I'm a stranger in this house now."

He stepped toward her and again took her upper arms in his strong grip. "Susanna, you must not go until you tell me that you understand that I still love you. I would never have caused you this pain if I had dreamed what my choice would do to you. Please look at me and tell me that you know that I love you." She looked into his eyes. She could see by his expression that he had spoken a truth so long held inside, that letting it go had nearly torn a hole in him.

"And I loved you, Jonathan. But that time is past. It is time we said good-bye." It took all her resolve to turn from him.

As he dropped his hands, she hurried from the room, unwilling to let him see the pain she was feeling. *I will deny it to others—but Jonathan, I still love you too.*

Chapter Sixteen

Susanna made her way to the kitchen, where Cook had begun preparations for the next day's meals. Fiona and Williams sat at the table. The eyes of both of them were still red-rimmed. Looking up in a startled manner as Susanna entered, Williams quickly stood. "How can I help you, Miss Thayer?" The usual hardness of her voice was gone.

"Would you tell Dan that Jane and I will be leaving in the morning? If he could bring the carriage around and take us to the harbor at about eight o'clock, I would be grateful."

"Yes, ma'am. Will you be eating breakfast before you leave?"

Looking at Fiona, she answered, "Yes, if Fiona would be so kind as to serve us in my room."

Fiona curtsied. "Yes, mum," she said quietly. "If I may speak out of turn, I want to tell you that we are so sorry that ye will be leavin'. You and your friend brought much life to this old house."

"Thank you, Fiona, and thank you, Williams, and you too, Cook. We will miss all of you."

As Susanna spoke with the house staff in the kitchen, Jonathan made his way up the stairs, where he knocked on Jane's door.

She was startled at seeing him when she opened the door. "How may I help you, Mr. Burnley?"

"Will you take this from me, Jane? It is my gift to you and Susanna." He pressed two bank certificates worth one hundred dollars each into her hand. "Please take it. I know you will need it for your voyage. There is little else I can do, but I can do this much."

"Susanna would not take it?"

"No, she will accept nothing from me." He could not hide his disappointment.

In her practical way, she responded, "I am not so encumbered with scruples in this matter as she is." Jane folded and slipped the bank notes up her sleeve. "It is true that we will need it. I will accept it on behalf of both of us. Thank you, Mr. Burnley." *And I shall hope that Susanna is not greatly angered if she discovers what I have done.*

"If I don't see you in the morning, I wish both of you God speed, safety, and happiness in your journey." He turned and walked back to his bedroom with a slowed step and rounded shoulders.

***

Old Dan had the carriage at the front door promptly at eight the next morning. Jonathan stood at an upper window and watched the two young women leave, his mouth set in a narrow, grim line. The words of Henry King, a seventeenth-century poet, flowed unbidden into his mind. *I am content to live divided, with but half a heart.*

***

"Young Mr. Burnley isn't coming to tell you good-bye?" Jane asked as she climbed in behind Susanna.

"No. We bid each other good-bye last night."

The old gardener closed the door and climbed onto the driver's seat. The carriage rolled gracefully down the long driveway. Susanna resisted the urge to look back at the great, old house and kept her eyes straight ahead, realizing that she was riding away from the happy future that might have been but now would never be. As the distance between the carriage and Thayer Hill widened, the sense of loss in Susanna's heart increased.

Jane's voice interrupted her thoughts. "Susanna, what will we do if we get to New York and find the ship for California has already sailed?" Her face was pinched with worry.

"I am hoping that we will have sufficient time to obtain our passage. If memory serves me correctly, the article in *The Messenger* said the ship was scheduled to depart on January twenty-fourth or shortly thereafter. If we can obtain passage to New York today, we will hopefully reach the port there in time to go directly to Mr. Brannan's office on Spruce Street and plead for space on the ship. Perhaps the departure may even have been delayed, but should we miss it, there will surely be other ships going to California. According to *The Messenger,* both Elder Brannan and Elder Pratt have predicted that thousands of Saints will make their way to the

Upper California Basin by sea. Should that be the situation, we will find some kind of acceptable way to support ourselves until the next ship sails. At this time, we really have no other choice but to carry out the plans we have made." She looked at her friend. "Please offer a prayer in your heart that it will all work out."

Her friend nodded.

***

When the carriage turned off High Street and toward the harbor, the forest of masts attached to the clipper ships, whalers, barques, and sloops stretched from the wharf north to the shipyard and docks that extended into the swift and wide channel of the Merrimack River. *Surely, at least one of these vessels is going to New York today or tomorrow,* Susanna thought.

Old Dan halted the carriage on the wharf in front of the weathered shipping office. He dismounted and opened the door. "Miss Susanna, if it's your intent to purchase passage on a ship, this is where you'll need to do that."

She took the old man's offered hand and stepped out of the carriage. She looked around. "Dan, will you wait until I speak with someone in the office about passage to New York?"

He spoke as he assisted Jane from the carriage. "Of course, Miss Susanna."

They stepped into the ticket office, where several people were standing about the room, many of them reading the sailing schedule for the week, which was tacked to the wall. While Susanna read the schedule over a young man's shoulder, Jane hurriedly looked around for the window where tickets were sold. When she saw it, she hurried to it, reaching it just as the man opened the little window behind the grill to begin the day's business.

"Sir, I desire to purchase passage for two on the next ship departing for New York. When might that be, and what is the cost?"

The bearded man looked at her. "If you're in a hurry, you're in luck. As today is Friday, that would be the barque *Runabout.* She departs in about an hour, right at ten o'clock from pier seven. Each adult ticket is $3.75; that includes a small stateroom, and you can board right away." He spit a wad of tobacco toward a spittoon near his feet.

Jane reached into the fabric handbag she wore on her left wrist and located one of the bank notes Jonathan had given her. She pushed it under the grill at the window. "When will it arrive in New York?"

"Three days, as it has a brief stop in Newport, Rhode Island." He looked the bank note over carefully, "Miss, it's a good thing that tomorrow is payday. That means that I can make change for this note. Had you come in on a Saturday, you might not have been so lucky." He pushed two tickets toward her and counted out her change.

She picked up the tickets and tucked the change into her bag. She hurried back to Susanna, who was speaking with a woman reading the schedule.

"Susanna, the ship leaves at ten and I have the tickets in my hand." The two young women hurried to the carriage, and Dan drove them to the pier, which was located two hundred feet farther down the wharf. When Dan halted the carriage, Jane sprang out and waved at the crewman who had begun releasing the heavy lines that held the ship in place. He paused as he saw her rush toward the gangplank.

Susanna gave Dan a quick hug, not something he was accustomed to receiving in his position as a servant. It touched him so much he had to wipe a tear. "We will miss ye, Miss Susanna. May God's blessing go with ye both."

"And God bless you, Dan." He slowly and sadly climbed back on the seat and turned the carriage.

They followed the crewman who led them across the deck and toward the captain. The great sails of the ship were being unfurled, and crew members were moving over the spars and up the shrouds and ratlines with bare feet, oblivious to the cold. These were men with faces burned by the sun and wind, some tanned the color of wood.

The captain touched his cap as Susanna neared him, and after glancing at the tickets Jane had extended toward him, he ordered one of the crewmen to show them to a stateroom below deck. The man had arms roped with muscle and a face as brown as a walnut. The stateroom was no more that ten by twelve feet, but it had double bunks attached to each long wall and a skylight in the deck above, which permitted some of the morning light to penetrate the cabin.

Before turning to leave the cabin, the sailor pointed to the whale oil lamp hanging on the wall near the door. In a clipped, Yankee rhythm, he instructed, "Ayuh, ye kin light the lamp while ye're here in the cabin, but never leave it burnin' when ye leave the room. 'Tis important that ye remember that."

"But we have no way to light it."

"When we're underway, ye kin purchase a box of lucifers from the quartermaster." He respectfully pulled at his forelock as he took his leave. 'Scuse me, ladies. I must get back to me dooties."

***

For the next three days, they ate with the other thirty passengers in a galley where the long tables and backless benches were bolted to the deck. The pea and pork soup, oatmeal, and hardtack were hardly edible by comparison to the food at Thayer Hill. Each day the passengers spent as much time on the upper deck as the elements would allow. Only occasional rough water or a queasy stomach could force them below.

The ship came into sight of New York Harbor on the late afternoon of the third day. Susanna stood at the deck railing with her heart beating rapidly. She whispered, "Papa, here I am facing another open door. This is another beginning—the beginning of a whole new life in a whole new world. I am both excited and more than a little frightened. Help me walk by faith. Surely God is guiding my steps."

The harbor was crowded with more masts and sails than Susanna could have counted—frigates, sloops, and cutters; merchantmen and whaleboats; barques and schooners. As they watched, the wharf drew closer and the passengers could see boat works, warehouses, and what seemed to be a countless number of sailors, businessmen, and passengers milling about, waiting to board one of the many ships. The dock was a city in itself.

Jane commented as they watched from the railing, "I am not so afraid of a long voyage now, as we have come through this one with some ease and comfort."

Susanna laughed. "Most of the time," she added. "May the next voyage be as easy, and may we never forget that Aunt Louisa said the Thayers should never be afraid of the sea. For many generations the sea has been a friend to my family."

As the ship was towed by two steam launches to the wharf referred to as the Old Slip, Susanna sought out the captain as he directed the preparations for unloading the freight. "Captain, it is our intention to take passage to California from a ship here, but to do so we must locate the office of the man who is arranging the voyage. His office is on Spruce Street. Would you know where it is?"

He touched his cap respectfully. "Miss, I believe that Spruce Street can be found about a half mile to the east of the pier where we will be berthed and runs north into the community of Brooklyn. Best of luck." He hurried off to direct the crew.

Susanna explained the situation to Jane as they watched the crewmen tie the ship to the pier with the great hawsers. The anchor chain rumbled with the weight of the falling anchor, making the entire ship shudder.

"While you wait with the bundles and the carpetbag, I will try to find Mr. Brannan's office. Give me what money you can spare, and I will arrange our passage with him, if at all possible." Jane seemed in a great hurry.

"But I should go with you, Jane."

"I will hurry along as quickly as I can. I will run most of the way, something I am sure you're not prepared to do, especially carrying the carpetbag."

Susanna acquiesced, and as soon as the gangplank was lowered, Jane pushed past the groups of people waiting with their bags and ran onto the wharf, looking for Spruce Street and asking directions of people on the street as she went.

Gradually, the others who had disembarked from the ship were met by acquaintances who had arrived to take them and their belongings away. As the sun disappeared behind the clouds on the western horizon, painting the sky in orange which faded to magenta and then to deep blue, Susanna became aware of the smell of fish oil, stale tobacco, sweaty clothes, and other unidentifiable odors, all smells of the sailors and the freight from the arriving and departing ships.

What is taking Jane so long? she thought nervously.

By this time, only Susanna and a young man of about twenty-five who had also traveled on the *Runabout* were standing on the wharf. The ship's crew swiftly cleared the deck and cheerfully took their shore leave, striking one another's backs and yelling in excitement. By the time they had disappeared into the city, dark had wrapped the dock. The only light cast on the area came from the lanterns that were hung high from the crossbar of the mainmasts of the ships tied to the pier.

Chapter Seventeen

Susanna spoke to the young man, breaching proper etiquette because they had not been introduced while on the ship. "Are you waiting for friends or family to come for you?"

He removed his cap respectfully. "Yes, Miss." He replaced it almost immediately for protection against the increasingly cold wind off the water. "I'm supposed to meet two men with whom I'm planning to travel to California on the ship *Brooklyn*—Mr. Cyrus Irea and Mr. John Phillips. We are acquainted by correspondence only, as I've not yet met them personally. I understand that the *Brooklyn* was originally supposed to depart on January twenty-fourth, but more recently, I've learned that the sailing has been delayed, perhaps as long as a week. If my acquaintances don't come this evening, I shall have to find a room to let."

"I fear that we have no one coming for us, so as soon as my friend returns, we shall have to seek a room for the night as well. May I ask if your group is of a religious nature? You see, my friend and I are planning to take passage to California with a number of members of our church on the same ship."

"As I will apparently be traveling with you, let me introduce myself. I am Samuel Johnson. Apparently, I am a member of the same religious group as you."

The sound of running feet drew their attention. Jane arrived breathless.

"Jane, is something the matter?"

"No, no, not really. I was just concerned about the way some of the men on the street were looking at me." She looked over her shoulder as she explained her nervousness and then looked Mr. Johnson over thoroughly. She turned back to her friend. "Susanna, the departure of the ship has been delayed, so we must find a room for several days. I paid the required amount for our passage and our names are now on the list of passengers."

Susanna motioned toward the young man standing near them. "Mr. Johnson has explained that he will be sailing with us." She stopped abruptly and turned to the young man. "I'm sorry, Mr. Johnson, for forgetting to introduce you to my friend Jane O'Neil and myself. I am Susanna Thayer."

He doffed his cap and gave a slight bow to Jane. "And I am Samuel Johnson, ma'am."

In the semidarkness, Mr. Johnson did not notice how Jane's complexion colored in a mixture of pleasure and embarrassment.

Susanna looked around a little nervously. "Now it seems that we all have the same problem. We need to find rooms for the night."

"I stopped at a boarding house not far from here on my way back from Mr. Brannan's office. It looks acceptable for our needs and the owner said he had available rooms for this evening. Just come with me." Jane led the way.

Mr. Johnson, who carried only one small bundle, noted Susanna's carpetbag by her feet. "Ladies, if you will permit me to be of assistance, I will carry the carpetbag for you." They started down the wharf with Jane urging them to hurry.

The streets were gradually filling with rowdy, laughing seamen and women with painted faces. The three of them made their way through the increasing darkness, lit only by an occasional street lamp or the light that spilled out through the windows of the drinking establishments facing the street. An occasional leer from some of the half-drunken seamen made Susanna very glad for Mr. Johnson's presence.

"It's not much farther," Jane encouraged the others.

Jane led the little group into an establishment of fairly decent appearance. Above the large, twelve-paned window next to the doorway, a sign read: "Bradford's Public House, rooms to let."

"Here we are. Mr. Bradford said that he would have a room for us, Susanna. I hope he will have a room for you, Mr. Johnson."

"As do I."

The patrons in the large room turned and thoroughly looked over the little group as they entered. Apparently finding nothing with which to concern themselves, they returned to their meals. The interior of the large room—walls, floor, ceiling, chairs, and tables—was all wood worn smooth and bleached by many years of use. The warmth of the fire in the fireplace filled the room. A large joint of beef was roasting there, and the fragrance of fresh bread filled the air. Susanna liked the establishment immediately.

***

"Will you be takin' supper with us?" the women were asked as they were shown to a room on the second floor by Mrs. Bradford, a tall, spare woman. She had pinned her gray hair high on her head, but damp tendrils were escaping from the various combs and hair clips. The wrinkles on her face looked as if someone had drawn the tines of a fork across her forehead. Mr. Johnson discreetly chose to wait downstairs until the landlady could find a room for him.

Susanna simply looked at Jane, wondering if they had sufficient funds left to pay for the meal. Jane nodded and said with confidence, "Yes, we will, and breakfast in the morning as well. If the room and meals are satisfactory, we will be staying several days."

As the landlady turned to leave, Susanna's concern for Mr. Johnson prompted her to ask, "Do you have a room for the young man with us?"

Mrs. Bradford nodded. "I can put him in with a gentleman in a room downstairs. I will be gettin' your meal on the table, then." She bustled out of the room and down the stairs.

When they returned to the main room, Jane said, "Will you please join us for supper, Mr. Johnson? You have been so kind, that it is surely the least we can do."

"As I am short of funds, I am forced to accept your offer, ladies."

The three sat down at the table. Mrs. Bradford set a plate before each of them of turnips, potatoes, and roast beef.

***

That evening, after a shared prayer, the two young women climbed into bed. Susanna asked sleepily as she lay her head on the pillow, "How much of our money was required to guarantee our passage, Jane? Do we have enough left to pay for our room and board until the ship sails?"

"Yes. We are well enough off."

Susanna stifled a yawn. "How much more are we required to pay before we board the ship? Will Mr. Brannan allow us to travel at less than full fare?" She yawned again.

"It is fully paid."

"Then we must be nearly out of funds."

"No, we have a substantial sum left."

Susanna's thoughts were struggling over the wave of sleep that was threatening to smother her thinking. "How can that be?" she mumbled.

Jane took a deep breath. She felt that this was as good a time as any to tell her friend. "I used the money young Mr. Burnley gave me before we left Thayer Hill."

Susanna forced her eyes open and sat up abruptly. "Jane, you took money from Jonathan? I can't believe you would do such a thing!"

"Are you angry with me, Susanna, for taking the money?" Her voice was contrite.

Susanna counted slowly to ten, as her mother would have done. Then she began to feel the warmth of gratitude and laughed quietly. "No, Jane. How could I be angry with you? Actually, it's a blessing that you took it. I'm not sure we could have made this voyage without it. I will sleep better for knowing that we are not penniless."

In the morning, as they waited for the landlady to bring their bowls of oatmeal porridge to the table, Mr. Johnson appeared, looking as though he had not slept well. When they invited him to join them, he said quietly as the color moved from his throat up his face, "I have sufficient funds to pay for my room for the next several nights, but I have little money to pay for my meals."

Susanna smiled broadly. "Your willingness to escort us to this place and carry our bundles is deeply appreciated and obligates us to look after your welfare. Will you allow us to pay for your meal this morning?"

He looked uneasy. "Ladies, I cannot accept such a generous offer. It breaches the bounds of proper etiquette. I am hoping that I will meet with Mr. Irea and Mr. Phillips, and perhaps the three of us will be able to find some temporary employment to cover expenses while we wait for the ship to depart."

"Then permit us to cover your meals until you locate your friends. In the meantime," she looked at Jane and then back at him, "we hope that you will continue to be our escort, as may be necessary. I'm sure that in a great city such as this, it is not entirely appropriate for two young women to go about unattended by a trustworthy escort."

"On that basis I will accept your kind offer." He sat and withdrew a folded newspaper from his pocket. "This extra edition of *The New York Messenger* came into my hands some days ago. Have either of you seen it?"

"No, the most recent edition we have seen came while we were in Lowell in November. We then relocated to Newburyport and have had no more recent information from the Church."

He handed the little newspaper to Susanna. She noted that it was dated 13 December 1845. By this time Mrs. Bradford had set the bowls of oatmeal before them. While they waited for it to cool, Susanna read aloud a portion of the article on the first page:

"*To emigrants: We have now on our books the names of about three hundred Saints who wish to go by water, and it grieves us to say that only about sixty out of that number will have means sufficient to carry them through. The final price for passage for each person will be fifty dollars, children over five and under fourteen, half price. Each one will need from twenty to twenty-five dollars worth of provisions; the whole amount, seventy five dollars.*" She looked up at Jane with wide eyes. "How close we must have been to being shut out of the voyage, Jane."

"The fact that we were able to pay the entire amount for passage and supplies for both of us made it possible. We have Mr. Burnley to thank for that."

Mr. Johnson paused with his spoon between the bowl and his mouth to ask, "May I ask your relationship to Mr. Burnley? Will he be sailing with us?"

Jane responded, to cover Susanna's brief embarrassment, "Mr. Burnley is simply a kind benefactor from Boston who has made our trip possible. We will always be grateful to him for his generosity, though we don't expect to ever see him again."

For a reason she could not have explained, Jane's words made Susanna suddenly feel sad.

Without saying anything more, they ate in silence until the bowls were empty. As the landlady cleared the table, Mr. Johnson spoke. "Miss Thayer, there are more articles of interest in that edition of *The Messenger*. May I read more of it aloud?"

She handed the little newspaper back to him. "Please do."

He shook the creases out of the paper. "*We have chartered the ship Brooklyn, of four hundred and fifty tons, with Captain Richardson, at twelve hundred dollars per month, and we pay the port charges; the money to be paid before sailing. She is a first class ship in the best of order for sea, and with all the rest, a very fast sailor, which will facilitate our passage greatly. Between decks will be very neatly fitted up into one large cabin, with a row of staterooms on each side, so that every family will be provided with a stateroom, affording them places of retirement at their pleasure. She will be well lighted with skylights in the deck, with every other convenience to make a family equally as comfortable as by their own fireside . . .*" He scanned the balance of the page and began reading again.

"*Bring all your beds and bedding, all your farming and mechanical tools, and your poultry, beef, pork, potatoes, and anything else that will sustain life.*" He scanned the article further for information of interest and began reading aloud again. "*Don't forget your pots and kettles with your necessary cooking utensils; have them, with your crockery, packed snug, for you will not need them on the passage; the ship will be furnished with tin ware that will not break.*"

He looked at Susanna. "You do not appear to have many of the items listed here."

She smiled and shook her head. "No, of necessity, we are traveling very light."

He folded the newspaper and returned it to his coat pocket. "I feel a need to walk to Mr. Brannan's office on Spruce Street in the hope that I might find sufficient information to locate my friends. Would either of you care to accompany me, or will you remain here?"

"I would like to accompany you, if you have no objection. I would like to meet Elder Brannan, if he is there," Jane responded. "Last evening, I was forced to pay our passage to his assistant." Her complexion colored slightly as she was embarrassed by her own forwardness.

"Miss O'Neil, it would be my privilege to offer you my arm."

Sensing that her presence was not sought, Susanna responded, "I think I would prefer to remain and rest, but would you please share any additional information you may obtain with me?"

"Of course. May I leave my small bundle of belongings with you to avoid its being pilfered?"

"Certainly."

Mr. Johnson touched his cap and offered Jane his arm.

Susanna purchased a sheet of paper and an ink pen from Mrs. Bradford and wrote to her mother again.

> *January 28, 1846*
>
> *Dearest Mama,*
>
> *As I write this letter, I am sitting in the room Jane and I have rented in a public house in New York, waiting for the*

day Jane and I will board the ship Brooklyn *to set sail for California. This is an exciting time. I do not want to admit that it is also a little frightening, but we are sailing with a large company of Saints, and I'm sure the Lord will watch over us. The journey is expected to take at least six months, so this will be my last letter for sometime. Give my love to all.*

Your affectionate daughter,
Susanna Thayer

Part Two

The Voyage of the Ship Brooklyn

Chapter Eighteen

"Sabbath meeting will be held on board the *Brooklyn*," Mr. Johnson told Susanna as the three sat down to supper in the public house. "Mr. Brannan was at his office today and said that the ship is being loaded as we speak, and the departure has been set for Thursday, February fourth. He told me that we should plan on boarding no later than the afternoon of the third." His excitement was evident as he spoke. "I did not locate my friends, Mr. Irea or Mr. Phillips, but was told that they had arrived two days ago and had paid the balance of their passage. I also paid my remaining financial obligation, and I am now nearly penniless, but I am content that my place on the ship is secured."

***

Johnson escorted the young women to the Sabbath meeting, which was held on the main deck of the *Brooklyn*. The hull of the ship was somewhat tubby in appearance and was painted black with a wide white stripe running its length. Black squares had been painted on the white band to suggest gun turrets to any distant ship which might hold hostile intentions. A strong, cold breeze made slack sails flap wherever they were not furled tightly against the spars.

After the large group sang the hymn "O God, Our Help in Ages Past" and listened to a prayer offered by Brother Quartus Sparks, Elder Brannan stood on a barrel and spoke in a stentorian voice loud enough to be heard by all of the nearly two hundred men, women, and children gathered there. "More passengers are expected to arrive before the ship sails, and the large number of individuals making this voyage requires that all regulations governing the company be obeyed fastidiously.

"Reveille will be at six, which is four bells on the morning watch, and all who are able will be expected to gather on the deck for a brief prayer meeting. Breakfast will be an hour later. The midday meal at noon will be marked by eight bells, the end of the forenoon watch; supper, at six o'clock in the evening, will be four bells. Every man will be expected to take his turn assisting in food preparation and cleanup under the direction of a member of the ship's crew appointed to that task."

Even those whose minds had wandered during the listing of the schedule and daily tasks returned their full attention to his words as he continued. "Upon our arrival in California, we expect to prepare to receive as many as twenty thousand more Church members who will come by water and others who will come by land, having crossed the continent. We will use the proceeds of the labor of all who are part of this effort to build a common fund from which all will draw their living for the next three years. This will be for the convenience and protection of the entire company.

"The migration of this group has the full support of President Polk, who has shared his hopes with me in a recent communication." Some excitement rippled through the crowd. "He believes that the landing of a large group of Americans on the California coast will increase the likelihood that the Mexicans there will refrain from joining in any open conflict with the US government. But for our protection, the warship USS *Constitution* will sail a few days after we do, to reinforce the likelihood that the Mexicans will not oppose our migration." This brought a cheer from the group.

Brannan announced that a brief sermon would be given on faith, and without previous notice, he called upon William Stout to deliver it. Evidently Stout did not hear that it was to be a brief sermon, and after forty minutes, Brannan stepped over and pulled on the man's coattail. The hymn "Praise God from Whom All Blessings Flow" was sung, and Samuel Johnson was called upon to give the benediction.

As the group socialized and introduced themselves to one another, Susanna was pleased to meet John and Marion Joyce again. Marion carried an infant, born while they had been in Lowell.

"May we see the child," Susanna asked her.

"Of course." Marion uncovered the plump and rosy little boy, who gurgled at everyone who let him grasp a finger.

"He is beautiful," Susanna commented in a melancholy way, thinking of the babies that would never come to her and Jonathan. "You must feel very blessed." The parents nodded and beamed with pride.

Samuel Johnson drew the attention of both young women when he hurriedly approached them. "I've found my friends, Mr. Irea and Mr.

Phillips. They are seeking better rooms and were wondering if there might be a room for them at Bradford's Public House. I have told them that they should come with us when we return."

Susanna nodded. "Let's go immediately. It is early in the afternoon, so surely there will be room for them before the evening lodgers seek a place to stay."

He waved his two new acquaintances over and introduced both of them. Mr. Irea was olive skinned and no taller than Susanna, possibly of Italian extraction. His black beard made him appear much older than his twenty-three years. Mr. Phillips's most notable characteristics were his British accent and the great shock of brown hair which was exposed when he removed his hat. He stood tall and thin in his worn clothing. Both men bent over the hand each young woman offered.

"Now let us make our way to Bradford's Public House and, hopefully, find lodging for my—our new friends." Mr. Johnson led the way.

***

Mr. Bradford cheerfully accepted the two new lodgers. At suppertime, as the three men and two women sat at a large, round table, a man entered in a drunken state with a lady of questionable occupation in his company and called out for a room.

The innkeeper, who was six feet tall and nearly three hundred pounds of beef and muscle under a broad apron tucked up under this black beard, moved swiftly toward them. The determination on his face needed no explanation. "Out with ye," he called out as he pointed to the door they had just come through. "Out, as we will have none of your kind under my roof. I run a respectable establishment here."

The man and woman retreated. Those who were eating smiled with relief and returned to their supper of beef stew. Jane whispered to Susanna, "I wish my father had run his public house in the same manner. It would have made my life much easier."

***

On Wednesday, the little group set out from the public house after offering their thanks to Mr. and Mrs. Bradford. Upon arriving at the ship, one of the crew, who wore a kerchief about his head to keep his hair out of his eyes, a gold ring in his ear, and a queue tied with a leather thong, led them down the hatchway to one of the staterooms between decks.

There, Brother Phillips unthinkingly stood upright in the dim light and hit his head on a support beam of the main deck. He dropped to his knees and held his head until his ears quit ringing. While Susanna and Jane expressed their concern, his two friends helped him to his feet, and in a stooped posture, they made their way to the staterooms assigned them. Only the children among the passengers could stand upright between decks.

One great difference from the little stateroom on the *Runabout* was immediately evident. This one was shared by five additional female passengers, all women traveling without husbands. Startled, they looked up from where they sat on the berths as Susanna and Jane entered. Dismay appeared on every woman's face for a moment, but Susanna quickly and cheerfully summed up the situation. "Well, it will be tight circumstances, but with two to a berth, we shall surely not get cold on this journey."

The first woman introduced herself as Fanny Corwin. She was a tall and slender woman in her midforties with salt-and-pepper gray hair pulled into a bun at the back of her neck. The second woman, Emaline Lane, was a young single woman of about twenty-one. Lucy Nutting appeared to be little more than twenty and was a diminutive young woman with chestnut hair. Mary Murrey was a stout, grandmotherly woman who spoke with an Irish accent. Just a hint of her formerly red hair color was still evident in the gray. The fifth woman introduced herself as Isabella Jones. She was a rotund woman of about forty. The music of the Welsh language colored her speech. Her face was marked by the smile lines of many years.

After all the travelers had shared a supper of salt pork, beans, and cabbage cooked into a stew in a huge, black pot by two crewmen assigned the task, all were encouraged to go up on deck for more instructions from Brannan.

As they gathered, Brannan climbed upon the barrel he had used Sunday, and for a moment he looked much like a squire surveying his acres and tenants with proprietary pride. "In the morning, when we are pulled out into the harbor by a steamer tug, those with children are asked to remain below decks, especially the children. There is always some danger if they get too excited and get under foot while the ship is setting sail.

"Some of you may find yourselves falling victim to seasickness. In those cases, it is recommended that you suck the juice of a lemon. They can be obtained from the quartermaster for ten cents each." At the mention of the exorbitant price, there was some murmuring among the passengers.

One man muttered, "I guess bein' seasick will be cheaper than them lemons."

"You were each served supper this evening by the courtesy of Captain Richardson, but beginning tomorrow morning, two men will be assigned each week to assist the cooks. The selections will be made alphabetically, so William Atherton and Jack Austin will begin tomorrow morning and will assist for the next seven days. The schedule for the following weeks will be posted on the door of my stateroom."

Jack Austin and his wife stood near his wife's sister, Emaline Lane, who was talking with Susanna. He said philosophically, "At least we get our time as cooks over with right away."

"You are not an experienced hand in the kitchen, my dear. Please do your best not to make anyone ill or lose any fingers in the stew," his wife responded with mock seriousness.

Brannan continued, "If you have loved ones here who have come on board to bid you farewell, please share your good-byes now so they can take their leave. As soon as they have departed, no one will be allowed on or off the ship. Be prepared to retire below deck by eight bells." Here he paused and cleared his throat. "There are two hundred and fifty passengers on this voyage in addition to the crew. That has created somewhat crowded conditions, so each one of us will be required to be cooperative and do our part to make the circumstances bearable. *If*, during this voyage, there should be any disagreements or difficulties, they will be brought to me to be addressed. Is that understood?"

All nodded in apparent acceptance of his instructions. As he climbed down from the barrel, several people bid family members a tearful good-bye, and by eight bells, all had returned to their cramped quarters between decks. The rumor quickly made its way among the travelers that those with children had been asked to stay below in the morning because the ship was carrying a larger number of passengers than was permitted for a vessel of that size.

That evening, Susanna and Jane climbed to the top berth that they would share and wrapped themselves in quilts. About midnight, Susanna turned over and noted that Jane's eyes were open.

"Jane," she whispered, "I'm sure the berths on the *Runabout* were not so hard as this."

Jane whispered her response. "I suppose they were. We have simply been spoiled by sleeping in the soft bed at Bradford's Public House for several nights and our memories have dimmed." She quietly giggled.

Susanna shushed her. "I dearly hope that we will soon become accustomed to the hardness once more. The quilts do very little to make the boards more comfortable."

From somewhere in the room, one of the other women whispered, "Amen to that."

In the morning, a sound like unending thunder woke everyone as hundreds of water casks were rolled across the deck and stowed in the hold. The noise continued for nearly three hours, making the ship shudder. Shortly after the midday meal was finished, the piercing squeal of a seaman's pipe was heard, prompting many of the men and older boys, and a few of the younger women, to rush to the main deck.

"Susanna, let's go up and watch the sailors as we leave the pier." Jane literally pulled her friend toward the stairs to the upper deck.

The spectators on the main deck stood out of the way of the crew and watched the preparations to set sail. The captain ordered full canvas, and the topmen poured up the rigging in an orderly upward torrent, their speed never lagging as they moved hand over hand up the top-gallant shrouds. Some ran out along the yardarms like circus tightrope walkers.

Twelve long bars were inserted into the capstan, and twenty-four crewmen began to march to their rhythmic singing of an old sea chantey, turning the creaking capstan as it raised the anchor. As if on cue, the mooring lines were cast off and the sheets were released and began to fill with the northeasterly wind which allowed the *Brooklyn* to up-anchor with full sails. The ship was guided toward the Narrows by the steamer tug *Sampson.* With the wind filling the sails, the vessel slid smoothly through the Narrows and into the open sea.

Jane looked at her friend and noted that she was quietly weeping. She pulled her away from those passengers standing close and with a worried voice asked, "Susanna, what's the matter?"

Susanna wiped her tears with the back of her hand and tried to smile. "I was suddenly wondering if we've made a wise decision. I'm afraid that I may never see my family again, and the thought fills my heart with regret—and yet," she turned and looked around the ship in wonder, "I'm almost overwhelmed by the beauty of setting sail. I feel so confused."

Jane couldn't think of anything comforting to say for the moment. Susanna took up her thoughts again. "The ship is being driven by an unseen wind into the unknown. Much of our lives have been moved by forces we can't see. Is God trying to tell us something . . . that perhaps the greatest forces in our lives will be unseen?"

In her practical way, Jane shrugged and responded, "I don't know, Susanna. It seems that you are more of a philosopher at heart than I have ever realized."

The slight rise and fall of the water in the harbor quickly evolved into the chop of winter ocean waves. In the strong wind, the ship lay over so steadily that there was little roll in her motion, even though she was pitching where she met the Atlantic rollers. Several of the passengers hurried back to their berths, suddenly looking ill. That group included the two women who had been described as being in "a delicate condition." Both were expected to give birth on the voyage.

After nearly two hours, Susanna and Jane retired between decks, their faces flushed by the brisk wind. Susanna's fears had faded. Excitement filled her voice. "Jane, wasn't it a glorious scene—the sailors raising the anchor and the sheets filling with wind? The captain was giving orders, and the men were climbing in the rigging with bare feet. It was thrilling to watch. I am determined to put my fears behind me. I expect that this voyage will be one of the most remarkable experiences of our lives."

***

Three days passed, and those who were not suffering from seasickness spent hours wrapped against the wind and walking on the deck. The occasional queasiness that Jane and Susanna had felt on the voyage of the *Runabout* no longer bothered them. The sea had to be very unsettled and choppy to send them below.

The children were fascinated with the broad expanses of snapping white sails. The wind whipped the waves into cats' paws beneath a blue and white dome of sky. The gulls and frigate birds screeched, wheeling with the wind behind the ship, seeking scraps from the refuse the cook and his helpers tossed overboard.

On the third day, two Sabbath meetings were held on the main deck. Those with last names beginning with *A* through *M* met at ten and the rest met at two. Captain Richardson attended both. As prayers were offered, he doffed his hat and a look from him made it clear that any crewman with his head still covered was challenging his authority.

Susanna found her eyes seeking out the captain whenever she was on the deck. He was a tall man, six foot two inches, with broad shoulders that filled his uniform jacket. His muscular build gave him an air of authority that he carried without self-consciousness. His dark eyes looked unflinchingly out from under heavy eyebrows. His black hair was sprinkled with gray above the temples but was neat and tidy and would remain so throughout the voyage, as one of the first mate's little-known skills was hair cutting. Each time Susanna saw the captain, she was filled with the same thoughts. *What a handsome and distinguished man. His presence fills me with confidence. Surely, nothing will go wrong with him in command.*

He stood near the binnacle on the quarterdeck, occasionally reading the compass and watching everything that was happening on the ship, in the water, and in the sky. He gave an occasional order to the helmsman at the wheel, a muscular man with a gold ring in one ear.

Susanna stepped over to Richardson and raised her voice to be heard above the wind that tugged at her bonnet and skirts. "Captain, may I ask a question?"

He nodded and smiled, melting the angles of his face into a pleasant expression. "Of course, ma'am. And how may I address you?"

"My name is Susanna Thayer, and please forgive my ignorance, as I know nothing of sailing ships, but I am fascinated by the fact that the wind blows from the northeast but the ship moves steadily southward."

"I'm impressed that you can read the direction of our travel. Most passengers could not do that without a compass or sight of the shore."

"As I have no navigational wisdom, I must admit that I looked at the compass."

He laughed heartily, exposing a row of good, white teeth. "The joke is upon me, as it had not occurred to me that you might have thought to do so." He chuckled again, "You see, ma'am, it's not so much the direction of the wind, but the set of the sail that permits us to direct the ship, a principle that can be applied to life."

She was quiet for a few moments as she thought about his statement. He had sent no signal that her presence was unwanted, and she was flattered by his attention, so she spoke again. "I've noticed that many of the sailors wear a gold loop in one ear. Is there a reason for that?"

"Aye. Those are experienced seamen who have sailed round the Horn. Most also wear a tattoo of a full-rigged sailing ship, and some even eat with one foot on the table. Those are the privileges of any sailor who has rounded the Horn."

Susanna found everything about the sea and the ship fascinating.

***

Five days into the voyage, Susanna and Jane climbed the open stairs from the main deck to the quarterdeck, where they heard Captain Richardson speak above the wind to the helmsman. "The barometer is falling. I fear we may be heading into a storm. To make matters worse, we're nearing the Outer Banks where the Labrador Current mixes with the Gulf Current. The area is called the Graveyard of the Atlantic for good reason. Be prepared to lash the wheel, if it becomes necessary."

"Aye, aye, Cap'n."

Looking around at the sea, Susanna noted that the ocean was an eerie gray-green color. In concern, she stepped over and put her hand on the captain's arm. "Sir, what makes you think there will be a storm?"

He respectfully touched the brim of his cap. "When the barometer falls as fast as it has for the past hour, it's a sure sign. If it gets bad tonight, I urge you to tie yourself into your berth. I will send the bo'sun's mate down 'tween decks with rope for those who have none."

Within a few minutes, the cold wind was driving the foaming, green water over the bowsprit each time it dipped into the sea. A sudden, hard rain started. Susanna and the other passengers on the main deck unsteadily made their way down the hatchway to the stateroom, where Susanna shared the captain's advice with the other women.

Stout Mary Murrey looked at Isabella Jones and said, "I'm not worried about needin' to be tied in my bunk. How about you, 'Bella? It would take a mighty storm to dislodge a body as large as mine from a berth." The other women tried to hide their smiles.

Isabella answered good-naturedly as she looked over her own girth, "I think you're right. You and I are likely the safest two on the ship."

Before she and Jane climbed into the top berth that evening, Susanna located the rope that she used to tie her bundle. She threaded it between the berth and bulkhead and tied it loosely near the foot of the wooden berth.

After all had made ready for the night and the oil lamp that hung by the door had been extinguished, Susanna lay in her berth and nervously listened to the thrumming of the taut rigging that was transmitted through the timbers of the ship. The vessel creaked and groaned as it was tossed on the waves like a child's top. Reaching for the rope in the dark, she pulled it up and tied it more tightly around herself and Jane.

The sounds of the storm increased and merged with the creaking noises in the timbers of the stressed ship, making the small children and some of the women cry in alarm. No one slept during the black night full of a howling gale that blew over the raging water. The bowsprit of the *Brooklyn* stabbed at the sky, and the yardarms dipped toward a black, invisible sea. The sails occasionally flapped with a sound like a cannon shot. The wind whistled through the shrouds and rigging, wailing like a soul in torment. The worst was the noise of the waves crashing against the hull and over the deck like a surging waterfall on which not even Noah's ark could have stayed afloat. By morning, passengers bore bruises from being tossed around, in, or out of their berths, including Isabella and Mary. But by midnight, Susanna had become severely ill.

Chapter Nineteen

For the next two days the ship trembled, rolled, pitched, rose on the great waves and repeatedly dropped like a stone into the deep troughs as the winds and waves battered it. The third morning, when the storm eased for a very short while, Jane climbed down and sloshed through two inches of water that had poured down the hatches before they were battened down. She lined up with a few other passengers, hoping to obtain a half dozen biscuits of hardtack. When she offered some of the biscuits to the other women in the cabin, each took one except Susanna, who was too ill to eat anything.

That afternoon, Jane left the cabin again in the hope of getting a drink of water for herself and her friend. She paused to listen to a group of nearly forty passengers who had chosen to leave their berths and gather around the long tables used for meals. They were holding hands and singing hymns. She joined them.

A surge of water bursting through the hatchway preceded a weary, unshaven Captain Richardson as he struggled down the stairs. His uniform was as wet as if he had been swimming in the sea, and his face was gray with exhaustion. He looked wooden and craggy in the poor light and hardly had the strength to raise his voice loudly enough to be heard above the storm.

"I regret to inform you that the crew has done everything that can be done under the present circumstances. The wheel has been lashed and the sails have been taken in. I have ordered the crew to tie themselves in their berths. In my twenty years on the sea, I have never experienced such a storm as this. We are in God's hands. I urge you to make your peace with Him."

As the group looked at one another in frightened silence, Marion Joyce said firmly, "We were sent to California, and we will get there."

As if that answered all questions, one of the men said, "Let us pray," and all went to their knees.

Within the hour, the wind and waves had lessened. By morning, those who had been the least ill began to take up life once more by presenting themselves for breakfast, but those who had been the most seriously ill, including Susanna, lay in their berths, too weak to eat or drink. The ship's doctor attended each. When he arrived to see to Susanna, he lifted her limp wrist and felt a thready pulse. "How long has it been since she had anything to eat or drink?"

"At least three days," Jane responded. "She is my best friend, but she is so ill she doesn't seem to know who I am. Can you do anything for her?"

"I'll try. I'll be back in a few minutes." He left the cabin.

"We must have the elders give her a blessing," Fannie Corwin insisted. "That will do her some good—maybe more good than anything the doctor can do."

Brother Joyce and Brother Sparks came at Fannie's request. When they noted Susanna's white skin—so white it was almost translucent—they looked at each other worriedly, but John Joyce stated firmly, "No illness is too great for the Lord to heal."

The women stepped back, allowing the men to lay their hands on their friend's head, and Brother Joyce commanded her to be healed.

She moaned weakly and rolled her head as the doctor entered. He urged all in the cabin to leave, but Jane refused.

"She is my friend; I will not leave her."

"Just give me room to work." He held her head up and put a cup to her lips. "Drink, miss." He looked to Jane and asked, "What's her name?"

"Susanna Thayer."

"Drink, Miss Thayer. This may help." Her eyes fluttered open, and he pressed the cup against her lower lip and commanded, "Drink."

She swallowed and moaned. "Drink," he commanded again. She did so. He was insistent that she drink all of the bitter liquid.

When the cup was empty, he laid her head back down and turned to Jane. "Keep her drinking and if possible, get her to eat. Call me if she worsens." He left the little stateroom and the other women moved back in.

"What did he say?" Fannie asked.

"He said she needs to eat and drink."

Isabella smiled and said, "I can get her to drink. I'll squeeze the juice of a lemon into some water and add some sugar. That will mightily improve the taste of the water on this ship."

Through encouragement, Jane got Susanna to drink the lemonade made by Isabella, and within two hours, the ill girl was able to sit up and eat a little stew. By evening, she unsteadily made her way to the dining area to join the others for supper.

That evening, a debate had begun between Lucy Nutting and Fannie Corwin as to who had saved Susanna's life, the elders and their blessing or the doctor.

Susanna ended the debate when she stated in a weak voice, "I felt the warmth of the hands of the elders upon my head. That is the first thing I remember. I believe it was the blessing of the elders that gave me the strength to drink the bitter brew the doctor gave me. I do not believe I would be among the living if it were not for that blessing."

That settled the matter.

***

That afternoon, Captain Richardson had the crew fill six large barrels of seawater and tie long ropes from one mast to another to be used as clothes lines. With bar soap from the ship's stores furnished to each family, the women began the task of washing the clothing and bedding that had become soaked and soiled during the storm. Susanna laughed when she saw the ship looking as if it had a multitude of small, colorful, variously shaped sails flapping in the wind to assist the larger sails that pulled the vessel southward.

Later that day, the infant son of Brother and Sister Nichols quietly died of dehydration and fever, passing like the sunset that drained the color from the sky. As Susanna watched the seabirds wheeling in the air above the ship, she sent up a prayer for the comfort of the weeping mother, who refused to be separated from his body until morning. Susanna's thoughts were filled with regret for the parents. *For some, the cost of this voyage will be greater than they could have guessed. May few others be required to pay such a price before we reach California.*

Early the next morning, many of the passengers stood silently in the predawn light for the simple service. As the sun began to rise, the luminous blue of the water gradually reflected back the orange of the east horizon, which faded to a thin layer of yellow. As the fiery ball rose, the radiant blue dome of sky covered the ship and its passengers from one horizon to the other like an inverted blue china bowl.

As the sun flowed over the crowd, a prayer was offered and one end of the plank was lifted. The tiny white bundle slid off into the water with hardly a splash. Only the flapping of the sails and the sobbing of the child's mother could be heard until someone started to sing "Rock of Ages." All joined and the melody swelled until it finally climaxed in the words, "Thou must save, and thou alone." Then it grew quieter as emotion tightened the throats of those present, and the words, "Let me hide myself in thee," were carried away with the wind.

The days became warmer as the ship neared the equator. As Susanna stood at the rail on a pleasant evening in mid-March, the captain stepped up next to her. "I see that your friend, Miss O'Neil, is spending time in the company of Mr. Johnson."

"Yes, I've noticed that they enjoy each other's friendship. I'm happy for Jane. He seems to be a fine man."

"I've performed a few marriages as a ship's captain. I would be glad to perform a few more on this voyage."

Susanna's smile was reflected in her voice. "I've noticed that Emaline Lane is spending time with Mr. Sirrine. Perhaps there will be several weddings on this voyage."

"Perhaps this is much too personal a question, but may I ask if you have a young man in your future plans, Miss Thayer?"

Susanna's complexion turned bright pink. "No, Captain, there is no one in my future at the present." Her voice dropped. "There was one once but no longer."

"A young woman as lovely and refined as yourself will surely have many suitors before this voyage is over." He smiled and touched the brim of his cap as he returned to his responsibilities.

But Susanna's heart was too bruised and wary to respond to the overtures from any of the single men on board.

***

As Brother Ed Kembel tapped his music baton on one of the tables in the eating area, he cleared his throat to gain everyone's attention. He spoke. "My dear Sister Thayer, will you be prepared to sing the second verse of this hymn for Sabbath services tomorrow? It lends itself well to a solo. I have a copy of the poem by Brother William W. Phelps entitled "O God, the Eternal Father" for each choir member, and I believe most of you are familiar with the melody composed by Felix Mendelssohn that fits it beautifully." As Brother Kembel sang the first verse, to familiarize the choir members with it, Susanna felt her face grow rosy with pleasure at being asked.

The following day as her rich alto rose above the sound of the wind and the water, Sister Nichols, who had so recently seen her infant buried at sea, wept at the words, "That sacred, holy offering by man least understood," but they were the tears of a comforted mother.

School classes were established and many of the Saints read some or all of the more than one hundred fifty volumes of the Harper's *Family Library* which had been brought on board. On pleasant days, Susanna would call out to the children on the deck, "Come and sit with me, and I will read to you." There, out of the way on the quarterdeck, she would read from the books to a cluster of children at her feet. On inclement days, they would sit at the tables between decks while she read aloud. Some of them followed "Sister Susanna," as they called her, around the ship, coaxing her to read until she was nearly hoarse. She loved all the children, but she loved little Jimmy Skinner, who reminded her of her brother Georgie, best of all.

***

As the ship came upon the equator, Captain Richardson invited Susanna to join him on the quarterdeck as he used the sextant to measure the sun's position in the sky. She enthusiastically invited Jane and Samuel Johnson to join her, and others followed them to see what the captain was doing. When he had everyone's attention, he aimed the sextant at the horizon. "We are extremely close to the equator."

"How can you know that?" Susanna asked.

"As I take a sight on the sun, its position in the sky and the time it is sighted can be used to calculate our latitude on a nautical chart. To check my accuracy, this evening I will sight the distance between the horizon and the star Polaris, which will be just barely above the northern horizon. Within the next few hours as we cross the equator, Polaris will disappear."

Long after Jane, Samuel Johnson, and the others had lost interest in the use of celestial navigation, the captain took time to answer all of Susanna's questions and demonstrate how the sextant worked. Her mind was hungry for learning, and she was pleased and flattered that he was so willing to share his time and wisdom with her.

***

The following day the wind began to abate, and by late afternoon the air was still and the heat had grown so oppressive it felt hard to breathe. The sea reflected the sky like a mirror of molten glass. Even the hours after sunset that had often been so pleasant were suffocating. The temperature steadily increased during the night, until Susanna, Jane, and three of the other women in their stateroom arose, threw on their clothing, and climbed to the deck, each taking a quilt to lie on. There, they found several others who were trying to find sufficient respite from the heat to allow them some rest. Those who could not, searched the dark sky, spangled with a million stars. As the sun rose the next day and the sea remained smooth and the air heavy with humidity, the captain ordered the crew to rig an awning to protect the passengers from the burning rays of the equatorial sun.

As temperatures rose to well over 118 degrees, the passengers lay unmoving, fanning themselves with anything they could use. About noon, the captain had three large barrels filled with seawater and set on the deck. Many of the boys and young men took turns jumping fully clothed into them from a ladder fixed to a mast, and then lying under the awning in wet clothing. Several passengers, including Susanna, noted that almost every sailor had taken to whistling—some quietly under their breath, but others whistled loudly, as if to awaken the sleeping waves and wind.

She raised her hand to stop the captain as he passed. "Why do the crewmen whistle?" she asked.

He stepped into a small spot of shade cast by the main mast before he answered. "Seamen hold to many superstitions, and one of them is that if they create enough disturbances in the air with their whistling, it will rouse the forces of nature and bring the wind."

"I hope they're right." She lay back down weakly on the quilt.

The next day, Captain Richardson, soaked with perspiration, without his uniform coat and with sleeves rolled to his elbows, made his way through the languishing passengers. "See that you and your children get enough to drink." Few had the strength to answer.

By the third day, drinking water was in great demand, but little food was consumed. The heat blunted appetites. At times a breeze would rise and push the ship a few miles and then fade to nothing, like the breath of a ghost. The cheers of the crew and passengers would quickly melt into disappointed groans. The sailors whistled more loudly.

The next time the captain passed Susanna and Jane, Susanna asked weakly, "Is this kind of heat common on a voyage such as this?"

He paused and shook his head. "Occasionally a ship will enter tropical doldrums, but this has been an unusually hot period to endure. There has been a time or two on this voyage—such as that terrible storm that struck when we had been out of port only a few days, and now this terrible heat—that it seems the very forces of Hades have tried to halt this journey. Perhaps, Miss Thayer, you would not be offended if I urge you to ask your leaders to offer a prayer that the Creator, who is God of Heaven and Earth, will see fit to bring the winds again."

Of course, why hadn't anyone thought of it sooner? The thought lifted her to her feet, and after asking several people, she located Sam Brannan. The heat had so sapped his strength that her suggestion met with little enthusiasm on his part. She continued through the group until she saw John Joyce. "Brother Joyce, could we have a group prayer to ask the Lord to bring the wind?"

He sat up and, after a moment during which he gathered his thoughts, responded, "You are right, Sister Thayer. We should be ashamed that we've not taken such action sooner."

By the time the sun had begun to set, a group of twenty-five men and women had gathered at the stern. Other adults, both men and women, made their way slowly toward the group, where they knelt. Brother Ed Kembel stood to lead the group in prayer.

As he prayed, his voice grew stronger and rose sufficiently to be heard by all who had gathered. "We recognize our dependency upon thee, Father, and ask that thy power over the elements move the winds so that we might continue our journey." After the group offered a fervent amen, all slowly returned to their previous places, avoiding any unnecessary expenditure of energy.

About midnight, a breeze made the sails flap, waking Susanna and Jane, who pulled themselves into a sitting position. Gradually the wind increased, the heavy air cooled, and the ship began to move again. Those passengers with sufficient strength offered a weak cheer.

"This experience has been a testimony to the power of prayer," Susanna said to Jane as she turned over on her quilt and finally drifted off to sleep.

Chapter Twenty

A WEEK AFTER THE HEAT of the tropical doldrums had become only a brief note in the diaries of many of the passengers, a great pod of dolphins swam near the ship, their sleek bodies weaving silver patterns under the water. They leaped over the waves as effortlessly as sea sprites. The children ran squealing to the railing to watch the dolphins leap and dive as they splashed and swam around the hull of the ship like children playing near their mother.

The cooling weather and a sun perpetually rising on the port side and setting on the starboard side of the vessel were all that confirmed the continued southward direction of the ship. The children played among the seamen like old friends, learning the language of the sea and watching their labors.

On a day when the wind had lessened and the ship made slower progress than was usual, a flock of tiny seabirds settled around the vessel, many perching on the masts and spars. Some of the crew became preoccupied, talking with scowling faces among themselves and watching the birds. Others were slow to obey the commands of the captain and first mate, as though they were distracted.

Jane and Susanna had been standing near the helmsman on the quarterdeck when Jane raised her voice to ask, "Why are the men so slow to follow orders today? Some of them look positively sullen."

The sailor waved one hand in the direction of some of the birds. He never removed the pipe stem he held tightly between his teeth as he responded. "See the seabirds that have settled about the ship? Some of the men believe them to be the souls of lost sailors bound to the sea in death as they were in life. They call them Little Lost Peters." His voice dropped. "They believe them to be a bad omen, Miss."

***

The next morning, the voice of the leadsman roused the passengers as it filtered below decks. "By the deep eighteen." The calls continued as Susanna and Jane dressed. "By the deep fifteen."

Lucy Nutting sat up and asked, "What is he saying?"

Susanna dressed quickly, prompted by her insatiable curiosity. "I don't know, but I'm going up on deck as soon as we have eaten breakfast to find out."

The helmsman's voice continued through breakfast, and after they had consumed their oatmeal, many of the passengers followed Susanna to the deck, where they could see a muscled crewman as he threw a long line with many markings on it into the water. The little birds were gone, and she noticed that the crew members had returned to their duties with greatly improved cheerfulness.

Susanna and Jane stood with several other passengers as they watched the heavy line soar out into the water. Within a minute, the leadsman called out, "By the deep ten."

The captain stood near the binnacle watching the compass readings and listening to the calls of the leadsman.

"By the deep nine."

At that call, the captain spoke to the helmsman in a raised voice. "Three points to port."

"Aye, aye, sir."

The next three calls from the leadsman were the same. "By the deep nine."

Susanna approached Captain Richardson. "Captain, what is the crewman doing with the rope? Is the water growing shallower?"

"Yes, Miss Thayer, but it is not worthy of worry. The leadsman throws his line into the sea ahead of the ship, and as the ship reaches the line, he pulls it up to check the depth marker. The sea is at nine fathoms at the present and . . ."

Her eyes grew wide in alarm. "But that is only fifty-four feet of water beneath us, is it not?"

"Yes, but now it will begin to grow deeper. We are some miles east of the mouth of the Rio de la Plata, where the ocean is as shallow as anywhere we will sail on this voyage, but put your mind at rest. The depth will increase now."

The leadsman's call was heard again. "By the deep twelve."

"The leadsman's reading says we are now at seventy-two feet, and according to my calculations, we're about halfway between the equator and Cape Horn." His smile was reassuring.

Susanna was very conscious of an increasing respect, perhaps even a fascination with this handsome man in the blue uniform, who seemed filled with such great knowledge—knowledge that everyone on the ship depended upon for their lives and safety. As she returned to the stateroom, she began to examine her feelings for the man. There was so much about him that reminded her of her father, but there was more than that; but just what, she wasn't sure.

***

The farther south the ship progressed, the weaker the morning sun became. It cast a deceptive, weak light that gave no heat. The spray from the waves was icy and most passengers remained on deck only briefly each day.

The morning of April tenth dawned with a heavy overcast, the slate gray of the sky nearly merging with the gray of the ocean. Only the white caps of the waves marked the separation between sea and sky. Elder Brannan announced to the first group gathered for breakfast, "Captain Richardson tells me that today we begin to round Cape Horn. If the sun could be seen through the overcast skies, we would have seen it rise behind us this morning. He says the temperature is twenty-six degrees but the barometer glass is steady, so despite the cold, he does not expect any bad weather. We are, at this point, about halfway in our journey."

A few men called out, "Here, here," or "Good news, everybody," and pounded the table with open hands a time or two in enthusiasm.

He continued, "Captain Richardson has also told me that he plans to dock in Valparaiso, Chile, in perhaps a week, where we will take on fresh water, food, and wood. He's hoping that the good winds hold until then."

Though all the passengers would have liked fresh air, only a few desired it enough to face the bitter cold and wet. They climbed the hatchway to the deck, where the dark and sullen ocean sent a cold spray splashing rhythmically across the deck.

At dawn each morning, a thin fog hung over the surface of the water, obscuring the whole circle of the horizon. The sun was a pale orb of silver instead of gold, barely visible to the east.

By midday the mist had usually melted into nothingness while the ship was driven steadily westward, away from the South American coast. Increasing winds intensified the creaking and straining noises in the great beams of the ship, and towering waves crashed against the hull.

By six bells on the morning of the sixth day after rounding the Horn, Susanna and Jane awakened to notice a difference in the feeling of the motion of the ship. "The ship rides so quietly this morning that had it ridden like this during the earlier portion of the voyage, I would never have become ill," Susanna commented. "The pitching and rolling have lessened. I wonder if this is what it will be like to sail on the Pacific Ocean. I fervently hope so."

As they and many others sat at breakfast, the captain descended with the second mate behind him. The conversations around the tables quieted as he raised his hands for attention. He was ruddy faced with the cold and his breath came in short gasps.

"Many of you have undoubtedly noticed a change in the feel of the ship. This is not a good change. During the night, the ice became so thick as to endanger our safety. I need every able-bodied man, woman, and child over the age of fourteen to come quickly up on deck and bring every tool that might be useful in chipping ice. That includes spades, shovels, pickaxes, clubs, *anything* that can be used to rid the ship of ice. If we are not quick enough, the weight of the ice will take the *Brooklyn* under." The volume of his voice increased with urgency as he urged, "Dress warmly, but come quickly!"

The alarm in his voice was like a cold hand around Susanna's heart. It prompted the passengers to rise from their bowls of half-eaten oatmeal immediately. The captain added loudly, "Appoint some of the women to watch the younger children. We need everyone—everyone who is able on deck immediately." His voice broke with the urgency of the situation.

Fanny and Isabella were left to help watch the younger children, many of whom cried when they saw parents rushing away, adding to the confusion.

"Jane, come with me. We may find some useful tools among the cooking utensils." Susanna opened the chest and located a large metal spoon and a large metal spatula with a wooden handle. She handed the spoon to Jane.

As they turned away, the other women and older girls began to search for suitable tools. The men and boys soon appeared with every kind of tool, including a three-pronged grappling hook. Some of the boys carried chair legs to use as clubs.

After each woman and young person reached the upper deck, a crewman handed her a ten-foot piece of rope. "Tie yourself to a railing or something solid so you won't slide overboard. Go over to the port railing and start there." The deck was leaning several degrees to port. "Get as much ice off that side as possible, so the ship can right herself." He was yelling above the wind and the thumping and cracking sounds of ice being pounded by the crew.

Susanna and Jane slid across the icy, sloping deck as if it were a frozen pond. When they reached the rail, they tied themselves to it as they had been told. Susanna quickly learned to slide the metal spatula under the ice so she could leverage it off. Jane pounded with the bowl of the big spoon and dug with the metal handle, but as quickly as the chunks of ice flew into the ocean, more would begin to form where they had been.

After three hours of frantic labor, the capes, coats, scarves, and mittens of the passengers were soaked with seawater and were freezing to the wearers. Susanna removed her sodden mittens and put them in the pocket of her cloak before returning to scraping, pounding, and breaking the ice with hands blue and stiff from the cold.

The ship began to right itself slightly, and that was a sufficient correction to allow three crewmen to be lowered by rope on bo'sun seats down the port side where, as they broke the ice, it would drop in great sheets into the ocean.

Susanna watched in alarm as the sea churned below the men. Her breath stopped for a moment when she recognized that the third crewman, a boy of no more than sixteen, was white-faced with fear. He seemed determined to obey orders as capably as any of the older men.

As he pounded the ice with a great curved hook, he nervously looked up to see if anyone was watching his success, meeting Susanna's eyes. She smiled her approval at him, even though her cheeks felt as if they would crack and break like the ice. He returned to his work with increased vigor, but as he swung the hook, the rope strung through the board he sat on gave way where it was tied to the railing. He called out as he dropped the great hook and grabbed the remaining strand of rope.

In panic, Susanna pointed and screamed, "Man overboard! Help him!" She screamed again as her feet went out from under her. Her nearly frozen left hand hit the railing. She pulled herself up and watched the young crewman as his frozen hands began to slowly slide down the icy rope, stopping only when they reached the wooden seat, which was still attached by one remaining knot in the rope.

Five crewmen rushed to the railing and began to pull the boy upward, calling out to him to hang on. They were slipping and sliding on the deck, unable to get purchase on the icy surface, but they braced against the railing and the last man reached the capstan, where he straddled it with his legs as they struggled to lift the terrified young crewman. When he was finally pulled over the railing, a great cheer arose from every mouth through nearly frozen lips.

The captain greeted the young man with a slap on the back and pointed him toward the crew's quarters. As the nearly frozen young man moved out of sight, the captain climbed the stairs to the quarterdeck and called out, "We've made much progress. Those men who are able are needed for another hour. The women and children may go below and get warmed."

After going below deck, Susanna's hands began to thaw and her bruised and cut knuckles began to bleed. Two fingers on her left hand were swollen and throbbing.

As she stood looking at her left hand, Fannie Corwin hurried to her with a clean rag. "Susanna, my dear, you're bleeding. Wrap your hands in this cloth and come with me. You must see the ship's doctor."

"I didn't realize I had hurt myself," she said, as she held up the cut and bleeding hand. Fanny took charge, leading her to the doctor's dispensary, where he was wrapping the injured foot of a young crewman.

"I hit my own foot with the spade instead of the ice," he said to the doctor sheepishly.

"I hope your aim improves before we run into another ice storm, young man, or I may be forced to fit you with a wooden leg," the doctor said with a chuckle.

The boy grinned embarrassedly and limped past Susanna. Fannie pulled her inside and insisted she sit. "She's hurt her hand," she told the doctor. She unwrapped Susanna's left hand with care. "I think she's broke a finger or two, Doctor."

He examined the left hand with great care. "You have one broken finger here. The other is badly sprained, my dear. How did you do this?"

"I have absolutely no idea, Doctor. It was so cold that I didn't feel anything when it happened."

He splinted the fingers carefully and wrapped them. He looked at her when he was finished and asked, "You're the young woman who was so severely seasick, are you not?"

She nodded. "Yes, that was me. I have wondered since what it was you gave me to drink."

"That was the drink made by boiling the bark of the slippery elm to which I added the juice of a lemon. It settles the seasick stomach."

"I wish I knew remedies such as that. I'm sure I will need knowledge of that kind when we reach California." She looked around the room. "Where did you obtain the bark of an elm tree on a ship?"

"You will note my many big and little bins on that wall. The largest one is full of slippery elm bark. The next holds willow bark. The third contains dried chili peppers; the next is full of dried pineapple. Another one holds garlic, and so on. Each is a remedy for a particular type of stomach misery. On the shelf above the bins are jars of spices used for medicinal purposes, such as cinnamon, flaxseed, parsley, chamomile, and honey. Nature furnishes us with many remedies for illness and injury if we learn how to use them." He turned and looked directly at her. "I occasionally need an assistant, Miss Thayer. You strike me as an intelligent young woman willing to learn. Would you be willing to assist me when needed?"

"It would be a privilege, Doctor Seagrave." She grew excited at the thought that here there would be much to learn.

Chapter Twenty-One

After the danger of the ice had diminished, the captain ordered his helmsman, "Make for the Juan Fernandez Islands. In this wind we will never make it to Valparaiso. We must set a westerly course." He was hoarse from yelling to be heard above the sound of the wind and waves.

As supper preparations were begun, the captain descended from the upper deck, his hair still covered with ice. "I thought that you would want to know that we are now—finally—underway toward the Juan Fernandez Islands. Some of you may know of this island group by the fact that it includes the legendary island of Robinson Crusoe. In a few days, you will feel the solid earth under your feet and have fresh water to drink." A weak cheer rose from cracked and bleeding lips and hoarse throats.

Within a few days, the doctor approached Susanna. "You will now have the opportunity to begin your medical education. I have in my dispensary two crewmen who have injured themselves. Would you assist me in treating and wrapping their wounds?" She nodded and hurried to follow him.

A week later, he asked if she would assist him in treating three passengers who were ill with stomach cramps. She followed his directions and boiled and strained the bark of the slippery elm and mixed it with lemon juice and a dab of honey. When her patients recovered quickly, she beamed with pride and pleasure. They each looked at her with an increased respect.

As the days passed, he asked for her assistance with some regularity. Jane finally asked, "Does Doctor Seagrave really need your help, Susanna, or is he perhaps a bit infatuated with you?"

Susanna laughed at the thought. "I know that I am not indispensable, Jane. He could find help from any number of people on the ship, and

I don't think he is infatuated with me. He has simply found me to be a willing student, and he is teaching me so many wonderful things."

***

On May first, the *Brooklyn* anchored off Robinson Crusoe Island. The passengers were impatient to leave the ship, and the women stood with skirts blowing in the wind until they were assisted by crew members down the accommodation ladder and into one of the longboats. Isabella Jones, Mary Murrey, and some of the other portly passengers were offered the bo'sun's chair where, amid flapping skirts, they squealed as they were swung out and over the railing and down to the boat. From there, all were rowed ashore, where they climbed out and waded through the shallows to be greeted by the eight inhabitants of the tiny island.

Captain Richardson arranged for rolls of unused sailcloth to be made into two large tents, and those women who preferred the island to the ship slept in a tent for the next several nights, making their beds on the ground. Several men camped in the other. For the next six days, the ship was loaded with wood and fresh water while the passengers bathed, did laundry, and traded with the inhabitants for potatoes, fish, and fruit. Without telling Susanna, Jane traded the scrimshaw broach given her by Aunt Louisa for fresh fruit for the two of them.

On the morning of the seventh day, with much regret, the passengers and crew returned to the ship shortly before high tide. Captain Richardson announced, "We will make our way toward the Sandwich Islands, arriving within four to five weeks, depending upon the winds, and there we will again replenish our food stores."

***

As the ship neared the Sandwich Islands, the first mate allowed some of the passengers to use his telescope in the evenings while he showed them how to locate the constellations that shone so brightly above them: Orion, Ursa Minor, Cassiopeia, Pegasus, and others. Susanna was his best student.

She couldn't help but think, *How strange that these same stars that looked down upon me and my family in Boston now look down upon us here, a world away in the great Pacific Ocean.* As she lay in her berth that night, she remembered a sermon given by Elder Parley Pratt where he told his listeners that all the great stars in the heavens were created by the same God. *And yet, He knows and loves each of His children.* She slept that night comforted by the thought.

On Saturday, the twentieth of June, all stood at the rail when the *Brooklyn* anchored in the great harbor of Oahu Island. The air was filled with floral scents and the breeze was a gentle caress.

The passengers waited impatiently to be shuttled to the jetty that extended out into the harbor. When they stepped out of the longboats onto the sand, they were greeted with leis of tropical blossoms and offerings of fresh fruit. A few of the Saints had sufficient funds to take board and room in the little hotel. Many of the men decided to sleep under the stars on the beach, and the captain again had the tents put up for the women.

While the passengers strolled the beaches and the sunny streets of Honolulu, which were paved with crushed coral, the crew spent their days loading fruits, vegetables, meat, fish, water, and wood.

The third day, Susanna and Jane sat on the beach with their skirts spread about them, feeling the sun and the warm breeze. Susanna took a small stick and drew randomly in the sand. "I have noticed that you have been spending a great deal of time with Mr. Johnson during the voyage. Has he said anything that would lead you to expect any change in your friendship?" When Jane didn't immediately respond, she added, "I would miss you dearly if you were to leave me to marry, but I would be happy for you."

Jane finally shrugged her thin shoulders. "I had hopes that he held special intentions, but now I have begun to think that I am simply a substitute for a dear sister he left behind and misses very much."

"I'm sorry, Jane. He seems such a nice fellow, and I thought he . . . well, I will tell you that I am a bit relieved that I will not be losing my dear friend to marriage—at least not right now." She leaned over and gave Jane a hug.

***

During the day while the ship was being loaded with supplies, the islanders regularly brought gifts of fruit to the passengers and crew members: watermelons, pineapples, grapes, bananas, even mushrooms. Those who had been sick with canker and scurvy grew noticeably stronger.

The two friends waded in the waves that rolled up and caressed the beach, holding their skirts above their ankles as they watched the playing children. "How I wish we could stay here—always. California can't be nearly as wonderful as these islands." Jane's voice was wistful.

Susanna sighed. She understood her friend's feelings. "All we can do is look forward and try to be prepared to walk through each door as the Lord opens it, and I believe the next door is in California."

***

On the first of July, the passengers stood at the rail and waved good-bye to those in the long native canoes, who paddled in graceful unison near the ship and escorted them well out into the ocean. That evening, Susanna stood at the railing watching the stars and the moon, a large radiant crescent that was reflected off the water. She wondered again why the Lord had apparently led her to this place in her life—this new, strange destination. *What does the future hold? Will I ever see my family again?* She grew melancholy for a few minutes until she remembered her mother's instructions at the train station in Boston. "Take life by the horns, Susanna." She took a slow, deep breath and promised herself she would face the future prepared to take it by the horns. *I am my mother's daughter, after all.*

A week after leaving the Sandwich Islands, word traveled through the ship that Elder Brannan's wife had become ill. His three-year-old daughter wandered on the deck alone, so Susanna picked her up. "Where's your papa?" she asked.

The child pointed and Susanna could see Brannan speaking with the captain. She approached the two men, and when it appeared they had finished their discussion, she spoke. "Elder Brannan, I understand your wife is ill. Do you need someone to look after her and help with your daughter?"

"Yes, I do. My wife is apparently with child again. Her seasickness is much worse than it was at the beginning of the voyage. I'm not sure what to do for her."

"My friend Jane and I will look in on her and keep track of the child, if it would be of help."

"Thank you, Miss . . . Miss?"

"Thayer, Susanna Thayer."

"Yes, yes, of course," he responded as if he had suddenly remembered her, but Susanna knew better. He had learned only the names of the men on the voyage and had dealt little with the women. "Whatever you can do would be appreciated." He returned to whatever important business always seemed to fill his time, leaving Susanna with the small child.

"What is your name?" she asked.

"Annie, like my mama."

"Annie, let's go visit your mother and see if we can help her feel better. We will take her a drink of slippery elm and lemon tea."

***

Over the next four weeks, Susanna spent time assisting Anne Brannan as she tried to eat the broth from the soups and stews provided for the passengers. She and Jane did the Brannans' laundry along with their own. Between the two of them, they kept close watch on the little girl.

The evening of the day before the captain expected to pass through what John C. Fremont had named the Golden Gate Straight, Susanna put her little charge to bed and asked Anne Brannan, "Is there anything you need?" When the woman shook her head, Susanna climbed the stairs and stood at the railing in the darkness, inhaling the fragrances wafting on the breeze from the unseen land ahead of the ship: pine, sage, warm soil. Occasionally the moon slipped out from behind a bank of clouds, spilling a silver light over the waves and the ship's rigging.

"It must have seemed like a very long voyage to you and the other passengers." The captain had stepped up to stand beside her. She was warmed by his voice.

"Yes, at times it has seemed unending, especially during the storms. But despite the hardships, there have been pleasant things to remember," she responded. Silence lay between them for a few minutes as they listened to the creaking of the masts and the sound of the waves rhythmically breaking against the bow.

Finally he spoke again. "And what will you tell your children someday about the pleasures of this voyage?"

"I will tell them of the brave and wise captain who guided the ship safely halfway around the world."

He cleared his throat as if a bit embarrassed by her praise.

To ease his discomfort, she added, "I will never forget the stop at the Sandwich Islands. I wonder if someday I might like to live there. The fruit, the climate, the friendliness of the people all seemed extraordinary."

"Admittedly, if those islands were on one of the routes between Britain and the coast of New England, I and my wife would not have hesitated to build a home there, but as I am an officer for the Black Ball Shipping Line and spend the vast amount of my time in the Atlantic, I have little choice but to live in one of the New England states."

At the mention of his wife, Susanna's heart seemed to miss a beat. She said nothing as she internally scolded herself. *What is the matter with me? Did I think that this man, who has only shown me courtesy and kindness, had come to feel something special for me?* She took a deep breath and asked, "Please tell me about your wife. You have not mentioned her previously."

"No, I suppose I haven't. That is unusual for me. I often spend so much time telling others about my wife and daughter that I'm sure they weary of listening to me." He chuckled. "My wife and I have been married more than twenty years. We have a daughter about your age. Perhaps that is why I have felt so protective of you—and your friend, Jane. Young women often remind me of her."

Striving for an increased emotional objectivity, she answered, "I'm sure I would enjoy meeting both of them someday."

"If you ever return to Massachusetts, I hope you will visit Salem. I would be glad to introduce you to them. You and my daughter would be great friends."

She was silent while she tried to cope with a double disappointment. She had to recognize that this man who had seemed so romantic, so handsome and courteous, was only being a good ship's captain—and suddenly, she faced a truth she had not admitted previously: *I will never return to Massachusetts. I will probably never see my mother and family again.* She saddened at that realization.

Keeping her emotions in check, she turned and offered her hand. "Captain, I'm sure that you will be very busy tomorrow if we reach the bay at Yerba Buena as you anticipate. I may not have the opportunity to wish you God speed at that time. Right now, I want to thank you for your able navigation and leadership and more especially for your kindness to me."

"You are more than welcome. I hope our paths cross again someday, but without the storms we have encountered." He tipped his captain's cap and disappeared into the darkness.

As she lay staring into the darkness that evening, listening to the even breathing of the other women in the stateroom, she asked herself several questions. *What did I expect from him? Why did I allow myself to develop feelings for him, feelings I was hardly aware of until he mentioned his wife? I must learn to abide by the philosophy of Socrates, who admonished each of us to "Know thyself." I must know myself more completely so I am not overtaken unawares by feelings such as these.*

***

After the passengers had eaten a simple breakfast in anticipation of disembarking, they gathered at the ship's railing. Some even gathered their personal baggage. Gradually, blue shadows came into view on the eastern horizon. They divided a metallic gray sea from a gray, overcast sky. Most of the women on board talked among themselves, some nervously laughing. Susanna stood apart, silently watching the scene and wondering what the future held now that the ship had reached its destination.

As the sun rose, the shadows grew into hazy mountains that looked as if an artist had smeared blue-gray oil paints in a landscape. By eleven, the midday haze had lifted and the sun had broken through the clouds and glanced off the water, like sparks from flint on stone, making the waves flicker as if they were ready to burst into flame.

As the wind pushed the ship through the gap in the hills of Fremont's Golden Gate, the clouds melted away, allowing the sun to burnish the surrounding hills in gold. The scene was filled with the colors native to a New England autumn, golden sand and bleached grass rising above streaks of yellow mustard in the crevasses of the hillsides that rose beyond the cluster of small buildings that made up the frontier outpost known as Yerba Buena. Muted grays were evident in the clusters of eucalyptus and Russian olive trees, and splotches of dun and taupe eventually took shape as clumps of dust-covered palms. Here and there, the smoky green of a few hardy pines and junipers added their deeper color.

As the ship slipped across the water of the bay, the high tide could be seen churning the pebbles against the beach, like pearls suspended in the murky water. The scent of seaweed and the tang of Spanish Oaks filled the air. The captain ordered several of the sails to be taken in to slow the speed of the ship, and with the grace of a sea bird, the vessel swooped toward the beach at the base of the tiny community. The anchor was dropped about two hundred feet from the shore. The crowd on the deck sent up a loud cheer as the crew moved rapidly up the shrouds and ratlines, securing the rest of the sails.

Part Three
California

Chapter Twenty-Two

As the passengers crowded together at both the port and starboard railings, watching the scene draw closer, Susanna commented to Jane, who had joined her, "It's little more than a small village. I can't imagine that there are more than a hundred people living here—certainly not many more than that."

"Are you disappointed?"

"Maybe a little."

Jane turned and looked directly at her friend. "What did you expect?"

"Frankly, I have no idea."

"Then how can you be disappointed?" They both broke into laughter.

"It doesn't matter what we expected. We're here, and we will make the best of it," Susanna said with a broad smile.

Yerba Buena was comprised of fewer than fifty buildings, perhaps a quarter of them constructed of rough-hewn wood, little more than cabins. The others were made of adobe brick and had the flat roofs that marked Spanish architecture. They sprang up about two hundred feet from the beach and straggled up the surrounding hills.

Jane pointed. "I can see a crucifix on the dome of one of the largest buildings. That must be the Spanish mission of San Francisco we were told about."

Susanna nodded. "I suppose so. But I wonder what the large adobe building inside the long wall is." She pointed in a different direction. "See? Way up the hill."

"I can just barely make out an American flag on a pole inside that wall. It appears to be a military fort with barracks." Jane turned and pointed to the north. "Look over there. Is that an American warship at anchor? I see cannons on the deck and an American flag on the mast."

"It certainly looks like one."

Impatient children pulled their parents toward the gangway, anticipating the lowering of the gangplank so they could leave the ship that had been an all-to-uncomfortable home for the preceding six months. Brannan pushed his way through the crowd and climbed on a barrel to address the group. "Keep hold of your children. We won't be going ashore for a while yet. If you keep a journal, make a note that today is the thirty-first of July, 1846. For the present, you and your families will need to continue to live onboard the ship while housing is arranged for everyone." An audible groan rose from the passengers.

The captain approached him and he stooped to listen for a moment. He straightened. "Some of you have asked about the other ship in the harbor. Captain Richardson tells me that it's an American man-of-war, the USS *Portsmouth* under the command of Captain Montgomery. It arrived here about two weeks ago and secured Yerba Buena on behalf of the US government. You may see some of its crew in the village as, at any time, about half of them will have shore leave."

After an hour of waiting while the ship was made secure, many of the passengers were assisted once more down the accommodation ladder into several long, flat-bottomed barges owned by Californios, a title the Spanish-speaking citizens gave themselves. For a few pennies each, they were willing to row the passengers to shore, all of whom were impatient to feel the earth beneath their feet.

The barges seemed to move with agonizing slowness. Once they scrapped onto the sand, the men were able to leap out, often without getting their boots wet. After assisting the women onto dry land, both men and women excitedly entered the dirt streets of the little village, which appeared to be little more than an enclave of adventurers, sailors, and Californios. The arrival of the *Brooklyn* more than tripled its population.

Jane and Susanna joined many of the other immigrants and walked first to the adobe fort on the hill where they had seen the stars and stripes flying from the flagpole. There they met a group of marines and sailors from the *Portsmouth*, who proudly shared the news that, in that area, the war with Mexico was over. While conflict between the Americans and the Mexicans continued in other parts of Alta California, Yerba Buena had been claimed without open conflict by the navy on behalf of the US government.

The captain of the fort welcomed them and expressed his approval that the *Brooklyn* had brought more Americans to settle the area, strengthening the claims of the United States. "To mark the occasion, all of you from the *Brooklyn* are invited to a celebration this evening, where we will all share food, music, and dancing," he announced.

At the celebration the new immigrants were fed fruit and cakes and entertained with Spanish guitars and dancing well into the night in the largest tavern in the community. Susanna and Jane modestly sat out of the way for the first few minutes, but that did not last for long. After Jane had accepted an invitation to dance from a sailor who insisted on a partner for the Virginia reel, she called out to Susanna, "Stop turning those soldiers down, and come out here and dance." She laughed as Susanna accepted the next invitation, and it was well after midnight before the music stopped and the passengers regretfully returned to the ship.

As they wrapped themselves in their quilts and lay down on the wooden berth, Susanna said quietly, "You seemed to enjoy yourself very much this evening, Jane."

"Yes, I did. I wasn't going to let Mr. Johnson and the pretty señorita he was dancing with ruin my evening." She giggled, something she seldom did. "I had a wonderful time, Susanna. I think I'm going to like it here. Did you enjoy the evening?"

"Yes, more than I had expected," Susanna said with a smile. "I think we will make friends here very quickly."

In the morning, the passengers again gathered on the deck. The fresh air and the sun, which painted filmy layers of color across the sky, added to the excitement of going ashore again. Brannan climbed the barrel and began the day's announcements. As he began to speak, the immigrants began to whisper and point. Wondering what was taking their attention from him, he turned in time to see another frigate sweeping into the bay, the USS *Congress.* As it moved across the water, in quick succession four of its cannons were fired in a loud salute. In answer, four cannons from the deck of the USS *Portsmouth* were fired. Then four of the cannons from the fort on the hill responded. The roar of the twelve explosions made the ground shake and caused dust clouds to rise from the adobe buildings of the village. The water of the bay trembled as if the ships sat in a giant soup cauldron that had been struck with a heavy metal spoon. Many of the women covered their ears, and the small children cried in fear.

After the excitement had quieted, Brannan cleared his throat and called everyone to attention again. "I regret that the *Brooklyn* had no guns to join in that salute." Many in the group laughed nervously, glad that the noise of the cannons had ceased. He continued, "I have a list here of some housing arrangements that have been made for some of the larger families and the single women. All others will be using tents for the time being. That should not present too much of a hardship as the present climate is mild. When I read the name of the head of the household, please step forward, and you will be handed a map of the location of the cabin or building where you will be housed. You will leave in the first or second barge."

He began to read names: "William Kettleman, wife and six children; Jerusha Fowler and four children; William Evans, wife and four children; Ambrose Moses, wife and four children; and George Winner, wife and six children." After a hand-drawn map was furnished to each family named, Brannan waved them over to one side of the deck, as if separating the sheep from the goats.

"The following single ladies will be immediately provided for: Prudence Aldrich, Emaline Lane, Angeline Lovet, Lucy Nutting, Mary Murrey, Isabella Jones, Sophia Clark, Jane O'Neil, Susanna Thayer, Eliza Savage, and Zelnora Snow. Arrangements have been made to house these women in the old mission.

"Those whose names have been read will immediately gather their personal belongings and climb into the long boats. The bo'sun's chair is available for those that require it. You will not be returning to the ship. Any of your larger possessions, such as crates, boxes, and barrels, will be unloaded by the crew later today or tomorrow.

"Yesterday, while I was ashore with some of the other brethren, we arranged to use the chapel in the mission at two o'clock each Sunday afternoon for worship services. The priest there says Mass at ten each Sunday morning, but he is willing to allow us to use the church in the afternoon. After our services, we will make announcements, conduct business, and notify everyone of any news we may receive regarding the likelihood of our being united with Brigham Young's overland company of Saints."

He stooped as if to jump down from the barrel that had been his informal pulpit during the voyage, when several men called out.

"Sam, don't get down yet. We have more questions."

"Elder Brannan, what about the cooperative?"

"Yeah, how's it going to work?"

He straightened up and looked around as if he were surprised that they had such questions. He pointed at John Joyce. "What's your question, Brother Joyce?"

"What about the cooperative we bought into when we paid for our voyage? How will that work and who will represent us on its board?"

Brannan cleared his throat and looked uncomfortable for a moment.

Quartus Sparks called out, "Sam, surely you remember—we were to live in a cooperative community for the next three years, until we were established here or relocated to join with the other Saints."

Recovering his aplomb, Brannan put up his hand to silence the group. "Admittedly, brethren, it has not worked out the way I had anticipated. The cost of the voyage, including the resupplying of the ship in the Sandwich Islands, was so great that the funds that were meant to establish the cooperative have been depleted."

An angry groan arose from the men in the group, and Brannan put up his hand again. "I'm sure no one will go hungry, but we will just have to make individual arrangements among ourselves." He paused, and before the discontent in the crowd could rise again, he called out, "For example, I suggest that the single women who will be housed in the mission combine their funds and work together as an extended family."

There were some subdued complaints, and many men turned away with emotions ranging from frustration to disgust written on their faces, but the grumbling quieted. Brannan called out, "This meeting is over. The next meeting of the entire group will be Sunday afternoon in the church." He leaped off the barrel and was quickly surrounded by a few men who were determined not to be put off so easily. The single women who had been named hurried down to their staterooms and excitedly gathered their belongings.

As they stepped into the second barge, Susanna and Jane could see the sunlight gold-leafing the hillsides above the village. When the barge scraped onto the shore, the crewmen helped the women out onto the pale, buff sand. The barge returned to the ship and brought the rest of the single women and some of the larger families. As the passengers stood on the damp sand, their feet left depressions which quickly filled with seawater. They stood or sat on bags, trunks, or bundles until Ed Kembel arrived and led them to the nearly abandoned mission of San Francisco. It was a lengthy walk up the hill. He explained as they reached the gate in the adobe wall, "The priest will continue to inhabit his rooms, but he won't bother you. He doesn't speak much English. His responsibilities amount to holding Mass once each Sunday morning for the Californios. He expects to be paid one hundred pesos rent for each room at the beginning of each month."

The rooms were small and dark, with one narrow bed, above which was a shadow in relief where a crucifix had once hung. Each had a musty mattress of straw previously used by the monks who had lived in the small cells a few years earlier, maintaining their vows of poverty, chastity, and humility. The rooms had no windows other than an opening above the plank door, through which the prayers of the penitent would have been audible to a religious leader standing in the hall outside the narrow rooms.

That evening, Susanna and Jane left the small rooms they had been assigned and walked throughout the small community and down to the beach.

As daylight faded into twilight, billows of fog from the ocean folded over and around all but the most prominent landforms. Susanna had not thought to bring a shawl or cape for their evening walk. "It's not so much the temperature that makes me shiver as the dampness, like Boston in the early spring or midautumn. It's an unusual climate for the middle of summer. If the weather is this cool and damp in July, I wonder what it will be in December." They walked a little farther in silence before she spoke again. "I didn't know what to expect when we reached California, but right now, I think the best way to describe how I am feeling is adventurous and," she admitted, "a little nervous."

"Susanna, we will take life by the horns, and we will make a good future for ourselves. That is how I feel."

Susanna was comforted by Jane's confidence, and they turned their steps back toward the mission. The moon was just barely discernible through the mist

***

After the end of worship services on the first Sunday in their new home, Susanna and Jane approached Brannan to share a concern expressed by many of the women. "Eventually we will run out of money and find ourselves without resources. Then what will we do?"

"There is a need for women who sew, and if you look around, you may find opportunities to sell baked goods. The men need haircuts and their clothing mended." He looked at the young women with a slightly patronizing air. "I'm sure you can find ways to support yourselves." At that, he turned and walked away.

As suggested by Brannan, the women in the mission had combined a part of their remaining financial resources to obtain food from the

Californios in the village. They bought fresh milk, meat, and vegetables daily for little more than a few pennies. Two native women from the village were hired to prepare the meals and, just as importantly, to teach the women from the *Brooklyn* how to grind the plentiful wheat for bread, and corn to make tortillas. Each afternoon in the mission kitchen, a mutual exchange of English and Spanish was carried on between the American and native women as they baked and tried to learn the language of the other.

Within the week, Susanna, Jane, and Emaline Lane were selling the tortillas they had made to the families living in the tents on the beach sand dunes. Susanna cut hair for several of the men with the precious scissors she had brought all the way from Boston. At the end of the week, they counted their profits. "Jane, we have two hundred fifty pesos and two US dollars," Susanna told her excitedly.

"We're just taking life by the horns, Susanna." They both laughed heartily.

The following Sunday after worship services, Brannan shared the news he had acquired from the captain of the USS *Constitution*. He stood in front of the altar in the small chapel. "I have learned that the United States officially declared war on Mexico on May thirteenth of this year. While conflict continues farther south in Los Angeles, San Pedro, San Diego, and other places, the Californios here have demonstrated no opposition to the troops that arrived on the *Portsmouth* and the *Constitution* and raised the US flag. We expect to continue to live peacefully."

***

For the next several weeks, the *Brooklyn* sat in the bay with sails furled, bobbing gently at anchor as the crews loaded supplies and made repairs. When the news traveled through the community that the ship would set sail the next day, Susanna purchased two sheets of paper, a quill pen, and ink and sat at the mission dining table to write a letter.

> *Dearest Mother, James, Rachel, and Georgie,*
>
> *I have reached California safely. It was a long journey, and it is very different than I had expected, but I must admit that I actually did not know what to expect. The weather is mild, and the community of Yerba Buena is small and, since the arrival of the ship, made up largely of Saints. Jane and I and many of the other single women are living at the*

old mission of San Francisco. We are supporting ourselves adequately by selling tortillas, cutting hair, and sewing. Brother Brannan is sure that the Saints who have left the United States will come overland and join us here. I hope you will not worry for my safety. I think of you all often, and miss you.

Your loving daughter and sister,
Susanna Thayer

The next morning she carried the letter down to the beach and after the captain shook Brannan's hand, she offered it to the seaman. As he took it from her hand, she noted that he carried at least a dozen other letters.

"I've no idea how much the post for this letter will be, but I have some American money with me. Do you know what it will cost to see it to its delivery?"

"From past experience, it will cost a dollar, Miss Thayer."

Susanna caught her breath. *Such a large sum for such a small letter.* With only a small hesitation, she reached into her pocket and pulled out enough two-bit pieces to make up the sum. As he took it, she smiled at him and quoted the common sailors' farewell that she had learned on board. "Fair weather and following winds, Captain."

"Thank you, Miss Thayer. And may the wind always be at your back." He touched his cap and walked toward the barge that was waiting for him.

The sun glinted off the high tide and the wind whipped the waves into white caps as the crew lifted anchor. A large number of the Saints and Californios watched from the beach as the crew climbed into the rigging and moved out along the spars to unfurl the sails. As the wind filled the sheets and pushed the ship westward, toward Fremont's Golden Gate, the large group of men and women standing on the shore waved hats and handkerchiefs. Susanna stood apart from the group, unmoving. She whispered, "*Via con Dios*," to the captain and crew, feeling for a moment that she was bidding yet another friend farewell, never to be seen again. After a few minutes, she hurried back to the mission, well ahead of the others, aware of a sense of homesickness, of finality. *There's no going back now. As we move forward in life, must we always leave behind those we have come to value?* She knew the answer even as she asked it.

The color of the evening sky melted from apricot to a rosy blush. A fog bank began to move in, with a wall of dark clouds rising against the cobalt blue of the western twilight sky. The temperature began to drop as the wind increased. Susanna sat on her cot and scolded herself back into a more cheerful humor before Jane arrived.

***

The following week, Brannan announced after Sunday meeting, "Brother Quartus Sparks has been appointed to lead a group of twenty men and their families to establish a settlement on the Stanislaus River that will be called New Hope. It will be located seventy miles east of here, where wheat and other crops will grow well. That way, the community will be well established when Brigham Young and the Saints arrive."

While the men and their families made preparations to relocate, the wedding plans of Emaline Lane and George Sirrine were announced.

Jane came running into the kitchen, where most of the women were working side by side with the village women, making chili sauce. "Emaline and George are going to be married tomorrow," she called out excitedly. "They will be married by Elder Brannan and there will be a fiesta to celebrate. Isn't this wonderful?" Her face beamed with the news. "Then they're joining the group that will settle New Hope."

Susanna paused in her bread making. "I'm happy for her," her voice caught, "but I will miss her." As she continued to shape the cornmeal dough into flat, round circles, she wondered: *Will there ever be such an announcement for me?* She hit the little ball of dough, flattening it into a lopsided circle, and finished the thought, determined to be positive. *Of course there will be—someday.*

The following week, a dozen men, most of them single, set out for the Sacramento Valley, where they hoped to find work at Sutter's Fort. Samuel Johnson was among them. Jane refused to allow that to depress her spirits.

Chapter Twenty-Three

As the weeks passed, Susanna, Jane, and many of the younger single women worked regularly in the big garden at the mission. Susanna was often the first in the garden each morning, her wonder at the rapid growth of the crops never lessening.

"Look, Jane, it's a squash bigger than a man's head, and it's nowhere near ripe. And the bean stocks are taller than any man in the settlement. This is a wonderland. It's no wonder that Elder Brannan wants President Young to bring the Saints here to settle." Brannan had rapidly established two mills and founded a newspaper, the *California Star,* with equipment he had brought on the *Brooklyn*. As often as once a month, Yankee trading ships and whalers stopped in the bay to take on water and food, their crews briefly flooding the settlement with greatly needed revenue, but on those evenings, the single women quickly learned to stay in the mission.

***

The Christmas season in San Francisco was an experience in a grand foreign culture for Susanna and Jane and the rest of the *Brooklyn* Saints—filled with the Spanish fiestas, fandango dancing, and parades considered a vital part of the holiday by the Californios.

In early February of 1847, Susanna and Jane sat at the table in the kitchen of the mission while Susanna read aloud from the *California Star.* Several women gathered around to listen. "*On January thirteenth, a treaty was signed between the United States and the government of Mexico, calling a halt to the conflict of hostilities in Alta California.*"

"That means that the war with Mexico is really over?" Fanny asked.

"Yes, it appears so." Susanna turned the front page and began to read another article. "Here it says that Lieutenant Washington Bartlett of the

USS *Portsmouth*, who has been serving as *acalde* of Yerba Buena for the past several months, has determined that the community of Yerba Buena will henceforth be known as San Francisco. He stated that too much confusion has existed regarding the name of the town because the old mission here has always been known as the Mission of San Francisco." She put the paper down. "Well, I don't suppose any of us will oppose such a change." The women shrugged their shoulders and went about their business.

***

By March, the first of four army transports dropped anchor in the bay and began discharging what would eventually total a thousand military volunteers who had joined up for the war with Mexico on the condition that they would be allowed to stay in California at the end of their enlistment. Before their arrival, San Francisco had been a town of fewer than four hundred, largely a Mormon community. These men brought with them army pay, badly needed skills, and an appetite for courting the single women that made Susanna almost as nervous about going out of the mission as the crude and rough sailors on board the whalers had. Their aggressiveness was explained by the fact that many of them wanted to homestead and wanted wives when they did.

By June, San Francisco was rapidly becoming a cosmopolitan city of many diverse ethnic groups with a surfeit of men of all types. In response to the influx of new visitors and settlers, Brannan announced that he would build a hotel.

In July, Jane burst into the kitchen at the mission, where the single sisters were making corn bread. "Susanna, have you heard?" She was breathless. "Brother Brannan and his friend Charles Smith have packed supplies and are taking a mule train to intercept President Young and his wagon company. Brother Brannan's sure he can convince Brother Brigham to bring the Saints here to Alta California, where they will find good soil, a mild climate, and cheap farmland, and he says he won't come back until the company led by President Young is right behind him all the way. Oh, I hope they get here before Christmas." In her excitement, Jane almost danced around the room.

***

In late August, as Susanna was selling tortillas on the street, she watched in amazement as a contingent of twenty-five men, led by Jefferson Hunt, marched into San Francisco. Their beards were shaggy and uncut. Their hair was long and rough, and their skin was browned as dark as the Mexican-born Californios. Their clothing was little more than rags, and worn-out boots were held on their feet with rawhide strips, but they marched double file with military precision, with their rifles over their shoulders.

The word went swiftly around the community that these were men from the Mormon Battalion recently released from their enlistment. Lieutenant Washington Bartlett, the acalde of the community, declared a holiday, and a fiesta was held the next evening to welcome them. The only place big enough to hold them and the townspeople was the chapel at the mission.

Susanna and Jane spent the entire day of the fiesta with the other single women preparing much of the food that would be served that night. The heat from the stove made Susanna's curls tighten as she fried the tortillas, watching them puff up enough to be filled.

"Jane, Isabella, do you have the refried beans ready for the tortillas?" she called out.

Jane hurried across the large kitchen, moving carefully between the other women with the pot of beans. "Here you are, Susanna," she said as she set it down on the large table by her friend. "Who has the tomato salsa?" she called out. Mary and Lucy jointly carried the large pot of tomatoes, chili peppers, and green peppers to the table, and a line of women gathered to assemble the tacos, burritos, and enchiladas, as well as several American dishes, including venison, sweet potatoes, and squash.

By six fifteen that evening, the kitchen was heaped with prepared foods, and many of the women had hurried to their rooms to change into dresses less wilted by the heat.

Susanna looked at Jane wearily. "I wonder if I can stay awake this evening. I'm much too tired to do much dancing." She pushed a stray curl out of her face. Jane just smiled as though she knew that no one would be too tired to enjoy the event.

By seven o'clock, all the backless benches were pushed against the walls, and long tables had been set up and loaded with the food. The smiles and thanks of the Battalion men quickly made the *Brooklyn* Saints forget the unkempt, disheveled appearances of the soldiers. After the men had eaten more food than they had seen since they had left Council Bluffs on July twentieth of the previous year, some found places to sit where they could watch the girls and women who put the loaded trays on the tables and carried away the empty ones.

As Susanna and Jane moved through the crowd, offering food to the men who sat along the walls, the smile of one young man caught Susanna's eye as he took the last burrito from the tray she carried.

He ducked his head in thanks and grinned. "Thank you, ma'am. This is the best grub we've tasted in a long time. They fed us good in San Diego, but not as good as this."

She looked past the scruffy beard and great tangle of sun-bleached hair and was suddenly aware of his thin and bony frame. He was lanky and long-legged, like a colt. His joints were all sharp angles under his worn buckskins, and his hands and face were as weatherworn as harness leather. He couldn't have been more than twenty.

Impulsively and sympathetically, she sat next to him, putting the tray on her lap. "You look like you've had a long, hard march."

"Yes, ma'am. Over two thousand miles just to get to San Diego, cuttin' a wagon road most of the way with tools not meant for the job. It was another seven hundred miles to get here." He took a big bite and swallowed with very little chewing. He put the last bit of burrito into his mouth and wiped his hand on his buckskin pants, which were soiled and as wrinkled as an autumn leaf. He bobbed his head in deference to her gender. "I'm Henderson Cox, but my friends call me Sonny."

"I'm Susanna Thayer. My friend Jane and I," she pointed toward Jane as she passed with a tray loaded with more food, "came on the ship *Brooklyn*. We left New York in early February of last year, so we haven't heard much about the Mormon Battalion or the war with Mexico. Did you see many battles?" Her eyes were wide with interest and never left his face as he talked.

His eyes were a deep blue, filled with an aching innocence and intensity. "The US government came to us while the Saints were camped at Council Bluffs and asked Brigham Young to give them a thousand men to enlist in the army to go off to fight the war with Mexico that President Polk had just declared a few weeks earlier. We didn't have a thousand men to spare, and most of us didn't feel that the government that had turned its back on us in Missouri and again in Illinois had the right to try to conscript us into the army to fight its battles, but Brother Brigham decided to do what the government asked."

As they were talking, another young man sat down on the bench on the other side of Susanna. He waited until Sonny had finished what he was saying before he introduced himself. "I'm Dave Rainey. And you would be . . . ?"

She nodded and offered him her hand. "Pleased to meet you, Mr. Rainey. I'm Susanna Thayer."

Where Sonny's hair was bleached blond by the sun and his skin was tanned like supple leather, Dave Rainey was dark haired with skin tanned almost as dark as cedar. She looked from one young man to the other with a perplexed look. "Can you tell me how letting the US government take a thousand men to fight Mexico benefits the Saints?"

One of the other women walked past them with another full tray of food, and Dave leaned out and stopped her. With a large hand, he scooped up a taco, which he ate in three bites. His answer had to wait until he had swallowed. "When Colonel Allen rode into camp in his fancy uniform and told us that the US Army wanted all the men from eighteen to forty to go fight a war with Mexico, I was downright indignant—and so was Sonny, here. I wasn't goin' to enlist even if they put a gun to my head—and I think President Young felt the same way. He got real red in the face as the colonel talked, but after a while Brigham called Heber Kimball and Willard Richards into his tent. About a half hour later, they came out and Brother Brigham told us that maybe this was a real opportunity to earn some money that the Saints needed to get them to Zion. When he saw that he was going to have a tough time convincing folks of that fact, he went so far as to tell us that this was an opportunity that could be the financial salvation of the Saints.

"He changed my mind and nearly everyone else's when he explained that the pay each man would receive plus the uniform allowance we would be given would be used to help the members of the camp there in Council Bluffs and would save some of the Saints from starvation." He nodded as if to agree with what he was saying. "And he added that it was a good way to show all our enemies who've condemned us for not bein' real Americans that they're wrong. Eventually more 'n five hundred men enlisted."

Sonny had finished another taco he had snatched from a passing tray. He studied his hands for a moment while he arranged his thoughts. "The only thing we fought was a herd of wild bulls. Brigham Young told us before we left Council Bluffs that if we did what we were supposed to, if we didn't dishonor God or our religion, that we wouldn't see any fighting." He paused, clasped his hands between his knees, and looked at the floor. His jaw tightened. "But we didn't expect that our real enemies would be Lieutenant A. J. Smith, the man who took over temporary command after Colonel Allen died at Fort Leavenworth, and that army doctor, Sanderson. Smith was one mean son of a gun, and Sanderson was either malicious or totally incompetent—maybe both. Most of us called him 'Doctor Death.' Both of those men hated the members of the battalion for no other reason than the fact that we were Mormons. It was rumored that Sanderson had been part of the mob that drove us out of Missouri."

Dave was evidently full, as he allowed a tray of food to pass without reaching for it. He folded his arms over his chest in a satisfied manner. "Smith marched us through the heat and sand without enough water or food. He wouldn't let the sick ride in the wagons. He threatened to tie them to the axles and drag them if they didn't keep up with the main body. He marched us through the cold winds in the mountains with our boots falling apart, and all the while, he sat up there on his big horse in his wool uniform coat. Thank goodness we got a new commander at Santa Fe, Colonel Cooke. He was tough but usually fair. Otherwise, I think we would have buried more men than we did."

Susanna's eyes widened, and she found it a little harder to breathe when she thought about the hardships these two young men had endured. "How many did you bury?"

"About twenty, I think. Sound about right, Dave?"

"Yeah, sounds about right—mostly from illness or hunger or thirst. Some died from accidents, like Norm Sharp. He knocked a rifle off a wagon. It went off and he died from the gunshot wound."

Sonny continued, "I remember two of those men real well. The first man to die was my friend Samuel Boly. He died just twenty-eight miles out of Council Bluffs. He had been real sick but felt that he needed to do his part, so he enlisted like all the other men. Felt it was his duty. Later, in mid-September, when we were on the south side of the Arkansas River, my friend Alva Phelps died. He begged Sanderson to just let him rest a bit and he'd be better in the morning, but 'Doctor Death' forced a spoonful of that calomel down his throat, and a few hours later he was dead."

At the mention of the calomel, Susanna involuntarily shuddered.

Dave interjected, "If he'd never told Sanderson that he was sick with stomach cramps, I think he'd be alive today, but he was all bent over and couldn't hide it. Most everybody felt that the doctor had killed him."

"It sounds like a terrible experience." Susanna's throat tightened with emotion. "Do you think anything good came of it, I mean besides the money that was paid by the government?"

Sonny nodded. "We carved a wagon road through the mountains for miles before we reached Santa Fe. We built a brick kiln in San Diego when we got there and then made real bricks and built the town a courthouse. We dug about twenty wells and built a blacksmith shop and a bakery."

Dave added, "Colonel Cooke believed in keeping us busy until our enlistment ran out. We whitewashed nearly everything in the town that didn't move. We repaired carts and wagons. Lieutenant Clift from the Battalion was even appointed acalde—I think that translates as somethin' like a mayor. I don't think he was looking for the job. People liked him and he had a good education. He served until his enlistment ran out."

Sonny took over the narrative. "In June, Colonel Stevenson, the commander of the Southern Military District of California, asked us all to reenlist. He sang our praises to the governor and to the US president in Washington. He thought we were the best thing that ever happened to San Diego. I think he thought he would keep us as long as he could, but most of us were tired and we just wanted to rejoin the Saints."

"Did *any* of the men reenlist?" Susanna couldn't imagine why they would. She was surprised when Dave nodded.

"Yeah, I think about eighty of them reenlisted for another six months. They continued to be garrisoned in San Diego. The rest of us were discharged July fifteenth and decided to march north. When our group of about fifty reached Monterey, we split up. We marched here and the others said they would march up to Sutter's Fort. They hope to find work there, and we'll join them there in a few days, after we've rested."

Looking around, Susanna noticed that the other women were cleaning off the tables so they could be moved out of the way for the dancing. "Excuse me, but I need to help clean up. I hope we can talk again." As she stood to hurry away to the kitchen, both men respectfully stood, unfolding their lanky frames.

When the big tables had been moved out of the way, the air was soon filled with the sound of Spanish guitars. When Jane left the kitchen, Dave Rainey approached her, and with a flourish and a bow that somehow didn't look absurd in his worn and tattered clothes, he escorted her onto the dance floor. Susanna noted that Sonny seemed content to watch the others dance. She sat by him but said nothing. He nodded shyly at her but did not speak until the first dance had ended.

He nervously turned his battered hat in his hands for a few minutes but then turned to her. "Miss Thayer, would you be . . . ah, be willing to try a dance with me. I'll try real hard not to step on your toes."

"Yes, Mr. Cox, I'd like that."

Susanna noted that Sonny's dancing was not polished, but what it lacked in skill, it more than made up for in enthusiasm. As they danced, one of the other soldiers tapped him on the shoulder, and he stepped aside as custom required, allowing the other man to take his place, but before the music ended, Sonny had tapped him on the shoulder and retaken his place as Susanna's partner. For the rest of the evening, Susanna had a rotating series of partners, with Sonny always returning to tap the new partner on the shoulder and take up the dance with her again.

At midnight, Brannan stood and announced, "The music will end with one more dance. We're glad to have members of the Mormon Battalion here in our little community. Every one of you has made us proud. Your officers have arranged for you to sleep in the barracks, as you did last night, for as long as you are in our fair city. If you are here on Sunday, we will look for you at our two o'clock services. We ask all able-bodied men to remain after the music is ended to assist in returning the benches to their proper places so everything's ready for Sunday." With that, he bid everyone good night and took his leave, not remaining to see if his instructions were followed.

Susanna and Jane joined the other women in cleaning the kitchen, and as they stepped outside into the darkness, they were pleasantly surprised to find Sonny and Dave waiting for them. Sonny cleared his throat as he turned his battered hat in his hands. "We, er, Dave and I were wonderin' if you would mind if we walked you ladies home. It's dark and we thought it might be unsafe for two ladies to be out alone so late."

Susanna chuckled warmly, as there were at least ten other women starting toward the mission. "Jane, should we let these two gallant men accompany us home?"

Jane just giggled, and the two young men accompanied them to the gate in the mission wall, which was not quite a hundred feet away.

When they reached it, Sonny cleared his throat again. "Could we, I mean, would it be proper for us to come and visit you ladies tomorrow, now that we know where you live?"

In the moonlight, neither man could see Jane's complexion color with pleasure.

"Of course," Susanna replied with a smile.

"I . . . I'm sure that would be just fine," Jane responded, trying to smother her pleased smile in the darkness.

Susanna added, "But I must make a request in return. When you come to call, will you allow us to cut your hair and trim your beards?" She was suddenly afraid that she had offended them with her forwardness. She didn't want to end the potential friendships before they had blossomed, so she added, "I mean, I think we both would like to know what the two of you really look like."

Both men grinned in an embarrassed manner, and Sonny responded a little shyly, "That would be just fine, ma'am. Won't it, Dave?" Dave nodded. "We kind of got used to how we look to each other, but we forgot what we must look like to regular folks." They tipped their hats. "See you in the mornin'." They started up the hill toward the barracks.

Susanna's thoughts were busy as she slipped into bed. *I don't know that I've ever been more tired.* She paused in her thoughts and closed her eyes. *Of course I have. How could I have forgotten the weariness of those first few weeks at the mill—but this is a wonderful tiredness. I haven't laughed or danced so much since . . .* She pushed the memory of that birthday party at the Burnley's out of her mind and deliberately concentrated on everything she could remember about Sonny.

His shy smile and self-depreciating manner had touched her deeply, and his blue eyes with that melancholy expression had reached out to speak to her. *Those eyes looked as if they had seen too much hardship for a man hardly more than a boy. If we become friends, perhaps those eyes will smile when his lips do.*

She turned over on the straw tick mattress and slipped into sleep thinking about what kind of a picnic lunch she and Jane could put together for the next day.

Chapter Twenty-Four

When Sonny and Dave arrived the next morning, Susanna and Jane were waiting with a basket of fruit, cheese, and baked goods. When they saw the two young men approaching, they hurried to meet them, trying not to look overanxious.

"Let's take a walk down by the beach, where we can have a picnic, and I'll open an unofficial barber shop." Susanna gave Sonny the basket to carry. In the bright sunlight, the sand was almost white, rippled by the wind and smoothed in places by the high tide. The surf rolled rhythmically against the shore.

They located a place a hundred feet from the water behind a sand dune where the wind was deflected and the sound of the waves was muted. There they could laugh and talk and eat without getting sand in their food.

After they had eaten a late breakfast or an early lunch—it didn't matter which it was to any of them—Susanna took out her scissors and comb and cut the hair and trimmed the beards of both men.

"Now you look more like refined gentlemen," she teased as she stepped back to view her handiwork.

Both men rose and offered a mock bow of appreciation, and Sonny murmured, "Thank you, Miss Thayer. Your skills are deeply appreciated."

"Deeply appreciated," Dave repeated. "We will be the envy of all our battalion brothers." Though they were both being lighthearted, Susanna found it endearing.

And now that you are both looking well groomed, you are by far the handsomest of all your battalion brothers, Susanna thought.

By midday, the wind grew cold and the sky in the west darkened with a ceiling of low clouds, so Susanna put the scissors and comb in the nearly empty picnic basket, and the four of them brushed the sand off their clothing and regretfully began the walk back toward the mission.

As they entered the town and passed another member of the Battalion, the man called out, "Hey, Cox, where'd you get that haircut? I'd pay two-bits for one."

Sonny responded, "If you mean that, then I'll bet this lady can give you one." He looked at Susanna to see if he had spoken out of turn.

She smiled and nodded. "We would be glad of the income."

"Just grab something to sit on," he called back to the man. Within a few minutes, someone had pulled up a barrel and a line had formed.

For the next three hours, until the rain ended their efforts, Jane tried to comb the snarls out of each man's hair, and Susanna cut it and trimmed the beards. "That'll be twenty-five cents," Dave told each man. "Just give it to the little lady right there." Jane collected the money. Sonny sat quietly nearby, exchanging banter with the men and watching Susanna work.

When the bell in the church tower rang, signifying that it was four o'clock, and the rain had driven other potential customers inside, Susanna and Jane had earned three dollars and fifty cents, a small fortune by their standards.

After the young men walked the two women through the light rain and prepared to take their leave at the gate in the mission wall, Sonny said apologetically, "I didn't mean to get you into a day of hair cutting, but I know the men appreciated your help so they could get lookin' a whole lot better. I think some of them want to do some courtin' while we're in town."

I wonder if that includes the two of you, Susanna thought as both the women laughed. She responded, "It was a blessing for us. We earned as much in an afternoon as we could have in two or three weeks of selling tortillas and doing laundry. We owe you our thanks. I'd be glad to cut more hair tomorrow."

For the next two days, the young women cut hair and trimmed beards and laughed with Sonny and Dave as they did so. After supper, Dave and Jane went for a walk on the beach while Susanna and Sonny sat on the bench in the mission garden and talked into the night under the stars about life and hopes and dreams.

Sonny explained that he had left his widowed mother and sister in the care of his fourteen-year-old brother when he had joined the battalion. "I sent her a letter from San Diego, but I don't know how things are at home. I don't even know where home is now. I sent the letter to Council Bluffs, but perhaps they're in the Salt Lake Valley by this time. It's been a worry. Perhaps she didn't even get the letter and is wondering if I'm still alive."

"I know how you must worry for them. My mother is also a widow, and I haven't seen her since I left home over two years ago to work in the mills. I hope to see my brothers and sister, and especially my mother, again someday, but I don't know that I shall." She paused and swallowed a lump in her throat. "I miss my family very much." The curfew bell for the single women rang at ten o'clock.

***

The following day, as the impromptu barbershop was cleaned away, Sonny grew somber, shuffling his feet a bit like a schoolboy. "There's something I been meaning to tell you." From the tone of his voice, both women knew it was something he had been putting off. "Captain Hunt has told us that tomorrow we'll be moving out to join the other battalion members at Sutter's Fort."

The sunshine noticeably dimmed as a cloud passed over the sun. Susanna said nothing but her outlook dimmed like the sunshine. As protection against the disappointment the news brought, she took a deep breath and said to herself, *We won't be any worse off than we were before they came.*

"What are you going to do there?" Jane couldn't keep the disappointment out of her voice.

"I hear that Sutter has about a thousand acres where he raises wheat, barley, corn, and even some grapes. He sells stock to the army, so he always has work for strong backs there." Sonny cleared his throat. "Would it be proper for me to write to you when I get there?" He was looking searchingly at Susanna.

"Of course, Mr. Cox. We'd be flattered to have either of you write to us."

"Will you write back to me?" His voice was earnest.

"Yes, as soon as you furnish me with an address to use," but she didn't dare expect that he actually would.

He suddenly looked very relieved. "You know, I hear that there are jobs up there of all kinds, maybe even some for women."

"When you write, let us know if that is the case."

They spent the balance of the day together, but the four of them were quiet and subdued. That evening as they stood at the mission door, unsure what to say, Susanna cleared her throat and asked, "When will you be leaving?"

"Jefferson Hunt wants to start right at six in the morning, so we won't have the chance to see you before then. He told all the men to say their good-byes tonight."

"So this is good-bye." It was a statement, not a question.

Both young men looked at their worn and dusty boots. Sonny kicked a clod of dirt and looked up at Susanna. "I'll write, I promise, so you must not forget your promise to write back."

"I'll remember," she said quietly.

The next morning, well before six, nearly fifty members of the community, including Susanna and Jane, had dressed early and were there at the barracks to watch and wave as the men marched off in formation with their rifles over their shoulders.

***

Brannan had returned from his meeting with Brigham Young and the other Church leaders whom he had met near Fort Bridger. He was bitter and angry about the outcome of the meeting, so he turned his back on his church responsibilities and put his full attention on the hotel, which was nearly completed. It was little more than a two-story adobe with eight rooms for guests and a patio with a few rough tables.

He stopped Susanna on the street and, putting a hand on her arm, stated, "Miss Thayer, I'm looking for someone to work for me now that my hotel is nearly finished. My wife suggested you and your friend Jane, the girl with the red hair—that's her name isn't it?" Without waiting for an answer, he continued, "She said you were both very helpful on the ship. I can hire any number of Californios to do laundry and to cook, but I need someone to supervise them, to register guests, and to keep track of the income and expenses. I've hired Alberto Garcia, the oldest son of the man who runs the general store, to be my manager, but he thinks I need someone to oversee the women who will work as housekeepers and in the laundry and the kitchen. Would you and Jane be willing to work for me?"

"I most certainly would, and I'll ask my friend if she would as well."

***

The hotel opened in October, and Brannan gave Susanna and Jane some simple instructions as to prices for the rooms and meals, then hurried off to prepare the next edition of the *Star*. "If you have any questions, ask Alberto," he called as he rode away. Both of the women would share a small room on the main floor behind the registration desk.

After the first week, Susanna commented to Jane, "I'm not sure just what Alberto is supposed to be doing; apparently not much is expected of him, though admittedly, he enjoys standing around and talking to you."

"He's useful when we have Spanish-speaking guests and need someone to interpret for us." Jane's tone was a little defensive.

"You like him, don't you?"

Jane colored a bright red and simply nodded.

"As much as Mr. Rainey?"

Jane nodded again. "And where Mr. Garcia is concerned, he has a very big advantage over Mr. Rainey."

"He does?"

"Yes, he's here, and Mr. Rainey isn't."

Fanny Corwin entered the hotel's main room and handed Susanna a letter. "This was waiting for you down at the store. Mr. Garcia, the postmaster, asked if I would bring it to you."

"Thank you, Fanny. How are things at the mission?" She didn't hear her friend's response as she took the letter from her hand and broke the wax seal. Jane and Fanny hovered close enough to read the letter over her shoulders. Susanna's hand shook a little with surprise and excitement. She was tempted to tuck it into her pocket and read it when she was alone, but her friends would not hear of it.

It was dated September 25, 1847.

My Dear Miss Thayer,

We are camped not far from Mr. Sutter's Fort at the present. It was a trek of about forty-five miles, but when we got here, Sutter hired us all. About half of us were hired to harvest wheat. He's built a gristmill about five miles from the fort. Others have gone up to Culloomah (as the Indians call it), where Mr. Marshall has been hired by Sutter to build a big sawmill, so lumber can be floated down the American River to the fort. When the wheat harvest and threshing are finished, I think I will go up to work on the gristmill along with some of the other men. The pay is better, I hear. Three men arrived from the Salt Lake Valley a few days ago. They were carrying a letter from Brigham Young. In it he said that the first company of Saints reached the Valley of the Great Salt Lake in July. Brother Brigham asked the battalion members to stay here in California for the winter as it is too late in the season to cross the Sierra Nevada range, and there isn't enough food or work for all of us there in the Valley right now. He instructed the men to earn as much as they could before they join the Saints next year. Since Mr. Sutter's fort is an outfitting station for anyone coming from the east to settle in Alta California, he has everything a traveler could need. He even has two old Indian women weaving blankets out of the wool from his sheep. He has carpenters here who fix the wagons of the travelers, and he sells horses, mules, and oxen. Every two weeks he sends a mule train to San Francisco along with several wagons full of wheat and other supplies that the folks there need. He says he needs more people to work for him, even women, as he has a bakery and sells bread and other things to the men who work here in the fort. It may be very forward of me, but I'm sure you and your friend Jane could find work here, if you want to earn more than you can there in San Francisco. It would only cost about a dollar for you to get here by riding back in one of the supply wagons when they return to the fort. My friend, Mr. Rainey, asked me to send his greetings to Jane. I must finish this letter as I am running out of paper. I hope you will write back to me soon.

Your friend,
Henderson Cox

Susanna said nothing for a moment as she reread the letter. Jane looked at her with raised eyebrows. "Do you want to go to Sutter's Fort to work?"

"I'm not sure, Jane. I really don't know." *This is another of those doors that open into the unknown. Should I walk through it?* She folded the letter and slipped it into her pocket. "But it was nice of Mr. Cox to write to me, and Mr. Rainey was kind enough to send you his good wishes."

"Yes, but good wishes are not as good as his presence."

Fanny missed the look that passed between them. "How is Mr. Brannan's hotel doing?" she asked.

Susanna responded, "When the mule train comes from Sutter's Fort, or when a ship comes into the bay, we're busy, sometimes too busy, but other times the place at most has only two or three guests."

"What do you mean by 'too busy'?"

"When the sailors are on shore leave, Alberto Garcia sometimes has to earn his pay. He occasionally has had to eject some of the rowdier guests." When Susanna mentioned Alberto's name, Jane colored slightly.

Fanny announced that she could stay no longer and started for the door. "I need to be getting back to the mission. It's near supper time." She halted and added over her shoulder. "Some of the younger women at the mission have heard that there are jobs for women at the fort that pay well, just like Mr. Cox said in his letter. I think some of them might travel up there to see if they could do better there than here." She grinned widely. "I hear there are many more unmarried men there." Without waiting for a response, she gave them a wave and was gone.

***

A whaling vessel entered the bay the next day, and the hotel rooms were quickly filled two to a room by men in a hurry to feel solid earth under their feet for a few days. They were willing to pay an additional twenty-five cents for bath water.

The subject of going to Sutter's Fort did not arise again until Susanna received another letter from Henderson Cox three weeks later. It was dated October 15, 1847.

> *Dear Miss Thayer,*
>
> *Mr. Rainey and I have begun working on the gristmill for Mr. Sutter. He is paying us one dollar and fifty cents each day. Many of the other battalion members have gone up to Culloomah to work on the sawmill. They receive nearly two dollars a day because the weather is colder up there and they must prepare all their own meals. Mr. Sutter is always in need of more help and is hoping to encourage some women to come here and work in his bakery. He said he would pay any woman working for him a dollar a day. I send my best regards to you, and Mr. Rainey sends his to Miss O'Neil.*
>
> *Your friend,*
> *Henderson Cox*

Susanna's response to him was full of news about the return of Sam Brannan after his talk with Brigham Young.

Dear Mr. Henderson,

Things here are very different now than they were before Sam Brannan went to talk with Brigham Young. He was greatly dissatisfied with Brother Brigham's response, as President Young could not be convinced to bring the Saints to Alta California. Mr. Brannan returned to San Francisco on September 17 and is telling everyone that Brigham is a fool. He has also been saying that the Saints will never grow a good crop in the Great Salt Lake Valley because it's too cold and the soil is poor. Most of us have noticed that he has shown a lessening of enthusiasm for his church responsibilities since his return, not even attending Sabbath meetings since he got back. It is whispered by some that Elder Brannan is a good Mormon only as long as it pays. Elder Amasa Lyman arrived from the Valley on instructions from Brigham Young to collect the tithing of the Saints. I've heard some say that Brannan refused to meet with him while he was here. I'm glad to hear of your success there. I will await your next letter.

Your friend,
Susanna Thayer

She deliberately made no reference to the possibility of relocating to Sutter's Fort, as she hesitated to face the unknown again when the known was as comfortable as the post she and Jane shared at the hotel, but she walked almost every day to Mr. Garcia's store in the hope that another letter might be waiting.

In response to Jane's teasing, she responded, "I must admit that I've been hoping for another letter from Mr. Cox, but though there hasn't been a letter in the last little while, my little visits to the store have produced another blessing. I've met William and Melissa Coray. They were part of the battalion. She is the only woman who traveled the entire distance. From what she has told me, it must have been a terrible journey. She gave birth to a baby boy in Monterey, but he died a few weeks later.

"Right now, they're living in a room behind Mr. Garcia's store. It's the only place they could find. Mr. Coray bought a freight wagon in Monterey with his army pay, and he keeps his animals in the stable behind the store." She looked up at Jane and added, "I've invited her to come up to the hotel and have lunch with us sometime when her husband is delivering a load of freight and she's alone, but frankly, I'll be surprised if she does, as she usually travels with him."

***

The announcement was made at Sabbath meeting on the first Sunday of December that Addison Pratt had been called as the president of the newly organized San Francisco branch of the Church.

When the two young women returned to the hotel, Susanna removed the sign on the front door that told potential guests that the hotel was not receiving guests until Sabbath meeting was over.

"Jane, I thought that Elder Brannan was the president of the San Francisco Saints. I wonder why President Young would send Elder Pratt to fill the post."

Jane removed her shawl and hung it on the hook behind the registration desk. "Do you think it has something to do with the fact that Elder Brannan refused to meet with Amasa Lyman when he came to collect the tithing of the Saints?"

"I suppose it might." From that time forward, Elder Pratt conducted two meetings every Sunday, one in the morning and another in the early evening. The mission priest seemed to have no objection to squeezing Mass in between the Mormon meetings.

***

To make the Christmas season even more memorable than the previous one had been, Jane and Alberto chose to announce their engagement on Christmas Eve. The festivities celebrated the coming nuptials for three days, even though the wedding would not take place for more than a month.

While Jane glowed with happiness, Susanna was feeling confused. She was genuinely happy for her friend, but she wasn't sure how to deal with the deep sense of personal loss.

Late on the evening of January third, after the celebrations for the new year had finally quieted, Susanna sat in the little courtyard of the hotel where the guests often ate. Only two hotel guests remained and they would soon be gone. She sadly studied the stars while she mentally debated the effect Jane's marriage would have on her future. *I think I shall be going to Sutter's Fort after all. The room Jane and I have used will become their room.*

She watched as the moon rose into view above the steep hills, a golden sliver on a star-spangled background of deep indigo. When the evening air grew cool, she rose and quietly made her way into the main room of the hotel, where Jane and Alberto were sitting in the corner, behind a small potted palm that Susanna had been nurturing. She could hear Jane giggle as he helped her with her Spanish and played with her hair. His fascination with her red hair was evident to anyone who knew the two of them.

Without disturbing them, Susanna threw on a shawl and then picked up a sheet of paper, pen, and bottle of ink in one hand and a lighted oil lamp in the other. She returned to the courtyard, where she began another letter to Sonny.

January 3rd, 1848

Dear Mr. Henderson,

It seems that I will be testing Mr. Sutter's willingness to hire women. I am planning to travel to the fort sometime in early February. My new friends, William and Melissa Coray, usually drive his freight wagon to the fort early each month, so I will obtain a ride with them. Jane will be getting married the first day of February, and it will be an appropriate time for me to look for a new place to start my life again. I send my regrets to your friend Mr. Rainey if his feelings for Jane were deep. I hope our paths will cross when I am settled there.

Your friend,
Susanna Thayer

***

"Susanna, we're going to be married twice. We will be married by Elder Pratt and you will be my maid of honor. Then we will go to the mission and be married by the priest, to keep Alberto's father happy. Aren't you happy for me?" Jane was radiant with happiness.

"Of course I'm happy for you, Jane." Susanna gave her a hug, but she was still aware of that nagging sense of personal loss.

Alberto's father insisted that the celebration fiesta last three days, as any wedding for a prosperous Spanish family was expected to do. The bride and groom were repeatedly fed and kept apart during the three days and nights. When they were finally allowed to leave the festivities, Susanna had arranged for them to have the largest room on the second floor of the hotel, which had been decorated as a honeymoon suite. Meals were sent to the room for two days, and the hotel help paused at the door several times a day to listen for Jane's giggles.

In all the excitement of the wedding, few acquaintances of the bride or groom took note of the small article on the second page of the February edition of the *California Star* announcing the discovery of gold on the American River. It was, after all, just a little piece inserted at the last minute by Brannan's editor, Ed Kembel, simply to fill space.

Chapter Twenty-Five

When the newlyweds finally left the room late on the morning of the third day, they found Susanna sitting in the lobby with her carpetbag, waiting for William Coray to bring his wagon to the hotel. She had given much thought to just how she should take leave of her friend without injuring her happiness. She had settled on the simplest way, a long letter waiting in the little room behind the registration desk and a quick, personal good-bye.

"Susanna, what are you doing? Why is your carpetbag packed? You're not leaving, are you?" Jane's questions came fast as she ran to her friend.

"No, no, Señorita Susanna, you must not go. A wedding brings friends together. It must not separate them." Alberto's sincerity was evident in his concerned expression.

Susanna rose and gave Jane a long embrace. She stepped back and looked earnestly into her face. "My friend, I am happy for you both, but now the little room behind the desk is your room. The two of you will make a good life here, and I must do the same but somewhere else. I'm going to Sutter's Fort, where there will be work for me—and maybe I will see Mr. Cox there." She gave her friend a weak little smile. "Don't be concerned for me. I will write to you, and you must write to me—and you must come to the fort to visit me." She brightened. "Perhaps Sam Brannan will build another hotel near the fort and permit the two of you to manage it for him, so this isn't really good-bye—just a 'see you after awhile.'" The sound of a large wagon could be heard. "Brother Coray is here. It's time for me to go."

Susanna gave Jane another hug before climbing onto the second seat behind Melissa. The reins were slapped against the horses' rumps and the wagon rolled away. From where she sat, Susanna turned and waved at

Jane and Alberto. Emotion had colored Jane's face with red splotches as her tears fell unheeded. She turned and buried her face in her husband's shoulder. Susanna turned away and wiped a tear as the wagon took her down the road to another open and unknown door.

***

As Brother Coray pulled the horses to a halt at the fort the next afternoon, Susanna noticed that the board on the front of the mercantile store where they had stopped read, "C. C. Smith and Company."

Brother Coray jumped down from the wagon, and as he threw back the tarp that covered the things in the wagon bed, he called out to Susanna, "You might want to talk to Brother Smith about employment. I hear that Sam Brannan just bought half of Brother Smith's establishment and is planning on expanding it. I think you'll be paid as much here as if you work for Sutter."

***

He was right. Susanna boarded in a home operated by a *Brooklyn* passenger, William Glover and his wife. She was paid a dollar a day, an excellent salary when she remembered her pay at the mill. In the beginning, the work was not demanding, but that began to change when Brannan bought up every shovel in San Francisco and the Sacramento Valley. He knew something was coming that few others seemed to recognize.

Sonny left his work at the gristmill and came to the fort a few days after he received Susanna's January letter. He waited until she and Charles Smith were closing the store, nervously shifting his weight from one foot to the other, half hidden by a large pile of tools. He had not drawn attention to his presence, so Susanna was startled when he stepped up to her and spoke.

"Miss Thayer," he cleared his throat, "it's me, Sonny Cox."

She turned from where she was straightening the baking soda, salt, and flour on the shelf behind the counter. "Oh, Mr. Cox, how nice to see you." Her smile lit her whole face.

"I know you must be tired after working all day, but if you will allow me, I would like to take you to supper."

"That would be wonderful, but I don't know anywhere we could go that would be a proper place to eat except the boarding house where I'm living. Mr. Glover only charges twenty-five cents a meal for anyone who isn't boarding there."

"That'll do just fine." His pleased smile was broad and infectious.

As they walked toward Glover's boarding house in the mild darkness, she couldn't stop her questions. "What kind of work have you been doing? Where have you been working? I had hoped for another letter after the one arrived in October, but I guess . . ."

He interrupted her. "I've been working at Sutter's gristmill about five miles up the river from here with some other members of the Battalion. It's hard work and I didn't get much chance to write letters. I was hoping that you might be here at the fort. I just got your letter last week. I've been asking around for you all day."

"I'm glad you did. It's good to see you. It's been busy here, but it's also been lonely."

"I know what you mean. Dave Rainey was sad for a couple of days when I told him that your friend got married, but I told him that he shouldn't be surprised. He didn't write to her. What's a girl gonna do if she never hears from a man who wants to be her beau?"

After supper with the other boarders at the long table in the dining room of the Glover boarding house, they sat together on the steps of the front porch of the unpainted, two-story frame house and talked into the night.

"Mr. Brannan's having all sorts of equipment shipped in," Susanna told Sonny. "He goes to San Francisco every two weeks and has William Coray bring back loads of things in his freight wagon that have come by ship."

He nodded and studied her face as they talked in the moonlight. "There's a rumor goin' around that there's gonna be a whole bunch of folks coming here to dig for gold. Some of the men who have come down from Culloomah have gold dust and nuggets sometimes worth twenty or thirty dollars. They say they can just pick it up in the sluice of Sutter's sawmill."

Susanna nodded. "Charles Smith taught me to weigh it so we can estimate its value when they come in to buy supplies because so many of the men use it for money. Frankly, I'm of the opinion that there couldn't be much more of it to be found since the men said they just picked it up off the ground."

Sonny laughed as he disagreed. "I think this could be a big gold strike. Brannan's counting on it. It might bring in hundreds or maybe thousands of folks looking to strike it rich." He stopped abruptly and said very seriously, "I'm gonna join Dave and take my turn at lookin' for gold. Brother Brigham wrote to the battalion members and told us to join the

Saints in the Salt Lake Valley this summer when the weather will permit travel over the Sierra Nevada Mountains and to bring as much gold or money with us as we can. I'm gonna join some of my buddies and dig for gold out on an island in the American River where the north and south forks join. Gold was lately found there. It'll take me longer to get back to the fort to buy supplies each week, as it's about ten or fifteen miles farther upriver than the gristmill, but I think it might be worth it."

"But you will still come back to the fort each week?" She wanted confirmation that his new plans would not end their friendship.

"Yeah, after all, a man's got to have enough food to eat—and some uplifting female company, if it's available."

She smiled in relief. "Do you have the equipment you will need—a shovel and pickaxe, things like that?"

He nodded in the faint spill of light that came through the windows of the front door from the oil lamp in the Glovers' entry hall. "Dave bought that stuff when it didn't cost so much. He's letting me use some of it." He threw his head back and laughed heartily. "Maybe I'll come back next Saturday night a rich man."

"Even if you're not a rich man by next week, I hope you'll come back." In the moonlight, Susanna could feel the color in her face rise. *How could I be so forward?*

At ten that evening, Mr. Glover came out of the big house. "I guess I need to tell you folks that my boarders are expected to be in their rooms by this time, so Mr. Cox will have to take his leave."

Sonny stood and nodded at Mr. Glover before he offered his hand to assist Susanna to stand. "Miss Thayer, I'll be purchasing supplies in the morning before I ride back to the mill. If it's acceptable to you, I'll take my leave of you then."

"Of course, Mr. Cox. I'll watch for you." As he sauntered off toward the stable where he kept his mare, Susanna stood and watched him, despite Mr. Glover's apparent impatience. *For the first time since Jane's wedding, I really enjoyed myself. He's a good man. I hope he comes to buy supplies often.* She entered the house with a light step.

***

On the front page of the April first edition of the *Star,* Brannan announced in bold type that gold had been found in the American River. He hired riders to take the papers east and paid them for every copy they delivered to a new city. Some of the men carried more than five hundred papers. They would be paid when they returned with a report and evidence of delivery.

By the end of the month, the *Star* was being quoted in the newspapers in the large cities of the East, and a steady stream of men looking for an easy fortune had begun to arrive like the water rushing down the sluice of the sawmill in Coloma.

It was rumored that Brannan had ridden through San Francisco yelling at the top of his lungs, "Gold, gold found in the American River! Gold in the Sacramento Valley!" in an attempt to stir up interest and generate business for the store he jointly owned with Charles Smith at the fort and for the hotel he was building there. It worked, and within the week, San Francisco was nearly empty. It had suddenly shrunk back to the obscure outpost it had been when the *Brooklyn* had arrived.

Late each Saturday afternoon, Henderson Cox saddled his mare and rode into the fort, ostensibly to purchase supplies, but really to spend some time with Susanna. As they sat on the front stairs of the boarding house porch on the third weekend he called, she asked, "Where do you stay when you're here, Mr. Cox?"

"I throw a blanket over the hay in the stable and sleep there. Nobody seems to mind. That way I can save some money and still attend Sabbath meeting with you."

"I'm flattered, Mr. Cox." She smiled. *That explains the stable fragrance he brings with him on Sunday.*

As they talked, their conversation covered many subjects. Eventually, as the evening grew late, it returned to their present situation, and she told him, "Mr. Brannan bought out Charles Smith. He wants to charge more for everything than Mr. Smith felt was right. Everyone has been calling Mr. Smith's store 'Sam Brannan's shirttail store' ever since they found out he bought a half interest in it, so now he can put his name on it." She changed position where she was sitting on the stoop and turned to look directly at Sonny. "Do you know, he told me that the shovels are now to be sold for fifty dollars? He only paid two dollars for them a month ago. Everything in the store is increasing in price so fast that I think it's unethical."

Sonny laughed heartily. "I suspect that Brannan will let the miners do all the work, and he will reap the benefits. I shouldn't be surprised if Brannan is the first millionaire in California, and he won't have lifted a finger to dig for gold."

The conversation changed direction. "Sonny, if you do strike it rich, what will you do with the gold you'll take back to the Salt Lake Valley?"

He was quiet for a minute, but in the moonlight, Susanna could see a slowly growing smile on his face. He looked out into the darkness. "I plan to build me a house and a harness shop with a corral out back where I can break horses and sell 'em. I'm good at that sort of thing."

She was about to respond when Mr. Glover stepped out onto the porch. "This is the first time I have ever seen my front porch used for courtin'. Young man, can't you find a more suitable place?"

"Nope." Sonny grinned up at the landlord in the darkness.

Susanna smiled. *So this is courting. How comfortable it feels. Not as refined as when Jonathan . . .* She pulled the blind of her mind down quickly, shutting out that thought.

As Sonny walked toward the livery stable whistling contentedly, Susanna looked at the sky and thought to herself, *How bright the stars have suddenly become. Why haven't I noticed how breathtaking the sky is here and how filled it is with God's jewels? Is the sky as beautiful over Boston tonight, Mother? I hope so.*

***

In the soft air of mid-April, as they sat on the stoop in the darkness, Sonny chewed on a piece of straw and mused, "There's more'n a hundred men diggin' out on Mormon Island now. Each one of us has a claim about five yards square and marked with tent pegs. That way, there's no disagreement over who's diggin' on whose claim. I hear that Brannan is going to open another store and a hotel on the island right away." He paused. "I was wonderin' if you could ask him if you could work in the store there. Then I could see you every night." He hurriedly added so as not to sound too bold, "Nearly everyone out there right now is a battalion member, so there's regular church meetin's—that's why everybody calls it Mormon Island." He stopped and almost held his breath while he waited for her response.

She hesitatingly answered, "I could ask if that would be acceptable to him."

Sonny exhaled. "That's great. It would be grand if I could see you every night."

Mr. Glover had stepped out on the porch, so Sonny stood. "I'll come by at nine in the morning for church, like usual." His hat went on, and he moseyed away, whistling as he went.

Why does ten o'clock come so quickly when Sonny's here? Susanna asked herself.

***

But plans changed quickly. When he rode to the fort on Saturday a week later, Sonny found her at the store a few minutes before closing time and talked to her excitedly as she straightened the merchandise on the store shelves after the front door had been locked.

"Some of the men have decided that we need to be heading out for the Valley. Things here are changing too fast. The kind of men coming in to dig for gold is different than before. Just a month ago, we could leave our gold dust sitting in a pan outside our tents and nobody would touch it, but now we have to sleep with a rifle by our bedroll. Bad times are comin' and most the battalion members know it."

Susanna motioned him to follow her to the rear of the store, where they could go out the back door. "What are you going to do?" she asked as she locked the door behind them. In the moonlight, Sonny could see the concern written on her face.

"Some of us are heading out for the Valley right away. We elected David Browett to be captain. We hope to establish a shorter, better route than over the Truckee River. There's nine of us, and we plan to leave next weekend, the first of May."

"Oh," was all Susanna could trust herself to say for a moment. She swallowed and finally added, "Isn't it too early to cross the mountains? Won't it be dangerous?"

He straightened a little, pulling the buckskin shirt tighter against his thin shoulders. "I can't pretend I ain't worried, but we won't know until we try." Then he waxed enthusiastic. "But if we're successful, it will make it much easier for all of you who will follow us to the Salt Lake Valley."

"The first of May—that's only a few days away." Her voice was almost a whisper.

"Yeah, in the morning, I'll need to get my supplies. I'll write to you from the Valley as soon as we get there." Without waiting for Mr. Glover to step out, he stood. "I promise I won't forget—and you write me back." He hurried away toward the stable.

The next morning the store was so crowded and busy that Susanna couldn't get across the floor to help Sonny with his purchases. All she could do was wave at him as he put his big sack of supplies over his shoulder. He waved back and was out of the door before she could speak to him. Her vision suddenly dimmed with unshed tears. She wiped them away quickly, in the hope that no one saw them. *I did so want to have the chance to talk with him before he left.*

Six days later, she was amazed and excited to see him waiting for her as she closed up the store.

Her heart skipped a beat and then raced for a moment. She couldn't smother her pleasure at seeing him. "What are you doing here? I thought you'd be well on your way across the Sierra Nevada Mountains by now." She was so happy to see him that it took all her self-discipline to keep from throwing her arms around his neck.

"So did we." They walked together toward the boarding house in the pleasant evening air. "We got three days up into the mountains and discovered that the snow was too deep to get through the passes, so we came back. We'll have to wait until well into June to try again."

"I would say that I'm sorry that you were unsuccessful, but it would be a lie. Now I can put off worrying about you until you leave again." They both laughed and he took her hand without self-consciousness.

Sonny returned to Mormon Island and continued digging for gold. In early June, he spent some of the gold he had found to purchase a second pack mule and another large store of supplies.

As they sat on the porch steps on Saturday night, he explained, "I'm anxious to get headed for the Valley, so I'm going to be leaving ahead of most of the other men. Captain Browett, Ezra Allen, and I are gonna set out on a scouting tour to see if we can mark the way for the others. It'll speed things up for everybody else. There's a group that's going to gather at Pleasant Valley, and they'll come close behind us."

Why is he in such a hurry to get going again? She couldn't ask all the other questions that came flooding into her mind or lay out the fears that churned in her stomach. She tried to smile at him, but her fears made her face stiff. "Where is Pleasant Valley?"

"It's about fifty miles east of the fort, and it looks like a good spot for the wagons to gather."

"You seem to be a big hurry. Is there a special reason?" Susanna's composure was weakening.

"Yeah, I figure that if I get to the Valley ahead of all the other Saints that'll be headed east from here, with the gold I have I can get started on a homestead and a cabin. I bought wheat and corn to plant as soon as I get there." He stopped and took her hands in his. "You see, I want to start a family as soon as I can, and I want you to be my wife."

Susanna's breath stopped for a moment.

He continued, his words almost tumbling over each other as he expressed what he had been thinking for several weeks. "When we met in San Francisco, I knew I liked you—a lot—but when the battalion men left to march up to Sutter's Fort, I figured I wouldn't see you again and there wasn't anything I could do about it. But when you came here and went to work in Brannan's store, I . . ." He dropped his head and seemed to be trying to order his thoughts. "I know we haven't known each other for very long, but I . . . I love you, Susanna, and I'm asking you to marry me as soon as you can get to the Valley. I knew you were special from the first time we met. I want to spend the rest of my life with you, and the sooner I get to the Valley, the better prepared I'll be to get married when you get there." He stopped and waited for her answer.

She closed her eyes and paused so long that he feared she was going to tell him that he had overreached, but she took a slow, deep breath and looked directly at him. "Yes, Mr. Cox. I'll marry you." Her heart had begun to pound, and she could feel her pulse in her temples. *I think my heart has been asleep since I left Boston. This is a wonderful feeling.*

"Then I think it would be acceptable for you to call me Sonny."

She laughed, a golden peal of pleasure. He pulled her to her feet. She threw her arms around his neck, and even the presence of Mr. Glover when he stepped out of the boarding house did not dampen their enthusiasm as Sonny lifted her off the ground. He turned her around and around before putting her down. He looked at the landlord. "We're going to be married. Will you congratulate us?"

Mr. Glover put out his hand. "'Bout time, I say. But now it's time for your bride to wish you a pleasant good night and to come inside. It's ten o'clock."

Sonny pulled her to him. "I'll be back again before I leave for the Valley. I'll tell you good-bye then."

***

That night, Susanna fell asleep thinking about the way Sonny's cheeks lifted and his eyes crinkled whenever he grinned. *And he loves me. Surely he won't leave me to marry someone else.*

Part Four
Journey to the Valley

Chapter Twenty-Six

On the nineteenth of June, Sonny returned to the store at closing time and asked Susanna to walk with him. "I want you to join the wagons that'll be gathering in Pleasant Valley and be ready to go east to the Salt Lake Valley with them. My uncle, John Cox, is going to be in that group, and he said you could ride in his wagon, and he would keep an eye out for you, if you could do some cookin' for him." He paused to watch her reaction to his request.

"When would they be leaving?"

"About the first of July."

"How would I get to Pleasant Valley?"

"Uncle John will come and get you. I'm just not sure exactly when. He's on Mormon Island right now."

"Would it be proper for me to travel with him unchaperoned?" Her forehead was wrinkled with concern.

He shook his head. "You don't have anything to worry about with Uncle John. He's a good man. He's got a wife and family in the Valley. Nobody will think ill of you."

"Then I'll be ready when he comes." Her face brightened. She was nearly overwhelmed with the sweeping realization that she had stepped through another open door and it would lead to a good life with Sonny. Her heart beat fast as she turned and faced him, her hands in his. "We'll have a good life together, Sonny. We'll have a big family and live with the Saints in Zion, and we'll have our own home. This is what I want—to have the gospel, a home, and a good husband and family in Zion."

He put his arms around her, and there in the street, for all to see, he gave her a gentle kiss. "Then we want the same thing."

He pulled a pouch filled with gold dust on a leather thong from his neck and pressed it into her hand. "You might need this. I've enough to get me there and get me settled. I want you to keep this for us." He looked into her eyes as if to impress them in his mind forever. "I know we haven't known each other very long, but this feels so right. Now I know why the Lord sent me with the battalion on that long march. It was to find you, and finding you made it all worthwhile." He grew quiet. "I'm going to miss you, Susanna. This is good-bye for now, and if we don't meet up on the trail, I'll be waiting for you in the Valley. Keep that thought in your heart."

She nodded. "I'll miss you too, Sonny." Her voice choked off, a tear traced a path down her cheek, and her heart began to pound against her chest as she realized that it would be months before she saw him again. As if to hold him there awhile longer, she put her hand on his arm. "You may be up to some high adventure. I will want a full accounting of it when I see you again." Her face reflected her anxiety.

He gave her another quick peck on the lips, and then it lengthened into a kiss of such passion that they were both startled. Susanna returned the kiss, ignoring the stares and grins of the men on the street. "And you shall have it." To avoid letting her see how hard the good-bye had become, he hurried away, rushing into the future. She watched the line of his back until he was out of sight, feeling a sudden emptiness. She bit her lip, determined to be as brave as she felt he would want her to be. *Separations are hard, but reunions are wonderful,* she reminded herself.

Clutching the pouch in her hand, she hurried to the boarding house filled with a confused mixture of feelings churning inside—feelings of nervous anticipation of the hardships of the journey and of excitement at what waited at its end. *He's a good man and we'll make each other happy. Soon I will have a haven, a haven shared with Sonny.* In her mind, she had already begun to arrange the furniture in the home they would share. That evening, she wrote her friend.

> *Dear Jane,*
>
> *I have happy news! Mr. Cox has proposed and I have accepted his proposal. Now I understand your happiness. We are going to be married in the Salt Lake Valley, but for now, he is going to go ahead of the wagon company as a scout. We hope to meet on the trail. We will be so happy and*

I promise to name our first daughter after you. Please keep me in your prayers and wish me happiness.

Your friend,
Susanna Thayer

On June twenty-first, John Cox tied his team of oxen to the hitching post in front of the store and entered with a long stride. Even from across the crowded aisles, Susanna recognized the blond hair and blue eyes so much like those of Sonny. She hurried through the crowd and offered her hand. "Are you looking for me? I'm Susanna Thayer."

"Yes, ma'am. I'm here to take you and your things to Pleasant Valley. Are you ready to leave?"

"Yes, sir. I can have my bag packed in about ten minutes, and I have warned the store manager that I might be leaving soon. Let me tell him the time has arrived." She pulled off her wide, white apron and hung it near the counter. She spoke to a gray-haired man, whose countenance became very unhappy, and hurried back to Cox. "I'm ready to go. Do you need to buy supplies right now, or can you take me over to the boarding house to get my things?" she asked as she excitedly followed him out of the store.

He pointed at the wagon."I got my supplies from Sutter. He doesn't seem set on scalping his customers the way Brannan does." He helped her into the wagon and turned the team in the direction she pointed.

At the boarding house, she explained to Mr. Glover that she was leaving, and as he took the seventy-five cents she owed, he told her, "I wish you well, Miss Thayer. You're a fine young lady, and that young man is getting a fine wife."

She impulsively gave him a quick hug and then hurried out to the wagon where Cox was waiting. He helped her climb onto the seat, and then he swung up and onto the other end of it in one smooth movement. He called out the commands to the oxen and the wagon lurched forward. Susanna grabbed the seat to steady herself.

The plodding oxen took four days to reach Pleasant Valley. John Cox slept under the wagon each night, and she made a lumpy place to sleep among his supplies in the wagon bed. When she asked about Sonny, he responded, "Sonny told me he would be leaving camp with Captain Browett and Ezra Allen towards the end of the month. Maybe we'll see him before they leave to scout out a way to the Valley. If we don't, then somewhere along the way, we'll most likely meet up with them."

When they arrived in Pleasant Valley on June twenty-fifth, Susanna was disappointed to learn that Sonny and the two other men had left the day before, but she was quickly cheered by the discovery that William and Melissa Coray were there. The women gave one another a great hug, pleased to know that they would have company on the journey. As they made supper that evening, a little black dog sniffed at their skirt hems.

"Melissa, look at this little dog. Does he belong to someone here in camp?"

Melissa shook her head. "When we arrived yesterday, I asked if anyone claimed him. It seems that he belongs to all of us. No one knows where he came from, but many of us have been feeding him the few scraps we have after each meal."

"Does he have a name?"

"Brother Muir, whose family came from Scotland, insists that he is a Scottie dog. They call him Scottie."

"What does he answer to?"

"He answers to food." Melissa reached down and patted his head.

Thereafter, Susanna saved him a portion of her supper each evening, and he quickly became her constant companion. In the evenings, when they sat around the fire, he would lie at her feet.

Brother Cox noticed. "Seems you have found a friend in that pup, Sister Thayer."

"I think so too, Brother Cox. He is a gentle, uncomplaining companion."

"I think you will find Sonny to be that kind of a husband." Susanna smiled to herself at his comment. *After all, John Cox would surely know his nephew's temperament.*

The battalion members had been given "pay in kind" from Sutter during the previous few weeks, which had included wild horses, mules, cattle, oxen, wagons, plows, picks, shovels, seeds, plant cuttings, and food supplies. Additionally, they had purchased two small brass cannons with gold dust; one was a four-pounder and the other a six-pounder.

"Brother Cox, what are the cannons for?" Susanna asked curiously.

"Perhaps they won't be particularly useful in fighting Indians, but they are impressive," he responded with a chuckle. "They have a certain scare value."

Eight men in the company were appointed to superintend the stock, and each night the animals were herded into a large corral made of recently felled timber. They had nearly a hundred fifty horned stock and a like number of horses. As they prepared supper, Susanna commented to Melissa, "If this valley was part of Zion, I would be content to stay right here forever."

But it wasn't, and on July third, sixteen wagons, drawn mainly by oxen, were lined up and headed toward the towering mountains to the east. The group of thirty-seven reached a green meadow three days later and called it Sly Park, after James Sly, who had ridden ahead and located it. They stopped there for six days while they waited, hoping the three scouts would return. The animals grazed and the men speculated about what might have delayed them. Whenever Susanna came within hearing, the conversations would stop. She knew the men were sharing their worries. Their unspoken fears made her anxious. While they waited there, John Eager from the *Brooklyn* and a very sick Elder Addison Pratt joined them.

Seeing how ill Pratt looked, Susanna approached him. "Elder Pratt, would you like me to fix you something to drink that might help your fever and settle your stomach?" He nodded, nearly too weak to speak. She spent the next hour boiling and straining elm bark to produce a medicinal tea. Pratt slept better than night.

In the morning, Cox congratulated her. "It seems we have a medicine woman with us. Where did you learn your skills, Susanna?"

"The ship's surgeon took me under his wing on that long sea voyage. He was kind enough to show me how to use certain natural herbs for healing."

Thereafter, Susanna was often called upon to treat stomach ailments and fever. "I fervently hope there are elm and willow trees along our way," she whispered to Melissa, "or my nursing skills will not be of much help."

From the green meadows of their camp, they began the ascent to the top of a ridge, and each day thereafter, four men were sent out ahead of the others to cut brush and roll large stones out of the way. When Cox took his first turn with the clearing crew, Susanna had to drive the ox team for the day.

He gave her brief instructions. "If they're laying down, tell them, 'Get up.' Then tell them firmly, 'Go,' and they should obey. Remember, you've got to show them in your voice that you mean it."

As a test, she called firmly, "Go." To her surprise, the great beasts leaned into the yoke, and the wagon began to move.

Cox walked beside the moving team as he completed his instructions. "To get them to go right, give them a 'Gee.' To turn them left, call out, 'Haw,' and about fifty feet before you want them to stop, call out, 'Whoa.' Give them some distance to get the wagon halted. They're well trained, so they shouldn't give you any trouble." With that limited set of instructions, he rode out of camp on a borrowed horse to catch up with the other men.

The wagons were able to make about ten miles a day. The humans and animals labored along a high ridge, where the road grew steadily worse, until they reached Leek Springs on July sixteenth. In the absence of Captain Browett, the company reorganized, electing Jonathan Holmes president, and Samuel Thompson captain. The reorganization was a quiet admission that something had happened to the three scouts. Most of the men avoided speaking of their fears in Susanna's presence, but she could not be insulated from the nervous worry that infected the camp.

Finally, she spoke of her fears. "Brother Cox, are there hostile Indians in these mountains?"

"Yes, Susanna. I won't lie to you. There are some fierce but primitive tribes of Digger Indians living here that have no love for white men."

"Do you think something has happened to Sonny and the other two men?"

"There's no way of knowin' at this point. Just keep a prayer in your heart."

She asked no more but she slept little that night.

The next morning, four men went ahead of the wagons and cleared several more miles of trail. They came upon a spring and the remnants of a dead campfire. Near it was a large mound that, from the moist soil, looked very recent. It had the appearance of a large, shallow grave.

When the four men returned to the camp, they quietly reported to Captain Thompson. "We spotted several Indians moving through the trees on our way back to camp. One was wearing a vest belonging to Jim Allen. We recognized it by the fringe on it. The Indians got away in the trees. We fear we will find our friends in that great mound at that camp site." They kept their backs to the women who were making supper near the wagons. Susanna noticed their whispered conversation.

"Brother Cox, why are the men whispering?" she asked quietly.

"Just be patient, Susanna, and we'll be told everything soon enough."

In the morning, the oxen struggled to drag the wagons up the steep grade the men had cleared the previous day. The group paused while Jonathan Holmes's wagon was repaired. They had covered a hard six miles by late afternoon when they reached the clearing in the forest where the four men had found the large mound of dirt a day earlier. The wagons halted, and the men climbed down. Cox had driven his team to the far side of the clearing so Susanna did not see the mound that some of the men went to investigate. She started to build a fire to begin preparing supper.

After William Coray spoke to several men, he returned to his wagon and searched for a spade. "Go get Susanna and keep her here," he said tersely to his wife.

While some of the men were stringing the rope line where the horses would be tethered, Melissa came to John Cox's wagon and insisted that Susanna come back with her to the Coray wagon. Susanna's heart grew cold.

The men gathered on the far side of the circle of wagons and began to dig. "What are they doing, Melissa? Why won't anyone tell me what's going on?" Susanna's voice was filled with quiet panic.

"William says it will be better for you to stay here with me." Melissa's voice was firm.

After about fifteen minutes, a combination of cries rose from the men. The shouting took on an edge, a frightening sharpness.

"It's them!"

"It had to be the Indians we saw."

"In the name of heaven, what did they do to them?"

"What will we tell Jim Allen's wife?" The voices came fast upon each other and were full of pain.

Susanna climbed down from the wagon seat, against Melissa's objections. "Susanna, stay here. Don't go over there!" But Susanna had heard enough that she had to know what had happened. As she hurried across the clearing, Melissa called out, "William, stop her!"

Coray rushed to meet Susanna and caught her by the waist. "Susanna, don't go. You don't want to remember him that way." His grip was like a steel band.

She looked up into his face. "Is it so very bad?" Her voice was a whisper.

"Yes, it's bad. You must stay with Melissa. After we rebury them, we will tell you what must have happened. Will you go back to Melissa?"

She looked into his eyes, and finally her stiff body relaxed with a sense of inevitable hopelessness. She turned and walked very slowly back to the Coray wagon, almost like a ghost. There she sat on the ground and drew her knees up. She put her face against her knees and cried like a motherless child.

Melissa took a quilt from the wagon and wrapped her in it, patting her shoulder in an attempt to console her. "He's in God's hands now, Susanna. It's over and done. He's in God's hands now," she repeated.

Only a few of the men ate any supper. Melissa insisted that Susanna sit on a large log that had been pulled up near the fire to help warm her. She shook as though she had been chilled in a winter snowstorm despite the quilt around her shoulders. When her friend brought her a tin plate of stew and insisted that she eat, the food was ashes on her tongue. She set it on the ground for Scottie, who had been sitting at her feet watching her face.

She asked Brother Coray when he finally sat down on the log near her, "Tell me what happened. I need to know."

"It looks like they were surrounded by the Indians and killed. The guard may have been so tired that he fell asleep—or maybe they didn't post a guard. The arrows were still in their bodies. The Indians stole their horses, clothing, supplies, guns—everything. We found Ezra Allen's pouch of gold dust lying under a bush. It must have fallen off when they were fighting with the Indians. We know it was his. Some of us watched him make it."

Unconsciously, her hand went to the pouch that Sonny had given her. It hung around her neck on a cord under her dress. "Did they suffer? Were they tortured?" Her words were hardly audible.

"No, it must have been swift." The other men who heard their conversation doubted that the fight had been swift or the deaths easy, but they understood that Susanna did not need to know any more details.

"Who buried them?" Susanna's voice was so quiet that William had to lean toward her to catch the words.

"The Indians often bury their victims to try to hide what they've done. The grave was hastily made."

The members of the company gathered while Brother Holmes gave a prayer over the large mound. Susanna stood unmoving as though she were in a dream, filled with a curious numbness and a burning in her eyes that felt like someone else's tears as she listened to him ask a benediction on the souls of the men and comfort for their loved ones.

Shortly after the prayer was finished, the horses began to whinny with nervousness and the cattle bellowed and churned. An earsplitting whistle from one of the guards pierced the air, and several men called out, "Indians."

The cattle began to push their way down the mountainside, working themselves into a frenzy. Thompson yelled, "Boys, limber up one of the cannons and let her speak. If we don't scare off those Indians, they'll drive off the whole herd." It took nearly three minutes to load the cannon, but when it was fired, the roar echoed through the trees and off the rocky mountainsides. "That ought to put some real fear in them. Now get the stock rounded up before we lose it all."

Melissa took Susanna by the hand and led her to the Coray wagon like a child. By nine o'clock, about half of the animals had been located and driven back toward camp. No Indians were seen.

"Brother Bigler, you and Jim Sly will stand guard until midnight. Then Coray and I will take over," Captain Thompson called out as others prepared for the night.

When Coray started to climb into the wagon bed, Melissa said quietly but firmly, "I put your quilt on the ground under the wagon, William. Susanna will be sleeping by me tonight. I'm sure you understand." He nodded but said nothing.

That night, after Susanna drifted off to sleep, Melissa heard her murmur, "Gone, everyone's gone . . . Oh, Sonny, why now?"

All Melissa could do was put her arms around the grieving young woman and whisper to her, "God is over all. Everything will be all right." Susanna hardly knew Melissa was there.

In the morning, most of the men were sent to locate the missing stock while a smaller group worked on a rock wall around the gravesite, filling it to the top with soil. Then they placed large rocks and a few small boulders on the grave to protect it from the wolves. Finally, two of the men located a rounded stone that resembled a headstone to put at the head of the grave.

Susanna sat wrapped in the quilt near the fire with Scottie at her feet while they were busy completing the protective wall. Brother Wilford Hudson took his ax and chopped the bark away on one side of a large fir tree. She watched as he carved the bare wood. It took him an hour. When he had finished, she rose on weak legs and made her way over to see what he had written.

To the memory of Daniel Browett, Ezra H. Allen, Henderson Cox, who were supposed to have been murdered and buried by Indians on the night of the 27th of June 1848. She returned to sit on the log again, unmoving for most of the day.

When Melissa sat on the log next to her and put her arm around her shoulders, Susanna whispered, "I'm a widow before I ever was a wife."

All but three of the animals were found that morning. The day was spent repairing wagons. Again, Susanna sat on the log unmoving throughout the day and was unable to eat anything when a supper of venison was prepared.

That evening, Captain Thompson gave a short sermon to the company. "Well-intentioned choices made in innocence or ignorance cannot be separated from the consequences that may follow. These three good men did not deserve to die. Brother Browett's and Brother Allen's wives did not deserve to become widows. But the decision they made to separate themselves from the main body of the company left them vulnerable to the violence that came upon them. They were nobler than we knew and better than we dreamed. In their memory, this place will henceforth be called Tragedy Springs." Susanna's fists were clenched like stones, her grief so heavy that, had she fallen into a river, it would have swiftly drowned her.

That night she lay unmoving, staring at the wagon cover while Melissa's even breathing told her the woman was asleep. Questions filled her mind. *Where am I going, Heavenly Father? What waits for me in the Valley? Why do such terrible things happen to such good people? Is this gospel worth the death of these good men? We could have stayed in California and been married there. How I wish we had.*

A voice spoke to her. Was it Sonny's? Was it her father's? She couldn't tell. "He that loveth father or mother more than me is not worthy of me; and he that loveth son or daughter more than me is not worthy of me" . . . *or she that loveth a sweetheart more than me is not worthy of me . . . so I must be prepared to give up everything to follow Him.* She had her answers, but they weren't easy answers.

Chapter Twenty-Seven

In the morning, Susanna quietly gave Melissa a hug. "Thank you for your kindness during this dark time, but I'll be all right now. The Lord has granted me the strength to carry the burden He has given me. I'm going back to riding with and cooking for Brother Cox."

"If you're sure. . ." Melissa looked dubious.

"I'm sure." Her voice was firm, but her eyes were filled with sadness.

For the next several days, every man with the strength to do so worked on the road to the top of the mountain, hacking and digging a wider trail. From that vantage point, several small lakes in a high valley were spread at their feet. In some places on the trail, the snow was more than two feet deep, and on the protected sides of the ridges, some drifts were as much as fifteen feet deep. Most of the sunny hillsides were covered with wildflowers.

Henry Bigler picked a bouquet and offered it to Susanna where she sat on a big rock near the Coray wagon. She took it with a weak smile and whispered, "I wish I could lay these on Sonny's grave."

Trying to be thoughtful, he suggested, "Just pretend that he gave them to you."

"I will try, Brother Bigler. Thank you for your kindness."

By the time the group left the campground at Rock Creek, several days from Tragedy Springs, Susanna had come to the realization that she was not the only one who would miss Sonny. John Cox had lost a beloved nephew, one he loved like a son.

She apologized. "Brother Cox, I'm so sorry that I have been so caught up in my own grief that I forgot that you lost someone you loved as well."

The voice of the quiet man rumbled in his chest. "That's all right, Susanna. Sometimes we can't see beyond our own losses—at least for a while. That's to be expected."

***

"Put up the tents tonight and for the next several nights. As long as we are in this high altitude, it's gonna be cold," Captain Thompson ordered as the camp ate supper. "We will need two guards in two shifts. The Indians are keepin' an eye on us."

In the morning, he ordered, "Increase the men on the clearing team to fifteen." President Holmes had the task of selecting the men for that duty each morning. The days were filled with hard labor as the men were forced to lower the wagons over steep ridges and cliffs with block and tackle, using ropes and chains wrapped around tree trunks.

Lacking heavy hammers or drills, they had only one way to deal with the biggest rocks blocking their way. "Add some more wood to that pile. We've got to get it roaring," Thompson would yell. The two women carried wood to the fires along with the men until all were exhausted.

"Stand back. The wood is green. The sap is going to spit sparks once it's lit," Bigler called out. The day would be spent in building large fires on each of the big boulders until they cracked into smaller pieces as they cooled and could be removed.

When they reached Pass Canyon, the work on the road proceeded at the slow pace of less than a mile a day for a full week. The men worked through the steep-walled canyon in rain and snow, their hands so stiff with cold they could hardly flex their fingers. Their work was made more challenging by Indians who threw large rocks from the tops of the cliffs and fired arrows at them.

Susanna and Melissa served as water carriers and prepared meals for the entire group so the men could push the work forward. As the women were passing around the water bucket and the ladle, Holmes yelled, "Look out! Rock fall!"

The roar of loose rocks tumbling down the side of the canyon focused everyone's attention. A spate of arrows followed. The men dropped their tools and scattered, but some weren't fast enough.

The rockslide only lasted three or four seconds, but several of the men were injured. Most of the men rushed back to the wagons to retrieve their guns. Thompson yelled, "Follow me. We're gonna end this problem." He led a dozen of them toward a crevasse where they could get a series of hand- and footholds for a climb to the top of the canyon wall.

Several men limped back to the fire holding their heads or injured limbs. Henry Bigler eased a wounded John Cox to the ground, where he could lean against a wagon wheel and was sheltered from any more arrows or falling rocks. "We've got to get the arrow out of his shoulder. Get me a sharp knife with a good point," he demanded.

Susanna handed him the only knife she possessed. Bigler cut the shoulder out of the shirt. "Hey, this is my one good shirt," Cox said weakly with a pale grin. Beads of cold perspiration stood out on his forehead.

Bigler's hands were shaking with the exhaustion of moving rocks all day and the excitement of the attack. As he lifted the knife to cut out the arrow, Cox objected. "Your hands are too unsteady, Henry. Get one of the women to do it."

Melissa was assisting her husband, who had a great gash on his scalp, so Bigler turned and spoke to Susanna. "Sister Thayer, I need your hands. You'll need to get that arrow out of John's shoulder." He handed the knife back to her.

Susanna froze for a moment. Grimacing, Cox added, "Please, it needs to come out."

"You trust me to do it?" she asked unsteadily.

He nodded. "Give me something to bite down on, Henry." Bigler handed him a stick to put between his teeth.

Susanna stepped over to the pot of boiling water that was meant to cook the venison for supper. She put the knife blade in it to clean it and then knelt by Cox. "I'll try not to hurt you, Brother Cox." She willed her hands to be steady.

He nodded, closed his eyes, and bit down on the stick. She carefully inserted the point of the knife into the wound and widened it so the head of the arrow could be pulled out without tearing the flesh any more than it already had. His jaw tightened, and he grunted in pain. When she had the arrow out, she looked around for a rag, and finding none, she bent and took a few seconds to pull the frayed ruffle off her slip. She tore it in half.

"Brother Bigler, please lift the pot off the fire. The water is too hot to use right now."

It took Bigler both hands to lift the pot by its handle with his feet spread to avoid the splashing hot water. When he set it down, she dipped the short piece of fabric into the water and held it up by one end to allow the wind to dissipate the heat. Then she gave it a twist and wiped the wound, which still oozed blood.

Bigler watched. "Cox, you're one lucky man. That arrow came mighty near hitting somethin' vital." Cox simply nodded, his face visibly white in the early evening darkness.

"Can you lean forward, Brother Cox? I need to wrap your shoulder." Susanna's face was almost as white as his.

He said nothing but leaned away from the wagon wheel. She wrapped the remaining fabric from her petticoat ruffle around his shoulder, making him grimace. "There now. Hopefully, that will help it stop bleeding," she said as she stood and dried her hands on her skirt.

He looked down at the white of the makeshift bandage. "Sister Thayer, you did a good job. Even my wife couldn't have done any better, I'll wager." His voice was weak but his smile was sincere.

"Thank you." Her voice was as unsteady as his. "I'm sure that is a fine compliment, but I hope I don't need to prove my nursing skills in this way very often."

By this time, more than a dozen men had climbed back down with news that the attackers were gone. Thompson assigned two of the men to guard duty. "Evans, you and Green are to eat some supper and then get back up to the cliff top and stand guard until midnight. At midnight, Judd and Garner will take over for you." He turned and called out, "Jim Sly, you're to have the cannon ready to fire, just in case we have any more trouble with Indians tonight."

During the night, John Cox developed a fever, so Susanna drove the ox team in the morning. While camp was made, she bathed Cox's head with cool water. "Brother Cox, I've got to change this bandage. It's soaked with blood, and if I let it dry, it will reopen the wound when I take it off." She turned away and tore another strip from her petticoat. "Can you sit up a little so I can wrap it again?"

He struggled to pull himself into a nearly sitting position. When she was finished, he whispered, "Thank you, Susanna," before he lay back down. She drove the team for three more days, while he tried to rest in the jostling wagon.

***

By the time fourteen battalion men riding horses and pulling pack mules arrived on August fourth, the fever had finally abated, and Cox was able to walk around unassisted. The new arrivals had left the gold fields only five days earlier, making good time using the road the Holmes-Thompson Company had carved in the mountains. They stayed with the company for three days but then set out for the Valley with ten men from the company joining them, sure that the wagon company had made its way over and through the worst part of the journey and would no longer need their road-building efforts.

Another two days of travel brought the remaining members of the company to the Carson River. When they camped that night, they saw at least a hundred fires flickering all over the mountainside.

"How could there possibly be so many Indians, Brother Cox? There must be a thousand of them out there around those fires." Susanna's nervousness was reflected in her voice.

"Not likely. I suspect that they're just tryin' to scare us. I think they're trying to get us to hurry away from what they consider their land."

When they left the Carson River, everyone was instructed to cut as much of the grass near the river as they could find. "There'll be little water and less feed except what we are carrying for the next several days," Captain Holmes warned the camp. "We'll cross the worst of what's ahead at night so get some rest this afternoon." At eleven o'clock that night, they set out by moonlight and traveled all night.

As the days passed, Susanna grew quieter. Cox finally asked her, "Sister Thayer, what makes you so quiet lately? You haven't even joined in the singing with the men after supper each evening. Are you still troubled by Sonny's death?"

She nodded as her words began to tumble out like spilled beans from a tipped jar. "I've come to realize that without Sonny, I have nowhere to go when I reach the Valley—no way to sustain myself. I've begun to wonder why God has brought me here. If he has a reason, I can't see it." Her voice dropped to a whisper. "I may be forced to marry a man I don't love to keep from starvation."

As Cox started to say something, she put up her hand. "I know other women have married without love, but that was never part of the future I saw for myself. I have always expected to marry for love. Now, I think I may never marry." Her voice was permeated with disappointment and hurt.

Cox patted her arm, trying to offer some comfort. "You will always have a place with me and my wife. You are as much a member of our family as if you had married Sonny. Don't allow yourself to feel alone. I'm sure there's a fine young man out there that will find you and you will love him very much."

She tried to smile at him, but it was a stiff, unsuccessful attempt. "Thank you, Brother Cox. You're a kind man. I guess I'm just feeling sorry for myself tonight." She stared into the distance. *But I think I shall never allow myself to love again; it's too costly,* she thought. *I must become self-sufficient.*

The company slept during the day in preparation for the night travel, but by late afternoon, thirst had awakened Susanna. She climbed out of the wagon bed and looked around at the shimmering waves of heat rising from the hard-packed, alkaline soil. The mesquite waved tauntingly at her in the hot wind, and the shadows of waterless clouds chased each other across the nearly barren earth.

She lifted a dipper of very warm water from the water barrel on the side of the wagon, water almost too hot to drink, and found it would not quench her thirst.

The order was given for the wagons to line up and renew their journey. The heat of the desert had weakened John Cox. "I'll drive the team. You rest," Susanna said as she climbed up onto the seat.

After four hours of travel, they reached the Humbolt River. While they made camp, Indians crept close, hiding behind the willows growing on the banks. As the sun pulled the light from the sky and sank in the west, a rain of arrows fell on the camp, hitting several horses, which quickly collapsed and thrashed about, showing signs of being poisoned.

Susanna found herself screaming at the Indians, "This is just too much! Is this what you did to Sonny?" In a burst of rage, she pulled Cox's rifle from its leather case in the wagon bed and took aim at the figures moving behind the willows.

"Susanna, do you know how to use that gun?" he called out weakly in alarm.

"I just point and shoot," she responded angrily with a tight jaw.

In quick succession, she cocked and fired the gun five times, the way she had seen it done. The Indians on the nearest bank scattered into the river. She watched as they rushed up the other riverbank and into the growing darkness.

Cox climbed weakly out of the wagon. "You did right fine with that rifle," he commented as he nervously took it from her. Her hands were still shaking with anger.

"It's bad enough when they shoot at us, but there's just no reason to shoot and kill the horses." She marched over to where the fire was to be built and began to stack the wood with an angry energy. She looked up at some of the men and asked sharply, "Is someone going to put those poor animals out of their misery?"

"Yes, ma'am," Captain Thompson said. He gave the orders.

The men looked at Susanna with less sympathy and more respect that night.

Chapter Twenty-Eight

For the next seven days, the company made its way along the banks of the Humbolt River, where grazing was poor but there was plenty of water. The Digger Indians continued to shoot the stock, and some of the cows that were too lame to keep up were slaughtered and the meat divided.

An occasional wagon company bound for California passed. Some of the westward travelers had wintered in Salt Lake City and brought good reports of the Saints' efforts to build a city and plant the area in grain and garden crops. The news meant little to Susanna. She was past feeling anything except a grinding, empty exhaustion. She and Melissa walked side by side, no longer riding in the wagons to spare the weary oxen. They spoke little. Even thinking took too much energy. The morning and evening prayers of the camp were brief, always ending, "Please give us strength and endurance to reach the Valley."

A westbound group that met the company on August twenty-sixth was led by Bishop Levi Ritter, who was headed for San Francisco to claim goods he and others had shipped on the *Brooklyn*. He informed Captain Thompson that it was five hundred miles to the Valley from that point.

"That sounds so far away," Susanna commented in a dispirited whisper to Melissa. "It might as well be five thousand miles." That night, Susanna sat unmoving under stars after most in the camp had retired to bed. Addison Pratt approached her and commented, "Something troubles you, Sister Thayer."

Susanna shook herself a little. "I suppose I am just missing family tonight. I miss my mother almost more than I can stand on nights like this. I'm so weary. If she were here, she would urge me to be strong, not to falter, and to take life by the horns. I need her strength right now."

"She's with you, Sister Thayer. Like all good parents, her influence is carried in your heart, and you can call on her strength anytime you need to. I'm sure you are your mother's daughter."

The familiar words warmed her. "I hope you're right, Brother Pratt."

***

The next day, Brother Pratt conducted a Sabbath meeting in the afternoon. Just as the meeting ended, Captain Samuel Hensley and a company of ten men headed west on horseback arrived in camp with heavily loaded mules. Hensley furnished Thompson with a map showing a cutoff he had recently found. "You can save a hundred and twenty miles if you use my map," he insisted. "That way, you can save eight or ten days."

Captain Thompson announced to the camp the next morning, "Since the cutoff will prevent the necessity of traveling all the way to Fort Hall, it's the best option."

The wagons began to work their way higher, twisting with the curves of the hills where the soil was hard and dry and, in places, so thin that great stones pushed up out of the ground as if the earth were slowly decaying, exposing its bones. The difficult, primitive trail stressed the humans, animals, and worn-out wagons. To add to Susanna's discouragement, Scottie disappeared one night. Though no one said so, it was known that the Indians were probably responsible.

The weather grew wet and overcast, reflecting Susanna's gloom. Finally, the hostile Digger Indians were left behind. The first time a group of Paiutes entered the camp to beg for food, Susanna ran to the Cox wagon and grabbed John's gun. He rushed after her. "These are Paiutes, Susanna. They just want some food. They aren't hostile," he explained as he took the gun from her hands. She still watched them with distrust.

Eventually, the Paiutes were displaced by better dressed and better fed Shoshones, who came to trade. Susanna traded a shawl to one of the squaws for a pair of moccasins to replace her tattered shoes.

Several days were lost as the scouts for the company tried to locate the Hensley cutoff. Rations dwindled; remaining strength melted like snow in the hot sun. When Bigler brought down a deer, many of the men were so hungry that as the venison was roasted on a spit, they would cut off a hot, hissing slice, juggling it from hand to hand, eating it while it was still hot enough to scald the mouth.

The night of September fourteenth, after an exhausting day of crossing cold rivers and coaxing weary animals up steep slopes, they made camp at dark and watched a total eclipse of the moon as it darkened the night. It equaled the darkness of Susanna's mood.

The long-sought Hensley cutoff, when finally found, was only a pack trail. Disappointment permeated the camp like the falling rain. The men could hardly face the fact that they would have to cut another wagon road with worn-out tools and worn-out muscles.

When camp had been made at the headwaters of Cassia Creek, Henry Bigler approached Susanna. "Brother Borrowman has an infected ankle. It looks real bad. He scratched it on something that has gotten into his blood. You did so well helping Brother Pratt when he was so sick and fixing up John Cox after he took that arrow in his shoulder—do you think you could help Brother Borrowman?"

"I don't know. I don't have much to work with, but I'll try." Her voice was a near whisper.

Brother Borrowman's ankle was swollen and red, and the inflammation and swelling were moving up his leg. Susanna asked for a pot of boiled water. Looking around, the only plants she thought might be of use were the willows growing in a clump near the stream. "Will you cut at least a dozen willows for me and pull the bark off them? Put the bark in the pot to boil in the water."

While the water was cooling, she excused herself while she returned to the wagon. She took her one remaining petticoat from the carpetbag, and with the scissors that had given so many haircuts in San Francisco, she cut it into strips.

She dipped the strips into the warm water, which had taken on a slick quality from the willow bark, and wrapped the wet strips around the ankle and leg. "I'm sorry if the wet bandages make you cold tonight, but I think this will help. I don't know what else to do. Have you got a saddle blanket to wrap around the bandages to keep your leg warm?"

"I'll find something, Sister Thayer. Thanks for your help."

In the morning, the redness and swelling were nearly gone. Borrowman's toes were almost blue with cold, but as Susanna removed the bandages, Borrowman laughed. He rose and walked around on his leg. "Sister Thayer, you worked a miracle. If we could just wrap all the stock with tender feet the same way, we could move double time."

For the next four days, the men spent their strength breaking and moving rocks, cutting brush, and widening the trail to accommodate the wagons, and on September eighteenth, they reached a pass in the mountains where they could look to the east and see the Great Salt Lake for the first time. They were on the northwest side, opposite from where the city was expanding, but the men cheered loudly. When Melissa Coray rushed to Susanna and talked excitedly about the sight, Susanna could only offer a stiff little smile.

"Susanna, don't you realize we're nearly there—that we're nearly home?" Melissa's voice was incredulous at Susanna's lack of enthusiasm.

"Melissa, I'm just too exhausted to feel anything. Perhaps I'm just feeling sorry for myself, but right now, I'm remembering the plans Sonny and I made . . . plans that will never be. The battalion men are hurrying to wives and children they haven't seen in two years or more." She pushed a lock of hair out of her face. "If I had known that Sonny would never live to see the Valley, I would have stayed in California. At least there I could have been self-supporting." Her voice had taken on an uncharacteristic bitterness.

"No, no, Susanna." Melissa led her to a large rock and pushed her down to sit on it. "There is a whole new life waiting there for you. You've got to believe that." She tipped her friend's chin up and looked into her eyes. "Do you believe me?"

Susanna forced a crooked smile. "I hope you're right, Melissa. Your friendship is one of the few things I will be able to claim when we reach the Valley."

"You'll always have my friendship, but more importantly, Susanna, you have the gospel. Don't let your exhaustion and your losses steal your faith from you." When her friend did not respond, Melissa shook her head and moved away to build the fire necessary to prepare another meal.

Susanna dropped her eyes to the blistered and calloused hands in her lap. She whispered, "I'm sure you're right, Melissa. I just need to be reminded at times."

She stared out at the valley so many had struggled and sometimes died to reach, the valley Sonny would never see. She heard her father's voice. "We determine our eternal future by the small choices we make each day, Daughter."

Without thinking, she responded, "Yes, Papa. I will try to remember that."

The voice came again. "Remember, by its very nature, faith must be tested."

Suddenly, the numbness of the past weeks faded, and she wept. She couldn't have told anyone why, but she wept with her back to the camp, hiding the tears and trying to keep her shoulders from shaking.

***

As the camp was cleared and preparations to move were completed in the morning, Captain Thompson called out, "We have to make our way around the north end of the lake, but take heart. We'll soon be there."

Five more days took the company north to the Malad River. The oxen were weak, and the cattle and horses were sore footed. Susanna's dress hung loosely about her, and her face was so sunburned that her lips were split and bleeding. Her exhaustion was so deep that every morning required a renewed reach for her faith to rise and face another day, and every step required a renewal of that faith.

The realization that they were nearing their destination began to fill the men with excitement and anticipation. They began to talk, laugh, and sing loudly, telling and retelling the stories of the lighter moments on their march.

One called out, "You remember when Bigler stepped in that cow pie and walked all day with the stuff on his boots? By nightfall, nobody would walk by him, and he hadn't even figured out why?"

After the laughter quieted, another called out, "Do you remember when Thompson gave that meat to Jim Sly and told him it was venison, but it was wolf? He boiled it for two hours, and it was still tough as leather. He never did figure out what was wrong with that cut of 'venison' until someone told him what it was." Again the laughter filled the camp, and so the sharing of the stories of their adventures filled the evenings after the last meal of the day was over. Their excited anticipation did not ease Susanna's emptiness.

When they reached the Bear River Valley, tired eyes finally recognized the southbound wagon ruts of the earlier wagon companies that had come from the east. The wagons were pulled steadily southward, with the Bear River on their right and tall mountains on their left. The lush greenness of the grass and willows on the riverbanks rested the eyes that had spent so many days squinting into the sun.

When they reached a settlement on the Ogden River in a beautiful valley, some of the men spurred their horses toward a familiar figure. "Hey, it's Captain James Brown," Holmes called out. He quickly dropped from his horse and grabbed the man in a bear hug. "How did you get here? We last saw you when you took the battalion sick detachment to Pueblo."

Brown swept his hand around the scene and explained, "President Young asked me to go to California to collect the mustering-out pay of the sick detachments of the battalion, and then I was instructed to use a portion of the money to purchase Miles Goodyear's fort here. Now we call this Brown's Fort. You're welcome to rest here as long as you like. There's only about six families in the fort and there's plenty of good farm land here. It's a good place to live, and here you're only about thirty miles from Salt Lake City."

The knowledge that they were so close to their destination prompted the men to suddenly become more concerned about their appearance. Remembering how Susanna had set up her little barbershop in San Francisco, some coaxed her to give them hair cuts and to trim their beards. They each paid her about a dollar in gold dust. That evening, they feasted on roasted ears of corn and melons. The good food and the cheerful spirits of the men made Susanna's spirits lift. A glimmer of her old courage returned. *Perhaps . . . perhaps things are really going to get better. Perhaps there really is a purpose to all this hardship.*

Several men were so excited about seeing their families that they determined to hurry on ahead of the slower wagons. Before leaving on horseback, Azariah Smith and Addison Pratt came to John Cox. "Brother Cox, if you'll herd our stock into Salt Lake for us, we'll pay you a penny a head per day."

John nodded. "Glad to, as I'm not going to go any faster with or without your stock." So Susanna drove the wagon again, while John used a borrowed horse to keep the stock moving steadily southward.

Finally, on Friday, October sixth, the remainder of the Holmes-Thompson Company, with nearly worn-out wagons, weary humans, and footsore animals reached Salt Lake City. Once the wagons were halted on the Eighth Ward Public Square, waiting families who had been told of the pending arrival of the company rushed to greet fathers, sons, and husbands.

Susanna stood in the shadow cast by the Cox wagon and watched while Eliza Cox and her children greeted John. She noticed that they held on to one another as if they would never be separated again. The children gathered around him, each coaxing for his attention. He teased the baby, Sarah, who had been born while he was away. He picked up four-year-old Anna, who did not remember him.

"Don't you remember your Pa, Anna? I'm back from the army. I've come home from California, and I have gold dust." He lifted the pouch from beneath his shirt and waved it. The children cheered, not sure just what it meant for their pa to have gold dust but excited about it if he was.

For Susanna, it was a painful scene. *I might have been greeting Sonny if things had been different. He would have scooped me up in his arms and turned me around and around, and we would have laughed and laughed . . .*

She wiped away a tear.

Chapter Twenty-Nine

Captain Thompson climbed into the back of this wagon with raised hands to quiet the group. "Some of the men are going to the Council House at the corner of South Temple and Main Streets to pay their tithing and report to Brigham Young. If you want them to take your tithing, they will do so."

Trying to shake off the self-pity that had been following her since Sonny's death, she offered herself some advice. *I must take life by the horns again.* She approached Henry Bigler. "Will you take my tithing to President Young?"

He agreed, so she counted out five dollars and handed the money to him, along with part of the gold dust given her by Sonny. She had twenty dollars and a portion of the gold dust left. *Now the Lord can see that I am trying to do what has been asked of me.*

***

When Eliza Cox and her children had arrived in the Valley, the men of the Ninth Ward had built them a cabin with three rooms at the corner of "the Sixes," Sixth East and Sixth South Temple Streets. It sat on a quarter of an acre with plenty of room for a garden and a cow.

Susanna was welcomed into the Cox home, where she offered her assistance in caring for the younger children. She slept in the bedroom with the three older girls, and Brother Cox immediately went to work to add another two rooms.

Susanna purchased a loom and spent her days assisting Eliza with the meals and the children and her evenings weaving blankets for women who brought her their carded wool.

When she insisted on paying John and Eliza twenty-five cents a week to help cover the cost of her board and room, he responded, "Susanna, you're a blessing to Eliza and me. You owe us nothing."

But she insisted. "I will pay my own way, Brother Cox. I am determined not to be a burden on anyone."

Throughout the winter, she had little reason to leave the little house except on the Sabbath to attend Sunday meetings, and she left those meetings directly after the benediction, gathering the children and waiting in the wagon until John and Eliza had completed their socializing. She carefully saved her money—for what, she wasn't sure, but she felt she would need resources if she were ever to become self-sufficient.

***

"It's a beautiful morning, Susanna. I've never seen a lovelier April day. John and I are going to leave Martha in charge of the children and ride to the Deseret Storehouse on South Temple to purchase some vegetable seeds. It won't take us very long and it's time you got out into the fresh air. Will you come with us?"

Susanna's immediate reaction was to politely refuse, as she had several previous invitations, but Eliza's face was so hopeful, Susanna hesitantly nodded. "Yes, if you like, I'll come with you."

They rode to the storehouse, and while John was carefully selecting vegetable seeds and talking with some of his friends, Eliza took Susanna's arm. "Come with me. We're going to walk down State Street and window shop. John will bring the wagon and locate us when he's finished."

Without waiting for her to agree, Eliza firmly pulled Susanna out of the door and down the boardwalk. They paused to examine the items displayed in the windows of the Zion's Cooperative Mercantile Store. They moved on to the second mercantile, which was a block farther down the street and was operated by two gentile men, Mr. Kinkead and Mr. Livingston.

"Let's go in and see what they have, Susanna." But when Eliza stepped toward the door, Susanna didn't move. She stood white faced and ridged. "What is it, dear?" She followed Susanna's line of vision and noted that she was staring at a small legal office across the street. The sign across the building above the doorway read, "Burnley Law Office." On the narrow panel next to the window was additional information. "Services offered: Wills drawn and probated, land titles registered, claims litigated, all necessary legal services available."

"What is it, Susanna? You look as if you've just seen a ghost."

"I have." Her voice was so tight it hurt her to speak.

"Well, ghosts are best faced down right away so they cannot disturb one's sleep." Eliza took Susanna's arm and pulled her across the wide street, avoiding the wagons and men on horseback.

When they reached the boardwalk on the other side, Susanna pulled back and whispered, "No, no, Eliza. I think it's best if we let it alone, just let it alone."

Eliza turned and looked at her, full of concern. "Susanna, I don't know what has upset you so, but we're going to address it. Nothing is as frightening as one anticipates." She took the young woman's hand and led her into the office.

A man in his midtwenties was seated behind a desk in the rear of the narrow office. He looked up from the sheaf of papers he was reading. "May I help you ladies?" He half rose from his chair but suddenly hesitated. He straightened more slowly and a quizzical look came over his face. "Susanna, is that you?" He quickly moved around the desk and approached the women. He put out both hands, his face bright with pleasure. "Susanna, it is you!"

As he reached for her hands, she stepped back out of his reach, as though his touch would burn.

It was Jonathan. Gone were the elegant coat and silk stockings he had worn in Boston. He stood before her in a rough linen shirt, leather vest, and homespun breeches. His boots were scuffed and worn.

"Susanna, I've been waiting for you to get here for more than a year. Tell me you remember me."

"Yes, I remember you," she whispered. "What are you doing here?"

"It's a long story. Please sit down and let me explain, or better yet, let me call on you. So much has happened. There is so much I need to tell you."

Instead of listening, she turned on her heel and ran from his office as if pursued by hungry wolves. As she reached the street, Cox saw her from his seat on the wagon and pulled the horses to a halt. She climbed in. "Hurry, Brother Cox. Take me away from here," she pleaded.

Eliza hurriedly followed her from the office with Jonathan behind her. When she reached the wagon, she looked at Susanna and asked, "What's the matter, Susanna? Why won't you talk to the young man?"

"Please, Brother Cox, take me away from here." Her voice was shaking. *Why did he come here? Did he come here to parade his wife and child before me—to remind me of the choice he made?* The thought jangled in her head like a loose coin.

Cox reached over and assisted his wife into the wagon before he slapped the reins on the horses' rumps. As the wagon moved down the street, Jonathan stood watching from the front door of his office in frustrated bewilderment, with his feet spread and his fists on his hips.

Susanna refused to speak on the way back to the cabin. There, she hurried into the bedroom and closed the door. Eliza pulled her husband aside and whispered, "You go outside and do something. Plant the garden, mend the fence—and take the children. Don't come in until I call you."

He shrugged his shoulders and herded the children out of the cabin, wondering what had gotten into the two women. After a minute, the sound of the ripsaw could be heard.

Eliza pushed the bedroom door open. When Susanna refused to speak, the older woman said firmly, "Susanna, you are going to have to talk to me and tell me what is troubling you. I will not leave until you do."

Eliza sat next to her on the bed and took her hand in both of hers. The story was finally told. "I loved him. I loved him from the time we were children, and I thought he loved me, but after my father died, he broke our engagement and married his cousin. The next time I saw him, he told me he didn't love her, that he married her to please his father." Her anger tightened her throat so much that she had to take a few seconds to swallow away the bile that was threatening to rise. "And because of his decision to please his father rather than keep his promise to me, my life became one hardship after another—one loss after another."

Her voice choked off in her throat for a moment. "Finally, when I found Sonny and thought a happy future was waiting for me here in the Valley, I lost him too." By now, the tears of frustration, loss, and anger were flowing steadily down her cheeks and dropping in great spots on her worn dress. "I'll never see my family again. I saw Sonny's grave where he was murdered by the Indians. I endured six months on shipboard and three months of travel by wagon over mountains and deserts. And there were so many other trials . . ." Her voice trailed off for a moment.

"And now, I live here in this foreign place on the kindness of others, unable to support myself because of the greed of his father and uncle." She paused long enough to take a shuddering breath. "He made the decision, but the consequences reached out and wounded me." Her energy and anger were dissipating. "Life wasn't supposed to turn out like this." She wiped her eyes with the sleeve of her dress. "And now he appears out of nowhere and expects to walk back into my life along with his wife and child."

Eliza put her arm about Susanna's shoulders and pulled her close. "But, my dear, blessings have come to you through these hard times. Would you have found the gospel if you had married him in Boston?"

She was drawn up short and hesitated for a few heartbeats. "I'd never thought about it. I suppose that never would have happened. I'm sure his family wouldn't have approved."

"Then you still have the greatest gift God can give. If you always remember that, all else will follow, if not today or tomorrow, then eventually—in this life or the next." Susanna nodded slowly, intellectually grasping what she was being told, but not embracing it emotionally. Eliza continued, "I think you owe this man the opportunity to explain why he traveled across three-quarters of a continent to find you."

She shook her head. "I do not want to see him again—ever. Maybe someday I can forgive him, but how would I ever trust him?" Her voice was almost inaudible.

"We will talk no more of it tonight. Another day will be soon enough for you to be brave." Eliza patted Susanna's shoulder as she rose from the bed and left the room. She began to prepare their midday meal, moving around the little cabin quietly shaking her head in frustration. After a few minutes, she remembered her husband and the children and stepped to the door to wave to him that it was time for them to come back into the house.

Susanna said little for the next week, and when Eliza and John asked her to go with them again to make some purchases at the co-op store, she shook her head firmly. "No, I'll stay here and watch the children and have a meal ready for you when you return." They were disappointed but not surprised.

As the wagon rattled away, Susanna sat down in Eliza's rocking chair and closed her eyes. Her head hurt. It had hurt all week. She had hardly slept for the past several nights. While the baby napped and the other children played outside in the mild spring air, she thought that perhaps she could get a little rest. She closed her eyes and slipped into a light sleep. The dream started almost immediately. There he was, standing in Aunt Louisa's sitting room, telling her that he loved her—that he would always love her.

She awakened and sat up with a start. Rising, she began to concentrate on preparing the meal to drive away the memory.

***

While Cox was purchasing several young chickens and fifty pounds of chicken mash, Eliza pulled on his sleeve and said matter-of-factly, "John, I'm going to walk down State Street past the mercantile. I need to go over to the law office of Mr. Burnley. I want to hear what he has to tell Susanna."

Jonathan Burnley was pleased to see Eliza. After they exchanged greetings, she stated in her direct manner, "I've come to ask you what brought you here to the Valley and what it is that you want to tell Susanna."

Glad to have someone to listen, Jonathan urged her to be seated then he told the story of his childhood friendship with Susanna and their unofficial engagement. "Upon the death of Susanna's father, my father concluded that the Thayer family had lost its previous social standing, so he began to pressure me to break off the engagement and marry my cousin. I was so young and dependent upon his good graces that I could not withstand the pressure. I was brought up to honor my father and mother—but there was never a happy moment in that arranged marriage, at least not until our son was born. Our love for him brought us some unity, but he only lived a few weeks. Three weeks after we buried him, my wife contracted yellow fever in the epidemic that swept over Boston. She was not a strong woman and she was dead in a week."

He swallowed hard. "But there is another reason I have been trying to find Susanna. Though I still love her, I realize that she has cause to be very angry with me, perhaps even to hate me. But to help put matters right, I have brought her a portion of the inheritance she should have received upon the death of her aunt. After she left to take passage to New York, I threatened both my father and my uncle with a lawsuit. I took the statement from the doctor who believed that a gift of calomel from Uncle Mortimer may have caused Louisa Thayer's death. After I announced to them that I was filing a civil suit and was planning to use the doctor's sworn statement against them, they both determined that it would be best for everyone if the case were settled out of court. We all knew that there was insufficient evidence to prove any crime had been committed, but just the scandal such rumors would cause would do great harm to the firm.

"Thereafter, I found little satisfaction in my work and less in the presence of my father. He set out to make my life difficult. I remembered that Susanna had told me that she had formally affiliated with a church whose members were sailing around the Horn to California. I read the newspaper accounts about the sailing of the *Brooklyn* and finally found two elders who were preaching that religion. After attending several meetings, I was baptized. When my father discovered what I had done, he disowned me."

When he grew quiet, Eliza urged him to continue. "I tried to establish my own law office in Boston, but my father made it clear to my potential clients that there would be serious business repercussions for anyone using my services. I eventually made my way to Nauvoo, Illinois, but the members of the Church had been cruelly driven out and were living in tents and dugouts in the Iowa territory. I traveled westward until I reached the big settlement of Winter Quarters on the Missouri River. I arrived after the Mormon Battalion had left, so there was plenty for me to do as one of the few able-bodied men there. I became part of the Charles Rich wagon company that left in June of last year and arrived here in early October. I've been looking for Susanna ever since." He paused and looked into Eliza's eyes searchingly for a long moment. "Will you help me? Please, I must talk with her. I have brought ten thousand dollars from her aunt's estate. She is a rich woman now, and she must be told."

Chapter Thirty

When John and Eliza arrived home, Susanna had bathed the smallest ones and had a meal on the table. Eliza said nothing of her meeting with Jonathan. At Sabbath services the next day, Cox preached a carefully selected sermon from Matthew 18:21–22, in which Peter came to Jesus and asked how often he had to forgive his brother. Cox closed his remarks with the quote from Doctrine and Covenants 1:32, "Nevertheless, he that repents and does the commandments of the Lord shall be forgiven."

Susanna had the indefinable sensation that somehow he was speaking to her, but she brushed the feeling away. As she waited in the buckboard for John and Eliza to finish their social conversations with friends and neighbors, she noted that Eliza carried one-year-old Sarah, but the other children were no longer with their parents.

As Eliza climbed into the wagon, Susanna asked, "Where are the children?"

"I have sent the three oldest girls and little Johnny to help Sister Jackson plant her garden in the morning. That house of hers is so empty with her husband and two children dead. Her arthritis makes it hard for her to put the seeds in the ground. She has needed the help of young, strong bodies to help with the planting and the harvesting the last two years. She loves having them around, and they will come home tomorrow afternoon, when the planting is finished. The two little ones, Mary Ann and Anna, have gone to stay with my sister. They love their Aunt Betsy. Little Sarah will stay home with us."

As the meal was cleared away, Eliza suddenly grew perplexed. "Oh, John, I have done something foolish. I promised Jenny Wheelwright that I would take her and her two little ones some supper this evening. She has been ill, and the two little ones do make it impossible for her to get any rest—but I completely forgot that we have company coming." Susanna paused with a large bowl of batter for tomorrow's corn bread in her hands, surprised that no one had thought to mention the fact that company was coming until then. *Who is this company?*

Eliza continued as she swept up the crumbs on the floor, "Well, you'll just have to drive me down to Wheelwrights in the buckboard and leave me there for a few hours to give her some relief. I'll put Sarah to bed before I leave. You can return to help Susanna entertain our guest. Come back to get me before midnight." John nodded.

"Who is this company?" Susanna's question hung in the air.

Eliza answered evasively. "John has some business to conduct with him."

That evening, the little play for Susanna's benefit proceeded, but when the "guest" arrived, her reaction almost ended it at the first act. The sound of a horse's hooves drew her attention twenty minutes after the wagon taking supper for the Wheelwright family had left. When she opened the door in response to the knock and saw Jonathan Burnley standing there with his hat in his hand, she closed it in his face and leaned against it, her heart pounding in her ears.

He knocked again. "Go away, Jonathan. I don't want to see you." The old hurt knotted in her stomach.

His voice was apologetic, but insistent. "Susanna, I'm an invited guest of Brother and Sister Cox. He has asked me to do some legal work for him. How can I do that if you will not allow me to come in?"

"He isn't here at the present. Now please go." Her voice caught in her throat. *Stop it, Susanna Thayer, stop it! This man means nothing to you any longer. Don't get so emotional,* she harshly scolded herself.

The sound of wagon wheels told her that John Cox had returned. She left the door and stepped into the little bedroom she and the oldest girls used. *If he must come in, let John Cox open the door. I will not.* She splashed water from the washbowl on her face to cool the burning.

John's big voice boomed through the little house. "Jonathan, come in, come in. Isn't Susanna here?"

"I believe she has left us to conduct our business out of her presence." Jonathan's voice was apologetic and regretful.

"Sit down while I get you a cold drink of well water. You look as if you had a dusty ride."

As the two men talked about a will for Cox, Susanna began to feel foolish. *If this man means so little to me, why am I hiding from him? I will not let him intimidate me into hiding like a naughty or frightened child.*

Pretending that she was no longer upset by his presence, she left the bedroom and, as both men turned to look at her, said with as much graciousness as she could muster, "I apologize for my earlier rudeness, Mr. Burnley. Let me cut a piece of pound cake for you both. Eliza made it yesterday."

As she busied herself lighting another oil lamp to brighten the room and cutting cake for the men, John asked casually, "Tell me about yourself, Mr. Burnley. What brought you out here to the Valley to practice your legal skills?"

"After my wife and child died in Boston, I was baptized into the Church, and my father disowned me."

Susanna stood as if she had been turned to stone for a full second. As he continued, she forgot the pound cake and took a seat in Eliza's rocking chair facing the fireplace. "I was forced to separate my legal practice from his, and thereafter, he saw to it that I did not draw many clients." The conversation continued with Jonathan repeating much of what he had told Eliza two days before, but this time for Susanna's benefit. He made no mention of the inheritance for fear that in her hurt and anger she would refuse it, as she had refused his financial help before leaving her aunt's home.

With her back to the two men at the table, she put her hands between her knees to steady them, moving only occasionally to put a piece of additional kindling on the fire. Cox continued to draw out Jonathan's story.

Abruptly, John looked out of the window into the April darkness that had closed around the cabin. He stood. "Please don't go yet, Mr. Burnley. I must round up my cow and her calf and get them into the stable, or who knows where they will be in the morning. It won't take long. Susanna, please give this man that piece of Eliza's pound cake you promised. He will certainly earn it before he has completed the details of my will."

Jonathan courteously rose as his host stepped out of the door. When he turned back to the table, he found himself looking directly at Susanna as she held a slice of pound cake to put before him. The light of the fire glinted off her auburn hair. He had never forgotten how lovely she was, or how easy it was for him to get lost in the green depths of her eyes.

"Susanna, let me apologize profusely for making you uncomfortable this evening by my arrival. I would not make you unhappy for anything in the world—at least, I would not add to the unhappiness I have already caused you."

"It is I who must apologize for my behavior." Her voice was formal and controlled. She laid the slice of cake on the table in front of him. "It was inexcusable. This is the home of Brother and Sister Cox, and anyone they invite should be made to feel welcome." She faced him with a stiffness that made her discomfort evident.

"Would it be proper for me to ask you to sit here at the table with me?"

She sat down but remained rigid and unmoving, looking at her hands.

"I will cut the cake in half and we will share it." His voice was insistent. As she raised her hand in protest, he added, "I insist. You must get yourself a fork and help me eat it."

Does he know how difficult he is making it for me maintain my self-control?

After they had each taken a bite, Jonathan looked at her with a look of regret that penetrated her defenses. "Susanna, we were once such good friends. Can we ever be friends again? Can you forgive me for my rash decision to marry someone else?" When she lowered her eyes and did not answer, he added, "I did not lie to you when we parted at your Aunt Louisa's home. When I said that I loved you and would always love you, I meant it. I still mean it."

His declaration nearly shattered what remained of that protective wall she was trying to hide behind. Her self-control finally burst like an overripe seed pod. She stood abruptly and turned away from him.

He rose and walked around the table. Standing behind her, he put his hand on her shoulder and whispered, "I'm so sorry, Susanna. I know these past four years have been difficult for you and it has been largely my fault. Perhaps I can never make it up to you, but I would like to try." He gently turned her to face him, put his arms around her, and pulled her against his chest. She did not resist.

They stood like that for a full minute before she stepped back and looked up into his face. "Jonathan, I've asked myself many times since I saw you so unexpectedly last week if I could ever again trust a man who hurt me so deeply. I've decided that I'm not prepared to cross that bridge."

He pulled her against him once more and put his face against her hair. "Sometimes a repaired bridge is much stronger than the original." His feelings of affection began to heat to a nearly forgotten passion, a passion he had tried for so long to smother.

With confusion written across her expressive face, she leaned back and looked into his eyes so long that it seemed she was searching for the answers to life's mysteries. "I don't know what to believe, Jonathan. It isn't just our broken engagement that troubles me. It seems that when I fix my affections on someone, fate or Providence . . ." her voice dropped, "takes them from me. I'm afraid of trusting too much. I'm afraid of ever trusting again. I have a hundred questions about my life, but few answers." She pulled away from him, smoothed her dress, and stood straighter. "I have determined that I must be prepared to provide for myself in this world and cease looking for anyone else to share my life or offer me protection."

He searched her face. "If you will place your trust in me, I promise that I will spend the rest of my life proving to you that you have not made a mistake. Will you give me a chance to rebuild that trust?" After a moment, he quoted from Henry King, who had been a favorite poet of both of them as children. "You art the book, the library whereon I look."

By this time, John Cox had found the cow and her calf and put them in the shed. He had straightened the farm equipment, filed a new edge on the plow blade, and mended a fence—not well, because of the darkness—but he had finally grown so chilled in the cold of the spring evening that he resorted to giving a quick knock on the door before he entered. Susanna and Jonathan quickly stepped apart. Susanna was embarrassed by the appearance of intimacy that their nearness to one another conveyed.

John rubbed his hands together and commented, "It's getting chilly out there, and I need to take the wagon down to Wheelwrights and pick up Eliza. You'll excuse me, I expect." He threw on his coat and grabbed his hat before he stepped back out into the night, more than willing to allow the two young people a little more time together. He smiled to himself, looking forward to telling Eliza that her plan was showing progress.

After they heard the wagon rattle away, Jonathan took her hand, turned it up, and held it against his face. Then he gently took her face between his hands. "The proposal I made to you before your father passed away is renewed. I'm not asking for an answer right now; all I'm asking for is the right to call on you so we can learn to know each other again. But I promise you that this time I am a different man—a better man than the one I used to be."

Susanna hesitantly smiled and covered his hands with her own. He dropped his head and placed his forehead against hers. She sighed and leaned into him, her cheek finding the hollow of his shoulder.

He encircled her with his arms. He had finally begun to undo some of the locks and bolts around her heart—and she knew it. Her throat tightened with tears she struggled to swallow, but these had no taste of bitterness in them. While she stood wrapped in his arms, she began to grasp the fact that the preparation of a will for a man as poor as John Cox had been a ruse, but she felt no resentment for it.

He held her tightly as he spoke. "There is something else I need to tell you—and this may end any likelihood that you will allow me into your life again. You will not need a man—any man in your life in the future. You see, I was able to obtain a portion of your aunt's estate for you. I transported it to the Valley in the bottom of a barrel of cornmeal. You are a wealthy woman now, Susanna. You now possess ten thousand dollars."

Her eyes rose to his face slowly as if she didn't understand. He continued, "I have little to offer you. You are now richer than I am ever likely to be, but I offer my love, my determination, my mind, and my muscle to you for the rest of your life. I ask you to consider my offer."

For a few moments, her mind could not grasp what he was telling her. She finally shook her head as if to order the unexpected thoughts and pushed away the news of unexpected wealth. She would deal with that later. Right now, she needed to figure out how to cope with Jonathan and their relationship.

She took a deep breath. "But we have traveled different roads to reach this place in our lives."

He traced the line of her cheek and throat with his finger. "Sometimes different roads can lead to the same destination. And 'journeys end in lovers meeting.'"

She had not thought about that quote from Shakespeare for many years. She looked into his eyes intensely, as if to force him to understand. "You are asking me to trust you. I'm afraid that if I permit myself to trust you—to love you again, you will be taken from me—again." She turned away from him. "You must give me time—time to learn to trust again."

"I promise to give you all the time in the world." He took hold of her shoulders and turned her back to face him. As he looked into her eyes, his expression was so open and tender that she felt another layer of her protective apprehension melt away.

It was after midnight when John Cox brought his wife home. In the meantime, it had been a good beginning for Susanna and Jonathan.

***

Despite her newly inherited wealth, Susanna continued to live with Eliza and John Cox, helping with the care of the children. The courtship progressed slowly. Jonathan would ride to Sabbath meeting each Sunday where he would sit with Susanna, John, Eliza, and the children. With that many chaperones, there was little concern about improper appearances.

By midsummer, they were taking long walks in the pleasant evenings. They talked of hurts and hardships. Jonathan's understanding of the depth of the pain and hardships his decision had caused her steadily increased. Gradually, tiny threads of hope and trust began to weave themselves into a fabric in which they could wrap their future.

***

At Christmastime, the engagement was announced, and a date for the wedding was set for April. On a warm day in the spring, the young couple stood before President Brigham Young in his office in the Council House, with John and Eliza Cox and several members of the battalion to serve as witnesses. The couple promised to love and to cherish one another throughout their lives and into the eternities. Susanna had chosen to wear a new, emerald-green dress with the pearls and the scrimshaw broach given her by Aunt Louisa, links to her past, but she was finally looking to the future with faith and determination.

"You may now kiss the bride," President Young said with a broad smile.

They shared a gentle kiss, and she colored from the lace collar of her dress to her hairline. They held one another tightly in an embrace that seemed to go on forever. She leaned back and looked into his face with a look that said she was searching her memory for some words that would help her make sense of what she was feeling. She smiled and whispered a quote by Henry King as she looked into his eyes.

My soul, sit thou a patient looker-on;
Judge not the play before the play is done:
Her plot hath many changes; every day
Speaks a new scene; The last act crowns the play.

He pulled her close, and as he whispered back to her, she could feel his breath gently moving her hair, "But today is the end of one play and the first act of another, a happier one for both of us." She laid her cheek against his shoulder. Her heart was finally whole. Only when she had ceased looking for it, did she find her safe haven.

Epilogue

In 1852, Susanna was eventually able to establish a correspondence with her mother and was grateful to receive twice yearly updates of Georgie's growth and development as he grew to be a fine young man. At seventeen, in the face of his older brother's opposition, but with his mother's blessing, Georgie was baptized into the Church, and in 1858 he was called to travel to Great Britain as a young missionary. After three years of faithful preaching, he led a group of converts financed by the Perpetual Emigration Fund across the Atlantic Ocean and the continent to the Salt Lake Valley, where he was finally reunited with his sister and her family. He lived with them until he was called to return to Great Britain and continue his missionary efforts.

Life in the Great Salt Lake Valley eventually became a little more comfortable, though Susanna and Jonathan were content to live modestly. She gave half the money from her inheritance to the Church Perpetual Emigration Fund to assist others to the Valley. The couple did not care that they were never likely to become rich—at least in earthly things. They had each other.

During October Conference in 1861, the names of three hundred families were read over the pulpit, each called by Brigham Young to the Dixie Mission. They were given thirty days to put their lives in order before they relocated to the far southwest of the Utah Territory. With their three children—Jane, Georgie, and Emily—Susanna and Jonathan packed their wagon and headed south, where Susanna was to become a vital part of the efforts of the Saints to cultivate cotton and weave the fabric so badly needed by the Saints in their isolated communities. Two more children eventually joined the family.

After the birth of her last child, Susanna embroidered a sampler, which was framed and hung in her sitting room. It read: "Take Life by the Horns." She explained the meaning of the words to her children as they grew, but they could never fully appreciate them until they faced life's challenges as adults.

Susanna and Jonathan lived to see their posterity gathered around them in their advancing years. Susanna learned well the wisdom of Psalm 68:6, "God setteth the solitary in families." How grateful she was for that truth.

Selected Bibliography

Bagley, Will, ed. *Kingdom in the West: The Mormons and the American Frontier.* Vol 3, *Scoundrel's Tale, The Samuel Brannan Papers.* Spokane: The Arthur H. Clark Company, 1999.

Levinson, Jeff, ed. *Mill Girls of Lowell.* Boston: History Compass, 2007.

Moran, William. *The Belles of New England: The Women of the Textile Mills and the Families Whose Wealth They Wove.* New York: St. Martin's Press, 2002.

Ricketts, Norma Baldwin. *The Mormon Battalion: US Army of the West 1846–1848.* Logan: Utah State University Press, 1996.

Stone, Irving. *Men to Match My Mountains: The Opening of the Far West 1840–1900.* Garden City: Doubleday & Company, Inc., 1956.

Talbot, Dan. *A Historical Guide to the Mormon Battalion and Butterfield Trail.* Tucson: Westernlore Press, 1992.

About the Author

Jean Holbrook Mathews has been a student of history, especially LDS Church history, and geography most of her life. She has taught public administration and state government at the University of Missouri–St. Louis, and she has served as the administrative director for an international foundation headquartered in St. Louis. She has traveled extensively in the United States and Europe, and she and her husband lived for nearly two years in the Phillipines while serving a mission for the LDS Church.